D1394571

NICOLA MARTIN

DEAD RINGER

CONTRABAND

Published by Contraband,
an imprint of Saraband,
Digital World Centre,
1 Lowry Plaza,
The Quays, Salford, M50 3UB
www.saraband.net

ISBN: 9781912235629
eISBN: 9781912235636

1 3 5 7 9 8 6 4 2

Designed and typeset by EM&EN
Printed and bound in Great Britain by Clays Ltd, Elcograf S.p.A.

At the time of writing, an app like the one in this novel did not exist, and no resemblance to any real app or software is intended or should be construed. All people and events described are fictional.

Walney Island, on the other hand, is a real place, albeit one that few people from outside Cumbria (or bird-watching circles) have heard of. It's wild and atmospheric, with a rich history. For the sake of the plot, this story focuses on the island's less charming points – bleak winters, a narrow range of opportunities – but, make no mistake, Walney is a gem of the Cumbrian coast. More people should visit it. Don't go out on the sinking sands alone, though . . .

Get ready to meet the other you.

Just upload your photo to get started. Using the latest facial recognition software, plus your votes, MeetYourDouble will find your doppelgänger.

She might be an astronaut or a model. He might live half a world away . . . or a few miles down the road.

You share the same face. Who knows what else you might have in common?

Start now.

Double Trouble

Roxanna Norris

MeetYourDouble is the hottest new app, with 200,000 new downloads in the last month alone. You might think you're one in a million – but, with seven billion people in the world, there are a fair few of you out there!

We've all seen the parade of celeb lookalikes. Some may be total pants, but some are uncanny. Wouldn't it be cool, then, to be able to meet your very own lookalike?

Users of MeetYourDouble say: yes! The app's following keeps on growing. It's become a cult phenomenon among the hipsters and shakers of everywhere from Shoreditch to Sandbanks.

All you have to do is upload some photos of yourself and click 'Find my doppelmatch!' A few seconds of digital crunching later and MeetYourDouble presents you with a selection of your closest counterparts. Other app users can then wield their votes to weigh in on which is the most uncanny match.

What if it turns out you share a face with an up-and-coming Hollywood starlet? (Awesome!) What if you share a face with a chavvy bruiser who spends Friday nights getting banned from Wetherspoons? (Criiinge!)

Either way, it's a glimpse into a different life – a life that might have been yours. With that in mind, who wouldn't want to meet their alter ego?

Doppelprofile – *MeetYourDouble*

Please fill in your details, so that other users can get to know you!

Name: Ella Mosier

Age: 24

Occupation: Still looking for the right thing

Location: Walney Island, Cumbria, UK

Interests: playing guitar, reading, avoiding drama, being ignored by my dog. I'm pretty boring, really.

Hi there, Ella! Based on the results of our doppelmatch software and 1,454 votes from fellow users, your photo has achieved a 98 per cent match with . . .

Name: Jemima Cootes-Mitchell

Age: 25

Occupation: Actress

Location: London, UK

Interests: theatre, singing, dancing till I die, give me adventure in all forms!

*Message **Jemima** now?*

1

WEIRD EARS

Ella

When I first met my double, I was disappointed by how little she looked like me.

'Ellie!' she called.

The woman waved her arms above her head, like I might miss her. Not likely. An oversize orange beanie bounced against her head and her mouth stretched in a theatrical 'O'.

'Ellie!'

It's Ella, I tried to say, but my lips were stuck together and nothing came out.

Over the course of the day's long train ride, I'd wondered if our first meeting might have the feel of a long-lost twins scenario. We'd scan the station's crowds until, miraculously, our eyes locked. Time would slow down, then speed up. We'd rush towards each other and fall into a hug.

No. Stupid.

That was a daydream borrowed from a bad movie.

In the broadest terms, we looked alike: pale skin and elfin features, with a mop of hair that was either dirty-blonde or dishwater-brown, depending on the light. But Jem, with her ugly beanie, wasn't my twin. She wore a brash smear of oran-gey-red lipstick to match the hat, and her hair looked in dire need of a hairbrush. Her appearance was far removed from the girl in the photo, with her sleek hair and minimal makeup.

I probably didn't look the same as my picture either.

As Jem's gaze bored into me, I ran a hand through my unwashed hair. I was all too aware of the dark circles under my eyes. The version of me on the app was the good Ella, the one I could just barely remember. The real me was much less impressive.

'Are you Ellie?' she asked, bounding over to where I stood.

In spike-heeled boots, my double was four or five inches taller than me. Despite the cold October day, she wore an ultra-short leather skirt with artfully-ripped tights. Her beaded top glittered when it caught the light, and was cut low to reveal the ample swell of her breasts. I wished I could be so courageous. In jeans and a faded green jumper, I felt bundled-up and dowdy.

'It's Ella,' I said in an undertone, but the blare of a train announcement swallowed up my voice.

I shifted my tatty backpack from shoulder to shoulder. It was Saturday afternoon and hordes of passengers streamed past us. The bump of a stray elbow buffeted me half a step backwards. I took a shaky breath and righted myself, but when I tried to speak again, I was interrupted.

'Who else would it be?' another voice said. 'Unless this place in swimming in your doppelgängers. Euston's turned into your own personal lab for Jemima clones.'

I turned to look at the guy who'd spoken. With black hair that fell past his chin, he looked Asian, maybe Chinese or Japanese. ('Foreign,' my mum would say with a sniff, triggered into a rant about immigration, even though our town was white-whiter-whitest.)

He was tall and wiry, and there was an eager, forward lean to his posture. Despite my nervousness, my toes curled inside my trainers. He was very good-looking. Jem elbowed him aside and stepped forward.

Without warning, my double hugged me.

In contrast to my daydream, it wasn't a tearful, thank-God-we-found-each-other hug. I didn't even have time to react to it. My arms hung limply at my sides, while Jem squeezed me tight for exactly two seconds. She air-kissed both my cheeks –

8

mwah! mwah! – and then pulled away again. When she spoke, her voice was newsreader-posh and bright with false cheer.

'It's so great to meet you!'

'It's great . . . to meet you . . . too . . .' I said.

Another person shouldered past us, shoving me aside. Jem seemed unaffected by the crowd, but I was beginning to feel lightheaded.

I glanced over at my train. It was departing again, going back up north. During the four hours I'd spent on the journey to London, my anticipation had crept higher and higher. Now I was on the downward swoop of the rollercoaster.

This stupid plan of mine to travel halfway across the country to 'meet my double' wasn't just a waste of money. I had a strong feeling I was about to make a fool of myself. In our messages through the MeetYourDouble app, I'd already lied to Jem to make myself sound more interesting. *I'm coming to London anyway.* (Lie.) *I've got some friends there.* (Lie.) *Might have a lead on a job.* (Lie.)

In truth, I'd come to London because . . .

Because . . .

'No shit, she really does look like you.'

It was the handsome guy at Jem's side. Like me and my double, he looked to be in his mid-twenties. When he peered at me, I shrank under his gaze. Jem was eyeing me, as well.

'Yuh, it's pretty crazy,' she said.

'I mean, she doesn't have the same mad glint in her eye, Ripper,' the guy said. 'But the rest of it . . . is kind of freaky. You're sure you don't have some secret sister out there? Maybe your dad played away one weekend in Blackpool?'

'My dad's never been north of Watford,' Jem said with a laugh.

The two of them spoke in a rapid back-and-forth, which – it couldn't be more obvious – was not meant to include me.

'Lemme see the ears,' he said, again examining me. 'Some

people have weird ears.' He cut his gaze to Jem. 'Weird ears. Band name. What d'you think?'

'Weird ears, weird ears,' Jem said. Then she shook her head. 'Nah, it strays. Say it too many times and it sounds like We're Deers. Or Weird Years.'

'Well, you say that like it's a bad thing – '

'If you're looking for a band name, how about Psycho Killer Strangers From the Internet?' I interrupted, the words slipping out in a rush of anger.

The two of them turned to look at me once more. My face burned, anger turning to embarrassment.

Voice faltering, I said, 'Sorry . . . but I don't have weird ears.'

'Hey, sorry about that.' The guy's expression softened. 'You definitely don't have weird ears. You have nice ears. Congratulations on your ears.' He raked his hair out of his face and looked at me intently. 'I'm Katsuhito. Don't worry, there won't be a spelling test. Most people call me Katsu. Like the chicken.'

Like the chicken? I didn't know what he was talking about, but his gaze was warm. For the first time, I felt like he was seeing me as a person, rather than as a prop.

'I call him Dicknugget,' Jem said. 'Sometimes Nippleface.'

Katsu put his arm around Jem (half loving embrace, half wrestling hold) and, when she tried to break free, he swooped in for a kiss. She leaned in to the kiss – sloppy, TMI – and then swatted him away, laughing. Her laughter came in a quick-fire volley, a fraction too loud.

Like Jem in her fashionably-torn tights, there was a hipster-ish vibe to Katsu. He wore skinny jeans, a yellow T-shirt, and a leather jacket. There was a piercing at his eyebrow and another nestled inside his ear. (Weird ears, indeed.) I didn't know any blokes in Cumbria who'd wear a T-shirt that read, *I'm just here to establish an alibi*, but that made me like him more, not less.

'What are we doing?' Katsu asked.

Jem shrugged and looked around at the station platform, which was beginning to clear. 'Coffee?'

'Addict,' Katsu said.

'Puritan.'

She stuck her tongue out at him. He laughed and drew her close. Their casual intimacy made my chest ache. Katsu hooked his finger around a strand of Jem's hair and pulled on it playfully. For a second, I felt a phantom echo of the sensation. Then all I felt was cold; they were indoors, and I was outside, face pressed against the glass. The two of them ambled away, without bothering to ask my opinion. I stood rooted to the spot.

What am I doing? Why am I here?

'Um,' I said.

Jem turned back to look at me. 'Coming?'

'Um, I'm not so sure . . .'

Out of the corner of my eye, I saw the train tracks glitter.

I don't want to be here anymore.

'Come on, we'll go get caffeinated and have some fun,' Jem said.

She shrugged off Katsu's embrace and advanced on me. I flinched as she squeezed into my personal space. She slipped an arm through the crook of my elbow. The scent of her perfume – oranges, sunshine – banished the grey day for a second. When her voice dropped to almost a whisper, it was as if her words were for me and me alone.

'I've been so excited to meet you,' she said. 'Honestly. It blows my mind how much you look like me. We could be sisters, I swear. We'll get some coffee, get some food, find something to do. It'll be marvellous.'

Jem's rapt gaze, the insistence of her words, disarmed me. Up close, I could see the resemblance clearly. Me and Jem, we dressed differently, we spoke differently, we held ourselves differently.

But . . .

I met Jem's gaze once more.

. . . the eyes. They were the same. Same shape, same shade: blue shifting into green shifting into grey; the colour of the Irish Sea on a cloudy day. The pointy nose was alike, too. We had the same wide mouth, the same angular face.

Looking at her was like passing an unexpected mirror and not knowing if it was your reflection you were seeing or another person.

Despite the cold day, despite my jangling nerves, I felt a rush of unexpected warmth. I'd experienced the same feeling when Jem's profile had loaded on the app. The fact that we looked alike, perhaps it was a fluke, a coincidence, an uncanny roll of the genetic dice. Yet I'd felt an instant connection with the stranger on the screen and I felt it in person, too.

Jem squeezed me into another quick hug and then released me. 'Come on,' she said again.

I nodded. In that moment, I recognised how cults recruited people on the basis of one charismatic leader. Katsu was a follower of the Cult of Jem, too. I saw that now. He gave as good as he got from her, but his soft-eyed looks betrayed him. As the three of us walked through the station, Jem was in the lead, hips swaying, and Katsu walked with a hand at her waist. I picked up the rear.

I took a deep breath and fluffed up my hair, trying to make it look less unwashed-dirty and more fashionably-dirty. Lifting my chin, I made an effort to walk tall, pushing through the crowds confidently. This was why I'd come to London: for the noise, the bustle, the sense of life in full colour.

I can do this, I can be this person.

Breaking into a slight trot, I jostled forward until I was level with Jem, not lagging behind. On the way out of Euston, we passed at least three coffee places in the space of 200 metres. There was a coffee cart, a name-brand coffee chain, an arty café with a chalkboard sign outside. We didn't stop at any of them. Apparently they didn't sell the right kind of coffee.

'I want Marco's dark roast . . .' Jem confided in me.

Katsu gave a sigh. 'The one in Chelsea?' He twisted his neck, also throwing a glance at me. 'You don't want to trek all the way to Chelsea, do you?'

I had no idea. Neither of them waited for a response from me, though.

'Can't help my cravings,' Jem said.

'You're a brat,' Katsu said.

'It's why you love me.'

Jem took a turn and Katsu followed. The world rotated according to her whims. I hesitated and then I followed too, down a set of steps and into an Underground station.

Chelsea. We were going to Chelsea. I only had the haziest sense of what might lie in this posh part of London. Money, tiny dogs, designer lives. Back on Walney Island, I knew someone named Chelsea. She was a bright, plainspoken girl who stacked shelves at Tesco, but maybe her parents had once dreamed of bigger things for her. You could give your child the name, but you couldn't give her the money, not if you were a nobody from a small town.

Inside the Tube station, a mangy-dog smell filled the air. Flickering fluorescents replaced the natural light. Someone pushed past me and their shoulder hit mine hard enough that my bones jumped in their sockets.

I fluffed up my hair again, straightened my spine.

I can do this, I am this person.

It was no good; the panic was creeping back in, prickling across my skin. A tide of people pushed me in the direction of the metal barriers. But I didn't have a ticket. Where could I buy a ticket? Craning my neck, I tried to locate the machines, but the crowd pushed me mercilessly onward in the opposite direction.

Jem and Katsu pulled ahead of me and passed smoothly through the barriers. I had no way to get through. The metal bar, slick and cold against my palms, stuck firm. A throng of people swelled behind me, impatient at the bottleneck I was causing. There were *tut*s and sighs.

I'd never felt more like a dumb hick from the country.

Beyond the barriers, my double's orange beanie disappeared from view. I had no choice but to turn around and fight my way back through the crowd. Scanning the sea of unfamiliar faces, it hit me in the stomach: I was alone.

Around me, strange accents and foreign languages blended together. Announcements blared over the loudspeaker. The rattle of trains arriving and departing sent shivers down my spine. Back home, I was used to life in miniature. Bus drivers who knew my name. Church services where fifty people was a big crowd. Towns where there were more seagulls than people.

Someone grabbed my arm. I flinched away, thinking: *Pickpockets! Muggers! Thugs!*

Again, I felt a hand reach for my arm. My vision cleared and I realised it was Katsu. He'd doubled back through the barriers.

'Come on, Weird Ears,' he said. 'Let's get you an Oyster card.'

Relief flooded my body, followed quickly by embarrassment. Of course. An Oyster card. I fumbled with the ticket machine's buttons, feeding coins down its metal throat. There were so many stages to the process, so many buttons to press. When I got confused, Katsu had to take over for me, selecting options on the screen with practised ease. It was several minutes before I got my card. Afterwards, my purse felt light – too light – but I pushed the worry aside.

'I guess the world is yours now,' Katsu said, as I swiped through the barrier.

I nodded. He'd meant it as a joke, but, plastic card clamped in my fist, I felt the truth of it all the same. For other people, for Jem, the world was a bright shiny pearl. Why not for me, too?

This was why I'd come to meet my double, after all: to see how a different version of my life might look.

I didn't want to be on the other side of the glass, peering in, anymore. I didn't want to live inside the last few years of regret. I didn't want to scroll blankly through other people's excitement on Facebook.

I wanted to be right there in the excitement. I wanted to become someone new; become the person I'd always imagined I could be.

2

DO SOMETHING

Ella

'Wait, you've never been to London before?'

We were seated on an Underground train and Jem was looking at me like I was a science experiment. It was a look that was becoming familiar.

I bet you've never been to Walney Island, either, I didn't say. I shook my head.

'First time in London?' my double asked. 'Seriously?'

I nodded and tried to fake a smile. Once upon a time, I'd planned to live in London, back when I'd still had hopes and ambitions and someone who loved me. I'd dreamed up a London all of my own; it was a room that existed inside my imagination. But I'd never actually set foot in the place.

'Well,' Katsu said, arching an eyebrow, 'there's a tramp.' He pointed at a bearded man, who was snoozing a few seats away, then widened his gesture. 'There's an arsehole in a business suit.'

'There's an ad for a liposuction clinic,' Jem added, pointing.

At that moment, the train burst out of its tunnel into sunlight. Jem gestured at the skyline, with its scaffolding-clad skyscrapers.

'There are some million-pound shoeboxes,' she said. 'Welcome to London.'

Over the course of our conversation, Katsu revealed that he was studying for a PhD in Chemistry. He spoke of it modestly, with an easy smile, like it was no big deal to be researching enantiomers (whatever they were).

Jem, who cut him off before he finished his explanation,

talked like she was performing on stage and people had paid for the privilege of hearing her. My double told me at length about her acting career.

'I'm up for a big role,' she said, leaning in close, her eyes glinting. 'Shit-hot director. Big-name cast. It'll put me on the A-list.'

'Cool,' I said in a low voice and Jem looked like I'd insulted her. Was I supposed to gush? Act like a fan and ask for an autograph?

In Cumbria, if someone got too big for their britches, you slapped them on the back and said, *Now, now, simmer down*.

I pretended to be interested in the view out of the train windows; graffiti swearwords and tinted-glass office buildings. It was naïve to believe that I could just step off a train and fit in. London was too big for me; I wasn't bold enough to belong here. Around Jem and Katsu, it was impossible not to feel meek and greyed-out.

'So what's your story?' Jem asked. 'What kind of things do you *do* Up North?'

There was a sarcastic note in her voice, or maybe I was imagining it.

'Um. I don't know. Normal things. Work and stuff . . .'

She didn't need to know that I'd recently lost my job – the last in a long line of minimum-wage gigs. Mine was a life that came without an IMDb entry. A life of church on Sundays and a pub roast if it was a special occasion.

Yet I couldn't help but feel defensive of my little island. I wanted to explain that, on Walney, rain had a smell to it. It was a smell that went beyond grass and earth and churning waves; a smell that could purify your soul.

I wanted to describe how, on a summer's evening, when the wind dropped and the last of the sun warmed the sands at Snab Point, it could feel like paradise. I wrote some of my best songs on those nights, melodies zinging through my mind as I scampered across the channel to neighbouring Piel Island, guitar strapped to my back.

Today, I couldn't give voice to any of it.

'I like music,' I said at last.

'Yeah?' Jem perked up. 'I'm starting a band.'

'Excuse me,' Katsu said, 'it's my band.' He turned to me, re-emphasising the words. 'It's my band.'

'I'm the star,' Jem said.

They continued their spat, sparring back and forth, only half serious. I sensed that they'd had the same conversation a million times before. I let them talk, relieved to drift into the background. I was used to it there.

*

When we emerged from the Underground station in Chelsea, I fell back into the role of a trailing puppy dog behind Jem and Katsu. A miniature pug on a bright pink lead snuffled at my shoes for a moment. Then its Barbie Doll owner yanked it away.

In contrast to where we'd come from, these streets looked scrubbed clean. Trees ornamented the pavements. The storefronts were sleek and polished, selling the dream for an undisclosed price. We passed high street stores, too, including a McDonald's, but even they retained an otherworldly glow.

Here, even the short people were tall. My eyes followed chic women in crisp colours and big sunglasses to shield against the non-existent October glare. In amongst the petrol sour of exhaust fumes, I caught an unexpected scent of cinnamon, like the whole place might be sugar-spun.

At the fabled Marco's coffee house, my double got a black coffee to go. I ordered a brew – four pounds for a teabag in hot water – which cleared out the rest of my change. I'd imagined we'd stay at the coffee house, chatting and soaking in the London atmosphere. It would be a salon, of sorts; Gertrude Stein on the Left Bank – another place I'd read about but never been.

Instead, Jem turned to Katsu and said, 'My place?'

'Sure,' he said with a shrug.

My heart drummed in my chest. I waited for them to consult me, but they didn't.

We were going to Jem's house?

Objectively speaking, I knew I hadn't made the best decisions today. I hadn't told anyone where I was going. It had sounded half-crazy (*I'm travelling across the country to meet someone who looks just like me!*) and, anyway, it was no one's business except mine. These days, I didn't have many secrets left, so I hoarded the ones I did have.

Make good decisions. That was what David always said. It was common sense to stay in a public place – a good decision. That was how you avoided getting murdered by a stranger who shared your face.

Of course, Jem didn't seem dangerous. A little self-absorbed, maybe, but not dangerous.

Still . . .

I licked my lips.

No one knew I was in London.

No one.

If anything happened to me . . .

Jem and Katsu were a few steps ahead of me. I could still turn and leave. Make up an excuse or simply slip into the crowd and lose them. It would be the sensible thing to do. It would be the Ella thing to do.

I tried to remember what Jem had promised me as we'd exchanged messages. What were her exact words? *Come to London and we'll do something.* I'd assumed she wanted to take me round the city, go see a show or attend a champagne gala. *Do something.* I'd imagined myself in a gallery, perhaps ordering a cocktail (even though I didn't drink). Maybe I'd filled in too many of the blanks. I'd wanted too much from this. *Do . . . something.*

'Wait up!' I called out, my voice louder than usual.

I broke into a run to catch up with them. Jem turned, reaching out a hand to me.

'Don't want to lose you, Twinnie,' she said.

She looped our arms together in a girlish pose, so that we walked down the road as a pair, with our steps perfectly matched.

I exhaled shakily, and then took a shallow breath in. I smelled cinnamon and oranges. Jem's perfume.

Do . . . something.

Minutes later, we turned down a side street and stopped in front of a bleached white building that looked fresh out of the wash. It rose in height to three storeys, with iron railings standing guard outside. Jem dropped my arm and bounded up the steps to the black front door.

Walney didn't have houses like this.

I'd guessed, based on her accent, that Jem was rich. But there was rich and then there was . . . this.

We walked into a light and airy entrance hall, with high ceilings and marble underfoot. An elegant staircase, carpeted in crimson, swept up to the first floor, but Jem waltzed over to the lift instead.

I was still processing the grandeur of it all when we arrived on the second floor and Jem moved to unlock the door to her flat. No, not a flat. An apartment. Once you paid a million pounds for a flat, it became an apartment. And a million would probably only buy you the bathroom in this place.

Everything here was rich. Casually, unassumingly rich. From the shabby-chic scuffed wooden floors to the perfectly-restored ceiling rose. The milky-coffee colour scheme and meltingly-soft furnishings reminded me of a hotel – the type of hotel where I could never, ever afford to stay. I caught my reflection in a huge gilt mirror in the hallway; I looked grubby against the surroundings.

I was struck dumb, but the other two were obviously used to it all. Katsu hung up his coat on the rack, but Jem didn't bother, letting hers fall in a heap on the floor. She kicked off her boots as she walked. The orange beanie whizzed off her head and landed at my feet.

'What's the plan?' Katsu asked.

'Food, food, food . . .' Jem stamped her bare feet in time with the chant. She disappeared in the direction of what I assumed was the kitchen.

'After that? I've got a buddy who's playing a show tonight. Should be pretty chill. Ella would probably enjoy it.'

He cast me a smile, and some of the tension in my neck eased.

I heard the fridge door open and then close again. Jem reappeared in the doorway, slurping noodles from a bowl.

'It's the promo party tonight,' she said thickly. 'Seven deadly sins.' She swallowed her mouthful and spoke more clearly. 'Only seven. But I could probably come up with a couple more.'

A frown crossed Katsu's face. He glanced at me and then back at Jem.

'So Twinnie's coming to the party, is she?' he asked.

Jem's face broke into a knowing smile that stretched her lips and showed too many teeth. Her eyes were lit with mischief.

It was weird to watch Jem's too-familiar features transform into such a foreign expression. Her face was the same as mine, but I didn't know how to smile like that.

'You never mentioned the party . . .' Katsu said.

My double pantomimed an *oops* face. 'Guess I forgot.'

'Right, you forgot,' he mumbled.

'Now I think of it' – Jem advanced on me, using her free hand to pull me into a side hug, so our skulls knocked together – 'wouldn't the two of us make for a glorious headfuck?'

3

THIS BAG CONTAINS MY FACE

Jem

God, what a little mouse. Squeak, squeak.

My double stood in the hallway. She was whispering into her phone. I poked my head out of the living room door, earwigging on her conversation.

'I'm just in . . . Lancaster,' she said.

Where the fuck is Lancaster?

'Staying with a friend . . .'

'. . . Well, it's a new friend . . .'

'. . . Yes, obviously, it's a girl . . .'

Ooh, intrigue.

I'd spent a couple of hours with Twinnie now – we'd eaten leftover pho and then ordered some more food – but I still couldn't quite get a read on her. Who was checking up on the little mouse? A boyfriend, deranged with jealousy? I wondered what the two of them did together. Played scrabble and drank tea, probably.

'I'll do the dinner tomorrow night,' she said into the phone. 'Promise.'

Ah, good little wifey. So why was she in London and lying about it?

'. . . And the sheep, okay.'

Sheep?

'I've already done their eyes . . . I just need to do their feet . . .'

What the fuck? Maybe Twinnie had escaped from a locked ward, not a sleepy little town. Or maybe her boyfriend was a deranged farmer uncle who made her sacrifice sheep to their cloven-hoofed god.

I stifled a laugh, but not well enough, because Ella, or Ellie (which one was it?) looked up and saw me. I smiled big and gave a wave.

'Would you like some tea?' I said in a stage whisper.

'ListenIhavetogo,' Twinnie said into the phone. 'Don't-worryI'llbefine. Seeyoutomorrow.'

She ended the call and pocketed her phone. It crossed my mind that she was probably one of those people who didn't have her phone set up with a passcode. So trusting.

'Tea?' I said again.

'No, thank you.'

She gave a prim little bob of the head, nodding even as she said no. I wanted to fit my knee into the small of her back and – *boof!* – make her stand up straight.

'Juice? Gin? . . . MDMA?' I said.

It was fun to watch her react, her eyes flicking from side to side. We got ourselves a proper pearl-clutcher here.

'Um, juice, I s'pose.'

In the kitchen, I sloshed into a glass some of the orange juice that Gabriela had squeezed for me. When Twinnie wasn't looking, I added a splash of vodka. She needed to relax. Her nerves were putting me on edge. My mouth was dry and my jaw was clenching. I made myself a vodka and orange, too.

'We should start getting ready,' I said and gulped at my drink.

Ella only took a tiny sip of hers. 'What kind of party did you say we're going to?'

'Just a party.'

I shrugged, playing it cool – playing it like my whole fucking career didn't rest on tonight's party.

'I get invites all the time.' I flicked my eyes skywards. 'It's a promo event for something, a new brand of drink, maybe. *Yeuch*. The booze will probably be horrendous, but the vibe should be good.'

The only reason to go was to see and be seen. I'd received a tip on who was on the guest list. I knew exactly who I needed to be seen by. And I planned to make a spectacle.

'Do you want to invite your friends?' I asked.

'My friends?'

'Yeah, you said you had friends in London.'

'Um . . .' Ella toyed with the hem of her jumper. 'I just got a message from them. They're busy.'

Busy or fictional. My double was a terrible liar. We had nothing in common at all. I narrowed my eyes, scrutinising her. That sad little expression on her face. Hunched shoulders, chapped lips, clothes from a bargain bin (or just a bin). What a disaster.

Despite all this, it was amazing how much she looked like me. Well, to be clear, she looked like the 'before' in a daytime TV makeover segment. But her features were still eerily like mine.

It was too bad my mum decided she hated my dad approximately five minutes after I was conceived. I would've made a marvellous big sister.

I looked again at Ella's threadbare jumper and un-made-up face.

'Let's get ready,' I said to Little Sis.

*

An hour later, the two of us were sitting cross-legged on the floor of her bedroom, facing each other. Concentrating hard, I stroked gel liner across Ella's eyelids.

'Stop moving!' I said when she twitched.

I take the art of make-up very seriously. I'm basically Michelangelo. The difference is that the Sistine Chapel had the good grace to stay still while he worked.

'Sorry,' she mumbled.

I resumed lining her eyes. Despite a few tremors, the job was going well. A bit of foundation and concealer were all it took to erase the stray freckles and flecked moles that the two of us didn't share. Twinnie's eyes were now dark with charcoal and smoke, just like mine. Her cracked lips were a shiny blood-orange colour. Perfect.

'Open,' I said, when I'd finished the eyeliner.

Ella blinked open her eyes, struggling against the heaviness of her lashes. I rummaged in my make-up bag – one that bore the legend, *this bag contains my face* – for the finishing touches.

'Why do you have knives on your wall?' Twinnie asked in her small voice.

I glanced up to see her gaze fixed on the far wall of my bedroom. That particular patch of plaster was painted in neon green; a 3 a.m. project sparked by too much speed. Mounted on the wall, there were about twenty ceremonial blades, mainly from Japan.

During the two terms I'd spent at drama school, I'd developed a fascination with fight choreography. My tutor was an intense thirtysomething with tousled red hair and pale eyelashes, who studied historical weaponry in between trying to fuck his students. He gifted me a small, evil-looking dagger and showed me where 'young gentlewomen' used to conceal them beneath their skirts. I lost interest in him right around the time I lost interest in drama school, but there was still something seductive about the glinting surface of a finely crafted blade.

'They're mostly daggers and swords,' I said. 'I collect them.'

'Ripper is a psychopath in training,' Katsu offered from the bed, where he lounged, absorbed by his phone.

'Okay . . .' she said.

I couldn't help but grin at the way Ella's eyebrows crept up her forehead. Even with all that make-up, her mousey expression of apprehension remained plain.

My phone whistled loudly. That was enough to wipe the smile off my face. I already knew who it was, but I checked to be sure.

Carlo.

Again.

Carlo, for the fifth time. I needed to get a new number. For that matter, I should probably move. Since that wasn't an option, I switched off the phone with a jab of my thumb. I sent it skidding across the floor. When it disappeared under the bed, I exhaled a sigh. Out of sight, out of mind.

Ella was watching me curiously. I pushed down my fear and pasted on a big smile.

'Come on,' I said, hauling Twinnie to her feet. I pushed her over to the mirror. 'Look at yourself!'

I admired her smoky eyes; her bright lips; the way her dark-blonde hair now held a hint of curl, deliberately mussed, like she'd just crawled out of bed with a hot guy.

'What do you think?' I said.

Ella examined her reflection in the mirror and . . . frowned. It ruined the whole look.

Twinnie obviously didn't get the memo that, when someone gave you a makeover, you were supposed to smile and say, *Wow! Oh, my God! Now I can finally live my best life!*

'I look . . . kind of like a doll? Not quite real, you know?' she said.

'You look hot!' I said, making an irritated noise in the back of my throat.

Ella glanced at me and ironed out her frown.

'Yeah . . . I mean . . . thank you,' she mumbled.

With her blank expression, I had to admit, she did look a little like a doll.

I turned to Katsu, who was studiously ignoring the whole exchange.

'What do *you* think?' I asked him.

He shrugged and made a noncommittal grunt. Exasperated, I picked up a tube of mascara and threw it at him.

'Ow!' he spluttered, rubbing his head. 'What d'you want

me to say? The two of you . . . you look the same. Congrats, you made her up into your own personal lookalike.'

Katsu's tone was sarcastic, but I never let sarcasm interfere with a compliment. I relaxed into a smile. Then I swooped down to bestow him with a kiss. God, he was sexy.

I deepened the kiss, sinking onto the bed next to him, but he pulled away after a few seconds. His eyes darted over my shoulder to Ella, then he gave me a long look – an I-know-your-secrets look – and frowned.

'You really know what you're doing, Ripper?' he asked in a low voice.

'Always.' I reared up off the bed. 'I'm having fun. I know you don't care about fun anymore, but I live on it.' I shook my shoulders in a jazzy little dance. My limbs were not quite coordinated, due to the fact that I was ever so slightly buzzed. 'I'm a next-gen sports car fuelled by F-U-N.'

He was laughing when I crashed down against his chest. I took this as a victory.

Making Katz laugh had become harder to do since he'd quit what he called the 'party drag bullshit'. He only went out on Saturday nights now, even though everyone knew the best parties were the secret Tuesday-night ragers. It was supposed to be Katz and me against the world; now he'd gone all grown-up on me. Traitor.

Ours wasn't a long and devoted relationship. More like a stuttering moped that crapped out at regular intervals on the road of life. The two years I spent in Los Angeles were our longest break. I was planning to be famous. I had no use for the little people of London.

In reality, I ended up sleeping with a series of psychopathic models-turned-actors who papered the walls of their Hollywood homes with black-and-white photos of their own faces. Meanwhile, on Facebook, I saw that Katsu started seeing some dull little mouse named Hannah, who grew tomatoes on her balcony and sold hemp hand cream from a market stall.

When I came back to London – tanned, tired, a faded version of myself – I fell back into old patterns with Katsu. It wasn't even very hard to break up him and Hannah. I dropped a few hints and he came running. The Hannahs of this world needed to take lessons in how to avoid getting hit by Hurricane Jem. Step one: get the fuck out of my way.

In my room, laid out on my bed, Katsu still looked entirely too serious. His laughter hadn't quite made it to his eyes. He disentangled himself from me and climbed off the bed. 'Going to the bathroom,' he said in an offhand way.

I groaned inwardly. Case in point: these days, for Katz, 'going to the bathroom' actually meant going to the bathroom.

'Don't let her bully you while I'm gone,' Katsu said to Ella on his way out.

'As if I would!' I called after him.

When the door closed behind him, my gaze returned to Twinnie.

'Let's play a game!' I said, clapping my hands together.

4

MAKE BELIEVE

Jem

In front of me, Ella blinked. 'What kind of game?'

'We'll get dressed for tonight,' I said. 'Then Katz can try and tell us apart.' I squeezed her shoulder, leaning in close. 'It will be hysterical.'

Twinnie gave a spasm of a shrug, which I took for assent.

I crossed the room to my walk-in wardrobe. It had seemed big when I'd first moved in to this apartment, but now it was getting cramped. I'd only been back in London for six months, but already everything about the city felt small. I didn't miss Los Angeles, but I was sick of going to the same places in London, seeing the same people.

Most of all, I was bored of being in this apartment. It was a beige investment pad belonging to my mother, and she was allowing me to live here only because it would look bad if her daughter were out begging on the streets. Mother never quite understood the concept of unconditional love. Living here, having my allowance drop into my bank account every month – there were big fat conditions attached. That was part of the reason I needed to make tonight a success, so I could be rid of her forever.

In the wardrobe, I switched on the light and rifled through the clothes, tossing different dress options over my shoulder and into the bedroom.

'Short or long?' I called to Ella.

'Um,' she said.

My double was quite the conversationalist.

'I'm going long,' I said. 'Full-on femme fatale.' I considered and rejected a couple of looks for me. Then I extracted a silver dress from one of my racks and tossed it to Twinnie. 'This would look cute on you.'

The dress had a metallic bodice and a grey tulle skirt that stuck out like a tutu. A sort of Astro-Ballerina-Barbie look. It was sexy-quirky enough that it would usually appeal to me, but tonight I didn't want to look quirky; I wanted to look like an A-lister. My hand brushed the cool satin of a red dress. Perfect. I yanked it off the rack and strode back into the bedroom.

Ella was getting changed using every trick she'd learned in PE lessons at whatever tragic comprehensive she'd spent her formative years. Her cheeks flushed pink when she saw me looking. I had no idea why. Her body was the only thing Mousey had going for her. She was a skinny bitch. I'd tried 100 diets while I was in LA to lose the extra bulge of flesh around my middle, with yo-yo-ing success.

I stripped off my clothes and stepped into the dress, admiring the way it clung to my boobs. Being skinny wasn't everything. At my hips, the dress fell in a dramatic curtain to the floor, revealing a slash of skin up to my thigh.

I heard footsteps trailing down the corridor.

'Katz!' I hollered through the door. 'Don't come in yet!'

The footsteps halted. I glanced over at Twinnie. Even in that knockout silver dress, she stood with rounded shoulders, her arms pressed against her sides like a mannequin. I wanted to grab her and shake her. *Be sexy! Own yourself!*

I didn't shake her, but I used my hands to push back her shoulders. Automatically she straightened her spine and lifted her jaw. Better. A smidge better.

'When he gets in here, don't say anything,' I said to her in a low voice. 'Katz!' I yelled again.

'I'm getting another drink, d'you want anything?' he asked, his voice muffled.

'No, stay here!'

'Thought I couldn't come in?' Katsu's tone was exasperated.

'Wait one second!'

I looked in the mirror a final time, fluffing my hair. Then I turned back to Ella, who wore a blank expression.

'Remember, just stay quiet' – should be easy enough for you – 'and completely still.' I raised my voice again, for Katsu's benefit. 'On the count of three, you can come in. Then you're going to guess who's who.'

'Who's *who*?'

'Who's Jem and who's not.'

'. . . Can I ask you questions?'

His voice was less muffled now, like he was standing directly on the other side of the door.

'No! That's the whole point. It's all based on how we look.'

'. . . Alright. Count of three, yeah?'

'Yeah!' I said. 'One . . . two . . . three!'

As Katsu pushed open the door, I tried to turn myself into a mannequin like Twinnie. Arms at my sides, vacant stare. It was tough to stay so still. My skin was prickling, the blood humming in my veins. I had to force myself not to grin.

What a riot. I'd found my very own Jem doll to dress up how I liked. Never mind that all my childhood Barbies had ended up headless after a couple of days of play.

Katsu stepped into the room. He paced its length, before turning and walking back again.

'Will the real Jem please stand up?' he said.

My double and I remained silent.

'I guess you're both standing, so that's pointless.' He paused, rocking back on his heels. 'First one of you to say "monkey funking" gets chocolate cake.'

My double and I remained silent.

'I guess you knew that one was a bluff. If I had chocolate cake, I'd eat it myself.'

Out of the corner of my eye, I watched as Katsu began an extravagant mime. He puffed on an imaginary pipe and twirled a moustache that wasn't there.

Under all his new seriousness, he was still the goofy-sweet kid I'd met as a teenager. He wasn't meant for the lab coat life; he was meant to be on stage, just like me. Why couldn't he see that?

I bit my lip to keep from laughing when Katsu pulled out a make-believe magnifying glass and peered through it. He leaned in toward Ella, examining her. Then he switched his focus to me.

'What have we here, Doctor Watson?' he murmured, dropping his face so that it was right next to mine.

I didn't look him in the eye, knowing that to meet his gaze would be to crack. My heart was jumping from adrenaline and a little something else, but I didn't want to spoil this. I wanted to know the truth . . .

How much alike did Ella and I really look? Could we actually fool anyone?

Katsu turned to examine my double once more. Then he straightened up. He made a show of pocketing his imaginary magnifying glass, before gesturing to Twinnie:

'Hey, Ella,' he said.

He leaned over and ruffled my hair. 'Hey, Jem.'

'How did you guess?' I exploded.

'I guessed because you're different people,' Katsu said, with a smug smile. 'And I am an amazing detective.' With one last twirl of his moustache, he gave a bow.

I slugged him on the arm, shooting a death glare. I'd done a flawless job with Twinnie's make-up. I knew I had.

'Oh, alright,' Katsu said. 'Your perfume smells like oranges, Ripper. Dead giveaway.'

I exhaled a long breath and my frown cleared.

'So you couldn't tell us apart.' A smile returned to my lips.

'It is pretty weird,' Katsu said, relenting, 'how much you look like her.' He narrowed his eyes, turning to Ella. 'You sure you're not related?'

'My mum and dad both grew up in Cumbria . . .' she said softly. 'I don't see how we could be.'

I'd had this thought, too. Maybe Twinnie was a cousin I'd never met. Or one of my dad's sown oats, all grown up. But I couldn't see Dada having much interest in some small-town Betty from a place I couldn't locate on a map. A sexy señorita from Barcelona, maybe, but not whatever Bible-basher birthed sad-eyed little Ella.

'There are some stories online,' she was saying, 'about people who were separated at birth. Like, um, one twin adopted in America, one in France. But most of the people on the app, they just look really similar. Just . . . a genetic fluke.'

'Yeah, humanity's little sense of humour,' I said. 'Anyway, we don't look completely alike. She's a little bit paler, a little bit skinnier. Thinner hair.' I leaned over and rubbed away a patch of foundation at her jaw. 'A freckle or two in the wrong places.'

This time, Twinnie flinched at my touch. She dipped her head and took a step backwards, arms still pressed to her sides.

'D'you have a wrap or something?' she asked. 'I'm cold.'

I swatted at the air, dismissive. 'You don't wear a dress like that and then cover it up.'

'Here, take my jacket,' Katsu said with a shrug.

He swiped his leather jacket from where it lay on the bed and handed it over. On Ella, it was slouchy and oversized, and she sank into it with a tremulous smile. Katsu reached over and squeezed her shoulder. It was only a gesture of comfort – good ol' Katz, lover of stray dogs and broken birds – but something in her eyes flickered to life when she met his gaze. Funny how she didn't flinch when *he* touched her.

Aw, bless, Twinnie had a crush.

'You should go on the site, Katz,' I said loudly. 'Maybe find a smarter version of you.'

'Nah, no point. All Asians look alike.' He paused for effect. 'That's what I've heard, anyway.'

I rolled my eyes and returned my attention to Ella.

'You're from Yorkshire or something, right?' I asked her.

'Cumbria . . .'

Moving to the mirror, I uncapped my lipstick and began reapplying. Twinnie loitered behind me, just visible over my shoulder, like a misplaced reflection.

'Whatever. Say something, y'know, Northern.'

'What?'

'Just say something.' I smacked my lips, evening out the colour. 'Y'know . . . *My name is Ella and I live Up North.*'

She shifted, eyes darting from me to Katsu, but he'd taken out his phone again and disappeared down a Wi-Fi wormhole.

'Go on,' I said.

'My name is Ella,' she said haltingly. 'I live in' – she emphasised the word – 'Cumbria.'

I nodded and then mimicked the words back, matching her accent:

'My name is Ella. I live in Cumbria.'

Katsu looked up from his phone. 'Hey, that was pretty good!'

'Hah!' I flicked my hair off my shoulder theatrically. 'Look for me in the new Stan Lembo movie.'

Katsu laughed, but Ella's smile was thin. In search of the perfect accessories, I rifled through my jewellery collection, picking up and then discarding a range of necklaces. I held up a silver statement piece studded with a big red ruby in front of Ella.

'Say something else,' I said.

'. . . What do you want me to say?' she asked, fingering the heavy necklace.

'What do you want me to say,' I mimicked, with a Cumbrian lilt.

'. . . Stop it, that's weird,' she said.

'Stop it, that's weird,' I said, taking the necklace back.

I was getting the hang of it now. Accents were kind of my thing. Not that I'd had much of a chance to show them off, not in marquee roles like Dead Prostitute #2 and Slutty Party Girl. All that was going to change soon, though.

'This is really weird, seriously!' Ella gasped out an exasperated laugh.

'This is really weird, seriously!' I parroted back perfectly.

'Cut it out, Ripper,' Katsu said. 'What are you, five years old?'

'It's fun!' I said, reverting to the expensively-educated vowels of my real accent. 'Ella doesn't mind. Tell him you don't mind, Ella.'

'. . . I don't mind,' she said, looking down.

'She don't mind,' I said, switching to her accent.

I looped a dirty-gold locket over my head and admired the way it hung heavy between my breasts. Katsu rolled his eyes and went back to scrolling through his phone. It was an obvious *I'm ignoring you* gesture. I tapped my foot, which made my whole leg jiggle.

'You try,' I said to Twinnie.

'Try what?'

'Say: my name is Jemima and I live in London.'

'I'm not good at that kind of stuff,' she said, shaking her head. 'Acting. Accents.'

'Come on, let's play.' Turning to face her, I swept Twinnie's hand into mine and tugged on her wrist. 'Let's make believe. You're not Ella anymore, you're someone else . . . Come on, say it. My name is Jemima.'

She looked up, meeting my gaze. Her expression was a shade more animated. 'My name . . . is Jemima,' she said slowly.

The game continued for a few minutes more. I flitted around my bedroom, finding shoes for the two of us to wear, considering handbag options. All the while, I drilled Twinnie on her accent. She gave little sighs the whole way through, but it wasn't like she told me to stop. It really was fun.

No surprise, she was a bad actress, but I was a great coach. Every time she'd speak, I'd find the flaws and correct her, getting her to repeat the same phrases over and over until they were perfect. Finally, she let out a defeated breath and said, for the tenth time:

'My name is Jemima and I live in London.'

I applauded and pulled her into a hug.

'What a good little pupil!' I said, smoothing a hand through her hair.

When I released her, my hand lingering on her arm, she looked dizzy.

'Thanks . . .' she said, biting her lip.

'We should leave soon.' I dropped my hand from Twinnie and turned away. 'Are you going to get ready, Katz?'

Katsu put his phone away at last.

'Sure, just give me a couple of hours to pick out an outfit, wax my chest, blow-dry my armpit hair . . .'

He ducked inside my walk-in wardrobe and emerged a moment later, still wearing jeans and a T-shirt, but with a slim-fit black DKNY dinner jacket slung over his shoulder. I knew it was DKNY because I'd bought it for him.

'Thanks for that single hanger you gifted me in your closet,' he said. 'Really makes a guy feel at home.'

He pulled his arms through the jacket and raked a hand through his shoulder-length hair. He raised his eyebrows at me, as if running a mental checklist of things to do. Then he broke into a smile.

'. . . Ready.'

'Men have it so easy,' I said, pulling him in for a quick kiss. My lipstick left a satisfying smear of red on his mouth.

Ella was watching us, but, when she saw me look, pretended she hadn't been. Damn right, you should be jealous. I normally took pleasure in chasing away girls who came sniffing around my man, but Twinnie was so unthreatening that there was no point.

Glancing at her familiar face, I felt strangely protective of her, like she was an extra hand of mine that had detached itself and scurried away on fingertip-feet.

I crossed the room and linked an arm through hers, breathing in her scent of wax-soap and gloom.

'Let's go indulge our worst sins,' I said.

5

SINS

Ella

A man, ten feet tall, ambled up and down the stretch of pavement outside the party. He wore a top hat and tails and, when he saw me looking, doffed his hat at me. It was bright blue and emblazoned with the word SYN.

The chill of the October night rose gooseflesh on my bare legs, but excitement stirred beneath my skin, heating me from within. It was Saturday night and I was going to a party. There was something blissfully simple about this fact.

I wanted to stay and watch the stilt-walker, ask how he stayed upright. He looked more solid on his four-foot wooden legs than I felt in the strappy black heels that Jem had lent me to wear.

Before I could open my mouth, my double yanked me along and we kept walking, arm-in-arm, while Katsu trailed behind. Despite Jem's bulldozer personality, despite her parlour games and her overbright gaze, I felt glad to be cinched in close to her. There was nothing she couldn't do, and it was inevitable that some of her confidence rubbed off on me.

The party was being held in an imposing Georgian house, somewhere close to the posh part of London where Jem lived. The house had sandstone pillars on either side of a red door, but as we climbed the steps to the door, a bouncer blocked our entry.

'Name?'

I lowered my head when he spoke, but Jem shot back, 'Ha fucking ha.'

'Alright, Jemima, how much trouble are you gonna be for me this evening?' the bouncer asked.

He was big and beefy, with black hair buzzed short and an overhanging brow. Yet, when Jem ran a hand down his arm, an incongruous smile cracked open his fearsome face.

'Oh, only a smidge,' she said, with an affected, breathy laugh. 'A teeny-tiny bit of trouble.'

'Yeah, yeah, yeah . . .' The bouncer angled his gaze over Jem's shoulder. 'Katz, you gonna keep her in check?'

'If only I could, man, if only I could.'

The bouncer chuckled. 'Go on in.' He reached to open the door and then hesitated, his gaze finally landing on me. 'Who's this?'

Though he was staring straight at me, his question pinged over my head to Jem.

'She your sister?' he asked.

My double leaned in close to him, her voice low and conspiratorial.

'She's me. You're wasted and seeing double.'

The bouncer was silent for a moment and then he let out a lusty belly-laugh.

At the kerb, a crowd of ten or twelve people, dressed in suits and silky dresses, arrived in a fleet of taxis. High-heeled shoes tapped against paving slabs as they huffed impatiently at my back.

'Whatever, Jem. Just try not to wreck the place,' the bouncer said and hurried us inside.

He cast one final glance in my direction. It was a flirty, knowing look; the same type he'd given my double. I wasn't used to people looking at me like that.

Giving him a small smile in return, I tossed my hair in what I hoped was a casual yet alluring gesture. Then Jem pulled me through into the house and the door closed behind me.

Inside, it was another world.

Like something from Versailles, the entrance hall was enormous, with a wide spiral staircase winding up to a cavernous ceiling. Two long strips of white fabric hung high above. I watched as a brunette woman climbed to the top, nimble as a monkey. She waved from her god-like vantage point. Then she wrapped herself in the fabric and flipped upside down in an effortless somersault. My stomach turned over in response.

If she fell . . . what would happen if she fell?

The acrobat righted herself and I pushed the thought away. There was something magical about the way she hung in the air. Much like I could pretend the stilt-walker really was ten-feet tall, I could pretend she really was flying.

Around me, there was a crush of people in elegant evening wear, chattering and laughing. Classical music created an atmosphere that was more sophisticated than I was used to. What was the last party I'd been to? It was probably at my friend Bethany's house: a summer barbecue on an overcast day; bottles of Peroni and undercooked meat.

'Take off that jacket, let everyone see you,' Jem said, tugging at the sleeve of my leather jacket. No, not mine – Katsu's jacket. If I breathed deeply, I could catch his earthy scent, along with a hint of something sweeter, like an apple plucked right from the tree.

Reluctantly, I shed the leather skin, revealing my silver dress. Jem banished Katsu to the cloakroom with our things and I felt a pang as he disappeared. I pressed my arms to my sides, reminding myself that my scars were faint now, barely visible to anyone but me.

A sandy-haired man nearby caught my eye. What was he looking at? A bubble of paranoia welled up in my throat.

He raised his eyebrows and lifted his glass in my direction. Oh.

He wasn't scrutinising me. He was flirting.

Relief made the blood rush to my face and I gave him a

blushing smile.

Before I could say anything to him, before I could contemplate if I wanted to say anything, my double was pulling me along. She passed through the crowd – Moses parting the Red Sea – and I glided in her wake. We ended up directly beneath the acrobats, which didn't seem to faze Jem at all, but I kept shooting glances heavenwards.

Waiters with blank expressions wandered by, holding trays with champagne flutes. They contained bright blue liquid. Presumably this was SYN. The swirling letters of the drink's name were on every glass. Jem grabbed one for herself and handed me another.

'*À votre santé!*' she said, clinking her glass with mine.

Was that French? What was I supposed to say in return?

I didn't reply and, to cover my flub, I took a tiny sip, even though I wasn't supposed to drink. The blue liquor was cherry-sweet with a chemical aftertaste that was almost metallic. I was disappointed. I'd hoped it might be the nectar of the gods.

Jem gulped down her drink and then replaced her empty glass with a full one from another waiter.

'Last one of these I was at,' my double said to me with a conspiratorial grin, 'the drink had tiny pieces of gold in it. What a riot. Idiots will buy anything.'

I tried to share in her smile, but the metallic taste in my mouth persisted. In Jem's world, whatever you wanted, no matter how ridiculous, there was no need to buy it. People gave it to you for free.

Someone slammed into me, hard. I turned, coming face-to-face with a tiger.

It was only face paint, but when he snarled, the man looked feral. 'Sloane-y buggers,' he muttered and was gone.

Part of me wanted to call after him. Not me! I'm not like these people!

Jem was drawing me close again, pointing out people in the crowd – the A-list actor who'd just got out of rehab; the opera singer who was sleeping with a Saudi sheik – and it was so tempting to let her coax me into the illusion. In my dress, in my makeup, in my disguise, I belonged among these people, our shared privilege making us seem ten feet tall.

All I'd ever wanted was to belong.

'This way, please!'

The instruction came from somewhere nearby and I craned my neck automatically. A flash blinded me. There was a flurry of sound – *chk-chk-chk-chk!* – as the camera's shutter went off several times in a row.

'Hold up the glass so I can see the branding,' the photographer said, 'and make it look like you're having the time of your life!'

He was a skinny black guy with a bootlace tie and a wispy moustache. His voice had an irritated, nasal quality that I guessed stemmed from saying the same thing over and over and being ignored.

I stared dumbly down his lens, but it didn't matter, because Jem elbowed me aside. She took up the whole frame. She raised her glass and gave an open-mouthed smile. It made her look like she was about to chomp down on something with her teeth.

The photographer's hand slackened around his camera. Bored. He snapped a single perfunctory shot and then turned away.

Jem's smile twisted into a sneer. She punched the photographer on the arm.

'Hey! You never seen a couple of clones?' she said and made a bleating sound like a sheep.

This time, she clamped an arm around me, presenting the two of us to the photographer. The guy shrugged and lifted his camera to take one more picture. It probably showed Jem with her mouth open, and me having my soul sucked out through my eyes.

I squirmed free of Jem's hold and darted out of frame.

'I don't like ... being photographed,' I said in an undertone.

'What, are you on the run?'

Jem's chummy smile was gone. She let out an exasperated huff, looking around for the photographer, who had now disappeared. 'This is my career we're talking about!'

I didn't know what a few photographs had to do with her career, but it unnerved me to watch Jem's too-familiar features darken with frustration. Her cloudy-grey eyes were the same shape and shade as mine, but now they narrowed, growing stormy.

'If I take a picture of you, will you stop your tantrum?' Katsu said.

I hadn't realised he'd returned, but he'd apparently witnessed the whole spat with the photographer. With a teasing smile, he slipped in next to my double and pulled her close. He raised his phone ostentatiously and snapped a selfie of the two of them. Now it was Jem's turn to squirm free.

'Yuh, because being seen in *Tatler* is absolutely no different to being seen by all twelve of your followers,' she said.

'Chill out,' he said. 'You're embarrassing yourself in front of Ella.'

Jem cast a contemptuous look in my direction and then swatted dismissively at the air, turning away.

'Going to find a bathroom,' she called over her shoulder.

As she stalked off, the crowd again parted mystically for her.

The classical music and the murmur of conversation around us wasn't loud enough to mask the awkward silence that Jem left behind her. I realised I was still holding the blue drink and I sipped at it again.

I shuffled my feet and then regretted it. My ankle went sideways in my too-tall heels. Katsu caught me by the elbow as I stumbled. His hand was warm and solid on my arm and I thought how nice it would be to slide closer to him. Instead,

I righted myself and took a step backward. His hand dropped. There was a moment more of silence and then Katsu spoke.

'Ripper is just a little on edge,' he said, rubbing at his face. 'There's this big role she wants . . . She's obsessed with, I don't know, exposure.'

I wondered how much time Katsu spent apologising for Jem. He seemed well-practised. I nodded, as if it all made sense, and then lowered my gaze.

'So what d'you fancy?' he said.

I sneaked a glance at him. His tired expression cleared and he leaned forward, bouncing his soles against the floor.

'Greed? Gluttony? Wrath?' he asked, gesturing to the rooms that led off the entrance hall.

'Oh . . .' I gulped down my disappointment.

'Greed's Monte Carlo and I'm telling you right now, I am the unluckiest bastard in this joint.' He whipped his phone from his pocket and scrolled through his messages. 'I hear they're doing Fight Club in the Wrath room, but that's gotta be a rumour. The first rule of Fight Club, y'know . . .'

I joined in with his easy laughter, my excitement about the party resurfacing. It was easier to relax without Jem's manic energy.

Through the crowd, I glimpsed a generous space off the entrance hall that contained croupiers in waistcoats. Roulette wheels hurtled in circles. From the Greed room, a brief roar rose up – either a big win or a big loss. I smelled Gluttony, too. The savage smell of sizzling meat mingled in the air with spun-sugar sweetness.

When, in my real life, would I get to inhabit a decadent world like this?

I was determined to enjoy it.

'Fight Club might be cool,' I said. 'You probably already guessed it . . . back home on Walney, I'm a bit of a brawler.'

Katsu's laughter redoubled, bright and genuine. He laughed

like he was being tickled. Pleasure wriggled through my stomach, releasing some of its knots.

The two of us roamed the ground floor, touring the Seven Deadly Sins that had been packaged up into neat zones for our consumption. At one of the roulette tables, a young man in his twenties – my age, if not younger – pushed a pile of black chips into the centre. Seconds later, he lost it all. He shrugged, like someone who'd dropped a penny and let it roll away. His bet probably could've paid off my student debt.

Greed gave way to Gluttony. There was an enormous doughnut in the centre of the room, twice the size of a lorry's tyre, and guests were invited to take a bite. The result was a pock-marked surface of the moon. A grill sizzled in the corner, producing steaks which people (mostly the men, suited and dribbling grease) ate on sticks made from bone shards, like they were lollipops.

'You want a cupcake?' Katsu asked.

I nodded. I was glad to hurry past the steaks, ditching my blue drink on a table along the way. At the far side of the room, a pâtissier (or, more likely, a cater-waiter who'd borrowed a tall white chef's hat) was icing people's names on to cupcakes.

The loopy letters drawn by the 'chef' looked more like *illa* than *ella*, while Katsu's cupcake read *catzoo*. We ate them anyway, the sugar high bonding us like little kids at a birthday party as we wandered back to the entrance hall. I giggled when Katsu got chocolate frosting smeared around his mouth and reached up instinctively to wipe it away. He retaliated by dropping a blob of chocolate on my nose.

I was sorry when a well-meaning waiter appeared and handed us napkins – and sorrier still when Katsu brought up Jem.

'Ripper will've calmed down by now,' he said, scanning the crowd. 'Probably be looking for us.'

He took out his phone and checked it for messages, but I

noticed he didn't bother to send any. Maybe he too liked it better when Jem wasn't around?

I squashed the thought. Stupid. He was my double's boyfriend, after all.

Feigning nonchalance, I glanced around. On a platform nearby, the tiger I'd met earlier juggled fiery batons. Flames streaked upward, ten metres in the air, and, for a second, it made the whole place seem alight. Following the high trajectory of the batons, I noticed the writing on the ceiling for the first time. A phrase had been stencilled above where the acrobats hung upside-down on the silks. *Pride comes before a . . .*

'That's quite a joke,' I said in a low voice, but I didn't think Katsu heard.

'Hey, tell me your deepest darkest secret!' he said.

My scalp prickled. *Illa . . . Illa, queen of the sickly and forlorn.*

Katsu wasn't paying attention to me. He gestured to a big wooden box with a slit in the top. On the table beside it, there was a stack of papers and a pen styled like a quill. *Confess your sins* was emblazoned across the box in blue spray paint. Katsu hummed the dramatic snatch of classical music they always used in cheesy reality TV and then winked at me.

With a flourish, he took the quill and wrote down something on a slip of paper – I caught the words *unicorn* and *naked* and *kill Hitler* – and then dropped it into the box.

'Your turn,' he said, his eyes crinkling in amusement.

I gave a little shake of my head, groping for a subject change. Now I almost wished Jem would come back and make everything all about her once more.

'What are the other rooms?' I asked, hoping to sound casual. 'Sloth and . . . and . . . Envy?' (I deliberately didn't say 'Lust'.)

'I think Envy's in the ballroom downstairs. Wanna check it out?'

'Sure . . .'

I was used to poky, damp basements in Cumbria where

you stored Christmas decorations. In Chelsea, basements were apparently a different matter altogether.

Katsu and I descended a flight of stairs into darkness and noise. The tasteful classical music of upstairs was gone, replaced by the thrum of electronic dance music. It took my eyes a few moments to adjust to the dim nightclub lighting. I was blind and my hands fumbled for Katsu's arm.

'Don't worry, Weird Ears, I got you.' His fingers closed around mine.

At the base of the stairs, I blinked rapidly. I'd thought Katsu's description an exaggeration, but no, this really was a ballroom – underground, cut into the earth, too big to be real. Its ceiling was high and its floor was shiny.

There were no windows, just mirrors. So many mirrors. They reflected knots of people dancing, laughing, embracing. Colours blurred as reflections bounced from one surface to the next.

Envy.

Look in the mirror. Look around. Look at everything you don't have.

'Wanna dance?' Katsu said in my ear.

I was still holding on to him. I didn't want to let go.

I also didn't want to make a fool of myself. Nervousness roared in my ears.

'Maybe we should go back upstairs . . .' I half-shouted to be heard over the swell of noise that accompanied a new song from the DJ.

'Aw, come on – one song.'

Katsu took a step backwards, still gripping my hand, and pulled me with him, on to the dance floor. I resisted, my shoulders stiff, but he gave me a smile – a lovely smile – and my body relaxed.

'Okay, just one . . .' I said.

I'd never been a club kid as a teenager, preferring to curl up with a book rather than visit one of Barrow-in-Furness's limited nightlife options. But, when I went away to uni, the girls on my floor took it as a given that, on Saturday nights, we hit the clubs. I wasn't a natural dancer, but on those fevered nights that sometimes stretched until dawn, I learned an important lesson:

Music and darkness and lust can let you lose yourself.

6

REFLECTIONS

Ella

In the ballroom, the bassline of the music throbbed at the front of my mind. It was already beginning to blot out my thoughts, my worries, my insecurities, leaving behind just one fact: I was dancing with a hot guy.

Katsu danced unselfconsciously. He was all cheesy moves and gangly limbs, but occasionally it came together with real rhythm. When the frenetic song that was playing reached its climax, he shot me a gurning grin. He grabbed my hand and spun me around, like a ballerina in a music box. My laughter, rendered silent under all the noise, shuddered through my body, right to the tips of my toes.

The song ended and I hoped he wouldn't remember that I'd only agreed to one dance. He raised his eyebrows and I smiled back.

We carried on dancing, through songs about love and betrayal, sex and revenge. Reflections from the mirrors danced around us, distorting our bodies like a trip through the funhouse.

'Jem!' someone yelled from a few feet away, waving an arm.

I waved back on automatic, but then turned away, sheltering myself against Katsu, my back pressed against his chest.

The photographer reappeared, the flash of his camera dazzling in the underground ballroom. I glided out of shot. Unlike Jem, I didn't want exposure.

I wanted . . .

What did I want?

My wants were vast and sludgy, like an expanse of quicksand.

Right now, I wanted to dance.

Katsu never strayed from my side. He swatted the photographer's camera away and put a protective arm around me. He was taking pity on me.

It was easy to pretend otherwise, though.

A slower, sultrier song rolled through the crowd. Instead of drawing away, Katsu pulled me closer, his hands resting lightly on my waist. My hands moved instinctively to his shoulders. He was close enough that I could smell him, his salty-sweetness, and feel the heat of his body.

My eyes drifted shut and I gave in to the intoxicating urge to let the music erase everything about me. Swaying to the rhythm, my hips pushed against him. His grip on my waist tightened. I shifted closer, my fingers twining together at the back his neck.

'You having fun?' he whisper-shouted in my ear.

My eyes blinked open, but I didn't reply. I didn't want to talk; I wanted to feel.

Our proximity meant it was inevitable that I thought about kissing him. I didn't know if it was real desire or another part of my carefully-constructed Jem costume. Perhaps it didn't matter.

I didn't kiss him, but I did crush myself closer to him. Turning my head to the side, I let it rest in the hollow of his neck. In response, one of his hands skated over the curve of my arse. We were rehearsing what else we could do in the dark.

If I were my old self, I would have been embarrassed by our closeness, the suggestiveness of it. But I existed outside of myself right now. That meant I could press my body against his and it didn't have to mean anything.

I closed my eyes again and a different face shuddered through my mind's eye.

Owen, with his too-wide, too-kissable mouth. Owen, with his tufty blond hair and sleek swimmer's body. I could smell the faint tang of chlorine in the air. I could feel his nimble fingers pulling at my dress. Owen, who'd promised to move with me to London. Owen, who'd promised me the world.

I hadn't seen him in years – it felt like months, but it was really years; time grinding on and on and on – yet I felt perversely like I was making him jealous. If I dirty-danced with Katsu, it might have a psychic effect on Owen. It might summon him from Berlin or Barcelona or whatever glamorous spot he'd ended up in, with a girl who wasn't me.

Again, I felt a tug at my dress.

I opened my eyes.

I was still dancing with Katsu, but Jem had grabbed a fistful of my dress, pulling me away from him. She pinched a patch of flesh on my torso in the process.

Using her other hand, my double stroked her fingers down Katsu's chest with a come-to-bed purr.

Katsu's eyes darted between the two of us. His girlfriend and the interloper. He wore a dazed expression, his posture slack. I wondered whether, in that moment, in the darkness and the heat, the difference between the two of us had blurred in his mind.

'Come on,' Jem said in my ear.

*

She dragged me through the crowd. The figures around us, reflected in the mirrors, advanced and then retreated, disappearing like ghosts as the mirrors fell away.

Katsu caught up to us at the base of the stairs. He said something to Jem, but it was swallowed up by a swell of music. She shook her head, shrugging off the hand he placed on her shoulder.

'You stay here,' she said to him, half-shouting. 'Only twinnies allowed.'

She yanked me onward, up the stairs. Unlike Katsu's loose, comforting grip, her fingers were a vice around my wrist.

When we pushed through the double doors into the entrance hall, it was like surfacing into sunlight. I was slammed once more by the casual opulence of it all: the creamy walls and austere oil paintings, the polished squares of the black-and-white floor, the gowns of the women, bright jewels against their suited partners. Jem's perfume filled my nostrils, sweet as an orange peeled at a summer's day picnic.

'Where would Stan go?'

My double looked at me as she asked the question, but it obviously wasn't meant for me. She barely paused before rambling on. Her speech came out rapid-fire, a shade too loud.

'Wouldn't want to mess up his pretty little face,' she said. 'Maybe he'd eat, but maybe not. Wasn't in the casino room. Wasn't downstairs. Must be upstairs. What's upstairs?' She let out a low chuckle. 'What's always upstairs?'

Her hold on me had slackened, but now she squeezed tight around my wrist once more. Was she angry at me for dancing with Katsu? Now that I was out of the dark ballroom, embarrassment churned in my stomach. I'd made a play for someone else's boyfriend; I'd made a fool of myself.

'Jem . . . I think I should go home . . .' My voice came out too quiet; more of a question than a statement.

My double shot me an icy stare.

'Don't be a prig, we're having fun.' With her free hand, she grabbed one of the blue drinks from a passing waiter's tray. She pushed it into my hand. 'Have a drink.'

Looking at it now, the resemblance to toilet bleach was obvious. Reluctantly, I took a sip.

'Have a *drink*.' She tipped my glass at a sharp angle, forcing it to my lips.

I gulped down one, two, three mouthfuls before I choked. I forced myself to swallow, but a dribble of excess escaped my lips. Jem cleaned it away with a rough swipe of her thumb. She pulled the champagne flute away from me and cast out her arm to dispose of it. I don't know if she imagined there was a waiter's tray behind her or if she meant to drop the glass. Either way, it slipped from her fingers and smashed against the polished floor.

To my left, a woman gasped. She pulled up her floor-length skirt and took a step away from the shattered glass.

Jem ignored her and stomped onward through the entrance hall, with me in tow. The heels of my shoes crunched against the broken glass. I imagined the blue bleach leeching down my throat, spreading through my bloodstream.

When we mounted the spiral staircase, we were moving so fast that I bashed my shin against the first step. Pain pulsed up my leg, nausea roiled in my stomach, but there was no stopping Jem. We spiralled upward, past portraits of nobility, who looked down their noses at me from three hundred years dead.

On the first floor, it was less crowded – and quiet enough that I could hear a grunting sound. I wondered if it was me; my pain given sound. Then we passed an open doorway. The man nearest to us wore a bright white shirt with the sleeves rolled up. He had straw-blond hair and a button nose. As I watched, someone took a swing at him, catching him right in the jaw. Jem tugged me onward before I saw him fall. In my imagination, he remained suspended in mid-air, blood blooming at his mouth.

A few steps later and we were on a different planet. The lighting was dim and tinted a dark pink colour. Cinderella gauze hung from the ceiling. There was no fighting or dancing here. Just beds and sofas. It was too dark to see much of what was going on, the gauze rendering figures as silhouettes. But, close by, we passed a couple kissing languorously, their clothes a thin barrier to more. Even as I watched, the man pushed the woman's skirt up her thighs. I could still hear a faint grunting sound, but I couldn't tell if it was coming from Wrath next door or here in the Lust room.

'Like to watch?' Jem whispered in my ear.

She let out a mocking laugh, loud enough to startle the kissing couple. I cut my eyes away, a blush crawling rash-like across my cheeks. My double leered closer to the couple.

'Hey, Stan! Fancy seeing you here!'

She plopped on to the oval-shaped bed that they'd claimed, pulling me down next to her. The woman glanced at us, her lips pinched together. She had dark skin that was glossed with sweat and her curls were mussed. The man beside her ran a hand through his corn rows. While his paramour sat up, smoothing down her skirt, he reclined, propped up on one elbow, regarding me and Jem from beneath hooded eyes.

'I know you, sweetheart?' he asked, his voice honey-smooth and American.

'I'm your Delilah,' my double said.

''Zat right?'

'All the way down to my tippy-toes, I'm her.'

Jem scooted across the bed, close enough to the couple that the woman let out a huff of irritation. My double reached out and lifted Stan's hand, placing it on her thigh. She guided it over the smooth satin of her dress.

'All the way down,' she said.

The rash of colour on my cheeks burned. I wondered if it was visible under the pink lights.

'You know we've already cast that role,' Stan said, but his hand lingered on Jem's thigh.

'So un-cast it. Re-cast it. I can prove it to you. I'm her. I'm everything you want me to be.'

'Stan, baby . . .' the woman said, draping herself against his shoulder.

Glancing at her, he patted Jem's thigh once and then pulled his hand away.

'You're a cute kid,' he said. 'I'll remember you for the next movie.'

It was a rebuff; a nice one. A thanks-but-no-thanks, served with a smile.

Of course my double wouldn't bow out gracefully. No one said no to her.

Annoyance flickered across her face, contorting my benign features. When she gave a smile, it was malevolent.

'You want to meet my double?' She clamped an arm around me. 'We're identical.'

'Twins, huh?' Stan lifted his eyebrows, unimpressed.

'Not twins, *doub-les*. She's from fucking . . . fucking . . . Yorkshuh or something.' Her voice succumbed to a slur. 'An' she's a perfect reflection of little ol' me.'

Interest stirred in Stan's expression, his forehead creasing. 'Not related?'

He looked at me. I shook my head.

'Two for the price of one!' Jem said, too loud. She nudged me. 'Say, *my name is Delilah and I'm a fucking – fucking hurricane.*' Her fingers dug into the flesh of my arm, hard enough to leave bruises. 'Say it!'

I was mute, paralysed.

'Say it . . .' Her voice dropped to a low rasp.

My double leaned in close, her chin hooking over my shoulder. The smell of oranges that oozed from her skin now seemed rotten-sweet.

'Isn't this a trip?' Jem went on.

Her mouth pressed against the curve of my neck. I tensed, but couldn't move. She had me locked in place. Then there came the wet drag of her tongue licking up to my earlobe.

7

PRIDE COMES BEFORE A . . .

Ella

Jem fell away from me, breaking out into gales of laughter.

'Isn't that what Delilah would do? Isn't it?'

Stan was looking at us glassy-eyed. He stifled a small cough and then said:

'Actually, maybe I like your friend for the role . . .'

I didn't have to look at my double to know that she wouldn't notice Stan's teasing tone. A surge of anger emanated from her.

It was the push I needed. I wrenched myself free of her grip and stood up.

The sense of nausea – bleach-blue sick creeping up my throat – renewed in a wave, but I forced myself to walk away. My foot went sideways in my shoe and I stumbled, but I kept going.

Jem's nasty voice followed me.

'You're not allowed to leave! You're me! You're *meee*!'

I turned and ran, out of Lust and Wrath, down the stairs and past somersaulting Pride. I needed air. I needed to leave the circus.

I needed to remember who I was.

*

I was halfway home in my mind. I was on a train, watching the London skyline rewind, replaced with a patchwork of fields. I was ready for sleep and something better in the morning.

It wasn't until I burst out through the front door that I realised I had no way to get home and nowhere to sleep. Cold air slapped me in the face. I didn't even have a coat. Katsu had taken the leather jacket, along with a handbag I'd borrowed from Jem, to the cloakroom, but I couldn't bear to go back in and retrieve them.

On my way out, the bouncer hailed me with a jovial smile. 'Leaving already?'

I ignored him, stumbling down the path and on to the pavement. Beside me, a sleek black car pulled up to the kerb. When the rear door opened, a trio of women fell out. For a moment, their perfume and laughter enveloped me. Then they were gone – into the party; into the Big Top – and I was alone on the street.

I managed a hundred yards more, walking almost to the end of the road before my feet gave out. My fingers clawed at the brick of a nearby building. I slumped against it. The houses around me slumbered – rows of identical Georgian town houses – and light pollution gave the sky an eerie purple cast.

I had no idea where I was.

I could find someone and borrow their phone, but who would I call for help? I knew no one in London. I had no money, no credit card, no train ticket, nothing.

I looked down at my bruised ankle and scuffed shoes; at my silver dress with its silly tutu skirt. There was a splatter of toilet-bleach blue on the hem. My stomach roiled again.

This was the stupidest idea ever.

My parents were right: my instincts were bad; I needed to be protected.

'Look who it is . . .'

My gaze flickered upward to see a man approaching me. His clothes were dark, rendering him a shadow on the dim street. But, when the streetlamp's light hit him, I saw that he was young, handsome, with olive skin and sleepy soulful eyes. He met my gaze, smiling big – yet there was something wrong about his expression.

'Hey, hey, hey . . .' he said.

My shoulders flinched inward and I angled my body away from him. Maybe if I ignored the man, he would go away. It could have been my life's motto, even though it had a terrible track record of working out for me.

'If it isn't Miss Marilyn Monroe herself . . .' He flourished a bow in my direction. 'What are the chances?'

'Sorry,' I mumbled.

It was the sort of general apology I defaulted to in life. Sorry for whatever's upset you. Sorry I don't have anything for you. Sorry for existing.

'What are you sorry for, Jemima?'

Oh, shit.

'What could you possibly have to apologise for. *Jemima.*'

Shitshitshit. My mouth was dry, my tongue a dead slug. It took me a few seconds to form a sentence.

'Sorry, you've got the wrong person.'

'I've got the wrong person? Oh, sor-ry.' His sing-song sarcasm rang out down the dark street. 'Isn't that a motherfucker? Got the wrong person.' He paced back and forth in front of me. 'Well, lemme tell you – you got the wrong person in me. Chose the wrong person to fuck over.'

He leaned into my personal space and I cringed away.

'I know it's all happy pills and Monopoly money to you, but I have to earn a living. And when you don't pay me, it's a big fucking problem.'

My heart jumped to my throat. Adrenaline kicked me into gear and I tried to shove past him. He caught my arm and slammed me back against the wall like I was a rag doll. My head cracked against the brick and it dislodged something in my brain.

I laughed.

I couldn't help it. This was all too absurd.

After everything that had happened, this was how I was going to die. Not as myself, but as someone else.

'Think this is funny?'

His face twisted into a snarl and it made me think of the face-painted tiger. Streak his cheeks with black and orange and he couldn't have looked more feral.

'I want my money, funny girl. Sell some of your jewellery, sell your goddamn cunt, I don't care. I want it all.'

Each word hit me like a physical blow. I closed my eyes, expecting him to crack my skull against the wall again, wrap his hands around my throat and finish me off. Instead, he pulled back, the press of his body against mine gone. When I heard him speak again, it was fainter. My eyes opened to see him walking away in the direction of the party.

'I mean it this time, Jem,' he called over his shoulder, 'I mean it . . .'

'Hey!'

A figure jogged down the road towards me. The voice was familiar, but it belonged to a different life.

'Hey, man, what's going on?' Katsu asked, as the big-fuck-ing-problem guy brushed past him.

'Ask your girlfriend . . .'

The guy squared his shoulders and kept on walking, disap-pearing up the path to the party's red front door.

The sight of him leaving sucked the tension out of my body. My head drooped on its neck like a wilting flower. I hunched over, breathing heavily, bracing my hands against my thighs.

'Ella!' Katsu said when he finally reached me. 'Are you okay? What was all that?'

He palmed the joint of my elbow, leaning in close to me; somewhere between a hug and not. I flinched, remembering the way the other man's words had lashed against my skin.

'I'm fine, I'm fine . . .' I whispered.

It was another default response. Don't worry about me, I'm fine. Everything's okay, I'm fine. I won't bother you with my pain, I'm fine.

'You're shivering,' Katsu said. He took off his dinner jacket and draped it over my shoulders. 'That looked kind of intense. Did he think you were Jem or something?'

'Yeah,' I gasped out. 'He wanted . . . money.'

'Really? Carlo can be a bit of loose cannon.' Katsu rocked back on his heels. His lips were thin, his face taut with worry. 'What's Ripper got herself into now?'

I thought of Jem's little display with Stan, offering herself up on a platter to him. Now this. There was obviously a lot that my double was keeping secret from Katsu.

I let him guide me back down the street to the party, even though the last thing I wanted was go back in there. His arm hovered at my back, perhaps worried I might faint. When I spoke, my voice had a groggy quality and I wondered if he could be right.

'I need to go home . . . get my stuff . . .'

'Yeah, we'll find Ripper and leave,' he said.

I yanked a hand through my hair, which had turned from tousled to bushy, wishing I had a band to tie it out of my face. It occurred to me that Jem was probably still in the Lust room. Perhaps her feminine wiles had worked on the director guy, after all. I glanced at Katsu. Guilt pinched at my windpipe, even though I didn't have anything to feel guilty about. I hated the way my double and I were bound together.

Should I tell him?

Or would that be betraying Jem, betraying this new sister of mine?

'What's up, Al?' Katsu said, as we passed the bouncer.

He waved us through the door and into the house. I almost asked to wait outside – the sight of the entrance hall raised beads of sweat on my skin – but I didn't want to be alone.

The acrobats, at least, were gone, and the crowd in the high-ceilinged room had thinned out. I sagged against the wall. Beside me, Katsu was typing, thumbs skimming across his phone. His jaw was clenched.

''Course she's not replying,' he said. 'Her phone's probably down a toilet somewhere.'

I nodded, but I was barely listening. My attention rested on the two strips of fabric that hung from the ceiling. They glowed eerie-white. Up above was the warning, *Pride comes before a . . .*

I let my eyes drift out of focus, reducing the words to a blur. Pride. Maybe that was my problem. My mother would be able to turn tonight into a parable. Her certainty would be unshakeable. If you had a bad day, God was warning you, testing you, or both.

The strips of fabric shivered. Silks, that was what they were called. Someone was climbing the silks. In my dazed state, it took me a moment to realise who it was.

Jem climbed with none of the finesse displayed by the acrobats who'd used the silks earlier. She only made it a few feet off the ground before her long red dress tangled around her feet. Dropping back to the floor, she wavered on the spot and then ripped at the slit in her skirt. It tore open, revealing a slice of skin and a black strip of lacy underwear.

She resumed her ascent. Higher and higher. The only thing she seemed to have going for her was natural agility, combined with unshakeable, drug-fuelled confidence. But that was all she needed to get two metres, five metres, ten metres in the air.

I watched myself climb to the ceiling; an out-of-body experience made real.

I reached out to grasp Katsu's arm, but he didn't need me to alert him. Jem was making her presence known.

'Heyyyy . . .' she called from her perch. 'Look at *meee* . . . Nine years of gymnastics . . . and I'm great in bed, too . . .'

She paused to wave and almost lost her balance. With a swooning sensation, I watched this woman – this woman who looked so much like me – hang on to life with one careless hand. I felt, once more, like I might vomit.

Katsu lurched into action, sprinting across the entrance hall. But when he grabbed at the bottom of the silks, that only caused Jem to sway dangerously above.

'Get her down!' he yelled at the people close by.

'Calm down, mate,' someone yelled back.

Above the crowd, Jem climbed even higher.

'She's fucked off her head!' Katsu said.

There was a burst of laughter from nearby partygoers.

'Aren't we all?'

'She'll *fall*.'

Katsu's desperation finally had an effect. It cut through the gawping apathy of the onlookers. The crowd stirred into action. A group of guys, dressed for acrobatics, many of them with smeared animal faces, assembled in the entrance hall. One began to climb the length of fabric, while the others formed a catchers' circle below.

'Noooo . . .'

When her rescuer reached the top of the silks, Jem swatted him away, her voice petulant as a child's.

'Katsu, look!' she called down, waving. 'I'm fiiiiine.'

Even as she spoke, Jem almost lost her balance, making the fabric sway.

'Katsuuuuu!' she said again. 'Loooook!'

He turned away from the spectacle. I wondered if it was because he didn't want to give her more attention, or because he couldn't stand to look at her.

It took a long time to coax Jem down, and the crowd of onlookers kept growing. The attention buoyed her mood higher. At last, though, she consented to let the acrobat help her down, using his shoulders as a makeshift ladder for the descent.

It was several tense minutes more before Jem finally dropped to the floor. Her face was flushed and unrepentant. Her torn skirt still revealed lacy black underwear. She made an extravagant bow. Several people in the crowd were applauding, wolf whistling and laughing.

Katsu was not.

*

My double's Chelsea apartment block, which had looked so lavish in creamy sunlight, seemed creepy and over-large at night. In the corridor that led to Jem's front door, she leaned heavily on Katsu's shoulder, while I trailed behind. He'd driven us home in Jem's brand-new yellow VW Bug, while she had dozed on the back seat.

'Jem, where are your keys?'

Though Katsu's voice was perfectly level, I noticed that it was maybe the first time since we'd met that he hadn't called her Ripper. Jem closed her eyes and pressed her face against his T-shirt. She made an indistinct noise in the back of her throat, like a child who didn't want to get out of bed on a Monday morning.

Katsu shook his head, working a muscle in his jaw. He grabbed the small silk handbag that was looped over Jem's shoulder and handed it to me.

'Find her keys, would you?'

I felt like a burglar, digging past used tissues and chewing gum till I found the keys. Fumbling with the lock, it took me a few tries to get the door open.

Inside, Katsu half-carried Jem to her bedroom. He pushed her on to the bed and she scarcely moved from where she fell. I had a paranoid sense that maybe she really was dead or dying. It was now obvious to me that my double wasn't just high on life. She'd avoided falling to her death on the silks, but what about the drugs churning through her system?

'I need to get home,' Katsu said to me. 'Working tomorrow. Need to get a few hours' sleep. Can I drop you somewhere? Train station? Hotel?'

I sunk my hands into my jacket – Katsu's jacket – and avoided his gaze. I'd implied earlier that I had a hotel room for the night. In truth, when I'd looked at prices, even the cheap ones were more than I was able to afford. Back home on Walney, when I'd been planning the trip to London, I'd had some romantic idea that I might wait out the wee hours in an all-night café, sipping hot chocolate and having stray conversations with fascinating strangers.

Stupid.

It would be best to go to the station, bundle myself up warm in a plastic chair and wait. There would be a train going north in four, five hours. Yet the idea of it was so pathetic that the strain must have shown on my face, because Katsu said:

'You can kip here tonight, if you want. Jem won't care.'

As if to punctuate the moment, my double let out an almighty snore and rolled over in bed. Her eyelids fluttered open and she murmured, '*Kaaaatz.*' A smile crossed her slack face and Katsu gave a rueful smile in return.

'It's okay,' he whispered and brushed a lock of hair off her cheek. 'You're safe.' When she settled back into sleep, he pulled back, stepping away from the bed.

'Get some rest, yeah?' he said to me. 'It's been a crazy night.'

Nodding, I took a dizzy step and almost collided with Jem's make-up table. I wished the night would end. I wanted to teleport somewhere else. Not home, just . . . an elsewhere of some kind.

Katsu reached out a hand, and I thought for a moment he was going to hug me. But he just reached past me to open the door.

'Jem'll be fine when she wakes up,' he said. 'A bit grumpy, but that's nothing new.'

I nodded again, ready to crawl into bed – any bed – and end it all. I followed Katsu out into the dark corridor. He didn't ask for his jacket back and when he spoke, his voice was distracted, like he wasn't talking to me but himself.

'Don't hold it against her, yeah? She's not usually like this.' He let out a long, sighing breath. 'Alright, she's always like this. She's always so set on being herself; she just goes too far sometimes. That's what makes her Jem.' He smiled and, though his voice was still irritated, there was a shine to eyes that was visible even in the half-light. '

On her best day, she'll make you feel like you're the centre of the universe . . .'

And on her worst day?

Katsu didn't finish his sentence.

'She's a force of nature,' he said instead.

I nodded as if I understood, but I could feel a tiny sob rising in my throat. I forced myself to swallow it down.

Even after her crazed behaviour, even in spite of his anger, Katsu still loved Jem. Who would ever feel that way about me?

8

OUT OF FRAME

Ella

Inside the mirrored funhouse, a clown jammed his fist against a big red button. *Bzzzzz.* His white face, with an oversized mouth painted orange, stared at me from three sides. *Bzzzzz.* I twisted away from his many reflections, kicking my feet. *Bzzzzz.* The mirrors shifted and I wasn't standing anymore but lying down, my body tensed on the edge.

I opened my eyes. A beam of sunlight made me squint them closed again. I'd slept on the sofa and I was right on the edge, my feet tangled in a blanket. I heard the sound again. *Bzzzzz.* Rubbing my eyes, I got to my feet.

I drifted through the apartment, the wooden floors warm against my bare soles. The dreamlike feeling wouldn't let go of me. I wondered if I was still asleep, or if I'd been asleep for years and this was real life.

Bzzzzz.

The intercom screen on the hallway wall showed a dark-haired woman. She tossed her hair and I imagined the sound of her high-heeled shoes tapping against the stone step. On automatic, I picked up the intercom's phone.

What was I supposed to say?

Hello, this is Jemima, how may I help you?

I slammed the receiver down again. Reality jolted back into place.

The woman pressed the buzzer yet again and its harsh call echoed through Jem's apartment. Still it wasn't enough to rouse my double.

I chewed my lip. If I waited, the woman would go away. If I did nothing, it would all go away, right? Even as this thought settled in my mind, a bald black man in a suit bounded into view on the intercom screen. He unlocked the door and held it open for the woman.

Oh, shit.

I scurried through the flat to find Jem, my bare feet slipping against the wooden floor. I almost ended up in the laundry room, before I corrected course and slipped into the bedroom. Inside, it was cave-like, curtains drawn, and smelling of sour breath. My double still slept like the dead, sprawled out across the covers of her bed. I crept over and put my hand on her shoulder.

'Jem . . .' I whispered.

No response.

I shook her shoulder. 'Jem!'

She took a snorting inhale of breath. Her eyes blinked open and then closed again.

I imagined the dark-haired woman cresting the stairs, flouncing down the corridor to Jem's apartment. As if on cue, there was a knock on the front door. It wasn't a polite little tap. This knocking was dull and continual, like angry applause.

'Jem, you need to wake up!'

I leaned in close, my whisper becoming urgent. She opened her eyes for real this time, meeting my gaze. Her face, slack from sleep, tensed. She jerked back, flinching away from me.

'Someone's here, you need to wake up,' I said.

When she spoke, Jem's voice was hoarse, edged with fear. '. . . Ella?'

I nodded.

She slumped against the bedcovers, a hand covering her heart.

'You scared the shit out of me. I thought that coke was cut with something.'

'There's someone at the door,' I said.

'Ugh, just get rid of them.' Jem rolled over in bed, pulling the sheet over her head.

I rocked back on my heels. The gloomy bedroom was airless. I couldn't catch my breath. The sound of the knocking on the door had merged with my headache. Was it just a hangover, or something psychological?

In the bedroom's full-length mirror, I caught a glimpse of my reflection. The woman had a fright-wig of hair. Her eye make-up was dark and her lips were red raw. Her silver dress was twisted around at the hips.

It was Jem who looked back at me in the mirror.

'Hello!' I said, swinging open the front door.

'So she lives,' the dark-haired woman said.

In one movement, she managed to kiss me on the cheek, slide past me (uninvited) into the hallway, and give me a swat on the shoulder. The woman had a dancer's way of walking, the sway of her hips contrasting with her business-y black dress.

'I'll be charitable and assume you forgot,' she said, 'because the alternative is that you deliberately blew it off.'

She had smooth brown skin and huge reproachful brown eyes. A hint of American surfaced in between the drawling upper-class English accent.

'Sorry,' I said, a reflex.

'It's been three years of sorry and I'm a little sick of it.'

The woman clattered into the living room and I drifted in her wake.

'Did I miss the part where you offered me a drink?' she said, waving a manicured hand. 'A water, if you have it.'

I was going use the faucet, then thought better of it. I dithered for a moment in the kitchen, but the huge American-style fridge was hard to miss. I grabbed a cloudy-grey glass bottle from inside, scanning the label to check it was water and not vodka.

'I know it's just a brunch, but it's not just a brunch.' The woman paused to take a sip of her drink. 'I've left Dave near the bottom of his bottomless mimosa. The play hasn't even opened and he's a mind to fire you. There's only so much damage-control I can do, Jemma.' She fixed me with a hard stare. 'You need to get your ish together.'

It was so weird, to have this woman – this stranger – look into my eyes and talk to me like we'd known each other for years. At any moment, surely, the façade would crumble. The clock would strike midnight and I'd turn back into Ella.

The woman took my silence for sullenness. She gave a little huff.

'It was a blow, not to get the Stan Lembo movie, I get it. I know this is' – her fingers gave a twitch – 'only theatre. But look at it as a stepping stone. Sometimes you have to spend some time in the trenches and fight for what you want.'

She raised her eyebrows expectantly.

'Okay,' I said. Then, catching her irritation at my answer, I added, 'I'm really sorry, about brunch, my mistake.' It was precisely the opposite of what Jem would have said. 'What can I do to fix it?'

'Get yourself smartened up.' Her lip curled as she regarded my silver dress, stained with flecks of blue and sitting wrong on my hips. 'Have a mimosa with Dave, smile pretty, maybe we can salvage this.'

I gave a tiny nod. 'Okay.'

She discarded her bottle of water on the counter and shot me another stare. It was a look that peeled layers off my skin, yet still she didn't see anything but Jem. The sensation left me lightheaded.

'I'm not one for threats, Jemma, but . . .' In lieu of finishing her sentence (her threat), she dabbed a kiss on both of my cheeks.

She swept out of the apartment without saying goodbye, leaving behind a breath of spicy cardamom.

*

It took me ten minutes to finally rouse Jem. My mother always used to threaten to throw water over me if I didn't get out of bed on time. I considered grabbing another chilled bottle from the fridge and dousing Jem with water, but she did at last return to the land of the living.

When I passed on my halting description of the dark-haired woman and what she'd said, Jem grabbed her phone and scrolled through her messages at speed. 'Shittingfuckingbollocks,' she muttered.

I'd expected her to laugh it off, but my double seemed rattled by the situation. Still dressed in last night's torn red dress, she paced the length of the room, massaging her temples like she was trying to get her brain to work.

'What did Savannah actually say?' she asked me. 'She's not firing me?'

'No . . . I mean, I don't know. She really wanted you to go to the brunch thing.'

'Ugh, that director guy is a freak. His play's completely wacko.'

'It's a stepping stone, though, isn't it?' I said, echoing the woman's words.

Jem wasn't listening to me. She disappeared into her walk-in wardrobe and I heard hangers clanging on the rails.

Left alone, it occurred to me that I should change, too. In a pile of dirty clothes on the floor, my jeans and jumper were jumbled up with a patterned minidress. I wrenched them free. They looked even shabbier than I remembered. I slid the silver dress off my body in a hurry, pulling scritchy wool over my head and pushing numb legs into my jeans.

I was fastening the button on my jeans when Jem stuck her head round the door of the wardrobe.

'Savannah actually thought you were me?' she said.

I nodded.

'God, people are stupid.' She gave a nasty laugh. 'You don't fancy going to brunch, do you? You can eat eggs benedict and flirt with Dave. I'll pay you.' Without waiting for an answer from me, she affected an old-timey advertising voice. 'Jemima's ver-ray own lookalike service. For all the tedious meetings you can't be bothered to attend.'

I felt like I'd been hit. I didn't like my double very much, but for a while last night, the two of us had been allies. This morning, it was obvious I was just a plaything to her.

'No, thank you,' I said coldly. I held up the shimmering dress. 'Where should I put this?'

'Keep it.' She shrugged. 'I can't be bothered to get it dry-cleaned.'

Jem, who'd changed into a mustard-coloured romper, waltzed back into the room and flopped on to the bed, apparently not in any hurry to go to brunch after all.

Did I even want to keep the dress? I wasn't sure, but I tucked it under my arm anyway. On the bed, Jem was scrolling through her phone. She let out a sigh that sounded more like a groan.

'Tell me the truth,' she said. 'How much of a tit did I make of myself last night? Was that a hallucination, or did I really climb up that silk rope thing, like some shitfaced monkey doing tricks?'

'Um . . .'

The noise Jem made this time was definitely a groan.

'Alright, that says it all.'

She rolled over, burying her face in the pillows. My cheeks flushed with second-hand embarrassment. I was torn between anger and pity.

'How pissed off was Katsu?' she asked, her voice muffled.

'He'll forgive you,' I said.

With cold certainty, I knew he would. I turned away, heading for the door.

'Hey, are you really leaving?' she called.

I paused, wondering if she might invite me to stay longer,

suggest we do something together after her brunch meeting.

'Get me a bottle of Lauquen from the fridge on your way out, would you?'

Jem didn't even look up as she spoke. She'd gone back to her phone. Whatever interest I'd held for her had now vanished; a Christmas toy cast aside on Boxing Day.

*

'*This is the 13:40 train from London Euston to Manchester Piccadilly, calling at Crewe, Wilmslow, Stockport . . .*'

Seated on the train, I stared out the window at the last-minute passengers who crowded through the doors. There was a lumbering gait to one of the men. My heart stuttered.

I recognised him.

It was the guy who'd threatened me last night, the big-fucking-problem guy. Carlo? Wasn't that what Katsu had called him?

The man turned, scanning the carriage with a bland expression. The nose was bigger, his brown hair cropped shorter. Of course it wasn't him.

I sagged back into my seat. The whistle blew and, at last, we began to move.

After the commotion with Jem's agent, I'd forgotten to talk to my double about him. Should I have told her? Warned her?

My skin crawled. I cast a look over my shoulder, making one last check that the man was nowhere in sight. It was Jem's big fucking problem. It wasn't mine. She had to pay him, that was all. Money could solve all problems.

The train chugged onward and London receded, countryside creeping in to replace the city. The miles between me and my double mounted up. It was a relief, yet disappointment swilled in my stomach like bleach-blue liquor.

My phone buzzed in my pocket. Probably more nagging, telling me to come home. I fumbled the phone and opened up the new message:

That was fun! Lets do in again sometime! Heres some pictures from last nite

I read the message twice. It was from Jem. We'd exchanged numbers back when I'd first agreed to meet her in London. Now, I felt an irrational urge to block her number or, at the very least, delete the message. Curiosity won out, though, and I followed her web link to look at the pictures.

These must be the shots taken by the photographer.

Filled with motion and colour, they were fluid and lovely. The party had turned nightmarish in my reality, but captured digitally, it was a wonderland. There were some panoramic shots of the mirrored ballroom and many more close-ups of partygoers.

I almost scrolled past the pictures of me. I appeared in the first shot off to the side, a bright, silver fish, writhing away from the camera, caught up by the stream of people. In the next picture, the camera claimed me, front and centre, dancing. My head was tipped back. I looked up to the heavens, face rapturous, as if the Envy ballroom were a church.

The name of the next station was announced over the loudspeaker, but I was deaf to it. I stared down at my phone, transfixed.

On the face of it, the picture was nothing. One shot among a dozen. A little bit arty, perhaps. One that an average person might choose to save. *That's a cute picture*, they'd say, before shrugging and moving on. But for me, it wasn't just that.

The woman in the picture didn't look like me. It was hard to pin down why, exactly. The shift of her shoulders, maybe? The gleam in her eyes? The twist of her smile? It was something about the way all those things worked together . . .

The woman didn't look like me, but it was me.

The thought was a simple one on the surface, but the more I turned it over in my mind, the more paradoxical it felt.

The woman in the picture had a life of her own. I couldn't help but wonder what would happen if she cracked her neck and climbed out of the frame.

*

Later, at home on Walney Island, I lay in bed, listening to the rain, bathed in the glow of my bedside lamp. Archie was curled up at my feet; a makeshift hot water bottle in the cold room.

I couldn't resist looking at the picture just once more.

The door of the caravan nudged open. I flinched and let my phone fall screen-down on to my chest. I covered it with my hand for good measure.

'So you're finally home.'

'Mmm,' I said.

'You'd better get some sleep.'

'I will.'

'Thought you'd be tired, after going goodnessknowswhere with goodnessknowswho.'

'It was just Lancaster.' I sat up in bed, disturbing the dog, who let out a low whine. I slipped my phone beneath the bed covers. 'Went to see an old uni friend.'

'I was worried about you; ask your father, I didn't sleep a wink last night.'

'Sorry.'

Mum swiped a stray tendril of grey-blonde hair out of her eyes and took two steps into the room. She brought with her a scent of disinfectant from the bottle she held. A rag dangled from the fingertips of her other hand. In the caravan's tiny kitchen, she spritzed blue cleaning fluid onto the work surface and rubbed hard at a reddish stain.

'Don't mind me,' she said. 'There's a family coming tomorrow, they might get here early.'

'I thought you said . . . the season's over . . .'

I swung my legs out of bed and Archie scrambled to take

my place in the warm spot.

'Half-termers, we're lucky to have them,' Mum said. 'Don't worry, I've put clean sheets on the bed in your old room.'

I lived near Snab Point, on the sparsely-populated southern tip of Walney Island, where there were three things: a lighthouse, ghostly-white against the grey landscape; a nature reserve, with bad-tempered seals clambering across the rocks; and a caravan park. I might have made a good lighthouse-keeper, creeping up its winding stairs with a guttering candle, but it had been unmanned and automated for years. Instead, the caravan park was my home.

My parents and my younger brother Simon inhabited a three-bedroom mobile home that was generous by caravan standards, but tiny compared to even a modest house. It was cold in summer, frigid in autumn, agonising in February. There was no room for any belongings beyond the essential. But what was unbearable was the lack of privacy. Even a quiet conversation could be heard anywhere in the caravan.

A year ago, after much begging, my dad allowed me the use of one of the rentals on site. It was a one-bed caravan clad in alpine green and decorated with flowery curtains and cushions. Out the window, there was a distant view of the sands stretching to the ruined castle at Piel Island. It wasn't much, but it was mine – some of the time.

I was turfed out of my 'home' anytime my parents were able to get a week's rent for it. Then it was back to the miniscule room of my childhood in their three-bedder. Most of what I owned (clothes, books and notes from my uni days, the guitar I rarely played) was packed up and stored in one of the site's sheds. There was no sense in unpacking and repacking it every time I rotated caravans.

We weren't travelling caravaners – my parents ran Paradise Point as a holiday park – but the result for me was a nomadic feeling, albeit a nomad stuck in the sinking sands of Walney.

'But . . .' I said. 'What about . . . ?'

I didn't finish my sentence, but Mum rounded on me like I'd started an argument.

'Renting this place out is what puts food on the table, my girl.' Her voice was shrill, her lips pinched. 'Don't you forget it. It's not your own personal hidey-hole. For that matter, I don't know why I'm the one cleaning.' She threw down her rag. 'It's your mess, you can clean it up.'

Anger made my jaw tighten and my scalp prickle. Was it so much to ask – to have a place that was mine? A caravan of one's own, in Virginia Woolf's parlance?

I had a fleeting image of what Jem would say in this situation: the devastating effect of her brazen laughter, her cutting sarcasm.

I wasn't Jem, though. And I was too tired to be drawn into the same argument.

'Okay, I'll do it,' I said in a monotone.

I shuffled over to the kitchen. In a normal house, that might have been ten or twenty paces. In my caravan, it was exactly three steps. I picked up the rag and pushed it robotically over the kitchen counter.

My mum let out a sighing breath, as if she were disappointed, even though she'd won. I'd seen pictures of my mum in her youth: big smile, matched by a big blonde 90s bouffant. She'd been a bombshell. Nowadays, Mum seemed literally faded: hair clipped into a bob; smile dimmed into something closer to a grimace. Maybe that was what life on Walney did to a person.

She leaned in close and, for a moment, I thought she was going to kiss me goodnight, like I was a child again. Instead, she swiped her thumb across my orangey-red lips.

'I don't like that colour,' she said. 'It's cheap.'

DAZZL! Magazine

Punch-Ups and Hook-Ups:

Double App Sparks Mayhem

Roxanna Norris

"It was just a laugh, right?" the sombre young man tells me over coffee. "Everyone I know has played on that app, so I put my photo on there, too. Turns out my double only lives 50 miles away. Crazy, right? I was sceptical, but he really does look like me. Obviously I had to meet him."

The lad I'll call Ryan hangs his head, clearly wishing he could go back and change the past. Ryan is now facing charges that could put him in prison for five years. There's a tag on his ankle and a thousand-yard stare in his blue eyes. All because he "met his double", Jake (not his real name), through the popular app MeetYourDouble.

"We went out for a pint," Ryan says. "It was a riot. Everyone stopped to talk to us, telling us we looked exactly like twins, couldn't believe we weren't related. The lasses loved it. I got so many numbers that night."

Before the night was over, things went from fun to frightening.

"I'm not gonna pretend I was stone-cold sober," Ryan says, "but Jake was *wasted*. Started ranting and raving, about how he was one of a kind and I was an imposter. He challenged me to an arm wrestle – to prove he's better, y'know? – and, when I won, he freaked out. I swear he threw the first punch."

Ryan's adamant about this, but some bystanders claim it was Ryan who initially attacked Jake. The incident escalated into a brawl. One onlooker captured part of the scene on his phone. The footage – which has racked up more than a million views on YouTube – shows Ryan and Jake rolling around on the floor of a pub, kicking, punching and screaming at one another. It's just another bar fight, except for the uncanny fact that the lads look identical.

Double vs. double; ding, ding, ding, round one.

What once seemed like an innocent craze has officially taken a sinister turn. Pull up the MeetYourDouble app and you'll find smiling photos of people posing with their doppelgängers. Now those photos are joined by a sober checklist: safety precautions that users should undertake when meeting their doubles offline. They include: meet in a public place, bring a friend with you, make sure your phone is charged, in case you need to call for help.

And maybe meet for bubble tea instead of tequila slammers, eh?

The so-called "brawling doubles" video, involving Ryan and Jake, might be the most high-profile incident connected to MeetYourDouble, but *DAZZL!* has dug up more dirt on the app. Think its users simply meet up and go frolicking hand-in-hand? Think again.

Our research reveals scores of doppelgängers behaving badly. For one young woman, her double didn't turn out to be her best friend – more like her worst enemy. She claims her double stole her boyfriend. She actually walked in on the two of them having sex! (Yes, it still counts as cheating, even if the other girl has the same face as your girlfriend . . .)

That's not the only tryst linked to the app, either. One proudly gay user is even *dating* his double. Talk about a modern-day Narcissus! "We're in love. It was all meant to be," the lad revealed to us in a telephone interview. Crikey! We're big supporters of same-sex marriage, but isn't this definition of 'same' a bit literal? Maybe, if you're looking for love, stick with Tinder.

Downloading MeetYourDouble could pierce your heart – or rupture your bank balance. A contact at the Metropolitan Police reveals that fraud cases linked to the doppelgänger app are on the rise.

No one likes getting their monthly bills and bank statements, but what if that envelope on your doormat is an overdraft notice for a bank account you never knew about? You might swear blind it's not your account – your ID was stolen – but what if the bank has video footage of a person who looks like you, opening up the account? This is the legal quandary facing dozens of MeetYourDouble users who allege they've been duped by doppelgängers that stole their identity.

MeetYourDouble provided the following statement: "We would like to remind users to stay vigilant when meeting their doubles offline. Negative incidents represent an extremely small proportion of the interactions facilitated by the MeetYourDouble app. Thousands of doppelgängers have had positive experiences using our platform to meet their doubles – and we'd like to continue our mission of bringing people together."

Bringing people together or bringing people a whole heap of trouble?

These days, it seems, doppelgängers are less doppeldo and more doppeldon't. Our online poll found that fifty-nine percent of you think that the double trend is on the wane, while thirty-four percent think the MeetYourDouble app should be shut down entirely.

9

THE RIGHT PLACE

Ella

'Checking in?'

The receptionist, a tall blonde with high cheekbones, lifted her eyebrows. Though she was smiling, I caught a hint of sarcasm in her expression. I was dressed smartly, in my best M&S pencil skirt and suit jacket, but still I didn't belong here. A man in crisp tennis whites elbowed past, apparently without even noticing me.

'I have an appointment with Mrs Brannan?' I said.

The receptionist wasn't even bothering to fake-smile now.

'Oh, the job interview.' She waved a manicured hand at the Swedish-looking leather chairs that lined the wall. 'Take a seat.'

It was a long wait.

Perhaps it was part of the interview process. A psychological test. They were sweating me out.

Or maybe I just wasn't worth hurrying over.

For its guests, the hotel was an oasis of effortless chic, selling a version of Cumbria I didn't recognise. Huge photographs on the walls showed the fells, a preternatural light making the grass glow green, the rock faces gold. The Irish sea stretched out in the distance, mist rendering it ethereal. Stylised lettering over the reception desk read, *Welcome to Eden!*

Classical music, faint and non-threatening, filtered through the hotel lobby, offset by the sound of a burbling water feature. The marble beneath my feet was caramel-coloured and polished to a high shine. It reminded me of Jem's apartment block.

I grabbed a magazine from the stack on the table. On the

cover, a blonde actress gave an open-mouthed smile, like it was the best day of her life. *DAZZL!* Magazine. Celebrity gossip and lifestyle chatter. A little downmarket for a place like this, but I guessed rich people liked to slum it sometimes.

My eyes skimmed over the pages as I twitched from article to article. Nervous energy. It was the piece about MeetYourDouble that stopped me. I read it breathlessly, hunching over the magazine. Then I glanced up at the receptionist, paranoid that she might be watching me for a reaction. My face flushed, but she either wasn't looking or was pretending she hadn't been.

It was only a month ago, but already the weekend with Jem in London seemed more like a hallucination than a memory. I could still recall the tingling sensation of euphoria, of power, as I'd stalked through the party like I owned the place, but the feeling was faint now. It was something that had happened to another person.

Cumbria was my real life. The real me.

I razored a thumbnail along the spine of the article. Glancing again at the receptionist – she wasn't looking; she was playing with her phone – I tore out the page. Part of me wanted to keep it, tuck it away under my bed for safekeeping; another part of me wanted to shred it into a million pieces.

Instead, I began to fold it. Each careful crease produced a sharp edge. A few minutes of folding and I held in my hand a crane. I puffed up its wings with my finger. Fly away, little bird, fly away.

Owen, my ex, had been mad on origami. Whenever he came over to my house in Durham, he left presents for me: a rabbit in the cereal box, a tortoise in the bathtub. I'd kept a few of them, but the colourful paper had grown faded in the three years since uni. Where was Owen now? Did paper rabbits still peer out of his cereal boxes?

The two of us met in a queue. Five years ago. The line of people snaked all the way around the side of a brick building; so long that it should've been a queue for a concert or a rollercoaster ride. It wasn't. It was just a queue.

Our story wasn't a meet-cute. Not a tale for the grandkids. Yet fate threw us together, one dreary day as we queued. Owen was damp-haired from his morning swim; I was one step behind, looking for reassurance. 'This is the right place, right?'

I bit my lip and then stopped myself, remembering my lipstick. It was my first day on campus and I wore a cornflower-blue dress, with lips stained red. Looking around, I realised I'd tried too hard. The other girls were effortless in jeans and T-shirts; I was playing at being grown-up, sexy. Yet Owen smiled at me and something fluttered in my stomach.

'Need to get your student ID?' he said. 'Yeah, you're in the right place.'

Later that day, Owen kissed away what remained of my lipstick. Later that year, he became the only thing in my life worth living for. But, just then, we queued – impatient, bored, excited – and waited for our lives to begin.

'Miss Mosier?' the receptionist called.

My hand closed around the paper crane. I tucked it into my suit jacket pocket and stood up.

*

'It says on your application you attended Durham University, but you . . . didn't graduate. Is that right?'

'Um, yes.'

Mrs Brannan was fiftyish, with glasses and greying brown hair that feathered to her shoulders. When I'd introduced myself, she'd given an unfocused smile, like she already knew me. Maybe she did. We were 15 miles from Walney and still everyone knew everyone. That was the way of it in these parts.

Her accent was broad Cumbrian, but she tripped over herself in attempts to emphasise every word. It was an obvious move to sound 'posh'. It made me think of Jem's coaching. In my pocket, the crane still wanted to fly away.

'Academia wasn't a good fit,' I said. 'I'm more . . . practical.'

I'd practised that answer. To add to the effect, I tried out my new smile.

'Great, great,' Mrs Brannan said, her teeth clicking over the end of each word. 'As I'm sure you're aware, this is a very important role.'

'Yes . . .'

We were seated in her office and the glamour of the reception area was noticeably absent here. It was barely big enough to house a desk and two chairs. The yellow paint gave the impression of an institution. The only thing that persuaded me it wasn't a converted broom cupboard was the small window that overlooked the hotel's gardens.

'A pivotal role.' She sliced a hand through the air. 'You know, I started in this role when I was your age.'

'Wow,' I said, trying to hold my sarcasm in check, 'and you've really . . . come a long way.'

'That's exactly right.' She gave an encouraging nod. 'The sky's the limit. It really is. There are so many ways you can go in the hotel industry. Small hotels, big hotels. Country estates, boutique hotels. You're lucky to live here, it's really a hotspot in the hospitality industry.'

I forced another smile, nodding along with her. Yes, chambermaid in a hotel was my dream job. I was lucky. So lucky.

I didn't mind cleaning toilets. I was good at scrubbing floors. But the fakeness of the hotel industry bothered me. This was the Lake District for outsiders, packaging up Cumbria as a product. The rich people who swanned through this hotel didn't know the brittle cold of the winds that blew in from the Arctic in February. They didn't have sandbags for when the floods came. They didn't know what it was to look out at the wide open spaces of Cumbria and feel hemmed in by them.

Mrs Brannan scrutinised my application form.

'You've held . . . various jobs over the last few years.' She gave me a well-now-young-lady frown. 'We're not big fans of churn here.'

'It's unfortunate,' I said. 'Those jobs weren't a good fit.'

I was repeating myself, but what else was I supposed to say?

I'd worked in a clothing shop in Barrow-in-Furness, until my voice had taken on a shrill edge every time I said 'Perfect!' or 'Right away!'

'I'd like to try this on . . .'

'Perfect!'

'Can you get me a bigger size?'

'Right away!'

'I need to return this dress, even though I bought it two years ago and there's a stain on the crotch . . .'

'Perfect!'

'My baby's crying because she doesn't like your face, can you change it for me?'

'Right away!'

I'd worked in a big-box pet shop, until I'd begun to feel I had too much in common with the snuffling animals trapped behind glass. In a call centre, where I'd been a customer care representative for a homewares firm proud not to outsource, I was required to say 'Yes, of course' in a reassuring Cumbrian accent, while old ladies yelled at me about their crockery.

My best job had been at an arts venue, run as a non-profit, in the countryside near the southern edge of Lake Windermere, not far from this hotel. It was an asymmetrical, steel-and-glass building; part space-age, part Mondrian. Offbeat theatre companies rolled through every week in the summer and there were revolving exhibits of modern art.

I only worked serving drinks, at the boho-chic café/wine bar attached to the venue, but I liked the atmosphere of the place. It hosted open mic nights sometimes. I was working up the nerve to bring along my guitar and perform. One day.

The venue only represented culture on a small scale, but it was still culture. At least it provided a glimpse of people from outside the Walney bubble. I remembered a performance by a London theatre group of *A Midsummer Night's Dream* that somehow involved a lot of hula-hooping. After a Saturday matinee performance, one of the actors – androgynous, his mass of curly blond hair tamed in a manbun – leaned across the bar to speak to me.

'Must be so inspiring,' he said.

'What?'

'Living here. All this scenery. Eden.'

He cast a glance outside, through the slanted windows. For a moment, I saw it as he did. It was June and sunny. Mountains slumbered in the distance and there were oceans of lush greenery. I tried to hang on to that mindset. Afterwards, I wrote a couple of poems-slash-songs about nature, but when I read them back, they sounded insipid. It was fine for Wordsworth to lose himself in nature, but I wanted to write about –

noise and bustle and dancing in the dark, city streets that changed past midnight, foxes sloping home as we were just getting started

– life.

What was so great about Eden? Eve got so bored she ate the apple.

Mrs Brannan interrupted my spiralling thoughts.

'I don't like to judge anyone based on a piece of paper.'

She reached over and patted my arm. I tried my best to return her smile. Out of the corner of my eye, I caught sight of the Cumbrian landscape. It was not the picture of life painted by the photographs in the lobby. On this November day, the icy-grey sky threatened rain; the tree branches were knobbly and bare.

A few weeks after *A Midsummer Night's Dream* at the arts venue, before I ever found the courage to sing at an open mic, the non-profit lost its funding and had to close. The building was sold and turned into yet another hotel. The job went away, like so many before. It became more ellipses on my spotty CV.

'I'm all about work ethic,' Mrs Brannan was saying. 'Work hard and you'll be rewarded.'

'Mmm,' I said.

Mrs Brannan finally noticed I wasn't paying attention. Her lips pursed.

'Hard work,' she said, louder. 'That's the message that gets lost for young people these days. Want everything handed to 'em.' Her careful enunciation was going by the wayside as she picked up steam. 'Like they'll get a medal just for showing up. That's not how the world is. You take what you can get and you're happy with it.'

I gave her a hard stare. Blood drummed in my ears.

Was it so wrong to want more than the bare minimum? Three hundred miles away in London, Jem took what she wanted. She'd never sit here in this cramped office, kowtowing to a frumpy old woman for the chance to scrub toilets.

'Don't just sit around and wait for things to be handed to you,' Mrs Brannan said, her eyes bugging out.

'I don't. Just sit around,' I said through clenched teeth.

Fuck this job.

Fuck this doll's house of a hotel.

I wanted more. I deserved more.

10

LIVE, LOVE, UGH

Ella

'Now, Ella' – Mrs Brannan exhaled a long breath through her nose – 'the staff at this hotel are very close-knit. I worry you won't be a good fit.'

You're damn right I wouldn't be a good fit.

I almost stood up and walked out. I almost did it.

Then I heard my mother's voice at the back of my mind. *You need this job. We need it.*

Just because I never got the degree didn't mean my student debt had been wiped away. I'd maxed out credit cards to pay for food and rent at uni and, even years later, I was still underwater. My parents, too, had gone into debt to help pay for my great shining experience of a university education. Our debt connected us as much as our blood.

The caravan park wasn't much of an earner and, thanks to a bad back, Dad could no longer pick up casual work as a handyman. My parents, as well as my younger brother, relied on what little I earned from my sporadic employment.

We need this.

'Sorry, I'm just a bit nervous,' I said.

In Mrs Brannan's office, I cleared my throat, concentrating on keeping my voice level. I pushed my anger all the way down into my belly.

'But I really feel like I could fit in here, do a good job,' I said. 'I love a challenge and I'm good at learning new things.' I could hear my voice becoming a robotic drone. 'I really like to teach myself things. I've learned how to play the guitar and that's one of those skills that really requires practice and dedication . . .'

Mrs Brannan's eyes were glazing over. She didn't want to know about me. She already had an impression of me fixed in her head. Feckless, don't-give-a-fuck young person. Millennial slacker.

Who was I to try and change her mind?

*

My old-banger of a car rattled a warning as I drove away from the hotel. Whenever I went above 50 mph, it felt like the seats might drop out the bottom of the car and hit the road while the wheels kept on going. Today I didn't care enough to worry about it breaking down. I hit the accelerator and let the rattling settle into my body, my teeth chattering, my skull bouncing on my neck.

A familiar weariness swept over me as I drove through Barrow-in-Furness, following the signs for Walney Island. Light rain had begun to splatter across the windscreen.

'It's not even a real island!' one of the girls I worked with at a clothes shop in Barrow had once said, with narrowed eyes, as if I were lying about my hometown.

My father would have turned purple at the accusation. 'Of course it's an island! It has a proud heritage dating back to the Bronze Age!'

In the shop, folding ugly clothes, I'd shrugged and turned away, saying nothing.

Technically, Dad was right. At five square miles, Walney was the largest of a cluster of islands off the Cumbrian coast. However, a hulking concrete road bridge connected it to Barrow on the mainland. It was an open secret that the bridge was decrepit and, with no public funds to repair it, when it finally caved in on itself, it would set our island adrift for real. Until then, we were tethered; the bridge like a baby's arm flung out, clutching at his mother's skirts.

My car juddered across the bridge. Tides were low and the channel below had turned into an expanse of pock-marked sands. Instead of veering left toward Snab Point and the caravan park, I headed right, into the maze of identikit brick houses that formed the bulk of Walney. Its settlements might date back to the Bronze Age, but most of the island looked like it had been built wholesale in 1975.

I parked in front of one of the brown houses and got out. The drizzle had turned to rain while I'd been driving.

'Why didn't you text me?' Bethany said when she opened the door. 'I'm on tender hooks!'

Tender hooks, not tenterhooks. It made me think of fat pink slabs of meat hanging in a butcher's window. Tender. Hooks.

'How did it go?' she asked, her eyes bulging.

I pushed a lock of hair out of my face, blinking away drops of rain.

'I got it.'

Bethany let out a squeal and flung her arms around me. It was an awkward manoeuvre, since we had to hug around the wailing three-year-old that clung to her neck and the basketball that protruded from her belly. I disentangled myself and edged past her into the dry hallway. She hadn't actually remembered to invite me inside.

'We'll be working together, this is so exciting!' she said, loud enough to be heard over the clamour of her child. She nudged the front door closed and deposited Talia on the floor. 'You walk like a big girl now.'

'Thanks for putting in a good word for me,' I said, but Bethany was focused on three-year-old Talia.

The little girl shuffled through to the living room and I shuffled after her. Talia had an eerie mini-me look to her: the same flat brown eyes as her mother, the same smattering of freckles, the same red-tinged hair that Bethany swore was chestnut, not ginger. Today, Beth's chestnut-not-ginger hair clashed with her pink bathrobe. She heaved herself down onto the sofa and Talia clambered up to sit on her lap.

'So when do you start?' Bethany asked.

I perched beside her and tentatively placed my leather shoulder bag (it looked like leather if you didn't get too close) on top of a pile of (clean? dirty?) laundry.

'Tomorrow,' I said. 'I guess they need people desperately.'

She nodded. 'To be honest, it's a bit of a crap job, babe. But Mrs B's not too bad. And last Christmas, they had a big party for us. Champagne and everything.'

Bethany broke into a grin at the memory. She looked fourteen when she smiled. Not like a mum-of-two and a part-time chambermaid. She transformed back into the girl who could conjugate French verbs faster than anyone in our class. The girl who dotted her 'i's with tiny hearts and swore that, when she was older, she was going to live in Monte Carlo with a handsome French lover.

The smile dimmed when Talia bonked her on the head with a magic wand. Bethany wrestled it out of her hands. ('Don't hit Mummy!') The wand was plastic. It had a star that lit up in rainbow colours. When you pressed a button, it played a tinny electronic version of 'Twinkle, Twinkle'.

I glanced around the room. Brightly-coloured cartoons leapt from the TV, their soundtrack held at bay by the mute button. On the mantelpiece, wedding photos of Bethany and Stuart jostled for space alongside tarnished football trophies. A mass-produced sign advised, *live, love, laugh*. The 'la' of the last word was obscured by a smear of what was either Nutella or poo, so it actually read, *live, love, ugh*.

'You get that picture I sent you?' Bethany asked.

'Which one?' I said, even though I knew.

'I want it.' Between us on the sofa, Talia was grabbing at the wand. 'Mummy, I waaant it.'

Bethany hesitated, then gave the child an indulgent smile and let her take the wand back. 'No hitting,' she said without conviction. To me, she said, 'C'mon, he's cute. He's a mate of Stu's from work. He has a job and everything.'

He's cute. He has a job. He has everything. If Prince Charming were on Tinder, that was probably what his bio would say.

'Hold on, lemme find my phone,' she said, excitement flooding her cheeks with pink. 'I'll show you his Insta.'

She lifted Talia off her lap and plonked her down on my knee. 'Look after missus here, would you?' Bethany's pregnant belly swelled into view as she levered herself up off the sofa. 'Thanks, babe. I think have to wee again. Every ten minutes, I swear.'

Without waiting for a reply, Bethany waddled out of the room. Talia gave me a long searching look and then bopped me on the head with her magic wand. I grabbed her under her arms and jiggled her, hoping this might distract her. She giggled and bopped me on the head again.

I sighed, my eye caught once more by the wedding photos on the mantel. Stuart, Bethany's husband, was in our year at school. He used to draw dicks all over the textbooks. His BO was legendary and he once pissed himself during a football match. Now he and Bethany had a house. They had a baby and another one on the way. How had we all got so grown up so quickly?

When Bethany got back, thumbing distractedly up the screen of her phone, Talia was crying and no amount of knee-jiggling from me was making her stop.

'My waaaan' . . . I wan' my waaaaaan',' Talia wailed.

Bethany leaned in and swooped up Talia, patting her on the back.

'What does she want?' she asked.

'I don't know,' I said.

'My *waaaaaaaaan*'!'

'Oh, her wand. God, where did that bloody thing go?'

Bethany and I searched the sofa – underneath, in between the cushions – but with no luck. As Talia continued to wail, I fumbled in my suit jacket pocket for the origami crane. I held it up for her to see, using my fingers to flap its wings.

'You want it?' I gave an encouraging smile.

Talia's sobs calmed fractionally. Her chest still heaved, but she gave a tremulous nod. I placed the crane in her sweaty little hand. She stared at it for a long moment. Then she ripped its head off.

'Bad girl! Very bad girl!' Bethany swatted at the child. To me, she said, 'She's not good with anything breakable, y'know? It's Stuart's genes. Destructive bugger.'

'It's fine,' I said. 'No problem.'

Talia's crying renewed and Bethany hugged her close, swinging her from side to side. I picked up Bethany's battered pink phone, which had fallen onto the sofa cushion beside me. From the smudged screen, a skinny guy stood beside a barbecue and gave a gangster scowl.

'Cute, right?' Bethany said, as Talia's wailing reduced to the odd hiccup.

I shrugged.

'Keep scrolling!'

I did as I was told, finding more photos of the lad looking would-be tough in various other places (in a dingy pub, at a packed football stadium).

'He's dying to meet you. Want me to give you his number?'

'Sure,' I said, faking a smile, knowing I'd never message him.

This was how it was in Walney. Unless you got out, you settled for the way things were. You carved out a career with the council or the NHS, and hoped public-sector cuts didn't gut your job. Maybe you ventured into the vast ivory boxes hiding secrets of nuclear submarines. I'd hoped my degree might vault me into a career I could brag about on Facebook.

Not a work-a-day job, but something I was passionate about. Of course, I didn't have the requisite degree (just the debt), and the need for money trumped passion.

As Bethany had done, maybe I should look elsewhere for satisfaction. I should hook myself a Stuart, pop out a kid or three. Maybe that would make me happy.

I kept scrolling through the photos, just for something to do.

My eyes glazed over, the surly blue-eyed lad replaced by a fleeting memory of Katsu wearing a half-smile. His hands rested on my hips, sending shivers through my thighs. In my mind, he licked his lips and leaned toward me.

I shook my head and dropped the phone. Katsu wasn't mine. He would never be mine.

'So Miss Moneybags with the new job, what are you up to at the weekend?' Bethany asked.

'Not much.'

'Oh my god, lucky. I need to bloody clone myself, I'm so busy. Did I tell you about Stu's mum coming to visit? Claims she wants to see her grandbaby then won't even lift a finger . . .'

Bethany unmuted the TV for Talia to watch, and a jingle for breakfast cereal fought for dominance over her voice. I nodded sympathetically as she talked about how her midwife was a bitch and pregnancy was making her constipated and Stu was never home and life life life life life.

'So what do you think?'

I'd zoned out and missed the first part of the question, but I nodded automatically. 'Yeah . . .'

'Babe, you're a lifesaver.'

'Ummm . . .'

'Talia would looove some time with her Auntie Ella.'

Oh, shit. I'd agreed to babysit again, hadn't I?

I'd known Bethany since I was eleven and still I could never figure out if my quote, unquote best friend was a master manipulator or if moments like this were accidental. She always seemed to catch me unawares and make me believe I'd agreed to babysit or help her weed the garden or give her a lift to see her other friends.

'You're so excited to hang out with Auntie Ella on Saturday, aren't you, bubs?' she said to Talia, who was whimpering and beating her fists against Bethany's chest. Maybe in toddler terms that meant excitement.

*

My car lurched to a stop in the empty gravel parking area outside Paradise Point. Opening the car door, I had to duck my head against the rain and run toward my caravan. Its green exterior looked grubby in the fading light, but at least it was mine again. No more visitors wanting rentals now that it was November. My heart lifted. For a few months, it was a little slice of home belonging to me.

All I wanted to do was change out of my polyester suit skirt and wash off the layer of stickiness that coated my hands after an hour at Bethany's house.

I turned my key in the lock, but it was already open.

Paranoia welled up inside me. Hadn't I locked it? I wasn't forgetting things again, was I?

When I opened the door, there was a man inside. He cast me a sidelong glance that suggested I was trespassing.

I edged in the door and put down my faux-leather bag.

'You been fiddling with this again?' he asked, poking at the heater with a screwdriver.

'It wasn't working . . .' I said.

'You've been overusing it, that's why it's packed up again.'

Dad banged the screwdriver against the metal exterior for emphasis and I flinched. Of course. If there was a way for it to be my fault, it had to be my fault. Why on earth would you actually want a working heater in winter?

'Sorry,' I said automatically.

'Don't be sorry, just don't do it again.'

Don't use the heater? Was that Dad's solution?

He dropped the screwdriver into his toolbox and slapped it shut.

'You get the job?' he asked as an afterthought.

Dad was stocky, with a greying beard and thinning hair. He had a permanent stoop, like something heavy was pressing down on him.

I raked a hand through my wet hair and shrugged out of my itchy blazer.

'Yeah, I got it.'

'Well, thank Christ for that.' He heaved up his toolbox and a twinge of pain showed on his face. 'Time to get on and do something with your life, young lady.'

No *well done, Ella.* No *I know things are hard for you, but . . .*

Dad was a hardy Northern bloke through and through. It would never occur to him to sugar-coat anything.

I murmured 'Yes, Dad' and stepped aside to let him out.

When he was gone, I changed into jeans and a sweatshirt, but I couldn't get back the feeling of returning home. I saw the caravan as it really was: dusty floral curtains, stained worktops; a bed that sank in the middle. All the cheap plastic kitchenware was borrowed from my parents; the crocheted blankets on the bed had belonged to my nan. Everything was a cast-off. I was a squatter.

'So you're, like, a traveller?'

When I was at uni, I scrupulously avoided talking about my home life. Those friends I did eventually tell asked this question in hushed tones. (Those that weren't woke enough to know that it was a slur asked if I was a gypsy.)

'No, no,' I said.

It was tempting to lie. The idea of being Romani at least had a mystique to it: firing up the caravan and trundling onward

95

every few months, recapturing a romantic past of covered wagons and nomadic heritage.

'It's just a bunch of static caravans,' I said. 'Holidaymakers and stuff. My parents run the place.'

'Ohhh . . .'

Disappointment and confusion clouded their eyes. Most had no idea what a static caravan was – if their family had a second home, it was more likely to be a villa in Provence, not a tin box on the Cumbrian coast – and those that did found the idea a bit, well, common. I watched them grope around for a reaction. Usually it was some variation on: 'Living there must be like being on holiday all the time!'

I gave a tight smile in response. 'Right.'

On the roof of the little green caravan, rain drummed an insistent rhythm. Inside, a trickle of moisture ran down the wall, betraying a leak. Maybe if the job at the hotel worked out, I could earn enough to get my own flat. One with real walls and real heating and a roof that didn't leak.

I slumped onto the bed, emptying out the contents of my leather-not-leather handbag. The spark of optimism was already dying. My parents would hate the idea. Their finances were so precarious, they relied on me to contribute. That wasn't all of it, of course. They liked me close by. They needed to check up on me.

The truth whispered to me: they didn't trust me to live alone.

Next to me on the bed, I tossed aside the old tissues and the dog-chewed hairbrush that had fallen out of my bag. I picked up the magic wand. When I turned it on, a rainbow of colours flickered over the shadowy walls of the caravan. A tinny rendition of 'Twinkle, Twinkle' unsettled the air. I waved the plastic wand and closed my eyes.

When I opened them again, everything had stayed exactly the same.

11

KEEP GOING

Jem

I woke up on a train travelling too fast. I had no idea where I was or where I was going.

The coarse red fabric of the seat back scratched at my cheek as I struggled into an upright position. Out the window, rows of poxy-boxy houses flashed by. The speed of it all made my stomach churn. When I pressed a hand against my middle, it aggravated a different pain. Bruised ribs. Broken ribs?

'We will shortly be arriving into Rossington,' a voice announced over the loudspeaker. 'The next station will be Rossington.'

Rossington? Yeah, still no idea. At least I knew I was in mainland Britain. I hadn't accidentally woken up in Amsterdam. Although, on second thought, Amsterdwhisam had the distinct advantage of being A Long Fucking Way Away.

I leaned forward, wincing as my brain rattled against my skull.

'Where's this train going?' I asked the man in the seat in front of me.

'Hull,' he said.

'Hull?'

Amsterdam was definitely feeling like a better bet than my current circumstances.

'Yep.'

The man, a middle-aged wanker in a business suit, tapped officiously on his scruffy-looking laptop to show that I was bothering him.

'Well, you know the old saying' – I summoned a jovial

smile – 'if you're going through Hull, keep going.'

Tap, tap. He ignored me. My smile faded and I sank back in my seat.

The smell of last night's whisky was oozing out of my pores. My ribs hurt. My head ached. And an unfamiliar sensation twisted in my stomach: fear.

My life was in shambles.

I still owed Carlo ten grand.

I couldn't go back to London.

At the next station, people shuffled off the train, their seats filled by identikit replacements. A businessman took the place of a businessman. A mother and child slid into seats vacated by a mother and child.

To be on a train was to be nowhere at all. Not a person, just a body packed into a slow-motion form of teleportation. It was a relief.

The train began to move again, onward to the fiery pits of Hull. When I was a teenager, before I passed my driving test, I used to take trains a lot. I figured out a hole in the space-time continuum. This discovery was so ingenious, there should've been a Nobel Prize for it. If I told my mum I was spending the weekend at my dad's house, and I told my dad I was staying with my mum, it basically meant that I disappeared. Poof! Into thin air.

I made it into a game. I'd go to a station in London and get on whichever train was leaving next. To Colchester, Totnes, Newcastle – I didn't care, as long as it was Elsewhere. Depending on my whims, I'd get a fleabag room above a pub, or a suite at a hotel (paid for with Mother's credit card). Usually, my dear parents would get their facts straight and figure it all out. But, more than once, I came home on Monday or Tuesday and they hadn't even missed me.

The train to Hull bore that persistent smell of new plastic and old trainers that I remembered from journeys past. The smell brought up feelings of loneliness and desperation.

I scrabbled under my seat, locating my bag. At least I hadn't lost it. Ignoring the fact that I'd landed in the quiet carriage, I pulled out my phone and scrolled through my contacts list.

'Hey, what's up?' Katz said.

His voice was muffled by distance and maybe the fact that someone had aimed a kick at my temple. I switched my phone to the other ear.

'Just having the time of my life here in Rossington,' I said.

Katsu was silent. On the train, a woman shushed her wailing child. The loudspeaker informed us that the refreshments trolley was now serving snot muffins and pigswill.

'Seriously, where are you?' Katsu said.

'I'm nowhere.'

I stretched, cat-like, in my seat, and then regretted it when my muscles pulled painfully.

'Okay, cool.' Katsu's voice was flat. 'So you're either on a train or you've invested in a very sophisticated sound effects setup.'

'Yeah, do you want me to switch to farmyard sounds or French brothel?'

I took a deep breath and launched into my best impression of a courtesan's orgasm. The man who'd told me we were going to Hull turned around in his seat and gave me a filthy look. Pervert. Probably liked it.

Katsu cut me off as I was getting into the swing of my act.

'Hilarious,' he said, without laughing.

'I'm going to Hull,' I said. 'Come meet me?'

When I was 17, on one of my jaunts across the country, I called Katz and said, 'I'm on a beach in Broadstairs. Come meet me?'

I did it because I was bored and lonely and K was closer to the beginning of the alphabet than M (Matthew) or S (Steven) or the initials of any of the other boys I was stringing along at the time.

An hour later, he texted me from the train. He actually came. All the way to Broadstairs. It was out of season and the only people on the seafront were old timers who'd probably never before seen an Asian kid with purple hair and an eyebrow piercing. He ambled across the wet sand toward me. His face did a cute little frowny thing.

'I was worried,' he said. 'Didn't think you should be here on your own.'

We walked along the beach (grey skies, pretty in a monochrome sort of way). I dared him to go for a swim (he got knee deep before he ran back inland, bellowing laughter). We ate chips off a missing girl's faded newsprint face, and I guess it was our first date.

On the train, I listened to the quiet rhythm of Katz's breathing on the other end of the call.

'Come meet me,' I said again.

'For God's sake,' he muttered. 'You've done this so many times.'

If I weren't hungover, if I weren't bruised, if I weren't frightened, his words wouldn't have stung. I'd have given a nasty laugh and told him to fuck off. But today his cold tone chilled me.

'Come on, let's tear it up in Hull together.' I was trying to sound breezy, but I only sounded pathetic.

Jesus Christ, was I crying? I blinked rapidly to get rid of the tears.

'Haha,' he said – not a laugh but a statement. 'I have to be in the lab all day.' He paused. 'See you Sunday, yeah?'

I grunted. Did we have plans for Sunday? I had no idea.

We'd been stuck in an on-again-off-again relationship for eight years now. He was different these days – grown up, no more purple hair, not into the party scene anymore – but he still looked at me the way he did that day in Broadstairs. Soppy and worried and all knotted up inside.

I did stupid stuff and Katsu humoured me. That was how it worked.

'Where are you going really?' he prompted, a sigh in his voice.

I imagined him making that frowny little face again, but I didn't want to find it cute anymore. He was supposed to come when I called. That was how it worked.

My eyes had dried up now. My lips pressed together in a sneer.

'Nowhere,' I said.

I ended the call and tossed my phone back into my bag. Seconds later, I felt the dull vibration of an incoming call travel down my leg. I ignored it. I was busy climbing through a hole in the space-time continuum. I didn't have time for useless boyfriends.

The trolley trundled down the aisle and I grabbed a dishwater cup of coffee. My stomach clenched and a little vomit bubbled at the back of my throat. I forced myself to keep drinking. Caffeine leeched into my bloodstream. My headache eased. Unfortunately, the details of my current predicament came roaring back to me at the same time.

*

Yesterday, the day from hell, I started my morning at the police station on Earls Court Road. I know what you're thinking, but I was the victim.

I leaned across the reception desk and banged my fists on its grubby white surface.

'Someone stole my car!'

'Take a seat, please, Madam.' The horse-faced woman stabled behind a computer monitor spoke without looking at me.

'My' – I banged my fist – 'brand' – *bang* – 'new' – *bang* – 'car!'

My brand-new car, with not an insubstantial amount of coke stashed in the glove compartment. I didn't say that. But withdrawal wasn't helping my mood.

I wasn't a princess about my possessions. I didn't drive a

spotless Range Rover around the mean streets of West London. I didn't drop ten grand on a handbag. But I loved my cute little VW Bug, its candy-yellow shell like a Smartie. When I'd got up to go to the theatre, it was gone.

Horse-face behind the desk twitched her gaze over to me. Maybe she realised I wasn't just another scrubber who could be ignored. I stared her down from behind Chanel sunglasses and drummed my fingers against the desk.

'Name and licence plate?' she said.

Moments later, she'd dredged up a report from the depths of the computer system.

'There's a claim on it,' she said, tapping the keyboard.

'What does that mean?' I asked with a huff.

'Hasn't been stolen, it's been repossessed.'

'That can't be possible,' I said, my voice rising. 'Check again.'

What followed was what my mother would call 'a scene'. I hammered my fists on the desk. I shouted loud enough to spook the horse-faced woman. Another pig, a balding bruiser, appeared. He tried to lead me out of the police station and, when he laid a hand on me, I screamed bloody murder.

Of course, it was all for show. I didn't want to scurry out of there with my tail between my legs. Better to leave with threats of arrest than admit to a bunch of strangers that my car really had been repo'ed – and I knew who was responsible.

It was what my mother would call 'a lesson'. Mother had never bothered to do much parenting when I was a kid, but now I was an adult, she couldn't stop meddling in my business. I still got my allowance from her (a measly few thousand a month), but she wouldn't lend me any money on top of it.

'You need to learn the value of money. You need to do something with your life.'

She'd sent the bailiffs round to get my car. Soon I'd probably come home to my apartment and find that she'd changed the locks.

After leaving the police station, I walked (walked!) across London to my job, shivering in the pissing drizzle. Not all my credit cards were maxed out, but it was becoming a game of Russian Roulette when I handed one to a cashier or cab driver. Shitting fucking bollocks. I really wished I hadn't left the last of my coke in the car.

I got into the habit in LA, when I wasn't skinny enough for casting directors. It was hard to go to the right parties and then get up for cattle call at 6 a.m. without shoving carbs in my face. So I graduated from taking MDMA on Saturdays and smoking weed on Sundays to snorting coke continually.

The drizzle in the air turned to real rain, dripping down the back of my neck, past the edge of my faux-fur gilet. I didn't even enjoy doing coke anymore. I just wasn't myself without it. I'd cut down since I'd come home – I'd put the weight back on, too – but I didn't like the shaky feeling I got when I went without. I'd quit sometime. When I was 30 or something.

'You look like hell,' Sam, the lighting tech with a bowl haircut, said when I got to the theatre.

'I'm hell's very own bitch queen.' I shook myself like a puppy and then peeled off my gilet. 'Would you believe someone stole my car?' My nipples poked through the material of my orange top and I could see Sam noticed. He lingered in the backstage lobby, even though it was almost showtime. I entertained him with an embroidered version of the day's events. I was in full flow (police harassment, crime-ridden streets, etc.) when Director Dave bustled up wearing a bitchface.

'You're late,' he said to me. 'Everyone else is already in place.'

Beside me, Sam dematerialised. I let my head hang down and reached out a clutching hand to Dave.

'I was robbed! I've had a very hard day!'

'Riiight.' Dave shrugged off my hand, his greasy topknot quivering at the crown of his head. 'Just fucking get changed and get in your box.'

My latest artistic venture was a starring role in a play about climate change. Well, 'starring'. I was listed second in the show's programme and that was only 'cause I fought for it. Originally, I was listed third. After I didn't get that Stan Lembo film, my agent Savannah had tried to convince me that real actors did theatre. They soaked in the rich history of being on stage, treading the boards, performing Shakespeare for the unwashed masses.

My play wasn't quite Shakespeare, though. It was immersive theatre with a storyline that seemed to change day to day. (However much the storyline shifted, it didn't matter, because I couldn't follow it, anyway.) It was my job to jump out of a box and scream at the eleven-minute mark and then don a metre-tall mask for the alien abduction scene.

Savannah had been my agent for almost four years, and I could read between the lines with her. *Take this role, it's your last shot.* She might as well have said, *Don't take it and I'm done with you.*

I sloped off to the dressing room, which was really just a storeroom that led through to the toilets. Posters from previous productions papered the walls, with marker pen messages scrawled over the top. ('There's no business like show business!' 'Teeth and tits and grit and determination!' 'The people who make it are the ones who didn't quit!') Everyone else must have already been dressed and ready to go, because the gloomy little room was empty.

I was digging out the purple catsuit I wore for my first scene when I heard footsteps behind me. Probably pervy Sam trying to get a look at my tits. I whipped around, wearing a coy little *uh-uh-uh* smile.

It wasn't Sam.

It was Carlo.

Shitting fucking bollocks smothered in cum sauce.

12

DO NOT DISTURB

Ella

Every few steps, the broken wheel on my trolley of cleaning supplies let out a squeak of complaint. I gave it a kick and it kept on spinning. I felt like a homeless old lady pushing a shopping trolley that contained everything she owned.

Each door that lined the hotel corridor was identical apart from the brass plate room number. When I reached the next one, I knocked and called out, 'Housekeeping!'

In my head, I counted *one-two-three-four*, waiting for a reply. On 'four', I pushed open the door. This was the moment when my world collided with a different one. As I scanned the room, I couldn't help but tense up. I'd been working at the hotel for less than two weeks, but I'd already stamped most of the items on my bingo card:

Bloke wandering round in the buff.

Couple having sex.

Woman on the toilet with the bathroom door wide open.

These were the classics; the ones every maid encountered. The old-timers among the hotel staff had better stories to tell, of sex workers and kinky bastards. One swore she'd saved a man's life after he hung himself. She'd found him dangling, half-dead, and cut him down. She told the story proudly; her great humanitarian effort. I didn't like to tell her that the man probably took his suicide mission on the road, to a different hotel, one with less conscientious chambermaids, where he could kill himself in peace.

Usually what I found when I pushed open a hotel room door

was much more banal than sex or death. The guest lounged in the bed or on the sofa, in a bathrobe or sweats, munching on something sweet and watching bad TV. It was the type of behaviour that was normal in private, but in the presence of a stranger, it became intensely embarrassing. Most of the time, they waved me away, but sometimes they beckoned me in and watched, hawk-eyed, as I scrubbed and dusted.

Who needed TV when you could watch The Maid Channel, live and in person?

Needless to say, I preferred it when the rooms were empty. I could go hours at a stretch without having a conversation. The performance repeated itself, over and over. Knock, knock, *housekeeping*, no answer. Push the door, scan the room, eyes down, *oh, sorry*. Knock, knock. No answer. Push door. Eyes down. Squeaky wheel. Scrub, scrub. Knock, knock. No answer. *Oh, sorry.* Eyes down. Eyes down. Eyes down.

I slipped into another empty room and began my cleaning routine. Take rumpled sheets and make them smooth and flat again, with crisp corners and plump pillows. Take grubby, water-flecked porcelain and make it dry and white again. Take a mess and make it pristine.

Twenty minutes of hard work could create the appearance of perfection. The trouble was, I knew it was all for show. My fellow maids and I never changed the sheets unless they were visibly dirty (even when the room was prepared for a new guest). We never hoovered if we could help it. We used the same grubby cloth to wipe down each surface (vanity, basin, toilet). 'Everything should look perfect,' Mrs Brannan told me on my first day. Emphasis on the word *look*.

In the bathroom, I misted the air with cleaning spray, so that it would at least smell like disinfectant. I dried off the remnants of water from the guest's morning shower and then scrutinised the room. Everything *looked* perfect. Just one task remained. It was arguably the most important task of all. The task which, if I failed to do it, would earn me a bollocking from Mrs Brannan. I folded the end of the roll of toilet paper into a sharp V. Perfect.

Back in the bedroom, I stripped off my rubber gloves to give my sweaty hands a break.

When I was actually working, I didn't mind the job. It was when I stopped that the feelings of frustration resurfaced. Two contradictory strands of thought wrapped themselves around each other, squeezing my insides tight.

You should be ashamed – university educated and stuck cleaning toilets.

You should be glad – what makes you think you're worth anything more?

I let out a half-sigh, my lungs heavy and constricted. I checked my watch. Ahead of schedule.

I felt a reckless urge to launch myself onto the bed, leaving a big, messy, Ella-shaped dent in the bedding. I wanted to grab one of the overpriced chocolate bars from the mini fridge and chow down. Pop off the cap of a teeny-tiny bottle of booze, put my feet up, and watch daytime TV.

I sighed again. No point in creating more work for myself. No point in getting in trouble.

Instead, I allowed myself a few minutes to snoop. It was a harmless way to pass an idle moment. I knew other maids who pranked the guests, lifting dark-coloured clothing from the suitcase and using them to clean the bathroom floor. One confided in me that she had figured out exactly the amount of cash that you could get away with stealing. Clear out their wallet and they'll notice, but grab a ten pound note and the guest will assume they spent it.

I never did anything like that. I just liked to look.

I uncapped a bottle of perfume from the vanity and sniffed. Apples, with a floral undertone. It smelled like springtime. Not actual springtime, but imagined springtime, which was almost preferable. In the guest's make-up bag, I found pearlescent lavender eyeshadow. I swirled a finger in the palette and streaked purple across my eyelid. My reflection in the mirror showed raised eyebrows. My cheeks were ruddy from exertion. My hair was falling out of its ponytail. I hadn't bothered to cover up the dark circles under my eyes. I couldn't even remember the last time I'd worn make-up. (Yes, I could. I was in London and I wasn't myself.)

Using the heel of my hand, I rubbed off the eyeshadow, leaving behind a ghostly trail of lavender. I moved to the wardrobe. Inside, ten or twelve garments were draped in a neat row. A lot of guests left their clothes to languish, wadded inside an unzipped suitcase. It said something about a person when they unpacked and hung up their clothes.

Dragging a coat out of the wardrobe, I swung it over my shoulders. It was upholstery fabric, heavy cream embroidered with green-and-brown swirls. The collar smelled like apples. I closed my eyes and breathed in, feeling the weight of the fabric on my shoulders. What was she like, the woman who wore this coat? How did she spend her days? Was she married? Was she happy?

I opened my eyes. It must be pretty easy to be happy if your world smelled like springtime. I hung up the coat, slotting it back into place as if I'd never touched it. I pulled out a deep violet robe, a sheer layer of silk that melted against my fingers. I rubbed the material against my face and smelled apples again, chased by something sour, metallic. Probably my sweaty body.

I hesitated and then drew my arms through the violet robe, wrapping the silk around me, concealing my black maid's uniform. Another moment's hesitation and I launched myself onto the bed. Fuck it. I'd make it perfect again later.

Gimme five minutes of escape.

The pillows were soft against my back and springtime filled my nostrils. I pulled my phone from my pocket and dived in.

During my induction, Mrs Brannan had given me a long list of rules. She'd emphasised the fact that I wasn't to take personal phone calls while I was working. I'd nodded and said, 'No, never.'

In that respect, I was a model employee. No phone calls; just the bottomless expanse of the Internet.

I scrolled through Facebook, slowing down and speeding up; absorbing photos and skimming text. Other people's lives trickled into my hands.

Beautiful sunset tonight in Geneva. Wouldn't be anywhere else.

I was challenged to show how much I love my kids by posting three photos of them. Can't imagine my life without them. #soblessed

"A dream without a plan is just a wish . . ." Planning for the future, making it happen! Watch out, Seoul, I'm coming for you.

Spending today in the sun. Having fun exploring gorgeous places with this gorgeous man.

Celebrating two years in the best job in the world. Amazing. Hard folk pays off, folks!

All I need in the world is that smile . . .

BF got me choccies 'cause I had a bad day #luckiestgirl

Anyone up for bloody marys at 12?

Yes, I'm up for it. Let's sit in the sun and drink cocktails.

In the airless hotel room, the thrum of rain against the glass was loud. The offer – of brunch, of drinks, of dinner and a show – was always from a friend in Edinburgh or Beijing or San Francisco.

Since graduation – the graduation I didn't get to go to – my uni friends had scattered across the globe. Their Facebook updates were snapshots of glamorous locations and exciting jobs. Here at home, my school friends from Walney were all having babies. *The most important job in the world,* an inspirational graphic decorated with pastel hearts might phrase it. Everyone on my Facebook feed was doing something different. But all of them, at least, were doing something.

Out of habit, I clicked on to Owen's page. When we'd broken up, we'd agreed to 'stay friends', although only in the virtual sense. I only checked on him from time to time. (I checked obsessively. Sometimes ten times a day.) His profile pic changed periodically – different travel destinations, posing with different friends – but he didn't update much. His current location was listed as Berlin and his workplace a charity that helped political prisoners.

His most recent status read:

Hey peeps. Sorry I haven't been around. Too busy liveing my life!

I wanted to hate the fact that he'd misspelled 'living', but it gave a rakish, too-busy-to-worry impression that clawed at my heart. My fingers twitched. Without wanting to, I scrolled all the way down his page, time rewinding. Owen updated infrequently enough that our past together lurked within easy reach.

Totally planning on becoming a gourmet chef. Amazing success with the cheesecake tonight. Ella will tell you all. I'm a cooking genius!

Mine was the first comment:

> Owen almost killed me tonight, lmao. Happy anniversary, honey.

I stared at the words long enough that they started to look like gibberish.

For our one-year anniversary, Owen had cooked from scratch a lavish, four-course meal. He even lit candles for the occasion. Although, they turned out to be scented 'man candles', borrowed from his housemate, which smelled like burned hair. We blew them out after ten minutes of coughing.

Regardless, the first three dishes Owen cooked (figs in ham, smoked salmon, creamy pasta) actually tasted pretty good. It even added to the ambience that they were served, in true student style, on chipped plates and accompanied by wine in plastic cups. The slight hitch was dessert, a caramel cheesecake rich with sugar. Well, in theory, except Owen mixed up the salt and sugar. I only managed a bite of cheesecake before I gagged.

We passed the wine bottle back and forth, chugging it to try and take the taste away. Then we laughed so hard and for so long that we forgot what we were laughing about. Our *folie à deux* gigglefit lasted days, annoying the hell out of anyone who wasn't us. For a while, 'cheesecake' was our code word. A banisher of bad days, it never failed to make us laugh.

The word was just another hole in my heart now.

I forced myself to click away from Owen's profile. I pulled up my Facebook messages instead, unanswered on my part for long enough that my friends had stopped writing. There were invites to come visit (to Lisbon, to Melbourne, to Singapore) and, when I said I had no money, helpful suggestions accompanied by cute emojis. *Could your parents lend you some money? Could you start a business? Sell stuff on eBay?*

What did I know about business? What stuff did I have to sell? All I had in the world were bad debts. When I was at university, I assumed I'd be able to pay it all back when I got one of those funcoolawesome jobs in the city. Instead, I was stuck in Cumbria, earning £6.70 an hour.

God, I missed uni and how simple everything had seemed. When I'd left for Durham at the age of 19, I'd thought it was paradise. Not everyone's idea of paradise, perhaps, but it was mine. Paradise that came with cobblestones and *Harry Potter* spires. To me, it seemed cosmopolitan. My new friends teased me at how I excited I was by the littlest things in Durham. A multiplex with more than six screens! Nightlife that stretched to more than one nightclub!

There were art galleries that hung more than insipid water-colour landscapes. A thriving live music circuit. Sleek shopping parades that sold more than fleeces and thermals. There were festivals in summer and ice skating in winter.

My fellow students were interested in the world and interested in me. They held rollicking 2 a.m. debates about politics. We filled up our lives to the brim with wine and laughter.

And, of course, there was Owen. Tall and athletic, with tufty blond hair and an irrepressible smile, Owen was a mystery to me in so many ways. It was baffling that he leapt out of bed at six every morning to go for a swim. He pinged messages back and forth to his family constantly. There was his doctor mum, architect dad, plus cute-as-a-button younger sister, and he laughingly relayed stories about them as if they were his friends. He talked about his course (ancient history) with the same enthusiasm other blokes reserved for footie results. Most mysterious of all was that he seemed to like me for me. It took some getting used to.

While Owen was on a history course, I'd chosen to study psychology. It was a wobbly decision that I almost took back more than once. A business degree would be more sensible. Law, perhaps. Or something practical, like nursing. Yet psychology enthralled me. It empowered me. At last, I began to get a sense of control over the brain chemistry that had blighted my teenage years. I felt less like a freak. Maybe, in time, I could even train to help other people who suffered the same darkness as I had.

Dreams. Just dreams. They'd drifted away like smoke when I'd failed to graduate.

My reality was earning £6.70 an hour cleaning up rich people's messes. It was an awkward enough amount of money that totting up my earnings took a long time. I'd become very good at torturing myself with maths games. If I spent twelve minutes cleaning this bathroom, how much would it earn me? How much was a spotless toilet bowl worth? (Precisely £1.34.) If I continued to earn £6.70 an hour, how many years would it take me to pay off my credit card debt? How many grey hairs would I grow?

My mental arithmetic skills had never been sharper. But the answers I came up with made my stomach clench. If I worked hard, I could become a supervisor in a couple of years, maybe even aim for Mrs Brannan's job. Was that what I wanted? Would that make me happy?

On Facebook, I almost wrote a message to Cait-in-Beijing (my uni friend, who had a mass of curly hair and a smile that showed deep dimples; lover of Bloody Marys and drunken talk of socialism), but the words stuttered in my brain. We'd been close once, but now she seemed far away. Not just in a different country, but on a different plane of existence.

Looking for a distraction, I tapped the search bar on Facebook. Was Katsuhito an uncommon enough name that I'd find him? I scrolled through the list of search results – guys I didn't recognise, in places I'd never been to – until my heart gave a jolt. Found him. I clicked on his profile.

I was curious. That was all.

I still had Katsu's DKNY jacket, the one he'd draped over my shaking body outside the Seven Deadly Sins party. It was folded inside my only drawer in the caravan, nestled next to my own clothes. Jem's silver dress and heels lived in a plastic bag shoved deep under my bed, like a Halloween costume waiting for next year.

Katsu's profile was a muddle of memes and web comics. To my disappointment, he didn't post much personal stuff. But he took a lot of pictures. They communicated a life lived at full speed: early-morning runs, sunsets at festivals. I scrolled until I reached a photo of Katsu and Jem. She was looking away, as if unaware of the camera. Her usual baboon grin was absent. No make-up.

She looked like me.

The door to the hotel room didn't squeak or sigh. It pushed open smoothly, footsteps deadened by the thick carpet. The woman was two metres away from me before I realised what was happening.

'Excuuuse me . . .'

A statuesque brunette, she stood with her hands on her hips. She smelled like springtime. And her face was scrunched up into a sneer.

13

LIFE LESSONS

Jem

'Congrats on your big role.' Carlo sidled over to me. 'Guess you don't have time for us little people anymore.'

In his best impersonation of a Mob don, he wore a Fedora. Even more absurd, he held a bicycle pump, which meant he'd ridden his vintage bike over to come and intimidate me. What a deplorable hipster. That was what made me laugh. And that was when he used the bicycle pump to hit me in the stomach.

Carlo. Motherfucking Carlo.

Third-rate actor turned pretentious drug mule. Bane of my existence. It actually offended me that I had to spend time worrying about Carlo.

Charlie, as he was once known, was a thesp who I met on the set of an indie movie a few years ago. The movie was a meditation on the Millennial mindset, where nothing happened, but the hero had a lot of existential angst. I played a party girl (my two lines were: 'Trevor is sooo hot' and 'Let's get this party started!'), while Charlie was the hero's rarely-seen brother.

Even in his scant scenes, he proved to be a diabolical actor, but that didn't matter to me, because he always had drugs on him. We used to smoke spliffs to kill the long wait between scenes. Bad movies tended to bind people together, so we stayed friends – albeit a friendship that revolved around drinking, drugs, throwing up, and then laughing about it all over eggs the next day.

I didn't see him during the two years I was in LA, but when I got back to London, I looked him up. In my absence, he'd sculpted the Carlo persona and gone full-on gangster. His parents were accountants and he'd grown up in Chelmsford, but suddenly he was pretending he was a Mafioso. Fucking idiot.

The bright side of his foray into the criminal underworld was that he provided easy access to good-quality shit. I started buying from him regularly. Sometimes I bought for friends, too; scaredy-cat wusses who liked nose candy, but didn't want to do anything so gauche as risk prison.

Thanks to Mother and her 'life lessons', my cashflow was unpredictable, so I racked up a few debts with Carlo. No big deal. He knew I was good for it. Eventually, he came up with a business proposition. I had rich friends; he had product to shift. I could be his middleman.

What a lark.

I treated it like method acting. I was the poor little high society girl forced into drug-dealing. It was a hell of a role and I played it with aplomb. Maybe, I thought at the time, I'd take it a step further; write a script with me in the lead role, like Matt Damon and Ben Affleck. Instead of *Good Will Hunting*, it would be *The Girl With Icing Sugar Up Her Nose*. I even looked into getting a gun. *Pow, pow!* All in the name of authenticity, you understand.

When it came to the job itself, I was good at shifting product. I just wasn't good at getting paid. I gave out free samples, so that people would know it wasn't cut with drain cleaner or something. Then I sampled a little myself. At a big country house party in the Cotswolds that I attended one weekend in September, I got so slaughtered I forgot I was supposed to be charging. I ran through a couple of grand's worth of coke in one night. *Poof!* Gone, like chalk dust in the air. It was a good weekend, though.

It was a mistake! Could happen to anyone!

I figured Carlo would forget about it. It was like he'd bought a round of drinks at the pub and I'd neglected to return the favour. No biggie.

He didn't forget about it.

In fact, he started getting aggro with me. Blowing up my phone with messages. Turning up at parties where he knew I'd be. I was usually able to calm him down, give him a few hundred pounds to shut him up for a while. But then he started talking about interest on the loan and 'this is how much you owe me' and blah blah blah. Honestly. What a drag. I had to get my coke from some skeevy bloke in the East End instead. I'd considered Charlie a friend. Then he'd morphed into a psychopath.

At the theatre, loitering in the dressing room, there was a weird sheen to his skin, like he was sweating oil. His eyes were glassy, blacker than I remembered. In the gloom of backstage, his large frame seemed too big for the small space.

He hit me again with the bicycle pump.

'Jesus Christ!' I said, doubling over. A remnant of laughter pushed out of my lungs.

He thumped me a third time and I staggered backwards.

'Seriously, Jem, I need my money.'

I cradled my stomach in my arms. Pain pulsed through my body.

'I'll get it,' I said, gasping. 'Fuck's sake, calm down. Take an oxy or something.'

He advanced on me, trapping me in a corner of the small dressing room. I could smell him now: body odour and dirty clothes. He was a fucking wreck.

'If you owe me money, that means I owe some other bastard up the food chain.' He gestured using the bicycle pump and it glanced off my shoulder. 'D'you get that? D'you get how much shit I'm in?'

I took another step backward, slumping against the wall. One arm still covered my bruised middle; the other, I held out in front of me, a vague attempt to ward off Carlo.

'I'm seeing my mum in a couple of days,' I said. 'I'll get it from her.'

Carlo took a step backward. His face slackened, his bicycle-pump-wielding hand dropping to his side. His voice was almost timid. 'Yeah?'

'Yeah, I swear.'

I squared my shoulders, shaking off my fear. This would make a great story. *Beaten up by a drug-dealer and I survived!* I couldn't help but laugh.

'Honestly, you look like the Incredible Hulk,' I said, grabbing my hair in a pantomime of rage. 'Veins popping in your forehead.'

Maybe the Hulk comment was prescient, because his anger roared back. Eyes wild, face ruddy, fists balled.

Don't do drugs, kids, I thought, remembering placid stoner Charlie who lent me his coat when I forgot mine one rainy Thursday on set. The thought fell right out of my skull when he cracked me over the head with the bicycle pump. It was a pathetic plastic thing, but the amount of force he put into the blow sent me reeling.

I collapsed onto the floor and he dispensed with the bicycle pump. He began to kick me instead, sucking in a ragged breath every time his foot connected with my ribs.

'You . . . need . . . to take . . . this . . . seriously.'

I was on the brink of passing out, so I couldn't exactly form a reply. Seconds dragged by, achingly slow, and at last I became aware that he was no longer kicking me. I still felt the reverberation, though, my body clenching against each imagined jolt.

'You put yourself in these situations, Jem,' he said, his voice sounding far away to my ears. 'You do it to yourself.'

My eyes had been squeezed shut, but now I opened them. He still loomed over me, but there was a hint of remorse in his face. He stooped to pick up the bicycle pump; the hand that gripped it was trembling.

'Sorry,' he said, his voice hoarse. 'Just get me my money. Ten grand. I'll give you two days, but that's it. Time's up.'

I always thought I'd be good in a fight. Scratch out the eyes, pull on the hair, hammer fist to the balls. Instead, given the choice of fight or flight, it turned out I was much better at running. A champion sprinter; Olympic gold medallist in Get the Fuck Outta Here.

Director Dave caught me staggering out of the dressing room ten minutes later and he was far from concerned for my well-being.

'Where are you going?' he asked.

'Home,' I gasped out, although I had no intention of doing so. Carlo could find out where I lived.

'We've got a performance to do! If you go, you're fired.'

I didn't have the energy to curse him out. Hands shaking, I gave him the finger and stumbled out the door toward the nearest bar. I drank myself numb, then a bartender I knew let me sleep for a few hours on the sofa in the break room. When I woke up, still half-drunk, I couldn't think of anything to do except climb through a hole in the space-time continuum. I used my last good credit card to buy a ticket on the first train heading out of London.

*

Halfway to Hull, I could still smell Carlo's stench of body odour and rage. I took another gulp of my coffee. At least my hands had stopped shaking. I still didn't know what to do, though. I could call Katsu back and tell him the truth, but that would be humiliating. He only knew Charlie-Carlo as my mate, not as my dealer. My face burned at the thought of owning up to all the stupid shit I'd done.

Carlo and my car and Director Dave and the whole London drag. All of it buzzed in my ears. I knew I'd fucked up with the play. By Monday morning, my agent Savannah would have spoken to Dave. I was down to my last chance with her. She'd probably fire me. Then who was I? An actress without an agent. An actress without a fucking chance.

I didn't want to deal with any of this. I just wanted to be someone else for a while.

At that moment, two serendipitous things happened at once. The kismet of it all had the quality of a kind-voiced god bending down from his perch on a cloud to whisper in my ear: *Hey, Jemima old girl, here's what you should do.*

First, I noticed the glossy tourist brochure shoved into the pocket of the seat in front of me. It showed a shimmering expanse of water, with craggy hills rising in the background. In loopy script, the headline read: *Where the Lakes meet the sea! Discover the majesty of the Cumbrian coast.*

Second, another god-like voice, belonging to the automated train announcer, boomed through the carriage.

'The next station is Doncaster. Change for trains to the Lake District and Scotland.'

Well, shit. I chugged the remainder of my coffee, feeling its heat travel all the way to the tips of my toes. By the time I crushed the empty paper cup in my fist, I was grinning.

I grabbed my bag and made my way to the nearest exit. The business wanker gave me a parting scowl, but I didn't spare him a thought. In my mind, I was already on another train, headed for where the lakes met the sea.

Hull would have to wait for another day. I had places to go, doubles to see.

14

FLIP A COIN

Ella

I scrambled off the bed, my phone falling out of my hands in the process. I bent to pick it up and, in a panic, ended up on my hands and knees. (Eyes down, eyes down, eyes down.)

'Are you wearing my *robe*?'

'Sorry, sorry, sorry.' I bundled my phone into my pocket and tore the silk robe off my arms. I heard the *riiip* of a seam giving way and so did the woman.

'For God's sake, what kind of place is this? You're supposed to clean the room, not make yourself at home!'

The ruined robe was balled up in my hands now. She reached over and yanked it from my grasp. I was still on my hands and knees. I wanted to crawl under the bed and hide.

While she stood examining the damage to the robe, I sneaked another look at her. She was beautiful in a Kate Middleton sort of way. Expensive clothes. Expert make-up. She was also my age. Looking up, she caught my gaze. Her dark eyes were cold.

'What are you waiting for? Get out!'

I climbed to my feet and grabbed the last of my cleaning supplies. The trolley's broken wheel made a screech as I shoved it out the door and along the corridor. I reached the next room – knock, *housekeeping*, no answer, push – and found it blessedly empty. I collapsed against the back of the door and closed my eyes, mortified.

Greasy little gremlin, grubbing around in someone else's life. Is that what you are, Ella?

My phone, still clutched in my grasp, vibrated. Paranoia

seized me. It must be Mrs Brannan. She'd found out what I'd done already.

No. Stupid. It was probably my mum checking up on me. Or a spam offer for something I couldn't afford.

I clicked my phone awake.

Hey its Jem. On my way to walny. Send me you're address

I stared at the words, heart thumping.

Jem? Coming to Walney Island?

What the hell?

The message's arrival was chased by another one, this time from Bethany.

Babe can you look after talia tonight? Mergency! Got a last minute appointment at the hairdresser

My fingers were numb as I typed a reply, but I didn't bother to fix the mistakes.

Sorry dont thnink I can

My eyes flicked to the time. I was way behind schedule. There were still three more rooms to do before the end of my shift. I couldn't overrun, not on a day when a guest would be making a complaint against me. Embarrassment throbbed in my veins. My face was hot. And Jem's message felt seared on to my skin.

Jem. In Cumbria. Jem. On Walney Island.

Why would she come here? What did she want from me?

Another message made my phone vibrate. My stomach dropped, expecting more from Jem, but it was just Bethany.

Plz? Cherry on top?

Ignoring the message, I tossed my phone on to the night-stand. Then I set about cleaning the room. I couldn't afford to lose my job. That was for certain. At least £6.70 an hour was better than nothing. Obviously, Jem would never understand the idea that, in the middle of the day on a Friday, a normal person would be working.

Even by the housekeeping staff's usual half-hearted standards, I took liberties on cleanliness in the next three rooms. I didn't change the sheets. I whisked a cloth over every surface, but at top speed and with scant regard for hygiene. Even though the remains of a muffin were mashed into the carpet in one room, I merely picked out the most conspicuous crumbs, instead of firing up the hoover.

As a result, I was able to clock out on time. Mrs Brannan was mercifully absent from the staff room, so I could slide out the door with my head down. Maybe the Kate Middleton guest wouldn't bother to complain about me? Maybe she'd let it go?

I heard again the *riiip* of her silk robe and knew that it was no good; she'd relish bringing fire and brimstone down on me.

I trudged down the hotel drive, a long walk to where the staff car park was hidden out of view of the guests. At least the rain had cleared up, but my nerves jangled each time my phone vibrated with a new message. I heard no more from Jem, however, just a steady stream of wheedling from Bethany.

Come on ill be ur best friend!!
Im sposed to get my fringe done I look minging
Plzzzzzzzzzzzzzzz

Bethany had been leaning on me a lot for babysitting recently. I didn't mind – even though Talia's main interests seemed to be screaming, crying and eating crisps. If there weren't any crisps to be eaten, she reverted to screaming and crying. We spent many hours sitting together by the frozen duck pond, bundled up in parkas, munching on prawn cocktail crisps. Life with a toddler was, at least, simple. Talia didn't plague me with the usual measure-your-worth-as-a-human questions. *Where are you working now? Got yourself a fella yet? Thought about the future? Life's short, y'know . . .*

I'd take idle chatter about cheese and onion vs. salt and vinegar from a three-year-old over probing questions from an adult any day of the week. Yet I resented the moments when I'd return to Bethany's house and find her cuddled up with Stu on the sofa, looking like the picture of marital bliss. Or, worse, when I'd let myself into her house and hear the tinkle of laughter from the kitchen; entering, bedraggled, to see her sitting at the table, drinking coffee with a different, more interesting friend.

A new message from Bethany arrived:

Cmon I know ur not busy

My skin prickled. Bethany wasn't my friend. I didn't have any friends left. She was the acquaintance who never stopped showing up. And, to her, I was a convenience.

I was about to type back *no fuck off* when my phone shuddered. This message was not from Bethany.

U there? Arriving at the statin in half an hour. Send me you're address

There was no *'please'*. No *'I was wondering if maybe . . .'* It was a command. Jem knew what she wanted and she took it.

I didn't have time to contemplate what I should send back when my phone lit up. Oh, God. Jem was calling me now. As I reached my car, I declined the call and shoved the phone back into my pocket, where it lay like an unexploded grenade.

My double and I had had no contact for weeks. There was no logical reason for her to show up. The idea of Jem on Walney Island was so outlandish that I struggled to wrap my brain around it. It would be like seeing a werewolf in the corner shop.

Slumping into the driver's seat, I wondered what she'd do if I continued to ignore her. Would she get on a train and go home? I chewed my bottom lip, turning over the possibilities in my mind. No, giving up and going home wasn't Jem's style. She would ask around. She'd make a nuisance of herself.

Everyone knew everyone on Walney. What would happen if a woman who looked exactly like me showed up at the newsagents, running her lipsticked mouth in her posh, drawling accent? What would happen if she ran into my friends, my family—?

My phone buzzed yet again. New message. Reluctantly, I opened it:

Got an address from google. This where u live?

My heart dropped to my stomach. Forget the newsagents; Jem was about to show up at the caravan park and start knocking on doors.

I bit my lip. Hard enough to hurt. Hard enough that the pain forced me into action. I tapped out a message to Jem.

*

On the way home, I drove my car fast enough that my entire skeleton rattled. I arrived at the caravan park and opened my car door to the sound of hammering.

'What are you doing?' I called out to Simon.

My brother held a plastic doll about the size of a newborn in one hand. In the other was his hammer. He spat out one of the nails he held between his teeth and hammered it through the doll's neck into a wooden post.

Maybe it was just my shredded nerves, but it felt like a nail was stabbing into my windpipe, too. I scuffed over to where he stood, next to the entrance sign that read 'Paradise Point'.

'I thought it could be a' – Simon's voice started as a mumble, then clarified when he spat out the last of the nails – 'Keep Out thing.' He flashed a grin. 'Beware.'

He pounded another nail through the doll's arm (she only had one) and then stepped back to admire his handiwork. His unkempt, sandy-coloured hair was even messier than normal and there was a smear of what looked like mud on his cheek. He smelled like he hadn't showered in a while.

'Found her on the beach,' he said. The tide had swept away the doll's clothes (she was naked) and her hair (she was bald), and given her skin a ghoulish green cast. 'Cool, right?'

I shook my head. 'Why would we want people to Keep Out? We want people to come in and rent caravans.'

Simon's smile dimmed. 'Whatever,' he muttered. 'I think it's cool.'

Did my brother do stuff like this just to freak people out, or was he really a certifiable weirdo?

The idea of Jem ambling up the lane to see Simon manhandling a feral-looking doll was so ridiculous I laughed. Then the laughter turned to churning anxiety in my stomach. What mad things would my brother say to her? What secrets of mine would she spill to him?

Simon's grin was back – he thought I'd come around to the idea of his new talisman – and he was swinging his hammer back and forth in a careless arc.

'You had lunch yet?' he asked. 'Wanna make me an omelette?'

'Not hungry,' I said, getting out my phone to check the time.

Jem's train would be getting in to Barrow-in-Furness station right about now, and it was only a ten-minute taxi ride to the southern tip of Walney. I'd tried to get her to meet me in town, but she'd insisted on seeing where I lived. God, she was impossible.

I glanced around the caravan park, which looked even more grey and desolate on this miserable November day. No sign of Mum or Dad. That was something, at least.

'Why don't you go into town and get us some burgers?' I pulled my purse from my bag and handed Simon a fiver. 'My treat.'

'What's the catch?'

'No catch,' I said with a tight smile. I wanted to shoo him. Go! Leave! Get out!

At that moment, Archie bounded over to where we stood, his paws landing on my thighs. My heart jumped into my throat – he'd startled me – and I pushed him away automatically.

Simon was quick to make a fuss of the dog, a mangy border terrier with a rough brown coat shot through with grey. ('Who's a good boy? Who's a prize-fighter? Yes, you are!') Archie was mine – a birthday present some ten years ago – but my brother was always pretending the dog was his. Story of my life. I was born and then, five years later, my brother came along and claimed ownership of what little the Mosier family had to offer.

'So I was thinking . . .' Simon rocked back on his heels, leaving Archie to run in circles around him. 'We should flip a coin.'

My brother held my five pound note in his hand, but he seemed in no hurry to leave.

'For what?' I asked, exasperated.

'The caravan.'

'Which caravan?'

Stupid question. I already knew.

'The green one. I think I should have it.' He squinted, his face taking on an expression of faux benevolence. 'But I wanna keep it fair.'

'It's mine!' My hands balled into fists. 'I've told you this isn't happening.'

Simon's voice was still airy, as if he were talking sense and I were being unreasonable.

'Dad's always wanted me to take over the caravan business – '

'What business?' I burst out. 'We're underwater.'

' – so I should have my own caravan.'

You fucking brat.

You live with Mum and Dad rent-free. You don't have a real job, just casual stints as a labourer or farm hand. You spend what little money you do make getting shitfaced with your mates on the beach.

You think because you're The Son, and Dad promised you a prize that doesn't exist, you can take my caravan?

I exhaled a long breath out through my nose. I didn't have time for this.

'You want a caravan? Take the yellow one,' I said.

Most of Paradise Point's caravans were rented on long-term leases, but there was a dilapidated one-bedder painted the colour of congealed custard that Mum and Dad used for short-stay tourists in the summer.

'The yellow one smells like mould.' Simon jutted out his lower lip.

'So clean it!' I swept away from him, stomping toward my – *my!* – caravan. 'And get those burgers!' I yelled over my shoulder.

Archie let out a bark, unsettled by my shouting, but he didn't follow me into the caravan. The moment my front door slammed, a new message from Jem made my phone buzz.

Whats with all the mud? Thought u lived on an island

I wanted to hurl my phone across the room. Before I could decide whether or not to actually do it, another message came in.

Im here now

Oh, shit.

I looked out the window to see my dad's white van, presumably driven by Simon, tearing out of the caravan park. On the bend of the lane, it passed a black cab. My stomach lurched.

She was here.

*

The woman who got out of the taxi couldn't have appeared more Other if she'd tried. Of the clothes Jem wore – a grey faux-fur gilet; a bright green bobble hat; a leather miniskirt – none of them matched. Yet the effect on her was arty, hip, knowingly eccentric.

I threw open the door of my caravan and hastened toward the taxi, scanning my surroundings for signs of other people.

From a distance, with her unkempt hair, her strange outfit, and her swaying gait, she looked like a stranger. But, when she turned her face toward me, I felt a jolt.

How could someone who looked so much like me be so completely different?

It was a question that had bugged me for weeks. I'd gone to London hoping to find a kindred spirit. A twin. Someone who got me, automatically, the way family was supposed to. Instead, I'd found . . . Jem.

'Heyyy!' she called out. 'What's up, Twinnie?'

The taxi did a sloppy three-point-turn and left. I tried to get a look at the driver. Did I know him? Was he an islander, or just a random bloke from Barrow?

'Nothing,' I mumbled. Then, louder, I asked, 'What are you doing here?'

Jem flung herself upon me in a hug that felt like a performance.

'I'm on a little holiday from myself,' she said, pulling away at once. 'Exploring the outer reaches of nowhere and nothing.'

I bristled. Right. What was that supposed to mean?

129

When I remained silent, she huffed, rearranging her wolf-like gilet.

'Just in the neighbourhood,' she said. 'Act like you're happy to see me, maybe.'

'Um . . . I'm just surprised,' I said. 'What are you doing in . . . the neighbourhood?'

'Oh, you know.' She grinned and gave a wink. 'Every day I'm hustlin'.'

I was again lost for words. The silence between us stretched. Jem's smile slid off her face. She made an exaggerated shivering motion.

'Fancy making me a cup of tea?' she said. 'You do have a house, right? You Northerners don't just live in the wild?'

My jaw seized. *Who the hell do you think you are?*

'Maybe you should go back to London . . .' I said, my voice coming out meek despite my anger. Jem's intent gaze made me feel cowed.

'You're not even gonna make me a cup of tea?' she asked.

There was a pitiful note in her voice. Now that her Cheshire Cat grin had vanished, I noticed how pale she looked. Her shoulders drooped and a hand lay across her ribs, as if protecting herself. Though she was fully made-up, with bright red lips, her eyeliner was smudged. It accentuated the shadows under her eyes. She was skinnier than she'd been a month ago. Her weight was closer to my own. Her tiredness, too, made the resemblance between us even more uncanny.

A cup of tea, a quick tour, maybe then I'd be able to get rid of her.

Even as I gestured toward my green caravan, I knew it wouldn't be that simple. A cup of tea wouldn't satisfy Jem.

15

A FAMILY AFFAIR

Ella

As we stepped inside, any pity I'd felt for my double drained away. Her lip curled, her eyebrows rose. In her presence, I was hyper-aware of the dingy floral curtains at the windows; the curled edges of the lino. I'd tried to personalise the space with a faded poster of the Paris skyline, but even that now seemed pathetic.

My home wasn't a multi-million-pound apartment, it wasn't even a modest house. It was a caravan.

'This is where you live?' she asked.

I jerked my head in a nod. *No, this is a hilarious joke. My mansion's round the corner.*

'Wow . . . cosy.' She sat down on the lumpen sofa that folded out into a bed, removing her hat and gilet.

I didn't reply. I turned away to fill the kettle, so that she wouldn't see the anger and embarrassment turning my face red.

There was a knock on the door and I jumped.

Jem stood up, like she might go and answer it. I sprang in front of her and opened the door an inch.

'What?' I said.

It was Simon, back already, but without burgers, because even that was too complicated a task for him. Archie whined at his feet. Traitor.

'Met Harvey down the lane,' Simon said, his tone bored. 'We're gonna get Domino's instead. Need some more money.'

Behind him, a black-haired teenager toed the gravel in knock-off Adidas trainers and spared me a scowl. Usually I would have told the two of them to piss off, but today I muttered, 'One second.'

I shut the door and grabbed my bag from the floor. With numb hands, I fumbled for my purse. I pulled out a ten pound note – the last of my cash. Behind me, Jem made an *ooh* sound in the back of her throat.

'Who's that?' she asked, darting to the window.

My mind raced. What were the angles like from outside? Would Simon and Harvey be able to see Jem through the window? If they could, would they assume it was me?

The thought made me feel dizzy. I grabbed my double by the arm and yanked her away from the window.

'Sit down,' I said. 'Be quiet.'

Again I opened the door a crack and shoved the tenner at Simon.

'Just go,' I said.

I slammed shut the door. Far from sitting down and staying quiet, Jem was speaking again and peering out the window.

'Who was that?' she asked.

I prayed Simon wouldn't be able to hear her from outside the caravan.

'Your boyfriend?' she said.

'I don't have a boyfriend,' I muttered. 'That's my brother.'

'Oh, sweet.' Jem's face was almost pressed to the glass now. 'I don't have any brothers or sisters. Does he look like us?'

Yes, Simon had the same green-grey eyes, the same pointy nose, the same dirty-blond hair. Like Jem, he was selfish and entitled. They had a lot in common.

'Sit down,' I said again.

'Don't you want to introduce me?' Jem's voice was sly.

'No,' I muttered.

She made a motion like she was going to tap on the window and then let her hand fall in a flourish.

No one in my family knew that I'd gone to London, attended

a crazy drug-fuelled party, stayed at a stranger's house, and, now, invited that stranger in for a cup of tea. I wanted it to stay like that. When I sneaked a glance outside, I was a relieved to see Simon and his friend climbing into the van. The dog leapt up into the front seat.

I went back to filling the kettle, flexing my fingers to stop them from trembling.

'Hmm . . . good shout,' my double said in a low voice, like she was talking to herself.

She still hadn't sat back down and was instead roaming the enclosed space like an appraiser at an estate sale. Picking up a book – a history of women in the SOE during World War II – she flicked through it at speed. Then she moved on to my guitar and strummed a single note.

I sloshed milk into two mugs and resisted the urge to slap her hands.

'How old's your brother, anyway?' Jem asked.

'Nineteen.' *And still acts like he's 14.*

'Huh.' Jem paused to shake my old ceramic piggy bank (empty). 'Where does he live?'

I scrunched up my face, anticipating my double's ridicule.

'Here,' I said. 'My parents run the caravan park.'

'Ahh.' She swept a hand through the air. 'A family affair. What's your surname? Moser, right?'

The kettle was boiling, its high whistle making my scalp prickle.

'Mosier,' I said. 'Why?'

Jem shrugged. She strayed to the compact bathroom area and began scrutinising herself in the small mirror mounted above the basin.

'Got any eye make-up remover?' she asked.

It was such a non sequitur, I didn't know how to react.

'No . . .'

'No probs,' Jem said.

She plucked a little pot of Vaseline that I used as lip balm off the edge of the basin and smeared a blob of it across her eyelid. Then she grabbed a tissue from the box and used it to wipe the Vaseline away, removing her eyeliner at the same time. With another swipe, she got rid of her red lipstick.

'I'll probably have to teach you to put on eyeliner,' she said. 'Otherwise you'll look like someone attacked your eye with a crayon. It can be tricky for beginners.'

'What?'

'You normally wear your hair tied back, right?'

She grabbed my hairbrush and pulled it through her tangled hair. This, at last, spurred me into action. Forgetting the tea mugs, I crossed the small space and snatched the hairbrush out of her hands.

My double apparently didn't notice my appalled expression. She was done with the hairbrush already. Sweeping her hair back, she secured it with one of my hair bands.

'Ponytail today,' she said. 'That's easy.'

She turned to face me, putting her hands on her hips. Even though she still wore her own eclectic collection of mismatched clothes, she had, in less than a minute, transformed herself.

She'd transformed herself into me.

'I'm Ella,' she said, slipping into my soft, Cumbrian accent. 'I'm a Northerner, but I don't live in the wild. I guess I don't have a boyfriend. I do have a brother. He's a dick and – ' She broke off, switching back to her real accent. 'Hey, what's your brother's name again? I should probably know that.'

'Don't,' I said, my voice rising. 'Don't make fun of me.'

'I'm not.' Jem actually seemed affronted. 'I'm just practising. You should practise, too. Start getting into character.'

'What?'

The worst part was that my double looked perfectly at home in my life. Her shoulders were relaxed, her foot tapping an idle beat.

Me, I wanted to scream.

'Don't you ever get bored of yourself?' Jem asked. 'Don't you ever get so fucking bored you want to climb out of your own skull and be someone else for a while?'

I stared back at her.

'Don't you ever feel that way?' she asked.

My thoughts were racing. My brain felt too big for my head, like it might bulge out through my forehead.

Jem was a lunatic. No doubt about that. I wanted to disagree with her. I wanted to yell at her to get out.

Instead I found myself giving the slightest of nods.

A sly smile broke across my double's face. Even though she wore no make-up and her hair was tidy, something about that smile was pure Jem. That kind of smile didn't live inside me.

'And we can do something about it!' she said. 'We get the chance to take a holiday from ourselves.'

Her plan was a simple one. Chillingly, exhilaratingly simple. Jem would stay on Walney Island and pretend to be me; I would travel to London and take Jem's place there. For a few days – for a week, perhaps – we would live each other's lives.

'It's not that easy,' I said, when she'd finished outlining her scheme. 'You can't just pretend to be me. You don't even know me.'

'I know where you live,' she said, glancing around my caravan. 'I know where your whole family lives. Two parents. A brother.'

My small living space felt even smaller with Jem in it. Her orange-scented perfume was strong and sweet-bitter. Her very presence seemed to taint the surroundings. This wasn't my sanctuary – my mum, like my dad, had a key, and she carried out frequent 'cleaning' sessions which left the contents of my cupboards subtly disordered, evidence of her snooping clear – but it was still mine, in some essential way. As Jem's gaze roamed through the objects on my shelves, I felt like she was taking it away from me.

'I bet you go to church like a saint,' Jem said. 'And work in some office where you' – her fingers danced against an imaginary keyboard – 'tap-tap-tap away on a computer.'

I wanted to interrupt – *no, I'm a cleaner and you have no idea about my life* – but Jem bulldozed onward.

'I know you read books, play guitar. I know you're not a big party girl. But I know you like to dance. I know you like music.' She gestured to my guitar. 'I know you won a prize for a song you wrote.'

'How do you know that?'

Jem shrugged. 'Google.'

The skin on my arms prickled. What else had her Google search revealed about me? There was nothing to find, surely? I wished suddenly that I could be sure.

'Come on,' she said. 'It'll be fun.'

Jem's smile was mischievous. One of her hands was outstretched, almost touching me.

'No!' I exploded. 'My life is not yours to play with.'

She rocked back on her heels, frowning. For once, she didn't say anything.

I crossed my arms, half hugging myself. I felt foolish, I'd overreacted. Jem only meant the scheme as a prank.

A shiver ran the length of my leg. It took me a second to realise it was my phone. The vibrations kept going as the phone rang and rang.

'I need to get this,' I muttered, looking for a way out of the conversation.

I fumbled open the door. The cold air outside was a relief after the stuffy caravan crowded with too many Ellas.

I let the door fall shut again. I didn't want Jem to overhear my call. I didn't want to give her more material for use in her grand new role as Ella Mosier.

'Ugh, finally,' Bethany said, when I answered. 'Why are

you ignoring me?'

'I'm not. I just . . . got busy.'

'No kidding.' Bethany sniffed. 'Your mystery plans that you can't tell me about. I had to miss that hair appointment, you know.'

If there was one thing my best friend could be relied upon for, it was complete and utter self-absorption.

'Sorry, I'll make it up to you.'

I threw a glance over my shoulder at the green caravan, hoping Jem was behaving herself inside, and drifted away in the direction of the shore. The wind rippled through my black hotel uniform. Looking at the sea, a shimmer of silver far out beyond the sandy channel calmed me fractionally.

On the phone, Bethany was still talking, talking, talking, but I was struggling to hear her over the clamour of my thoughts. Was Jem's plan ludicrous? Or was it so ludicrous it might work?

'Can you take Talia for, like, one hour?' Bethany was saying. 'My friend invited me to go do a Zumba class.'

'A Zumba class?'

'Yeah, I mean, you could come, too, but it's kind of a pregnancy fitness thing . . .' Her voice rose abruptly. 'Talia-baby, don't put that in your mouth!' There was the sound of a tussle and then she returned to the call. 'Can you do it or not?'

'What?' I said distractedly.

I'd reached a wooden shed we used for storage at the edge of the caravan site. I sagged against it, breathing in its smell of mould and rotten wood. My eyelids felt heavy. It had been such a long day.

'Babysitting,' Bethany said in a *duh* voice. 'One hour. Maybe two.'

'No . . . Sorry.'

'Oh, come on. I'm not asking for a kidney.'

'How about tomorrow?' I said.

'What's wrong with today?'

The whine in Bethany's voice reminded me of school. *Why can't I copy your maths homework? Why won't you write my essay for me?* It was a special kind of purgatory to be stuck living in the same place you grew up, squabbling with your brother, and plagued by people who treated you like you were 13 years old.

A spark of anger overcame my tiredness.

'I'm busy!' I said, louder than I'd intended.

Bethany let out a little snort of disbelief. Before she could form a response, there was a beep on the line.

'That's someone else calling,' I said. 'Have to go. Sorry. Bye.'

I rang off and answered the new call.

'Hello, is that Ella Mosier?'

I was so distracted, I didn't even recognise the voice. It was probably just someone selling.

'Yeah, it's me, but I'm not really looking to buy anything right now.'

'Ella, it's Mrs Brannan.'

My throat closed up. I barely managed an 'mm' of acknowledgement.

'Ella,' she said, 'I just wanted to have a quick chat with you about what happened today.'

I imagined Mrs Brannan sitting in her mental-ward-yellow office, pushing her glasses up her nose and pursing her lips.

'Okay . . .' I said in an undertone.

'One of the guests made a very serious complaint about you.'

For one bizarre moment, I wondered what Jem might do in this situation. Lie, probably. She'd paste on that big smile and lie through her teeth. *What are you talking about? There must be some sort of misunderstanding.* Either that or she'd laugh and say, *So what? Uppity bitch got what she deserved.*

Ella, slumped against a rotten shed, desperately in need of £6.70 an hour and a good reference at the end of it all, remained silent.

'Do you have anything to say?' Mrs Brannan prompted.

'I'm sorry.'

'I'm not sure that sorry is going to be good enough . . .'

On the other end of the call, Mrs Brannan droned on about 'inappropriate behaviour' and 'immaturity, plain and simple'. I took her tongue-lashing in silence. My eyes were fixed on the horizon. I watched a little red boat heading out to sea, destination who-knows-where. The view was blurred by my tears.

At the edge of my consciousness, a car engine rumbled.

I imagined myself plodding across the sands and, when they turned to sea, I'd start to swim. Upon reaching the little red boat, I'd tug on their ropes and say, *Take me with you. Take me anywhere.*

The red boat disappeared around the headland.

I glanced away from the shore, barely taking in what was happening. Gravel sprayed up as a vehicle motored across it. It took me a moment to come back to myself, to realise what I was seeing.

A car. My mum's car.

On the phone, Mrs Brannan was saying, 'Ella, are you listening to me?'

'Yes, I'm listening,' I said. Anguish made my voice sound sarcastic.

From a distance, I watched my mum get out of her car, a silver Volvo she liked to remind me was older than I was. She called out, 'Someone help me with the shopping? Ella, you home?'

Even in the midst of everything else, this tiny irritation rankled. Of course she didn't call for Simon. When did she ever expect anything of Simon?

'This is an extremely serious matter . . .' Mrs Brannan said in my ear.

'I understand that,' I said, trying to keep my voice level.

I began walking toward where my mum's car was parked, my footsteps sluggish. That was when I heard another voice yell out, 'Coming!'

I stopped, paralysed. Fifty metres away, the door of the green caravan swung open. A familiar figure bounded over to Mum's car.

16

TWO FOR ONE

Ella

Jem was dressed in jeans and a khaki jumper so old, it was slightly misshapen. Thumb holes had been worn through the thin fabric at the sleeves. I knew this because my thumbs had created them.

One of those thumbs pressed the red icon, cutting off Mrs Brannan mid-sentence. I let the hand holding my phone drop limply to my side. At this distance, I couldn't hear what Jem was saying. I could only see her addressing Mum and smiling. Mum smiled back and opened the boot of the car.

My breath was coming in ragged bursts, my chest tightening. On automatic, I took a step to the side, so that if Mum glanced over, she wouldn't see me. I weaved around the old yellow caravan, moving closer. The wind had strengthened and it tangled my hair, pulling it loose from its ponytail. Jem's voice carried toward me.

'What have you bought?' she asked.

'Oh, just some bits and pieces,' Mum said.

She handed two plastic bags full of shopping to my double and heaved out another two for herself to carry.

'Anything exciting?' Jem asked.

Mum stopped to retrieve a few apples that had escaped one of the carrier bags and then slammed the boot shut.

'Not unless you call two-for-one on pork sausages exciting,' she said.

'That's pretty exciting!'

I wanted to scream. Jem sounded like a moron. Her accent

was wrong. The way she stood – hips jutted, boobs pushed out – was wrong, too. Everything about her was wrong.

'Oi, missus, where d'you think you're going?' Mum said.

Shopping bags grasped in her hands, my double was strutting in the direction of my green caravan. She stopped, half-turning back to look at my mum. Of course she had no idea which caravan belonged to my parents.

My heart stuttered. Concealed behind the yellow one-bedder, I leaned out to get a better look at Jem's expression. In her place, I'd have crumbled, eyes wide, hands trembling.

You caught me, I imagined myself saying. *Sorry, sorry, sorry –*

'I'd lose me head if it weren't screwed on,' Jem said and let out an airy laugh quite unlike mine.

'C'mon, then,' Mum said.

She traipsed over to the big caravan the colour of soured milk and my double followed. The plastic of their shopping bags crackled. I retreated a few steps to stay out of sight.

It would happen. It had to happen. Any minute now, Mum would notice how wrong I looked and sounded.

'Brrr, it's cold outside,' Jem said, in a crappy imitation of my accent.

'Going to be colder tonight.' Mum shifted the bags in her grasp in order to yank open the caravan door.

I wanted shout after them, *She's not me! Can't you see that?*

I bit my lip, hesitating for a moment, and then moved clear of the yellow caravan, hastening toward my parents' three-bedder.

This game had gone too far. It needed to stop. I needed to end the charade.

So what if Mum found out I'd lied and gone to London? It was a white lie. I was a grown woman. I could make my own decisions.

For a moment, the cold blustery day fell away and I was back in a stuffy little room, too small to be packed with three people and all their neuroses. Bald-headed David was working his jaw like he had a seed caught in his back teeth. I'd always thought therapists were supposed to be calm, implacable. David – with too-pale skin and too-big eyes – gave the impression he was more strung-out than most of his patients. He was constantly twitching or fidgeting.

'I know you're upset, Elizabeth,' David had said to Mum on that day. 'But it helps to voice your feelings.'

'She lied to us!' Mum burst out. 'For months. For months and months and months.'

'That can be a symptom of it.' David was bouncing his thumb against the arm of the chair. 'It's something we need to work through, all of us, together.'

Funny how my mental health had turned into a group project, especially when my problems still felt all my own. I sat in silence, toying with the hole I'd worn in the sleeve of my khaki jumper.

'I just can't stand it. It eats me up inside.' Mum turned in her chair to face me, laying a hand at my arm like she might shake me. 'Ella, this needs to change. No more lies. Please, no more lies.'

David held up his hands and aimed a weird, rubbery smile at me. 'I think we can all agree on that, make it a part of your recovery plan.'

No more lies.

Outside my parents' caravan, I slowed to a stop.

I couldn't bring myself to step inside and see the disappointment in my mother's eyes when I revealed my extent of my lies about London and Jem. I didn't want to see what lurked beneath her disappointment, either – something closer to loathing. Who are you? What daughter of mine would act this way?

The door to the spoiled-milk caravan yawned open. I took a step back, eyes darting for somewhere to hide.

It wasn't my mum who stood in the doorway.

It was me.

I watched as Ella scampered down the steps of the caravan. She swung her hips as she walked and smiled like the cat that got the cream.

*

Jem was ready to accept an Oscar, a Golden Globe, a Tony Award, and maybe even a Nobel Prize for contributions to humankind. She bounced around my caravan's interior, excitable as a puppy, giving me a play-by-play of what had happened.

And then I was like . . .

And then she was like . . .

The five minutes my double had spent pretending to be me lasted at least twenty minutes in the retelling.

I sat on the sofa-bed, legs drawn up to my chin, tea mug balanced on my knees. Jem kept firing rhetorical questions at me ('How crazy was it when – ?'), but never paused long enough for a reply.

'What a fucking rush,' she said, her eyes glowing. 'Wasn't it a rush?'

My double talked like I'd been involved somehow; we'd shared a brain for those few minutes Jem had spent putting away the shopping.

I remained mute. The emotions of the last hour congealed inside me. There was the needling feeling of embarrassment, as Jem bulldozed through my life. There were the background irritations of Bethany and my brother. The shame of the bollocking from Mrs Brannan. The fear of what would happen next time I went to work. I felt sick and tired of everything.

'This isn't okay,' I said quietly. 'What you did . . . it's not okay.'

'Don't worry' – Jem's smile was impish – 'you have my full permission to torture my mother however you choose.'

'I think you should go,' I said.

Even to my ears, my voice sounded unconvincing. I wanted

Jem to leave, right? I wanted this whole mess to end. Didn't I?

'I need to take the tools back,' Jem said. 'I promised.'

'I can do it,' I muttered.

My double put a hand over her heart, faux-solemn. 'I gave our dear sweet mama my word.' She pronounced it *mu'mar* like she was in a nineteenth-century TV drama.

While they'd been taking in the groceries, Mum had foisted on Jem a box of tools that needed returning to Ol' Roy at the pub on Piel Island. I knew for a fact that Simon was supposed to return the tools, since he was the one who'd borrowed them.

There was no sign of my brother or the van (or the pizza, for that matter). He'd probably scarpered to get high with his mates. It rankled that I had to do his chores for him yet again. And there was no choice but to go on foot, since my car's suspension couldn't hack the sinking sands.

I swung my feet down onto the floor and peered at the clock. It was almost three. It would be dark in a couple of hours. If I wanted to get to Piel and back, I needed to go now. Was it better to leave Jem here to wreak havoc or take her with me?

I sighed. Stupid question.

'Are those the only shoes you have?' I asked, eyeing her narrow pointy shoes, the patent-leather shined up a lurid turquoise colour.

Jem shrugged. 'Yeah, so?'

'So wear those out on the sands and you'll probably die,' I said.

*

My double splashed through the puddles wearing my wellies. She let out an occasional whoop as her soles got sucked into a patch of quicksand and she had to wrench them free. I followed behind more carefully, in a pair of Mum's old wellies that I'd grabbed from the storage shed. They were half a size too small and, once we got out on to the sands, I realised there was a pinprick hole in the heel letting water in.

'What fun! It's crazy out here!' Jem said breathlessly. 'I feel like we might fall off the edge of the Earth.'

I nodded, nosing into the scritchy fabric of my green scarf. It was scarcely more than a mile from Walney Island to neighbouring Piel Island, but the walk out onto the sands was like entering a ring of desolation. The rumbling of traffic along the road at your back receded. It was replaced by silence, stirred by a wind strong enough to rip the breath out of you.

Soon we were clear of the knee-high grasses that grew thick and tangled at the shoreline, and past the green nub of uninhabited Sheep Island. The ruined castle on Piel rose up in front of us, craggy and gothic.

'What's that?' Jem asked. 'Your second home? Lemme guess, you've been holding out on me. Ella of the manor born.'

Her laughter, tinged with cruelty, made the hairs on my back of my neck stand on end. The weight of the toolbox I carried in my hand dragged at the skin of my palm.

'Piel Island,' I said, swallowing down a nasty retort. 'It's where Lambert Simnel and his men hid out, tried to take the throne from Henry the Seventh.'

Jem wasn't listening.

When I was young, the local kids scared each other with stories about ten-year-old Lambert, a crofter's son who pretended he was King Edward VII and got his head chopped off. I later learned it didn't go down like that – the boy lived – but we still imagined his rotting head jammed on a spike on the castle walls. As teenagers, we had to prove the stories didn't frighten us anymore. *Dare you to climb to the top of the ruins. Dare you not to die.*

I remembered golden-hued summer evenings with Bethany and Stu and my other school friends. We tramped across the sands, laughing and shouting, tossing our empty beer cans over our shoulders to sink in the quicksand. On Piel, we scrambled up what remained of the battlements and yelled our small-town frustrations into the wind. It was almost possible to believe ghosts were there with us, stroking our cheeks with their invisible fingers.

No, it was the wind. And it wasn't the castle that was treacherous. It was the channel that stretched between Walney and Piel.

I eyeballed the sands around me, noting their texture and colour, steering clear of an almost imperceptible danger. I mostly followed the fresh tracks of a 4x4 (probably belonging to Ol' Roy, pub landlord on Piel). Vehicles were technically banned on the sands – it was a protected wildlife area – but those were city folks' rules.

'Careful!' I called out to Jem, who'd strayed twenty metres away from me.

After the initial slipperiness at the shore, the sands were hard beneath our feet. You could be tricked into thinking it would be the same easy walking the whole way, and you could stride clear across to the channel to misty Barrow-in-Furness. If you tried to make that trek, you'd almost certainly get caught up in a patch of sinking sands.

Without warning, terra firma could give way, replaced by sands that were wibbly-wobbly like fat under loose skin. Cow belly, islanders called it.

There was an old joke told on Walney. I'd first heard it from my grandpa, his breath stale with cigarette smoke, the skin at his eyes crinkling with laughter. 'Here's what you do if you get stuck out on the sands, little Ella.'

'What?' I'd asked, cuddling up to his chest.

'You fall forward' – he'd dipped his head, pantomiming a fall – 'right onto your face and you give up. No one coming to rescue you. Nothing to do but die.'

A joke, but a true one. Once the cow belly sucked you

ankle-deep, then knee-deep, the only thing to do was wait for the tide. It would come trickling in at first, along the gullies and channels that cut through the sands. Then the trickle would turn to a rush, a great weight of water, strong enough to knock you off your feet. One gulp of seawater was all it took to drown you.

Grandpa had passed away a year later. Lung cancer. Maybe drowning on the sands would have been kinder.

'For real, who lives on this island?'

Jem skirted close to me again. With her scrubbed-clean face and her shabby stolen clothes, she appeared as my reflection, hiding in my peripheral vision.

'There are a couple of houses, and the pub . . .' I said.

I still got the feeling my double wasn't really listening to me. She was analysing me, shifting her stance to look more like mine.

'Say you live there . . . what do you do when the tide's up?' Jem said, making her shoulders rounded and adopting a slouch that pulled her chin low.

'I don't know' – my voice came out irritated; I purposely thrust my shoulders back – 'wait for it to go down?'

'Batty,' Jem murmured. 'Total crazysauce bats.'

Her eyes were shining. She seemed entranced by the whole errand to Piel, even though it was me who was carrying the heavy toolbox. As far as Jem was concerned, she was visiting an exotic country and indulging in the local customs.

My phone vibrated in my pocket.

Tomoz for babysitting yeah?

When I ignored Bethany's message, it took less than a minute for my phone to start ringing. With a loud breath of frustration, I declined the call.

We were almost at Piel Island now. To get there required

a dash across a patch of quicksand, the ground turning soft and dangerous beneath our feet. I'd drop off the tools and then – what? Strong-arm Jem into a taxi and out of my life?

It would be a relief to get rid of her. Everything would go back to normal.

I heard the ringing of a phone and thought it was Bethany again, but my phone was black and silent.

'Hey, Katz-ooh,' Jem said in a sing-song greeting, pressing her phone to her ear.

She was silent for a moment, apparently listening to Katsu talk. She mimed a blabbing mouth with her hand for my benefit.

We passed the rusted shell of a car, half buried in the quicksand. It had only been lost a few years ago – kids on a joyride; they'd made it to safety, the car hadn't – but it looked like an ancient artefact today.

'Oh, you know, this and that,' Jem was saying into the phone. 'Just because you didn't want an adventure doesn't mean I can't have fun on my own.' She gave me an exaggerated wink. 'Getting away from it all. Taking a little *drama workshop*.' She paused again. 'Yep, see you when I get back! Love you too!'

She ended the call and let out a raucous laugh.

Drama workshop? Everything was a joke to Jem. My whole life was a joke.

Thud.

The sound made Jem jump. It startled me, too. I looked down at the box of tools I'd dropped on to the sands. My double hesitated and then bent to pick them up.

'Don't bother,' I said, a warning note in my voice.

The heavy toolbox was already beginning to settle into the soft sand. Let it sink. Let the tide roll in and wash it away, the same way it washed away the bodies of hapless wanderers.

I turned on my heel, so that the castle was behind me. I began walking back the way I'd come.

'What are you doing? Where are you going?' Jem called

after me.

'I can't be fucking bothered with this,' I said.

Close by, there came the panicked *peep-peep-PEEP-PEEP* of an oystercatcher's call.

'What? What about the tools?' Jem let out a breath of laughter. 'How will the poor batty people of Pale Island survive without their tools?'

I stomped onward. For the first time that afternoon, I didn't notice the trickle of cold water inside my boot. I felt warm despite the icy wind.

My double was trotting now to keep up with my pace. When I shot her a sidelong glance, I noticed she wasn't smirking or sneering or raising her eyebrows in a mocking way. Her face was slack, her grey eyes uncertain.

'So, first of all,' I said to her, 'you keep saying *fun* wrong. It's not an *uh* sound, it's an *ooh* sound. You're walking wrong, too. I don't meander the way you do. I don't shake my arse. And just . . . shut up once in a while. I don't talk that much, usually. When you're pretending to be me, try keeping quiet. Gives you less scope to screw up.'

'Waitaminute,' Jem said. 'Does this mean . . .'

Her familiar wide mouth stretched into a grin. She actually sounded impressed.

I thought of what she'd said earlier. *We get the chance to climb out of our skulls and take a holiday from ourselves.*

'I want a holiday,' I said.

17

IMPROV

Ella

Back in the caravan, I'd shut the floral curtains tight, fussing so that not even a sliver of what was going on inside could be seen from outside. The sun was setting fast – no light pollution to prolong the twilight – and I knew the lit-up caravan would become a beacon in the darkness. I didn't want to give my family a reason to come knocking.

The other Ella had arranged herself against the counter in the kitchen. She watched as I pushed a Spanish omelette around a pan, but didn't offer to help.

'Brother's name?' I asked.

'Simon,' Jem said, her voice edged with boredom. 'What's mine?'

'Trick question. You don't have any brothers or sisters.' I paused. 'Favourite food?'

'Ugh, something tedious . . . Blueberries.'

'Strawberries,' I said.

'Fine, whatever. Mine's steak. Rare.'

'I know.'

I made a face, because I'd watched videos of slaughterhouses. I didn't share Jem's zeal for barely-dead flesh.

My double sloshed some more peach-flavoured artisanal gin into a plastic cup and waved the bottle in my direction. She'd magicked the gin from her bag an hour ago and it was already half empty. I'd seen that brand at the supermarket. It cost forty pounds a bottle.

I shook my head. I'd had a cupful to try and calm my

nerves – what was I doing, agreeing to hand over my life to Jem? – but it had only made my skin tingle and my mind zing with too many thoughts.

Jem reached over and plucked a hunk of potato, gooey with half-cooked egg, from the pan. I tried not to wince when a splatter of egg ended up on her jumper (mine).

'My middle name?' I asked.

'Theresa,' she said thickly. 'Very holy.'

'Yours is Constance' – my words were coming out a shade too fast – 'after your great-aunt.'

'Seriously.' She swallowed the last of the potato with a glug of gin. 'No one is going to ask you about my crazy racist Aunt Connie.'

'They might do,' I said.

Jem rolled her eyes. When she tried to steal another potato, I batted her hand away. She scowled and began to gnaw on her thumbnail instead.

I clenched my jaw. 'Stop biting your nails, I never do that.'

With a *pop*, Jem extracted her thumb from her mouth. She glowered at me.

'I guess you'd better start, because I can't stop,' she said.

I glowered back at her, until she dissolved into a fit of laughter.

'You are way too stressed about this,' she said. 'Chill out. You can do whateverthefuck you want while you're in London. Scream and yell at the top of your lungs about Aunt Connie, for all I care. I don't give a shit what anyone thinks of me. You can spend all your time eating strawberries and pronouncing "fun" with an *ooh*. I don't care.'

While Jem's attitude to the switch was laid-back ('just wing it – haven't you ever heard of improv?'), I was treating it like a uni project where I needed to get a first. I nibbled on my littlest fingernail, gnawing gently, but without breaking the nail. I'd quit biting my nails years ago.

A smell of burning filled the air, shaking me out of my

thoughts. I snatched the pan off the heat and slopped the omelette onto two plates. Archie nudged his head against my leg, angling for a share.

Part of me wished to see him barking and whining at Jem's presence (the way dogs always knew something was wrong in gothic literature). Instead, the two of them were getting on famously. My double bent to scritch at his belly and he fell over in ecstasy like a cheap harlot.

Jem began to eat, leaning against the counter and rubbing at Archie's belly with her bare foot, but I was still preoccupied.

'What am I going to do in London?' I asked softly, wondering aloud. I pushed the omelette across my plate, but didn't lift my fork.

She shrugged, her mouth going chomp-chomp-chomp. 'Shop. Eat. Go out,' she said at last, swallowing. 'If you really get bored, you can hang out with Katz.'

Katz. Katsu. The name chimed inside my head like bells.

'Alright,' I said. 'I guess that's what I'll do . . . Wait, don't you have a job?'

'My play's on hiatus.' Jem flapped a hand dismissively. 'I'm on hiatus from it, anyway. Bunch of pretentious fuckers.'

I lapsed into silence, relieved I wouldn't have to act while I was in London. Well, I wouldn't have to act on top of my role as Jem. I gnawed on my knuckle. A mad giggle was building in my throat. On Sunday morning, 'Ella' would show up for work and Mrs Brannan wouldn't know what hit her.

'Do you know how to clean a toilet?' I asked.

My double looked so appalled that I couldn't suppress my laughter any more.

'Why don't I just call in sick?' Jem said.

'Nope, that's not how this works.' I swallowed down my giggles. 'Oh, just pour loads of bleach down it and give it a quick going over with the toilet brush.'

Jem's lip curled, but she nodded.

'I played a cleaner in a TV show once. Ended up shoved inside a broom cupboard, dead. Anyway, I had to fake-clean for two hours on set.' She mimed spraying and polishing. 'Real cleaning's probably not any different, right?'

I rolled my eyes. Jem was a brat, but her best dead-cleaner impression would do fine. My job was so mindless, I didn't see how even she could screw it up. If the job was even still there, of course. My insides writhed at the memory of Mrs Brannan's you-should-be-ashamed-of-yourself tone of voice.

'If Mrs Brannan – that's the boss – if she wants to speak to you about the, um, incident, just say sorry a lot.'

Jem's reaction was cheetah-quick. 'What incident?' She leaned forward, sniffing out gossip.

I wanted to say *none of your business*, but the queasy reality was that everything about my life was now Jem's business, and everything about hers was mine. Talk about a deal with the devil.

In a halting voice, I told her about the Kate Middleton woman, the violet robe, the ripping sound. Far from being scandalised, Jem laughed so hard she actually slapped her thigh.

'Score one for Little Mousey,' she said. 'Sounds like that bitch got what was coming to her.'

My double's amusement was so unbridled it was contagious. I lifted a hand to my lips, shielding a smile. *Yeah, that bitch got what was coming to her.* Chewing at my thumbnail, I took a deep breath. Then I bit down. My nail tore off between my teeth, leaving behind a ragged edge.

*

Cumbria flowed out behind me as the train sped south. Out the window, it was a crisp, clear November day, made of pearly-grey skies and fields that retained a ghostly tint of white frost. It was easy to love Cumbria when you were leaving it.

It was still early in the morning and inside the train remained slumbering quiet. The Saturday-morning passengers were an odd mix of bright-eyed daytrippers and sallow-skinned partygoers, returning home hungover.

One of the latter category, a man, squeezed down the aisle. As he passed my seat, he slowed to look at me. My heart dropped. He was an islander and he recognised me. He was a friend of my parents, maybe.

Eh up, Ella! he'd say. *Where you going? Why you dressed like that?*

I looked up at him, but he didn't say anything. He dawdled a moment too long, his gaze lingering over me. Then he pushed on down the aisle and was gone.

I breathed out unsteadily, shifting my gaze out the window, to the rise and fall of the countryside as it ebbed past. It was still early. Perhaps I could try and sleep away the rest of the journey. My double was almost certainly still sleeping.

Jem had spent the night nestled in a nest of blankets and cushions on my floor, Archie curled around her feet, but when I'd been preparing to leave, she'd crawled uninvited into my bed. I'd left her like that, faded pink duvet pulled up to her chin, hair spread out across the pillow; someone who looked like me, but wasn't me, asleep in my bed. The sight of it was surreal. I wondered for a moment if I'd climbed up out of my body. Astral projection or something.

But, no, I was definitely inside my own body. I knew it because my toes felt pinched and my lips were dry.

This morning, Jem had made up my face – sleepily brandishing make-up brushes with one eye open – and then styled my hair, so that it fell in soft waves. I was now dressed in her assortment of 'hobo chic' clothes, though I'd shed the hat/gilet when I'd got on the train, reluctantly revealing an orange top (tight, low-cut) and a leather miniskirt, worn over hole-y green tights. My feet were squeezed into narrow, patent-leather shoes.

The outfit seemed clownish to me, but the hungover men

slowed their pace as they passed my seat. The train conductor dropped a meaningful note into the word *darlin'* when he clipped my ticket and said, 'Thanks, darlin'.'

My double and I were physically identical in so many ways, but Jem – even my uncomfortable imitation of her – grabbed attention to exactly the same degree that I evaded it. I was struggling to get used to it.

I couldn't stop my shoes from pinching, but I could fix my dry lips. I reached automatically for my bag, with its little pot of Vaseline that I used as lip balm. But, of course, now I carried Jem's bag, which was bright purple, scuffed up, and bore a picture of a kitten whose eyes had been X'ed out. The bag was full to bursting, mostly with cosmetics. I couldn't even decipher the purpose of most of the tubes and pots. Almost all the labels seemed to be written in French. After a lot of rummaging, I found something that was – probably, possibly, perhaps – lip balm.

I also unearthed Jem's phone in the process. We'd made the exchange late last night. Without ceremony, she'd tossed in my direction a sleek, expensive phone. It looked brand new.

'Oh, I guess you should have this . . .'

The idea that swapping our real lives also required swapping our virtual lives had not occurred to me. I didn't even have time to think about what I was laying bare before Jem grabbed my own phone (much older and severely battered) from the counter.

Jem set upon my phone, her thumbs skimming over the screen.

'Let's see . . .' she said. 'New status update.' She paused to shoot me a devious grin and then tapped out a sentence, which she read aloud with gusto: *'Ella is taking a little time out from herself right now.'*

'That makes me sound crazy . . .' I said.

'So? It's funny. You post something as me. *Jem's not quite herself today . . .*'

She laughed uproariously, but I frowned. I reached out to grab my phone away from her, but she pulled back her hand, hiding it behind her back.

'Delete it,' I said. 'I don't want people to see it . . .'

'Why not?'

'It's stupid. It's not a joke if no one gets it.'

'Touchy, touchy,' she said, but brought out my phone and made a couple of taps on the screen. She held it up. 'Deleted, see? Happy now?'

In my hand, Jem's phone beeped. A new message flashed up on the screen.

'Listen . . .' I said. 'I can't reply to your friends. I'll do something wrong, give the whole thing away.'

She seemed about to argue, but then rolled her eyes, lifting her shoulders into a shrug.

'Alright . . . We just keep an eye on each other's messages. No status updates. No pointless stuff. Only reply if it's, like, urgent. Deal?'

On the train, I looked down at Jem's phone. Last night, I'd nodded. Now, I wondered what counted as 'urgent'. As if on cue, it gave a loud whistle.

I read through the flurry of messages that had arrived for Jem in the late hours of Friday and the early hours of Saturday. There was a rollicking group discussion between friends named Imogen, April and Stee; a continuation of what seemed to be an endless conversation about nothing. There was a 'let me know you're okay'-type one from Katsu. Flirty ones from a selection of other guys – Adrian, Daniel, Lukasz (*Lou-kaz?* I didn't know how to pronounce it). There was a long, involved anecdote from Jem's dad that I couldn't follow.

I gnawed on my fingernails, most of which were now ragged and bitten. I could leave Jem's friends to chat amongst themselves. I didn't know how to respond to Lou-kaz and the rest. The message from Jem's dad didn't seem to require an answer right now. That left Katsu.

Reading through the back-and-forth of Jem and Katsu's messages to each other made me feel like I was peering through a window into someone else's bedroom. After spending a torturous minute thinking, I typed:

I'm okay can't wait to see you

Even this innocuous message made my stomach twist. I imagined Katsu reading the message, smiling, thinking of me (no . . . Jem). Even clicking out of the conversation didn't make me feel better, because Jem's lock screen was a picture of Katsu. He was shirtless. It was summer. On a beach somewhere. He squinted against the sun, smiling at me (no . . . Jem).

I hesitated and then, taking a deep breath, switched off the phone completely. The dead black screen stared back at me. Its blankness was a relief. I didn't want to think about the fact that I'd sent the message to Katsu not as Jem, but as me.

18

WHO IS THE FAIREST OF THEM ALL?

Ella

'Tell me what it'll be like . . .' I said, in my dream, in my memory. 'After uni . . .'

Owen let out a long slow breath, as if gathering his thoughts. We were in a park, it was summer, and the fair, freckled skin of his face had already turned pink from too much sun. When he wrapped his arms around me from behind and nosed into the curve of my neck, I breathed in the faint smell of chlorine from his damp hair.

'We'll rent the biggest flat we can afford in London,' he said. 'So that means it'll probably be the size of a postage stamp . . .'

He made vague hand movements as he spoke, conducting lazily.

'Like . . . you open the door and you just' – his hand flopped down on its wrist – 'fall forward onto your bed. Because our flat will be precisely the same size as a double bed. And the shower curtain will hang over the oven. But we'll love it, because it'll be ours.'

He nuzzled against me, his voice growing drowsy and contented.

'And I'll become one of those loony people who swims in the Thames . . . and you'll play open mic nights and gain some kind of cult following. We'll drink too much and hang out with weirdos just like us. And it'll be a hell of a life. You and me.'

In the park, in my memory, in my dream, he kissed me.

On the train, I awoke with a start.

*

In London, I kept my head down as I walked along Jem's tree-lined street. Instead of my usual scurrying gait, I ended up shuffling, reluctant to reach my destination. I caught myself and made an effort to saunter instead, trying to mimic the careless, swinging way my double walked.

The night before, I'd written up pages and pages of notes about my life and the people in it. Jem, griping over 'all this bloody homework', had reluctantly done the same. During the train journey, between fitful sleep, I'd read and re-read Jem's notes, thinking it would make me more confident in my new role. I knew now that it was useless. I couldn't even get right the way Jem walked. Forget about copying the rest of her life.

It was early afternoon when I reached the bleached-white building where my double lived. It looked imposing in the day's grey light, with its severe iron railings and heavy black door. Heart pounding, I stepped up to the door and dug Jem's keys out of her bag. There was a whole raft of them, six or seven in all, strung on a mirrored key ring that read, *Who is the fairest of them all?*

I picked a key at random and stuck it in the lock. When I tried to open the door, it stood firm. I twisted the key again, but it wouldn't turn. It looked correct, it fitted in the lock, but it wasn't the right key. What a stupidly perfect metaphor for this whole day.

I glanced around, looking for anyone who might be watching as I dithered on the front step. I felt like a burglar – a particularly inept burglar. I took a deep breath, shaking out my trembling hands. Then, working methodically, I began sorting through the keys once more. Picking the likeliest culprit, I shoved it into the keyhole, jiggling hard, until the lock gave. The door swung open, revealing the marble-floored, high-ceilinged entrance hall.

The key drama had almost been enough to make me forget that the second I opened the door I would have to *become* Jem.

Since leaving my own house this morning, I'd been pretending to be Jem. But it had been pretending without consequence; playing dress up. Once I stepped over the threshold into her life, everything I said and did would become Jem's words, Jem's actions. As far as the world was concerned, I *was* Jem.

One of her neighbours, a glamorous redhead in an emerald-green coat, skip-stepped down the sweeping staircase toward me. My voice shrank to the back of my throat. *Don't talk to me, please don't talk to me.* I was aware that my eyes were wide and staring. I gave her a nod, hoping that seemed neighbourly. She brushed past without acknowledging me.

Upstairs, outside Jem's apartment door, I repeated the key farce, my fingers even more fumbly than before. I had a paranoid sense that the flat wouldn't be empty. Someone would be waiting, ready to spring out from the shadows and confront me. When I found the right key and the door gave, I pushed it open an inch, then a little more, sliding my body through the gap.

I called out, 'Hello . . .?'

The word came out soft – more of a whisper than a yell – and it sounded distinctly Cumbrian. I tried again to summon Jem's carelessly-posh, sing-song accent.

'Hello!'

The result was closer to a convincing copy of Jem's voice. But it yielded only silence. I groped for the light switch and the shadows receded.

Just me. Only me here.

I closed the front door and moved through the apartment, falling once more into a hunched, creeping gait. The huge gilt mirror that hung in the hallway glinted in the shifting light. The empty rooms were as beautiful as I remembered and I felt out of place in every one.

In the living room, yards of sheer cotton hung in front of the windows, creating an odd gloom, as if Jem wanted to prevent anyone from looking in. The velvet cushions scattered on the sofa seemed positioned by a designer. The glass-topped coffee table was polished to a high shine. The closer I looked, the more the whole thing seemed staged. Like a movie set just after the actors had left. None of it screamed 'Jem'. Too tidy, too perfect.

It was almost a relief to end up in my double's bedroom. Though garish, with its bright green wall, it was lived in, dirty clothes strewn on the floor and a strong scent of oranges from her perfume. When I opened the door to her room, I half-expected to find Jem herself in there, preening in front of the mirror. *Hey, Twinnie! Hey, Little Mouse!*

Jem's room, like the rest of the apartment, was empty.

I roamed the over-large space, caught between curiosity and a sense that I was invading my double's privacy. I reached out to touch one of the ceremonial swords mounted on the green wall – what a pretentious thing to collect; how knowingly provocative – and then snatched my hand away at the coldness of metal against skin.

With a shudder, I thought of Jem, 300 miles away, rifling through my stuff in the same way. I consoled myself with the fact that there would not be much for Jem to find. I'd cleared out my secrets and burned my diary long before she came into my life. I kept my thoughts locked up in my head now.

I picked my way across the carpet to the bed, which was also heaped with clothing. Automatically, I began to sort and fold the clothes into a neat pile. Then I realised it wasn't what my double would do – Jem left her bedroom chaotic; whoever tidied the other spaces, it wasn't her – so I stopped myself. I rocked back on my heels, trying to think what she *would* do.

If I was alone, did I need to act like Jem? If there was no one to see me, was I myself or was I Jem? The questions made my head hurt. The strange feeling that I was not alone renewed. This oversized flat was full of eyes. Watching me.

I exhaled a shaky breath and it sounded loud in the empty room. One thing was for sure: I needed to get out.

I thought of Jem's casual answer to what I should do in London: *Shop. Eat. Go out.* I pulled her phone from my pocket and switched it on. Ignoring the inevitable influx of new messages, I tapped out:

Wanna go shopping?

*

'Hey Jemster, I see you've dressed down . . .' came the greeting from a tall woman with long chocolate-brown hair. For a split second, her appearance reminded me of the Kate Middleton woman at the hotel.

My face flushed. The make-up Jem had applied for me that morning had smeared over the course of the train journey, so I'd removed it, intending to reapply. Unfortunately, I'd ended up wearing eyeliner that looked – in Jem's words – like someone had attacked me with a crayon. I'd had no choice but to take it off again and opt for simpler make-up choices.

In preparation for my new role, I'd slicked on plenty of orangey-red lipstick and chosen a nondescript white top from Jem's wardrobe, which I'd teamed with black skinny jeans and a fitted, fawn-coloured wool coat. Each item was designer, visibly expensive, and cut in a way that gave me a figure I'd never had before. I'd thought the effect was passable, if not a perfect Jem impersonation, but now I wondered if I'd totally messed it up.

Without waiting for a response, the woman bounded off her wooden bench and swooped in to kiss me – *mwah! mwah!* – on both cheeks.

'You look like shit,' she added cheerfully, as she pulled away.

She wore a grin that was full of big white teeth. Standing several inches taller than me, at perhaps six foot, she had the broad shoulders of a warrior. Her feminine good looks, contoured with lots of makeup, were a contrast to her voice, which was low and gravelly. From looking at the profile pictures of Jem's friends online, I knew her name was Imogen.

She was flanked by two others, who lounged on a set of benches in a pedestrianised side street. Surrounded by huge leather handbags and oversize shopping bags, they took up far more room than they needed to. They appeared not to notice the woman with a double-wide pushchair who hovered close by, hoping to nab a seat.

Soho, cold despite the winter sun, was noisy and dirty and packed with people who all seemed to be scrutinising me. I'd got lost on the way to meet Imogen and the others, and my heart rate was up. All the twisty-turny streets of this part of London looked the same to me.

Imogen removed one of her bags from the bench so that I could sit down.

'Not . . . feeling well,' I said, my voice coming out stilted with the effort of maintaining my double's accent. 'Think I'm getting the flu.'

I'd worked out this excuse in advance. It would be a convenient reason for anything that was wrong about my behaviour or appearance. If I got overwhelmed, I could fake a stomach ache and leave.

'Oh, you poor lamb!' Imogen leaned in to give me another hug, though turned her face away to avoid sharing my air.

'You should take it easy.'

It was the girl to Imogen's left who'd spoken. With her long waves of blue-green hair, she was easy to identify. Her name was April and her Twitter profile read 'artist, lesbian, sick of your shit – I am all of these things'. She was plump, with brown skin and big eyes. In most of the selfies she posted, those eyes shone with a smile. Today, she was frowning.

'Seriously,' she said to me, a warning in her voice.

Her eyes were trying to communicate something to me, but I had no idea what. I looked away, fussing with a tissue from my pocket.

'She's fine,' a bracing voice cut in, 'you two hens stop your clucking.'

The final member of the group was Stee. Stee was not a girl. Or maybe she was. Her face held the soft traces of girlhood, pixie-ish and delicate, but her silver-blonde hair was cropped short and she wore boy clothes – ripped dark jeans and a button-down shirt, with a red bow tie peeking out at the collar.

Stee shot me a conspiratorial glance and, once again, I had no idea how to react.

I was saved from having to come up with a response by a young girl, perhaps six or seven, who scampered up to where we sat and asked April, 'Are you a mermaid? Are you a real mermaid?'

'Yes!' April gestured to the folksy green maxi-dress she wore. 'I can't show you my tail right now, because the mermaid elders wouldn't like it, but look – ' She put her legs together beneath her skirt and made a kick like the flick of a tail.

The little girl's eyes rolled back into her head in sheer ecstasy. She ran away, brown pigtails bouncing, back to her mother to tell her all about her mermaid encounter.

'Kids are cute,' April said with a sigh, watching her go. 'They just grow up into arseholes. If only we could figure out a way to stop the arseholification process . . .'

'Shut up,' Stee said. 'You love being an arsehole.'

'True,' April said, pausing to swig from her gigantic coffee, 'but I actively monitor my arseholiness. I do my best to focus it, like a laser, at other arseholes. Who, like, fucking deserve that death ray of arsehole . . . arity.'

'I have literally no idea what you just said.'

'Yeah, well, it was deep as fuck and you're thick as shit.'

I tensed, wondering whether the exchange was going to

escalate into an argument, but the two of them just laughed. April offered Stee a sip of coffee.

Judging by the number of bags they carried, I thought Jem's friends might be shopped out. Not so. Imogen leading the way, we strolled the busy streets of Soho, ducking inside boutiques with quirky names like *Yellow Octopus* and *Retro Foe.*

Stee drew Imogen into a conversation about their respective Friday nights ('. . . didn't even know my own name . . . that coke was cut with something, dude . . .'), while April looped her arm through mine. The gesture was so casually intimate, it reminded me of Jem's behaviour the first afternoon we met, when I'd fooled myself into thinking I'd found a friend or even a sister.

'Hey,' April said softly, 'you been MIA the last few days . . .'

'Um,' I said, 'yeah. Just needed to . . . get away from it all.'

I gave a spasm of a shrug as my mind raced. All those hours spent drilling Jem on the facts of her life and I'd missed the most obvious pitfall of this switch. What went on in Jem's head? How could I know?

How could I ever really become her?

19

NONSTOP CALAMITY

Ella

'Where did you go?' April asked.

'Edinburgh,' I blurted out.

Where did that come from? I'd never even been to Edinburgh. I only thought of it because something about April's sweet smiles and arty vibe reminded me of my uni friend Cait.

Last year, before she moved to Beijing, Cait and a couple of others planned a road-trip to see me on Walney. Then we'd all head up to the Edinburgh Fringe together. The plans fell through at the last minute – for complicated reasons involving a sick dog and a fake-sounding cousin – and I never did go to Edinburgh.

'Cool, you get to see Bean?' April asked.

Was Bean a person or a place? I had no idea.

'No, I was only there for a bit,' I said.

Maybe April twigged my panicked expression, because she reached over and squeezed my hand.

'You're really okay? Sure it's just the flu?' she asked, her concerned expression making her look more like a Disney mermaid than ever. 'You're not mad at me?'

'No! Of course not!' I cast around for a change of subject. A few feet away, Stee was telling yet another outrageous story of partying gone awry. 'Stee's crazy, right?'

We were in a cute little vintage clothes shop, with distressed wood floors painted teal. April thumbed through a rack of patterned dresses. 'Nothing new there,' she said, lifting her eyebrows.

'She's gonna get herself killed one of these days,' I said.

April looked at me sharply, then checked to see if Stee had heard.

'*He*. Don't even joke about it,' she said.

'Sorry,' I muttered, before remembering Jem would never apologise.

April just shook her head, leaving me to wonder what I'd done wrong. I squirmed out of her grasp under the pretence of looking at my phone. In reality, I scrolled without reading, taking deep breaths and trying to slow my heart rate.

Even in my distracted state, I noticed there were no messages from Jem. I'd thought maybe she'd send me a text or two. Radio silence was unnerving. What was she doing right now? Who was she talking to?

Would the people in my life even detect a difference? My mum's eyes followed me obsessively, but it was so long since she'd actually seen me. Maybe Mum and the rest of them wouldn't notice the change at all.

Should I text Jem? No, I wasn't sure I wanted to know what was going on.

I forced my thoughts back to the situation at hand. Beside me, Imogen was talking, in drawling, tragic tones, about her sometime-boyfriend who'd perhaps (she wasn't sure) broken up with her.

'I just give with too much of my heart . . .' She was making doleful cow eyes at me. 'You know what I mean, Jem?'

'Mmhmm,' I said, while Stee guffawed and April made *aww* noises.

A phone rang. My heart jumped – maybe it was Jem – but, no, it wasn't my phone.

'Yuh,' Imogen answered the call, her voice filling the whole shop. 'Yuuuh . . .'

Just for something to do, I rummaged through the same rack of dresses April had been looking at. I fingered a pretty blue one, wondering about the price. Back home, I did a lot of my shopping in charity shops, but they didn't look like this one. I eyed the animal skulls mounted on the walls, festooned with fairy lights.

'Well, for fuck's sake, Audrey, why didn't you bring this to me yesterday?' Imogen was saying, her tone a far cry from the lovelorn teenager of two minutes ago. 'You mean yet again you take a shit and I have to clean it up?'

I turned over the price tag on the blue dress. It cost £400. I had to look twice to check I hadn't misread it. *Four hundred pounds*. Okay, so this wasn't second-hand clothes shopping as I knew it.

'You do this again and I'll make sure no one in the city will hire you – not even Starbucks.' Imogen stabbed at her phone. 'That fucking ingrate' – she aimed her voice approximately in my direction – 'I hired her and she repays me with nonstop calamity.'

I nodded, worrying the price tag between finger and thumb. The idea that, at 25, Imogen had enough clout to hire and fire people made me feel like I was the recipient of her tongue-lashing, not poor Audrey.

'Don't let it get to you, it's Saturday,' April said with a yawn.

Imogen glowered a moment longer and then abruptly revived her grin.

'Hey! That's super adorable, you should try it on.' She swept the blue dress off the rack and held it up against me. 'So cute!'

In front of the mirror in the dressing room, I smoothed the dress down over my hips and fluffed up my hair. The dress had a billowing dramatic skirt that contrasted with its fitted bodice. Shades of blue and purple were divided up by thick black lines reminiscent of stained glass. I uncapped my orangey-red lipstick and reapplied, but when I practised my smile in the mirror, it still had a tremulous quality.

'What d'you think?'

I drew back the curtain. It felt like I was stepping out on stage.

In the fitting rooms' communal area, Imogen was adjusting the tie on a cream wrap dress, but when she saw me, she clapped her hands together. 'Love it!'

April was trying on an ostrich-feather fedora, frowning at herself in the mirror. Stee was the only one of us not in the fitting rooms. He'd grown bored of the cooing and preening and gone outside.

As Ella, I might have agreed that it was stupid to waste so much time trying on clothes. As Jem, it was fun to bask in the attention. Imogen spun her finger and, on command, I did a little twirl in the stained-glass dress. I felt pretty.

'You're looking skinny . . .' April said. 'Cute, but skinny.'

'Shut up, she looks like a model,' Imogen said, fussing with my zipper, which hadn't quite made it all the way up my back. 'But your boobs have shrunk. Dieting's cruel.'

A shiver started at the nape of my neck where the metal zip lay against my skin and shuddered all the way down my spine. I didn't like their appraising eyes.

Jem was curvier than me. Not massively so, but to a degree that someone looking closely would notice. There were subtle differences between the two of us – freckles and moles in the wrong places – that might be obvious to a keen observer. I should never have tried on the dress; I should never have courted their attention.

Imogen was still too close, smelling of rose and sugar, like Turkish delight. She was tugging at the neckline of my dress, repositioning it against my collarbones. I had a crazed thought that maybe she was looking for a name label, the type we'd had sewn inside our clothes in infants' school. Inside the dress, it would say *Ella*.

I flinched against the cool touch of her fingers. I wanted to run away.

'You're getting the dress, right?' Imogen said.

I managed a tiny nod and she yanked off the dress's tags.

'Wear it now,' she said. 'Stinky's getting us in to that new Lebanese place in Shoreditch.'

'Okay . . .'

I grabbed my other clothes from the fitting room and shoved them into the oversized handbag of Jem's that I carried. I scarcely had time to think before I was standing at the till, handing a credit card to the cashier. It was one of five credit cards Jem kept in her wallet. Back on Walney, she'd casually told me her pin for all of them was her birthday (11th June). I gulped at the £400 charge – but Jem could afford it, right? – and lightly tapped in one-one-zero-six.

Transaction failed.

The cashier, absurdly glamorous in red-glitter lipstick, gave a tight smile. 'Probably my fault,' she said and repeated the process.

My hands were shaking as I hit one-one-zero-six again.

Transaction failed.

'Maybe try another card?' the cashier said.

I tried two more. Both times, the transaction failed. The others grew restless behind me. April was complaining of hunger, Imogen had gone back to talking about her not-quite-boyfriend.

Why hadn't Jem warned me her cards were maxed out? On the flip side, who was I to spend her money, anyway? The cashier's eyelinered eyes were narrowed. She was looking at me like I was a thief, and maybe I was one.

This whole thing was a colossal mistake. I wanted to back away and tell the cashier to cancel the purchase, but I was wearing the dress. I'd have to get changed, make a big scene.

Every moment as Jem held inside it the potential for danger. You never knew when you might look down and realise you'd strayed into sinking sands.

'Oh, for God's sake,' Imogen said with a tinkling laugh.

'My treat.'

She handed over her credit card and, moments later, we were exiting the shop.

'Problems with your mum again?' April asked me in a low voice.

'Yeah . . .' I whispered, though I had no idea.

Putting on the stained-glass dress for the first time, I'd felt beautiful. Brave. A new Ella. Now the pitiful old Ella threatened to climb back out of my rib cage and smother me.

*

At the Lebanese restaurant in Shoreditch, there was a queue down the street. I'd never seen people queue for a restaurant, but then pub grub and old-fashioned Italian were what passed for good food on Walney. It was only 7 p.m. now, but it looked like the restaurant would be full until midnight. No way we were getting in.

Maybe now was the perfect time to scurry away. *Transaction failed* flashed in my mind. It came with a beep-beep-beep sound, and a taste like metal against my tongue. *Transaction failed*.

I'd wanted so badly to be convincing as Jem. It was a test for myself, to prove I was bold enough to thrive in London, to live the kind of life I'd once dreamed of with Owen. Instead, this experience was crystallising my greatest fear: the small-town girl from Walney Island was all I'd ever be.

'Sorry,' I said in an undertone. 'I think I should go, not feeling well . . .'

'Oh, shut your mouth,' Stee said amicably. 'You'll be fine once we get inside.'

He disappeared round the side of the building. April and Imogen looked unfazed. Stamping their feet to keep warm against the cold, they talked about April's plans for an art show of her work. 'Daddy thinks holding it in Shoreditch is uncouth,' she said with a sigh. 'He wants me to find a venue on the Southbank.'

Jealousy spiked against my windpipe. It must be easy to be an artist – or an actress – if your parents would pick up the tab. I drew Jem's fawn-coloured wool coat more tightly around myself and mustered the courage to say I was leaving once and for all.

Before I could speak, Stee reappeared at my shoulder. 'Hasim can get us in.'

'Sweet,' April said, rubbing her belly. 'I could eat, like, five pounds of halloumi.'

Where was Stee going? I had no choice but to follow.

The couple who were standing beside me in the queue – a man with a bushy black beard and a woman whose brown hair looked like it had been dipped in purple – began muttering, and their whispers spread down the line.

Around the corner, a white door, unmarked, was partly concealed by industrial-size dumpsters. People from the queue were craning their necks to look. Some appeared curious, others were pissed off.

I slipped through the door, the last of our four-person party, and immediately I was descending. The staircase was dark and narrow, but the air was warm and smelled of honey and spices. At the bottom, I emerged blinking into a brightly-lit kitchen. A handsome man, with brown skin and sleepy eyes, beckoned us past the throng of kitchen staff who were chopping and frying and stirring.

Imogen paused to dip her finger in a vat of what looked like golden sludge. 'Mmm, so good,' she whispered to me. Before any of the staff could complain, we were out on the restaurant floor.

The guy, who I assumed was Hasim, pulled out a chair for me at a table in the middle of the room. He gave me a flirty smile, but all I could do was gawp at him.

All those people outside – many of whom looked like they'd

been waiting for hours in the cold – and we were going to bypass them? I'd never be able to do this on Walney. I wouldn't have the courage – or the connections – to pull it off.

Food came without us ordering it. Grilled meats, rice, stews, cheese, and pots of golden sludge weighed down the table. Even as Jem's friends dug in to the food, I couldn't process what was happening. I glanced around the crowded restaurant. We were underground and the walls were exposed brick. The lights were covered with dark red lanterns, giving the room a dramatic crimson glow.

Hasim uncorked a bottle of red wine and poured me a generous measure.

'You're looking stunning this evening,' he said to me in a throaty voice. (Stee made a gagging noise beside us. Hasim swatted at him.)

I met his gaze. I felt more stunned than stunning. But his smile was dimpled and genuine. When he looked at me, he saw Jem – self-assured, sexy Jem. I wore an expensive dress, my hair hung loose and glossy around my shoulders, my lips were bright and kissable. From looks alone, I was indistinguishable from my double. I just needed to learn to act like her.

'You charmer,' I said, giving my voice a mischievous purr.

This time, when I smiled, there was no bashful quality to it, only a certainty that I was deserving of Hasim's compliment.

My admirer was called away by another member of staff. He bobbed his head as he was leaving, giving me a mournful look.

'Have some halloumi!' April said, shoving thick slabs of grilled white cheese at me.

I stabbed at a piece with my fork. The cheese was chewy, a little like rubber, but with a salty taste that exploded in my mouth. I reached for a second slice before I'd even finished my first. Suddenly I was ravenous.

I piled my plate with great slops of everything. The golden sludge Imogen had sampled earlier, served studded with pomegranate seeds, was indeed delicious. I swallowed it down with a gulp of wine. I knew mixing alcohol with my medication could make me woozy and dizzy, but in that moment, I couldn't bring myself to care.

Right now, it seemed unfathomable that anything could go wrong. In my new dress, I felt carefree, I felt pretty, I felt . . . like I had a place in the world.

Jem's friends were so confident. It was unthinkable that their lives' trajectory could go anywhere but up, up, up. Their certainty was contagious. Every moment as Jem held inside it the potential for excitement.

'You still coming on Friday?' April asked.

'Friday?' I echoed.

'My birthday, you bitch.'

'Right,' I said, reaching for another glug of wine. 'I only forgot in the sense of not remembering. But now it's burned into my brain.'

April gave a *huh* of a laugh, mollified.

'You bringing that man of yours?' she asked.

I knew the right response: 'Which one?'

'You're terrible,' Imogen said, making a face. 'I can't find one decent fella and you're always stringing along five.'

'Not five.' I paused, courting their laughter. 'Maybe four on a good day.'

I grabbed another slice of halloumi. April was right; I was too skinny.

Over the hour that followed, I found that I didn't need to try so hard to summon up Jem's accent anymore; it flowed out of me easily. I forgot I was pretending. I dropped comments into the conversation without thinking. I began having fun.

I forgot . . .

I forgot I was pretending?

*

When the four of us tumbled out of the restaurant's doors two hours later, the bearded man and the purple-haired woman who'd been in the queue next to us were seated at a tiny table next to the toilets. They were poring over menus; it looked like they hadn't even ordered yet. The woman cast me a dark look. I laughed, fluffing up my hair as I swept past her.

Don't be jealous, darling. It's not a good look.

On the pavement outside the restaurant, Imogen threw out the question, 'What are we doing now?'

'I was up at six, painting, so I'm shaht-tered,' April said, hiding a yawn behind her fist.

I checked my phone for the time. Past nine o'clock. I'd been hanging out with Jem's friends for more than six hours, but the time had flown by.

I was torn between wanting to stay – I was having such a good time! – and feeling like Cinderella at 11:59. I'd convinced the world I was Jem for an afternoon, but if I pushed it, the façade might fall away.

'Think I might head home for a quiet one,' April continued.

'Me too,' I said, and a hint of Ella's Cumbrian accent crept into my voice. 'I should probably get going.'

'Both of you, shut up,' Stee said. 'You're such lightweights.' He turned to Imogen. 'What can we do that's fun?'

'Hm, what's around here?' Imogen scanned the street and began to rattle off intel like Stee had asked her for stock market tips. 'There's a speakeasy place on the corner. That railway yard plays soul music, R&B. The circus-y place – '

'No, not the usual bollocks,' Stee said. 'I'm so sick of hipsters.'

'. . . Okay, I have an idea.' Imogen stuck out her arm for a taxi.

'Where?' April asked.

'It's a surprise.'

'I hate your surprises,' April said, but she was grinning.

20

LAY OF THE LAND

Jem

I leaned on the pinewood bar at Jackdaw's, showing off my boobs in a cornflower-blue dress of Ella's that I'd found buried at the bottom of her drawer. I was waiting for Bethany to arrive. While I waited, I sipped on a Martini and played with the barman.

'I've never . . .' He rubbed his beard. Big, black and furry; the type of beard that would read 'hipster' in London, but was more 'woodsman serial killer' up here. 'Never had sex on a plane,' he said.

'Oh, please.' I took an unladylike swig of my drink.

Jackdaw's was the kind of bar-restaurant that people on Walney Island probably considered 'fancy'. The tables were laid with checked table cloths, and tacky tea lights flickered on every surface. Decorative plates bearing cursive Italian slogans and cartoons of moustachioed men lined the walls. Tinny Michael Bublé songs played over the sound system. The only good thing about the place was the stink of buttery pasta wafting out from the kitchen.

I dabbed at the corners of my mouth with a paper napkin, thinking about my next words.

'I've never punched anyone in the face,' I said at last.

The barman took a nip of whisky and I let out a cackle of delight.

'Who did you punch?'

'Long story,' he said, his eyes glinting.

They were good eyes. Brown shifting into amber, like a cat's.

Soulful, despite his beefy build and don't-fuck-with-me beard. I was tempted to take him for a spin; tease all his secrets loose. I sipped at my drink and trapped him in my gaze.

'Ella?'

I was having such a good time, I'd forgotten where I was. I'd forgotten *who* I was.

'Ella?' a woman's voice said again.

The barman raised his eyebrows and I remembered.

The woman heaved herself onto the bar stool next to me. In the flesh, Bethany was ginger-haired, with freckled skin and crooked teeth – and she was very pregnant. Jesus. I tried not to stare at her big round stomach. Who got pregnant in their twenties? Who stayed pregnant in their twenties?

'Hey . . .' I said. 'How's it going?'

My voice didn't sound right – too rah-rah hockey sticks; not enough of a scummy Northern burr – but I brushed that thought aside. In general, I was doing a great job of mastering the Ella effect. I'd spent the day traipsing around, getting the lay of the land, practising her round-shouldered posture and dead-puppy-dog stare.

'Oh, you know,' Bethany said, shifting in her seat, 'my ankles are all swole up, but I'm fine once I'm sitting.'

'You look cute.'

'Do I?'

Dipping her head, she smoothed a hand over the shapeless orange tent she was wearing. She looked like an escapee from a death cult.

'Super cute!' I pulled her in for an air kiss and her chin bumped awkwardly against mine. 'What are you drinking?'

'Uhh . . .' She scanned the bottles on display.

I gulped down the last of my martini and raised my head to stare down the backwoods barman. He'd strayed to serve another customer, but when he saw me looking, he ambled over to us.

'Make me something lethal,' I said to him. 'Dust off all those bottles that never get used.'

'I've never . . . put anyone in a coma,' he said under his breath, meeting my gaze dead on.

I licked my lips. 'Try me.'

Bethany rudely interrupted the pornographic thoughts filtering through my mind.

'Excuse me, could I have a half pint of lemonade?' she asked the barman. 'And could you put a little umbrella in it? Maybe a cherry?' To me, she said, 'I need to feel like I'm drinking a real cocktail, so we can celebrate.'

'Celebrate?' My voice was distracted; my eyes were still tracking the barman's movements.

He spun a dusty bottle of rum in the palm of his hand and caught it a split-second before it crashed to the floor. I knew a thing or two about massaging men's egos, so I applauded. The glance I shot him was admiring. He could copy and paste it from his mindspace and imagine me fawning over his dick.

'Yeah!' Bethany nudged me. 'Because we've been friends for so many years. Like you said.'

'Mmm.'

I tried to remember what line I'd spun when Bethany had called Twinnie's phone earlier. She'd been bugging me about looking after her spawn, but I'd knocked that one on the head. Instead, I'd suggested a girls' night:

'I've been trying out this new thing, read about it online,' I'd said, 'where you, like, really appreciate every day' – total improv – 'so when I saw on Facebook it's our friendiversary' – blatant lie – 'I knew we had to celebrate.'

Bethany had gone squishy like putty in my hands. 'Aww, babe! How lovely! I'll ask Stu if he can look after Talia . . .'

It was kinda fun to manipulate her. She probably knew Twinnie's secrets, too. All the better to get in character. I also needed a guide to Arse-Crack Island's social scene and

Bethany was convenient.

The barman plonked down an over-adorned lemonade and a dark mixed drink that bubbled ominously. Bethany grabbed her glass and began fiddling with the umbrella. 'These are on you, right?'

'Sure.'

Covertly, I rolled my eyes, missing Imogen's deep pockets. I pulled a twenty pound note from my bra and presented it to the barman, dewed with a little boobsweat. He gave me a wolfish grin. Basking in his attention, I took a swig of my drink. It was rich and smooth, sweet, but with a bite of bitterness. The strength of the alcohol made my lips tingle. This was a drink to lose yourself in. Perfect.

'Had an absolute 'mare yesterday . . .'

Beside me, Bethany had launched into a long and involved story about a mix-up at the post office. It was so boring, I was going to suggest she record it as a go-to-sleep podcast to help insomniacs. But polite little Twinnie would never be so rude. I wondered what went through Ella's mind when she sat and listened to Bethany. I'd found a bottle of antidepressants hidden under her bed; they obviously numbed her out enough to tolerate it.

Maybe I needed a pharmaceutical fix of my own. Alcohol was chasing away my blues – and making my Carlo-induced injuries hurt less – but it was always nice to have a kick of cocaine to keep you awake and ready for anything. I shrugged off the thought. I wasn't going to do anything so boring as detox, but after the scare with Carlo, I wondered if I should take it easy, give my body a break.

The barman returned with my change. He dropped a handful of coins into my outstretched hand and the skin of his fingers brushed mine.

'Let me know if you need anything else,' he said, with a meaningful look.

I sucked hard on my straw. 'Uh huh.'

Our eye-fucking was interrupted by Bethany.

'So I was thinking tomorrow afternoon, right?' she said, buzzing like a fly on the edge of my consciousness.

I drummed my fingers idly. 'Hm?'

'Some quality time for Talia and her auntie!'

'I'm not her auntie,' I said without checking myself.

'You know what I mean.' Bethany twirled her tiny umbrella between thumb and forefinger. A dimple appeared in her cheek as she smiled.

'Not sure tomorrow works,' I said. The only way babysitting was a viable option was if the child was old enough to make me a G&T.

'Oh . . . okay, maybe one evening this week?'

God, Beth-a-me-me-me really wasn't getting the message. I'd thought I could have some fun with her, but Mrs Pregnant Dimwit was turning out to be a drag.

'She's your kid, why don't you bloody well look after her?' I stopped myself from adding, *Or pay a nanny to do it for you.*

The smile slid off Bethany's face. Her eyes got all big and round, like her fat stomach.

'That's not a very nice thing to say.'

I spluttered out a laugh. 'What are you, eight?'

'Look . . . tonight was your idea and now you're saying mean things to me, making slut eyes at Darryl.'

'Who's Darryl?'

Her eyes flicked to the barman, an *uh-duh* look on her face.

Oh. Darryl with the beard. The name made me like him less. No one ever moaned *oh, Darryl* in ecstasy.

'He's only interested in getting into your pants,' Bethany said huffily. 'Been like that since school.'

'Well, at least someone's interested.' I paused to gulp down a few centimetres of my drink. 'No one wants to go near your huge Granny pants right now.'

Bethany went bright red. 'That's a really' – she mouthed the word *shitty* – 'thing to say.'

She folded her arms across her chest, her stomach supporting her crossed arms like a pillow. The result was accidentally hilarious, so I laughed.

'Shitty?' I said. 'You're one to talk.'

'What's that s'posed to mean?'

'You treat me like shit. You know that, right?'

'I'm your best friend, I've supported you through . . . everything.'

'Please. I've seen your messages. It's all *wah, wah, wah*, do me a favour, Ella, babysit for me Ella, lie down on concrete and let me walk all over you, Ella.'

'That's not true!'

'It fucking well is. You're a selfish little bitch.'

Twinnie had surely been wanting to say these things for years. She'd probably thank me for unloading on her behalf.

Bethany tried to get up and storm out, but the act of dismounting from the barstool sent her careening sideways into a country-bumpkin-type in a flat cap. In the process, she spilled her own drink (the paper umbrella fell onto the bar, drenched in lemonade) and capsized Flat Cap's drink as well. Dripping sugary residue, she flung a couple of weak insults at me on her way out the door. They bounced right off me. I was bulletproof.

'Bye, then!' I called out.

I angled my body away from the spillage and chugged at my drink. My skin was hot, my heartbeat drumming loud in my ears. It felt good to let loose. What Twinnie's life was missing was a good fight. My eyes darted to the barman. And a good fuck.

Darryl dragged a filthy rag from under the bar, wiping up the spilled drink.

'Catfight, is it?' he said. 'Should slather the both of you in baby oil and charge money to watch. The preggo belly would pro'ly be a big draw.'

Darryl was laughing, but I let out an irritated breath. It turned out I liked the backwoods barman more when he talked less. I took a final slug of my drink.

'What time do you get off work?' I asked.

'Couple of hours.'

His eyes crinkled into a smiling squint. Dammit. He was still cute.

'You ever been to Ireland?' My thumb bounced against the bar. No, Ireland was cold. I wanted to go someplace hot. 'Ever been to Rio?'

'Shit, I was thinking my place, but you got big plans.'

I was enjoying this – being someone new. I always thought I'd make a hell of a spy: keeping false papers in a secret compartment in my suitcase, donning a blonde wig, sleeping with the enemy to gain intelligence. Did Ella have a passport? What was stopping me from making a getaway for real?

'Yeah, I got plans.' I let my eyelids flutter shut, stretching my neck. 'Plans and schemes, ideas and dreams . . .'

'Never used to be like this when I sat next to you in maths,' he said. 'You're full of surprises, Ella.'

I opened my eyes. 'That I am.'

21

HUSTLERS

Ella

The taxi deposited us in front of a grand, sandstone building, with pillars and arched windows. Union Jacks on flag poles flopped in the wind, as if this were a stronghold against military attack.

'Ah, Sugar Daddy Land,' April said, making a face.

Po-faced doormen in navy-blue uniforms held open heavy glass doors for us. Inside, it was wood-panelled and strangely hushed. We perched on red-velvet-upholstered stools at the bar, beneath a glittering chandelier.

'Two in ten,' Imogen said in a low voice.

'I'll go three in ten.' Stee thrust back his shoulders and cast his gaze around the opulent room. 'Old dudes are hungry for a little snack like me. What about you, Jems?'

I gave a twitch of my shoulder and summoned a haughty look of disinterest.

Stee leaned in close to Imogen. 'She's hustling us, Jem's a born hustler.'

What were we doing here? What were they betting on?

This place was lavish, but it seemed too fusty for my new friends. A marble bust looked down at us imperiously from its place above the bar. The majority of the clientele consisted of over-50s in expensive evening wear. By contrast, Stee's ripped jeans, Imogen's plunging neckline, April's hippy-dippy maxi-dress, marked us as garish interlopers in this upscale bar. Even my stained-glass dress was wrong. I shifted on my bar stool, trying to copy April's look of bored nonchalance.

'Well, I'm buying my own drink,' she said pointedly.

April ordered a vodka cranberry from the bartender, who was beautiful, with waist-length black hair and completely dead eyes. I muttered, 'Same.'

'I'm fine for now,' Imogen said to the bartender. Her smile was suspiciously syrupy and she was angling her gaze over my shoulder.

April's phone was on the bar, the stopwatch running down from ten minutes. I sipped my drink and realised Stee was gone. He was in the corner of the room, leaning against the wood panelling, having what looked like an intense conversation with a portly man whose slicked-back hair did little to hide his bald spot.

When I turned back around, a martini had appeared in front of Imogen like magic. 'From the gentleman in the green tie,' the dead-eyed bartender said. She slid a business card across the bar. 'He also sent you this.'

Imogen's smile turned from treacly-fake to triumphantly real. 'One,' she said, tapping the business card.

'Six minutes,' April said, her cool, commanding tone reminiscent of an umpire.

Stee returned, swaggering. He flicked a business card between his fingers. 'He's going to mentor me,' he said, giving an exaggerated wink.

'Mmhmm,' April said.

As the particulars of their game came into focus, I couldn't help but laugh. Imogen only allowed herself a second to join in with my laughter. Spurred on by Stee, she took a slug of her martini and slid off her stool, heading for a trio of men at the other end of the bar. April called after her, 'Five minutes!'

'Shit.' Stee shot off in the opposite direction.

Torn between amusement and horror, I watched the two of them work the room. Imogen was shameless, throwing back her chocolate-brown hair and leading with her boobs.

Stee was more cunning, cultivating a little-boy-lost persona, all bitten lips and big eyes, that succeeded in sucking-in men three times his age.

For all their success – I saw Stee tuck another business card into his breast pocket – a hot-and-tingly feeling of embarrassment rose in me. Weren't they worried about making fools of themselves?

I cringed, waiting for the men to rebuff them. Yet even when a jowly man, expansive in a banana-yellow shirt, shouldered away from Imogen, the result was a shrug. She gave a titter, tossed her hair, and moved on.

Beside me, April was whispering commentary, imitating the men in the room. *'Do you like fox hunting, old gel? How about you let me stick my rifle up your – Oh, excuse me just one minute, I'm having a minor heart attack . . .'*

I snorted out a laugh and joined in. *'Oh, no wait, that's just a bad gherkin I ate with dinner. Do you like gherkins? I've always considered them an aphrodisiac – '*

The bartender reappeared and placed a drink in front of me. It was creamy and extravagant, adorned with a wedge of pineapple. Beside it lay an off-white business card.

I was still struggling with how to react when Stee returned, displaying two more business cards. 'I win, right? Three in ten.'

April held up her phone. 'Twelve minutes.'

'I came the closest.' Stee gave a disgruntled snort. 'Where's Im, anyway?'

We all looked around. Imogen was cosied up next to a good-looking man in a bright white shirt. Silver crept up his temples, threading through his brown hair, but at least he looked closer to forty than fifty. She'd clearly forgotten all about the game.

'Harlot,' Stee said, with a dismissive flick of his hand. 'How about you, Jem? New round.'

Before I could reply, I felt a hand on my forearm.

'Enjoying the drink?' came a creaking voice. 'Thought a girl like you might fancy something fruity.'

I caught a glimpse of April's face. She was open-mouthed, trying not to laugh. I swallowed down my own giggles and swivelled to look at the man.

His face was weathered – he looked about seventy – but his smile was broad. Despite the stiff joints of his hands, the lines of his black suit were sharp. His burgundy shirt was unbuttoned to reveal a curl of white chest hair. The ghost of a handsome young man surfaced as he spoke. Ten years ago, the rasp of his voice might have been sexy.

'I do like fruit,' I said solemnly. 'Apples, oranges, kiwi fruit . . .'

'How about passionfruit?' the man asked.

'Too many seeds.'

Next to me, April gave a yelp of laughter that she covered with a cough.

'Ahhh, I see,' the man said, as if my conversational stylings were fascinating. 'So tell me what you do with yourself, young lady.'

'She's a policewoman,' Stee cut in. 'Long arm of the law and all that.'

I gave a sage nod. The absurdity of the situation had chased away my nerves. I took a long drink of the coconut-sweet cocktail. (Piña colada?)

We continued our conversation, every addition from Stee or April sending it swerving into new heights of ridiculousness, until I became a policewoman who dabbled in Olympic-level gymnastics and also churned her own cheese from her country estate in Dorset. He bought all of us a fresh round of drinks. The man was surprisingly charming, smelling of whisky and liquorice. His blue eyes fixed me with a magnetic gaze.

I didn't like to admit it, but his attention was flattering. At uni, blokes had only ever bought me watery beers. No one had ever sent me a cocktail before. And few people had ever been so interested in my life and exploits (fictional or not).

After a few minutes, the man – Helm – tottered off to the men's room. 'You stay right here,' he said to me and I fluttered my eyelashes.

As he walked away, I turned to Stee, making myself go cross-eyed.

'Ready for more?' he asked, clapping his hands.

I sipped at my second piña colada and shrugged. The alcohol had gone to my head; the ultimate painkiller. Before, I'd been mortified by their games. Now I felt intrigued.

'Let's do dares,' April said. She nudged Stee and then made an eeny-meeny gesture until she landed on a man across the room. Her target slouched in all black, with the thinning shoulder-length hair of an aging rockstar. 'Bet you can't get *him* to buy you a bottle of Moët.'

'Challenge accepted,' Stee said. 'But only if you go over to Im and pretend to be her jealous girlfriend. I'm talking screaming, shouting, a whole scene.'

The two of them hopped off their bar stools and linked pinky fingers, giving a solemn finger-shake. I was both relieved and disappointed to think that they'd forgotten about me. Then Stee leaned in close and muttered:

'Jem, dare you to – look, he's coming back – dare you to steal his wallet.'

I opened my mouth to reply, but Stee and April were gone, leaving me alone. Well, not quite alone. Helm leaned heavily against the bar, giving me a misshapen smile.

Steal his wallet? Seriously? None of them needed the money, but this was clearly what these people – these hustlers – did for fun.

What would Jem do in this situation? Stupid question. What wouldn't Jem do.

I slid off my stool and took a step toward Helm.

'This is a beautiful suit,' I said, stroking a hand down his black lapel. 'Who's your tailor?'

Helm harrumphed and began an in-depth review of his favourite and least favourite Savile Row establishments. I let my hand linger on his chest, feeling the outline of his wallet, but there was no way to get at it.

I rocked back on my heels and slugged down the remains of my drink. 'I'm so thirsty,' I said.

On my command – wave a magic wand, *zing!* – he extracted his wallet and signalled to the bartender.

In my peripheral vision, I caught an arc of red liquid fly from a glass. A yell rose in the quiet bar. It was April. 'You dirty bastard, what are you doing?'

I turned to see her advancing on Imogen and her freaked-out-looking gentleman friend. There was a splash of red down his white shirt.

April's face crumpled up in an exaggerated cry. 'Sweet pea, you promised you'd never do this again . . .'

Helm was looking at the trio, as well. His wallet lay on the bar. The surly bartender was putting the finishing touches to my new piña colada. Any moment, she'd plonk it down in front of me and Helm would turn around to pick up his wallet and pay.

On the other side of the room, April was doubled over in mock-agony. Helm was completely entranced, his gaze angled away from me.

I didn't hesitate. I didn't think. I didn't breathe.

I just reached over and seized the wallet like it belonged to me. I tossed it into my bag and murmured, 'Little girls' room, be right back.'

It felt like I was coasting on air, rather than walking. Stee was closest to me – sweet-talking a man who looked more confused than turned-on – and I slipped an arm through his.

'We're going,' I said to him.

He gave an irritated sigh. 'Oh, but – '

'We're going,' I said again, my voice like steel.

'Wait, you didn't really – '

'Get the other two.'

I gave him a push in the direction of April and Imogen, still play-acting a lovers' tiff, and then glided in the direction of the door. The uniformed doormen ushered me out and I gave them my best Jem smile.

It was the cold air outside that brought me back to myself.

What had I done? We were just playing, it was just a prank. But now a man's wallet was in my bag and I was walking away.

Stee, April and Imogen spilled out of the bar after me.

'What's going on? Why are we leaving?' Imogen asked.

Stee aimed a howl at the sky. 'Jem, you didn't. You fucking didn't.'

I wasn't gliding anymore. I was scurrying, slipping as I rushed in Jem's uncomfortable heeled boots. The other three trailed in my wake.

'What did I miss?' April asked, skip-stepping till she was level with me.

My voice came out wheezy. 'We need to get out of here.'

'I'll call a car,' Imogen said, waving her phone.

'No time,' I muttered.

We were a hundred metres clear of the bar's flag-adorned entrance now, turning the corner on to a busy street. I scanned the passing traffic.

'Can you see a taxi?' I asked wildly.

'We'll never get one from here,' April said. 'We'll have to walk to – '

'Jem's on the lam, we need to leg it,' Stee interrupted, guffawing.

At that moment, there came a shout from behind us. My heart squeezed in my chest. We were caught. They were after us.

'Shit, the police!' Stee screamed, although I didn't have time to turn and look.

April hoiked up her long dress and grabbed my hand. Paralysed by fear, I'd slowed down, but April yanked me forward in a run. Stee kept pace with us. Even Imogen, who'd been dawdling at the back of our group, like she was tempted to go back to the bar and resume her meet-cute, began to run.

'These shoes were made for sitting down and looking pretty,' she called out, but I could hear the fizz in her voice. She was having fun. Beside me, Stee gave another howl. Even April, when I cast a frantic glance at her face, was grinning.

We ran the length of the busy road, exploding through throngs of people crowded onto the pavement. Blood rushed in my ears. My bag slapped against my thigh, the wallet inside a lead-weight reminder of what I'd done.

Stee guided us in a sharp left down a side street.

'Quick! Down here!' he said.

Were the police really chasing us? How had they got to the bar so quickly? I cast a glance over my shoulder, but I could see nothing.

We scrambled down the narrow set of stairs, a side entrance to a Tube station. On the fifth step, I almost tripped and fell, but April saved me. 'No man left behind,' she said breathlessly, shooting me a smile.

She locked her arm more tightly into mine and we ran together through the garishly-lit tunnels of the station, with Stee leading the way and Imogen close behind him. The four of us skidded through the barriers, me fumbling past the stolen wallet to find my Oyster card.

We dashed around three or four corners, before emerging on a platform, where a train waited to depart. There was a mechanical beeping sound.

'Shiiiiiiiiit,' Stee said, running headlong for the train.

Holding onto April, I could do little except follow. The doors were closing, but she shoved me through. The beeping reached its crescendo. With a whoosh, the doors shut.

The train was moving. And I was on it.

April released her grip on me, and I stumbled into a seat. Nearby, Stee was bent double, breathing heavily.

'Oh my God . . . I need to start doing cardio . . . I'm not fit enough for a life on the run . . .'

'That took five years off my life.' Imogen slumped into the seat next to mine. Her once perfectly-made-up face glistened with sweat. 'At my funeral, all you bitches better say nice things about me.'

As the train hurtled along, April leaned against a pole. She smoothed a hand through her blue-green hair.

'Just one question,' she said, her voice still betraying a slight gasp. 'Why are we running from the police?'

'Jem just carried out an armed robbery,' Stee said. 'Except all she was armed with was a pair of brass balls.'

'What?' Imogen said.

Hands shaking, I reached into my bag and held up the wallet. 'I stole this from Helm.' When Imogen's mouth dropped open, my voice grew tiny. 'Stee dared me to.'

'Jem,' Stee said, his grin huge, 'it was only a joke. I didn't think you'd actually fucking do it.'

Shitshitshitshitshit. What had I done?

It now seemed obvious to me that the police probably hadn't been in pursuit of us. But what if there was CCTV of me at the bar? What if there was a warrant for my arrest being written up at this second?

I wasn't a cool criminal, doing a flawless impersonation of Jem. I was a lunatic. I'd ruined everything. My whole body trembled. I sucked my lips into my mouth, wishing I could disappear.

We sat in silence as the train clattered onwards. My friends – no, Jem's friends – eyed me like I was a feral cat who'd bitten them once and might do it again.

I felt a confession welling up in my throat.

Listen, I'm so sorry, but I'm not who you think I am. I'm not –

It was Stee who broke the silence.

'So today we got chased by the po po, I broke my own record at the Sugar Daddy Game . . .' he said, settling back in his seat on the train.

'That halloumi was good, too,' April said.

'Not a bad day, all things considered,' Imogen said. 'What do you think, Jemster?'

My voice was gone. I could only manage a nod.

'Jem's a madwoman, but that's why we love her,' Imogen said, putting an arm around me and squeezing me close.

The easy chatter of my friends – Jem's friends – resumed. I remained mute as they opened up Helm's wallet and cackled over its contents. Along with cards and a wad of cash, it contained a photo of a Dalmatian, a small bundle of dental floss, and a handwritten note that read, *Whatever happens will be for the best.*

Over the course of the conversation, the three of them also pulled apart and sewed back together their memories of the night. They transformed my misfire into a funny story; a lark, a riot, something that was *ohmygod so Jem.*

22

INTRUDER

Ella

We left Helm's wallet lying on a seat on the Underground train. Maybe it would get stolen for real. Maybe it would be handed in as lost property. My new friends didn't seem to care. The whole thing was just a lark. We wouldn't really get arrested and, if we did, we had rich parents to bail us out.

Back at home (home?), I stepped into Jem's hallway and glimpsed myself in the oversized gilt mirror. My hair was tangled; my eyes retained a feral gleam. Even once I scrubbed my face clean, still I was not quite Ella, not quite Jem, not quite anyone at all.

The apartment was creeping me out. In this late hour, its minimalist, high-ceilinged rooms were dark and yawning, hiding who-knows-what. I couldn't get comfortable here.

At least the chaos of Jem's room felt cheerful; lived-in. I compromised on the no-cleaning rule, shifting some of her dirty clothes and clutter, but still leaving the room recognisably Jem-like. I also changed the sheets on the bed, rooting through a cupboard in the laundry room to find clean linens. The laundry room wasn't much smaller than my green caravan on Walney. I felt a thrum at the base of my skull, my scalp prickling. What was Jem doing right at this moment?

I was tired and drunk enough to push this thought from my mind, climbing between clean sheets and escaping into sleep from this life that wasn't mine.

*

I woke up early the next morning and lay in bed for a long time, listening. The apartment was quiet. I couldn't even remember the last time I'd woken up to silence. Sundays were always busy. Often, I had an early shift at work and awoke before dawn to a beeping alarm clock. Even if I wasn't working, there was church and then chores to do around the caravan park. A day of rest, it was not.

I had no idea how Jem used her Sundays. Surely not for chores. Definitely not for church. Work? No, Jem's play was on 'hiatus', whatever that meant.

I stretched like a cat. A day of nothing. A day unplanned, unwritten, unsoiled. The possibilities were tantalising.

I was recognisably hungover – limbs aching, head sore – but it was a comfortingly banal sort of pain. I was confident I could shake it off within a couple of hours. Yesterday, I'd felt frightened of this strange life that didn't belong to me. Today, I felt invigorated. I'd go exploring; drink in the buzz of the city. I rolled over in bed and saw Jem's phone light up and then go dark again.

I'd turned it on to silent last night. Now I seized it and saw that several new messages had come in while I'd slept.

Dada – Princess. In London for a flying visit. What's Her Royal Highness up too?

Twinnie – Bethanee is a fucking bitch then lolololol. Finding ways too entertain myself tho

Imogen – ME: Jem, come meet us in Stokey. JEM: *steals a jet plane*

Katsu – :sushi emoji: :knife emoji: :saxophone emoji: :aubergine emoji: :honey emoji:

Imogen – ME: Jem, Sunday afternoon picnic in the park!
JEM: *stages a heist in Waitrose for tiny sandwiches*

Gabriela – Swish swish made you some polenta cake
lazybones swish swish

Imogen – ME: Jem, we're going to Paris for the weekend.
JEM: *nicks the mona lisa from the louvre*

Stee – Hahahahahahahahahaha! Fly us to the moon in your
stolen jet Jems!

Bitch Mother – Let me know when you're ready to talk like
a grownup.

Twinnie – Eight is to early to get up on a Sunday you must
be fucking crazy. :microphone emoji: :girl with hand out
emoji:

I let the phone fall from my hands. It landed face-down,
enveloped by the soft duck-down duvet. What was Jem doing
on Walney? How had she come to the conclusion Bethany was
a 'fucking bitch'?

I should have felt panicked. Instead, laughter spilled past my
lips. It sounded harsh in the silence of the room, much louder
than my own cautious giggles.

I didn't care.

Walney seemed so far away. The Ella who scrubbed and
prayed and did what she was told – she was on holiday from
herself. The woman who lounged in this big bed at 11 a.m.,
she could do what she liked with her Sunday. She could steal
a wallet if she wanted. She could steal a jet plane.

I got out of bed. The wooden floor was warm beneath
my bare feet. It was like walking on the sun-roasted sands

of Piel Island on an August evening. At home, in winter, I'd been known to sleep wearing three jumpers with thermals underneath. In Jem's world, November was balmy as a beach getaway. I wandered through the apartment naked, my usual self-consciousness absent.

My double kept her rooms gloomy, but I swept aside the sheer cotton from the windows and let the winter sun fill the apartment. In the process, I swept away my discomfort about being alone here.

Time to get ready. From Jem's wardrobe, I chose a scarlet mini-dress, with long sleeves and an ultra-short hem, which I teamed with black-and-grey tights that striped up the back of my legs. I looked good. Objectively, I looked good. Like a woman from a magazine.

I decided against washing my hair. It looked more Jem-like tousled and dirty, anyway. I made myself up as best I could, skipping the tricky eyeliner, but smearing on smoky eyeshadow and adding plenty of mascara. I slicked on femme-fatale-red lipstick, too. The result was *look-at-me, look-at-me, look-at-me* and, for once, the idea of eyes following me wasn't scary. I found Jem's perfume and sprayed it on my neck, on my wrists. The air was suffused with a sunshine smell of oranges, undercut with the sweetness of vanilla, the earthiness of ginger.

To complete my Jem costume, I grabbed an oval-shaped, tarnished-gold locket from her jewellery stand. It hung between my breasts and the weight of it pulled at the back of my neck. I remembered Jem wearing it to the Seven Deadly Sins party. Curious, I pried it open and peeped inside.

I wasn't sure what I expected to find. A stash of white powder? A vial of blood sacrifice for Lord Lucifer? Instead, it contained a photograph of a much-younger Jem, smiling, beside . . . her mother?

Apart from the few honey-blonde tendrils of hair that fell in her eyes, she was impeccably groomed, in tan slacks and an Oxford shirt. There was a lift to her jaw, a glint in her eyes, that was foreign, yet still I saw a passing resemblance to my own mum. It was enough that the sight of her made my heart judder.

I thought of the text message, Jem's mum listed as Bitch Mother in her phone. Theirs obviously wasn't a sentimental relationship, and yet Jem carried her around in secret. Closing the two of them up inside the locket with a soft click, I felt guilty, as if I'd strayed into a secret room in my double's home.

Still, I didn't want to take the locket off. An imagined warmth radiated from it. Maybe it commemorated a good day; a trip to the zoo, perhaps, crowned with strawberry ice cream cones and a stuffed polar bear from the gift shop.

Leonora.

The name rose to the top of my mind.

I'd memorised the name Leonora, along with Jem's dad's name (Max), her middle name, the preparatory school she'd attended, her childhood dog that had died (a pug named Puggy), plus a hundred other tiny fragments of a life. The name of Jem's mum didn't tell me much, but I turned it over in my mind anyway. *Leonora, Leonora, Leonora*. A melodic name. A refined name.

I was both relieved and disappointed to know I'd probably never come face-to-face with Jem's mum.

In the kitchen, I found the fridge bare (a lone steak oozed blood in its shrink-wrap; a block of forgotten cheese had turned green), but, nestled beside a six-pack of craft beer, there was also a bottle of milk. I ate a leisurely breakfast of sugary, name-brand cereal. While I ate, I turned on the giant TV screen in the living room, revelling in its hundreds of channels.

When I grew bored of channel surfing, I found a music channel and cranked up the volume. The living room felt less sterile with a bassline reverberating off the walls. I danced alone on a sugar-high, delirious.

Clunk.

The noise wasn't even very loud. Just the sound of an object being put down. Undramatic, but insistently there.

It came again.

Clunk.

I stopped dancing. I stood motionless, my ears straining to hear over the sound of the music.

Clunk. Clunk.

My heart was already beating fast from the exercise, but now it raced at sickening speed. I fumbled for the remote and turned off the music. The room drowned in silence. I heard it again.

Clunk.

The empty apartment wasn't empty anymore.

I tiptoed across wooden floorboards to the living room door. My earlier giddiness had evaporated. I wasn't at home here. I'd never be at home here. As I eased open the door an inch, my stomach churned.

Clunk. Clunk.

The noises were definitely coming from inside the apartment. Someone had broken in. I craned my neck to get a glimpse of the hallway, but I couldn't see anyone. Were they hiding? Would they leap out and come charging towards me at any moment?

Clunk. Clunk.

Oh, God, could it be the police? There was CCTV footage of me stealing the wallet and now they'd tracked me down.

No, no, that wasn't right. I knew from TV that the police would ring the doorbell. If someone was going to break in, it had to be –

The big-fucking-problem guy who'd cornered me the night of the party.

Sunday morning was the perfect time to catch someone unawares. He'd planned to murder Jem in her bed.

I needed a weapon. A frying pan from the kitchen – or was that just a slapstick gag? Then I remembered Jem's showy wall of knives. I imagined myself unsheathing a dagger and dashing, ninja-style, toward the intruder. Too ridiculous for words. I was going to die and what could I even do about it?

Like a lamb offering itself up for slaughter, I swung open the living room door.

A figure bustled towards me down the hallway, armed with a cheery smile and a wide-open stance.

'Hello, Jemima!' she called out in a hearty voice.

The woman was petite, with black hair piled up on top of her head. Her olive skin was loose with age, and there was a slight hunch to her posture, but she looked at me with warm familiarity. And I had no clue who she was.

'Don't turn off your music on my account, dear,' the woman was saying. 'I like it. It keeps me young.' She paused to give a shimmy and then laughed.

I looked back at her, mute.

The whiplash of receding fear was turning my vision to static. I wasn't going to die. Not unless the middle-aged woman was a well-disguised assassin sent by the big-fucking-problem guy. I wasn't in danger, but I'd been plunged back into my role as Jem.

Who was this woman? Fear had shorted my brain functions, but now I remembered Jem mentioning that Leonora also had keys to her apartment. Was the woman another family member? A family friend? Perhaps Leonora paid her to drop by and check on Jem? Wouldn't that make sense, since my double seemed likely to fall face-down into a drug coma?

'Hi,' I managed at last, a tiny squeak.

'You're quiet today,' the woman said. 'Usually I can't get you to shut up. Is it me? Do I smell?' She mimed sniffing her armpits and laughed again. 'Don't forget to eat that polenta cake. I'll leave it in the kitchen for you.'

Whatever confidence I had developed in pretending to be Jem was unravelling fast. What was I supposed to say to this woman? What was I supposed to do?

She stepped into my personal space and I panicked. She was clearly a family friend, someone close to Jem, and now she was exasperated at my rudeness, suspicious of my blank reaction.

I should do something. I should . . . what should I do?

I sucked in a breath and, haphazardly, reached out to hug the woman. There. A hug. A hug was how you greeted a family friend.

As soon as I touched her, I knew it was wrong. The woman pulled away. She tilted her head and frowned.

'Little Miss Jemima . . .' The woman gave another laugh, lower this time – forced. 'Always playing games. Like a puppy. Piddle on the carpet and then you want to play.'

I stood frozen. I was still too close – to this woman who was not, evidently, a relative or friend – and she swatted me away.

'Work to do,' she said. 'You leave me be now.'

Heat rose in my cheeks; prickling shame made it all the way to the tips of my ears.

Now I saw what I'd missed in my panic. There were the cleaning supplies that had gone *clunk, clunk, clunk* when the woman had placed them on the floor. The clothes she wore were drab – work clothes. The way she spoke was without refined vowels or a snooty vocabulary, in an accent closer to my own.

She was the cleaner. And I'd just hugged her like a long-lost relative.

Through a fog of embarrassment, I heard the *bzzz* of the intercom. I looked dumbly at the woman, who had now snapped on a pair of rubber gloves and was brandishing a can of spray polish. I half expected her to strip off the marigolds and rush to the intercom.

Bzzz. Bzzzzzzzz.

'You going to get that, dearie?' the woman asked, a hint of irritation in her voice.

I cringed at my own stupidity. This woman wasn't a butler. She wasn't a *servant*. She was like me in my other life, trying to do her job surrounded by useless rich people.

Bzzzzzzzz.

I scanned the hallway for the intercom, wincingly aware that you were supposed to know where things were in your own home. The woman's eyes bored into me (suspicious, judgemental), though when I glanced at her, she was pretending to polish a silver photo frame. Finally, I located the intercom on the opposite wall and dived towards it.

'Hello?'

'Hey, it's me. Let me up.'

The intercom's screen showed a tall figure with a mop of dark hair. The angle of the camera concealed his face, but the sound of his voice stirred memories in my belly.

23

STEALTH

Ella

I hesitated for a fraction of a second and then mashed my hand against all the buttons, hoping one of them would open the outside door.

The cleaner was still hovering behind me, watching me for signs I wasn't really Jem. I ran a hand through my hair and tried to work out my next move. Before I could formulate a plan beyond 'panic, freak out, lose mind', I heard knuckles scraping the door in a light knock.

Without pausing, I ran to the front door and yanked it open.

'Hey, gorgeous.'

His easy, familiar smile greeted me. A smile that made my stomach flip over.

Katsu crossed the threshold in a single step. He grasped me under my arms, sweeping me into a hug that lifted me off my feet. All the breath was sucked from my lungs. I couldn't breathe, I couldn't speak, I couldn't think. And Katsu was kissing me.

It was a real kiss, open-mouthed and insistent; a kiss full of wanting.

Maybe I could have stopped him, corrected him. Maybe there was a split-second between opening the door and being kissed when I could have done that, but I didn't.

How long was it since I'd been kissed like this? A year? More. My lips had become dry, sucked into a thin line. Now they bloomed against his. The kiss sent a fizzing sensation through my body, travelling all the way to my toes.

Katsu broke away and spun me around once more. Then he set me back on my feet. I wavered on the spot; dizzy, overwhelmed.

'Where've you been?' he asked, grinning. 'Gallivanting somewhere up north? Keep me in the loop, hey?'

I blinked at him, still wordless. Then I twisted my neck to locate the cleaner. She'd disappeared into the living room.

'Katsu,' I said in a low voice, 'I'm not – I'm not her.'

The smile slid off his face.

'. . . Ella,' he said.

His face was blank, but two bright spots appeared in his cheeks.

'Shit, I'm sorry,' he said.

'Don't . . . be sorry,' I said faintly. My lips still tingled from the memory of the kiss.

He looked at me sharply and I looked away.

'Jem never said anything. *Shit*.' The anger rose in his voice. 'Is she here? Where is she?'

'No . . .' I glanced over my shoulder again, worried the cleaner might reappear. I slipped into my own accent. 'She's in Cumbria. Pretending to be me.'

'She's *what*?'

I shrugged helplessly.

'And of course she didn't say anything to me.' Katsu narrowed his eyes. 'What was all that guff about an acting workshop? God, this is just like her. She'll do what she pleases, to hell with what anyone else thinks.'

He paused, taking a few deep breaths.

'Did she bully you into this?' he asked. 'I bet she did. Jem's good at that.'

'No . . . I wanted to . . . Well, maybe I did. I don't know anymore.'

Katsu was quiet for a long moment. I looked down at my feet, wishing I could unlive every second of the last ten minutes.

I sneaked a glance at him. Maybe not every second. Maybe I'd keep a few of those. I looked away.

'Well . . .' he said at last.

He sounded normal again. Easy-going. He reached out and chucked me on the chin, forcing me to meet his gaze.

'Let's start again,' he said. 'Hey, Ella. How's it going?'

*

We went for a walk. I was desperate to escape the cleaning lady's gaze. Despite her cheery smiles, she unnerved me. I could too easily imagine myself transposed into her body; a servant creeping around after vibrant Jemima.

Outside, breathing in the cold, petrol-sour air, these thoughts retreated. At Katsu's prompting, the experiences of the last few days were transformed into harmless anecdotes.

'She did what?' Katsu said.

'She just started helping my mum with the shopping,' I said. 'Casual as you please. Chattering away.'

I released a big breath. I was glad to talk about it. It made the whole thing feel less sinister.

'And you were where?'

'Hiding, behind a . . .' I didn't want to say *caravan* and have to explain my living situation. 'Behind a wall.'

'And did she sound like you?'

'I mean, I s'pose so. But . . . sometimes she was a bit like one of those child actors you see on TV, playing Oliver Twist. You know, public school kid, trying to sound Cockney.'

Katsu laughed, long and hard, and I couldn't help but smile. I wasn't used to having a captive audience when I spoke. He was a good listener, too. He leaned forward, eyes shining, lips slightly parted; concentrating hard. He laughed in all the right places and made little theatrical gasps when the story got dramatic.

'The accent got better,' I said. 'Once she got into character.'

'What about you? Are you in character yet?'

I made a squinting, shrugging gesture. 'Maybe, I don't know.'

'When I saw you at the door, I literally couldn't tell you apart,' he said.

I dipped my head, thinking of the kiss and blushing in spite of myself. My mind jangled with what-ifs. What if I'd kept up the charade a few minutes longer? What if we'd strayed into the bedroom? What if . . .

'Now that we're talking, though,' he said, 'it's like . . . I can't even imagine mixing the two of you up. The way you talk, the way you act, I don't know. You're so completely different.' He paused, apparently lost in thought. 'But then you'll look a certain way, say a certain thing, and . . . you suddenly look so much like her. I'll think: *that's Jem* . . . even though I know it's not.' His eyes scanned my face. 'It's weird.'

The intensity of his gaze made me feel exposed. *But I don't want you to look at me and see her,* I wanted to say.

I stayed quiet and we kept walking, the silence thick with unvoiced thoughts.

'I don't think people necessarily notice other people,' I said at last. 'Not every detail, not the way we think they do. They're too much up in their own heads.'

'Yeah.' Katsu scuffed the heel of his trainer against the pavement. 'I guess we all think we're special snowflakes, but most of the time . . . People just fill in the blanks, see what they want to see.'

His voice was wistful and I got the feeling his thoughts were drifting away from the conversation again.

'Yesterday, I was so worried that one of Jem's friends would call me out,' I said, plucking a leaf from a tree that loomed over the path. 'I'd do something wrong and they'd say, *hey, you're not Jem!*' I began to shred the leaf. 'But they never did. I made so many mistakes. Did so many things Jem wouldn't do and somehow it didn't even matter.'

I let what remained of the leaf flutter away on the breeze. 'Because . . . the thing is, no one's primed to say: *hey, you're an imposter!* They'll only ever say: *hey, you're in a weird mood.* Or . . . *hey, did I do something wrong?*'

'Yeah,' Katsu said. 'Whenever someone's weird with me, I always think I'm the problem.'

'When I hugged the cleaner, she just thought I was playing.'

'Waitaminute. You hugged the cleaner?'

'Well,' I said archly, 'I don't know how things are done in London, I thought maybe that was a normal thing to do.'

Katsu was silent for a moment and then he burst out laughing.

'You're funny.' He nudged my elbow. 'You're one of those stealth funny people. Serious on the outside. Funny on the inside.'

I looked down; I didn't want to show how much his comment pleased me.

'You're not missing Jem?' I said.

'Oh, God . . .' He made a so-so gesture with his hand. 'I love her to death, but Ripper can be exhausting. She'll do this all the time. Disappear for a few days, few weeks. Once, she ran away to LA, stayed for two years. Life without Jem is a hell of a lot more peaceful, but it's a mite empty, y'know?'

Love her to death. My insides clenched.

'You told me . . .' I cleared my throat. 'You said she's always so set on being herself, she goes too far sometimes.'

'Did I?' he said, raking a hand through his hair. 'Yeah, that sounds about right.'

He was quiet for a long moment and, when he resumed speaking, he sounded a little sad.

'She's been going too far a lot, recently. Don't judge me' – Katsu gave a cringing smile – 'but I used to be kind of a party beast, too. Maybe that's what happens when you were the scholarship kid at a private school. All your friends are trust-fund babies and you've got that perfect-Japanese-student bollocks clogging up your brain. I didn't want to end up a fun-sponge engineer, so I went the other way.'

I gazed at him, surprised. Katsu was the cool guy; uncomplicated and easy-going. To my chagrin, I realised I'd never really thought about him beyond that archetype.

'Finally got bored of the scene,' Katsu said, 'bored of waking up with a hangover.' A car whipped past, red and sporty, and his eyes followed it, lingering on the horizon long after it had disappeared. 'Jem's still in it pretty deep, though. When she got back from La-La-Land – this was only a few months ago – there was this shell around her. This hardness. Too many drugs, too much rejection, I don't know. Used to be I could look at Jem and know exactly what she was thinking. Not anymore.'

I thought of the big-fucking-problem guy, of the flirtatious messages to other men on Jem's phone. I wondered how much about Jem's life Katsu really knew. Maybe I should tell him – warn him. I bit my lip, torn. He didn't deserve to get destroyed by Hurricane Jem.

Yet I couldn't shake the feeling that it would be a betrayal – a betrayal of Jem, and a betrayal of the whole situation. After all, I was not even technically in London right now. I stood here in Jem's shoes – literally, in Jem's pointy, uncomfortable heels – and that came with the expectation that I'd keep her secrets for her.

The further I burrowed into Jem's skin, the more secrets there seemed to be. What else was she hiding? I'd assumed that switching lives was just a joke to her, but now I wondered if there was more to it.

Why hadn't Jem told her friends she was pulling off this grand switcheroo? Why hadn't she told Katsu at least? At the party, she was open about the fact that I was her double. Now she was hiding it. Something had changed. Jem had come to Walney ready to bulldoze into my life. Why? What was she up to? Was I part of a bigger scheme? What exactly did Jem want with my life?

I was still a plaything to her. Even from 300 miles away, she was messing with my head.

I heaved out a long breath. This was my Sunday, my holiday. I didn't want to waste it worrying about Jem. On a simple, lizard-brain level, I wanted to hang out with Katsu. I couldn't bring myself to spoil the moment.

Beside me, he'd slipped his phone from his pocket and was thumbing through his messages. When he saw me looking at him, he raised his eyebrows.

'God, what a mindfuck,' he said. 'I wasn't even thinking. I was about to send Jem a message, but . . . you have her phone, don't you?'

I nodded. Then I said, hesitantly:

'You could text her on my number. If you needed to get hold of her.'

'Nah, it's just . . . Jem was supposed to come to Sunday lunch today.' Katsu mimed pulling a noose tight around his neck. 'We already rearranged it twice, my mum and dad are expecting her. Figures she'd forget. Why go to Sunday lunch when you could be stealing someone's identity?'

'I could come instead,' I said in a rush.

'Pretend to be Jem?'

'Yeah . . .'

I bit my lip, waiting for him to reject the suggestion.

'You seriously want to sit through lunch with my parents? You know it'll be excruciating, right?'

'What else am I doing? I mean, I s'pose I could go back to Jem's house and try to hug the cleaner again. That might be fun. See if she takes out a restraining order against Jem.'

Katsu laughed – another deep, genuine laugh that made me glow with warmth.

'Alright,' he said. 'But don't say I didn't warn you.'

*

Katsu lived a couple of Tube stops away. After the tree-lined streets and casual grandeur of where we'd come from, I couldn't hide my surprise.

'Based on Ripper's place, did you think everyone in London lived in a mansion block?' he said, reading my expression. 'My parents are scientists, not hedge fund managers.'

We stopped outside a modest Victorian house, which had been sliced awkwardly into flats. I followed Katsu down a narrow flight of metal steps to the basement level. There was a collection of plant pots outside the front door; a poor man's garden. All the plants were dead.

'My dad's a handyman,' I said faintly, 'but growing up, everything of ours was always broken. It was . . . ironic.'

'Yeah, my dad's working on a cure for cancer, but he can't figure out how to use the grill.' Katsu toed one of the plant pots. 'Or keep a plant alive.'

He pulled out a key and fitted it in the lock. A moment before he pushed open the door, he turned to me.

'Oh yeah,' he said, 'you should probably know. My mum and dad hate Jem.'

I froze, but Katsu was already barrelling through the door, calling out, 'Burglars! Hello!'

24

SWEETHEART

Ella

Horrified, I could do nothing except follow Katsu into the flat.

In contrast to the neutral tones of Jem's apartment, here, splashes of bold primary colours dominated the walls. There were floor-to-ceiling bookcases that squeezed the hall passageway even narrower. An oversize floor lamp, enormous in the small space, half-blocked my way as I tried to get into the living room.

I almost walked straight into the sofa, because that, too, was awkwardly positioned. As I tried to navigate the overstuffed flat, Katsu's parents bombarded me with questions.

'Jemima, how are you?' a petite Asian woman asked. Her English was slightly accented – her native language Japanese, I assumed. 'How was the journey? What have you been doing?'

I knew from Katsu that his mum was called Yuka. She had a sleek curtain of black hair and she wore bracelets that clinked every time she moved. She was pretty, with inquisitive eyes and a big smile. If it weren't for Katsu's warning, I might have missed the tight line of that smile; the wariness that hid in her eyes.

'Yes, Jem, tell us what you've been up to!' the man said.

Katsu's dad, Malcolm, was white; tall and beanpole thin, with too much straggly brown hair on his chin and not enough on his head. When I didn't answer, Katsu's parents forged onward with more chatter.

'Would you like a drink?' Yuka asked.

Malcolm, frowning, placed a hand on his wife's shoulder,

qualifying her statement.

'A soft *bev*erage,' he said.

'Yes . . . a beverage. I'm sure Jemima didn't – '

'We have a wide selection of soft beverages!' Malcolm said.

'Yes, yes,' Yuka said, 'lots of beverages. Tell us which beverage you would like.'

'That,' Katsu said, cutting in, 'is the most times anyone has ever said beverage. An average of eight thousand beverages per hour.' He turned to me. 'Band name: Average of Beverages. What d'you think?'

I still couldn't find my voice. Beside me, Malcolm gave a long-suffering sigh.

'Why don't you show Jem the drinks in the kitchen?' he asked.

'Don't you mean the *bev*erages?' Katsu said, laughing, while his dad let out another sigh.

Katsu put his arm around me, guiding me through the cramped living room and into the even more cramped kitchen. The door swung closed behind us. When we were alone, he seemed to realise that he was standing too close to me. He dropped his arm. I tried not to react – to the touch, or to the absence of it. I sagged against the worktop.

'So . . .' I said in a low voice. 'Could you please tell me why your parents hate me?'

'Last time Jem came to dinner at my parents' flat, she showed up drunk. Threw up on the rug.'

'What?'

Katsu grinned, like it was a great joke.

'She claimed it was food poisoning. And, you know . . . my parents are pretty dozy. They might have bought it. Except she smelled like a brewery. It was a fun night.'

I stared at him, appalled, but he still wore a smile, as if it were a good memory. He flipped open the fridge and began pulling out cans and bottles.

'Couple of years ago,' he said, 'my dad had a barbecue for

his birthday, invited Jem. She gave him a cock ring as a present. Then *I* had to explain what it was. Jesus.' He flicked his eyes heavenwards. 'Ripper does it for sport, but to be fair that was the most memorable barbecue we ever had.'

My throat closed up, even as I recognised it was my cue to laugh. I turned away, busying myself with choosing a drink – a *beverage* – and wished I could be somewhere else. I'd been wrong to volunteer to impersonate Jem. I didn't want to stand in this cramped kitchen and hear the affection in Katsu's voice when he talked about my double.

*

'Jemima, have you been well?' Yuka asked over dinner.

'Yes, I've been well,' I said robotically. The answer was too prim to pass as a good impression of Jem, so I scrambled to rephrase. 'I mean, I've been . . . tremendous.'

The four of us ate seated on the floor, arranged around a low table. I wasn't sure whether this was cultural or because the flat was so small – possibly both?

The selection of food was, frankly, bizarre. There was a spread of sushi, beautifully prepared, like something out of a magazine. Plus, there was a sloppy beef dish that looked microwaved, served with Yorkshire puddings. I ate a little of everything, out of politeness, but the Yorkshire puddings had the consistency of polystyrene.

The conversation flowed freely – because conversation always did around Katsu. He seemed to have inherited his ability to talk about everything and nothing from his parents. The family's digressions were continual and always lively. Even so, I dreaded the moments when the focus of the conversation would switch to me.

'What have you been up to, Jem?' Malcolm asked.

It was a simple question, but I blanked on an answer. What was I supposed to say? If Katsu were to be believed, Jem had returned from California and spent the last few months careening off the rails. *Well, gosh, Malcolm, I've been getting high a lot recently and racking up debts with terrifying men . . .*

No, I definitely couldn't say that. Even telling the truth about how I'd spent my Saturday sounded insane. *I've been spending a lot of time fleecing old men and running from the cops, Malcolm . . .*

'I've been . . . I mean,' I mumbled. 'Work. Mostly.'

From the other side of the table, I saw Katsu covertly roll his eyes.

'Oh, you're in a new play, is that correct?' Yuka said.

'No,' I said, thinking of Jem's *on hiatus* comment. Out of the corner of my eye, I saw Katsu jerk his head. 'Um, I mean, yes. The play is very exciting,' I mumbled. 'Everyone's really nice.'

'Oh, wonderful! Malcolm and I should come to a performance. What's it about?'

'Uh . . .' I racked my brains, trying to remember what Jem had told me. 'Climate change and, um, alien invasion.'

'Sounds . . . unusual.'

Katsu let out a loud groan. 'Would you stop torturing her?'

'We're not torturing her. We're interested,' Yuka said, turning back to me. 'How have you been spending your free time, sweetheart?'

Katsu, hidden from view of his mum, made a face in my direction and mouthed *sweetheart*. Then he relaxed into a smile. I felt a fluttering in my stomach as our eyes locked for a moment too long.

When Yuka's question remained unanswered, he jumped in.

'She's been finding herself,' he said. 'She's really been going through a lot of changes. Spiritually, I mean.'

I couldn't help but laugh, even as Katsu's parents looked on, bewildered.

*

'Um,' I said to Yuka, when the meal was finished, 'this food was really nice. *Arigatou*.'

Yuka nodded eagerly.

'*Dou itashimashite*,' she said. '*Nihon-go o hanashimasuka*?'

'Um. Sorry. That's the only Japanese word I know.'

Yuka smiled and reached over to squeeze my arm.

'It's a good word to know. You're welcome, sweetheart.'

She began gathering up the plates from the table, but I stopped her.

'Katsu and I will clear up,' I said.

'We will?' Katsu asked.

'Yes, we will.'

We spent the next few minutes ferrying dirty plates through to the kitchen. Katsu acted like he'd never loaded a dishwasher before. The chore made him huffy.

'I come over for dinner for a break from this . . .' he said, scraping beef residue off a plate using sluggish swipes.

I reached over and closed the kitchen door. Yuka and Malcolm's conversation reduced to a murmur.

'Oh please, you're one of those men whose mum still does his washing for him, aren't you?' I said in my real voice.

'Only . . . sometimes!' Katsu had the grace to look embarrassed.

I tutted, nudging him with my elbow. He nudged me back and I felt warm all over.

'So' – Katsu cleared his throat – 'you know they officially love you, right?'

He mimed throwing up and then lapsed into a smile. I shook my head.

'They don't,' I said, my real accent slipping out with a huff of laughter. 'I was a moron. All that stuff about really nice people at the play. No way Jem cares about how *nice* the people are.'

'Are you kidding? That's catnip to them. They just want me to find a nice, normal girl.'

I ducked my head, hiding a smile.

'I didn't do a very good impression of Jem,' I said.

'That's why they liked you.' He picked up another plate and scraped it clean. 'At least now maybe my dad will stop trying to set me up with my cousin.'

I raised my head, laughing. When he met my gaze, my stomach squirmed pleasurably.

'What's your cousin got to do with anything?'

'She's not really my cousin. She's half of a second cousin or something. *Louise*. My dad drew up a family tree once, to prove to me that it's not incest. Not really bad incest, anyway. Dad loves her. Because she's, like, a genius doctor. He wants to lock those genetics down for his grandchildren. Like we're Amish and I should be married by the age of 26. He's dying for me to go out with her.'

'You're not serious.'

'Maybe. Sometimes it's hard to tell when my dad's joking – '

'Goodness, what must that be like?' I cut in.

Our eyes met again, his gaze lingering on mine for a moment too long.

'Anyway,' Katsu said, clearing his throat, 'I guess I'm free of Louise now. My mum called you *sweetheart*. She's already planning mother-daughter spa days with you, I know it. Want to share how you came by your extensive Japanese vocabulary . . .?'

'Uh, I used to like anime?'

'Right. Don't tell Mum that. Pretend you have a deep-seated affinity for the culture and history.'

I shook my head, trying not to smile too broadly.

'Tell me why we ate sushi and roast beef,' I said, picking up a leftover Yorkshire pudding from one of the plates.

Katsu snorted. 'That's what happens when your mum spends hours making amazing sushi, but your dad thinks Sundays are for roasts.' He raised his eyes to the ceiling. 'My mum thinks roasts are disgusting. My dad loves them. But my dad can't cook, so we get whatever *this* ready-meal crap is . . .' He scrutinised a stray smear of beef on one of the plates. 'I'm not even sure this is real meat.'

'This has been going on literally my whole life,' he continued. 'Can you believe they actually want me to move back home? Save money for a deposit? I don't think they realise it would be like moving into the loony bin.'

I felt a swell of kinship in my belly. Jem, with her multi-million-pound, paid-for apartment – that was a life completely foreign to me. But Katsu and his family weren't like that. His parents' cramped flat wasn't so different to my parents' miniscule caravan. He worried about money, too. If I told him how claustrophobic my life on Walney Island was, maybe he'd even understand.

I went to toss the Yorkshire pudding into the food waste bin, but he swiped it from my grasp and took a bite.

'Hey, Yorkshire pudding!' he said, waving it in the air. 'For the girl from Yorkshire! It's like you're right at home.'

'Cumbria's not the same as Yorkshire,' I said.

'It's . . . nearby, right?'

'It's a completely different place!'

I grabbed the Yorkshire pudding from his hand and punched him on the arm for good measure. Katsu made a wounded face and rubbed his arm. I wondered if I'd really hurt him –

'Sorry!'

– but he broke into a grin, dropping the wounded puppy-dog act.

'Trust me, you'll have to try harder than that,' he said. 'My other girlfriends have hurt me way worse. Jem once clocked me on the mouth. Chipped my tooth. She said it was an accident, but . . .'

'Well, I'm sorry anyway,' I said, turning away to stack a few more plates in the dishwasher.

I reminded myself that I could never entirely tell if Katsu

217

was joking or not. But I couldn't help noticing . . .

He just called me his girlfriend.

*

Malcolm wanted us to stay all afternoon – I couldn't tell if his offer to teach me how to play the bongos was a joke or not – but Katsu stressed that we had to get going. I was glad. I liked his parents, but I also really, really didn't want to learn the bongos.

'Do you need to be somewhere?' I asked Katsu, as we climbed the metal steps back up to street level.

'Oh no' – he cracked a smile – 'I just needed to get away from those crazy people.'

'They're nice,' I said, wishing I could better express what it meant to have parents who loved and supported you.

'I kinda fancy a walk,' he said. 'How about you?'

'Sure.'

Katsu and I walked slowly, aimlessly, not talking much. The silence was a comfortable one. Winter sunshine gave the streets a bright sheen, but a cold wind pulled at my hair. The only thing that would make the walk better were if Katsu were to wrap an arm around me and tuck me against his chest. Instead, we walked side by side, each of us careful not to touch the other.

'Can you sing?' he asked suddenly.

The question startled me.

'Um. A little . . .? Not very well.'

'Great,' he said with a laugh. 'That officially makes you a better singer than Jem.'

'What?'

'We were supposed to have band practice later today. Another thing Jem decided to ditch. You can come along instead.'

I wasn't sure how I felt about being The Replacement yet again. I looked at Katsu, trying to gauge whether he was making the suggestion because he wanted me there, or because he had no choice but to settle for the fake version of Jem.

'You like music, right?' he said. 'I remember you told me that.'

'Yeah, I . . . play guitar.'

'Shit, the band won't know what hit 'em. Jem can't even clap in time most days.'

'. . . I won't know any of your songs.'

'We don't have any songs,' Katsu said. 'We're trying to write some, but we're mostly pathetic. A bunch of musos sitting around, trying to jam. We usually start every practice with a twenty-minute argument about Aretha Franklin.'

I looked at him uncertainly. 'Why . . .?'

'I guess you'll have to come along and see.'

25

SPARROWS

Jem

'Ready . . . go!'

I leaned hard on the cleaning trolley and set off. With one foot wedged up on the trolley, I pumped the other one against the carpeted floor like a skateboarder. By the time I reached the corridor's halfway point, I was flying.

'I think it is three, two, one and go,' an out-of-breath voice just behind me said.

'Suckersssssssssss,' I yelled, ignoring her.

My trolley crashed against the far wall.

Towels leaped off the shelves of the trolley. A bottle of disinfectant toppled over and rolled away, blue liquid swishing inside.

'I win!'

The metal casing of my trolley reverberated, creating a sound like a bell. Vika, the other competitor in the Cleaning Trolley Olympics: Corridor Dash, rammed her trolley into the same wall seconds later.

I collapsed on to the carpet and let out a cackle of laughter. The way I fell roused an echo of a bruise on my side, but the pain was worth it.

'Is three, two, one and go, no?' Vika said, frowning. 'This is how it go, no?'

My smile hardened. 'You saying I cheated?'

'No, Yella, no.' She took a seat on the floor and patted me on the arm. 'I misunderstand.'

'Go again? Best of three?'

Vika, with her long plait of blonde hair and washed-out

blue eyes, shook her head.

'I work now. Five more rooms.'

'Come ooooooon,' I said, reaching out and tugging her hair like the chain on a lavatory. 'Best of three.'

Ella's colleagues in shit-scrubbing were a dismal bunch, but at least Vika was persuadable. She had a timid look about her that made me think maybe she'd been sold into sex slavery and escaped her pimp by running barefoot across the Yorkshire moors.

'No, Yella, sorry.'

She claimed to be a business studies graduate from Bulgaristan or somewhere, but that was much less interesting. Imagine going abroad for a better life and ending up in Cumbria. I'd been here two days and already I felt like I'd been marooned in the boonies.

This afternoon, I'd driven Ella's tinpot car fifteen miles through Cumbria to the hotel where she worked. The wide open spaces filled with nothing made me feel like I was in the first scene of a horror movie.

Vika collected her scattered cleaning supplies. She pushed her trolley away ('bye bye, Yella'), each revolution of its wheels letting out a squeak.

I'd thought Twinnie's job might give me the full Cumbria experience. I was keen to gather enough material for a dozen or more hysterical pub stories where my admirers would be wowed by my chutzpah. '*So I went to the Lakes and pretended to be someone else. I even took up her job as a chambermaid. I had everyone fooled. What a riot, what a rush, what a God-like feeling . . .*'

So far, it was so predictable. Sweaty grunt work and no time for fun.

I unlocked one of the heavy wooden doors ('Housekeeping!') and found the room empty. I still had seven – or was it eight? – rooms to clean, but what I fancied was a bath. The piss-dribble that came out of Twinnie's showerhead wasn't cutting it for me. I spun the taps in the en suite and filled the room with steam.

This was the type of hotel where my mother would drag me for a spa weekend. She was always doing that. 'Making up for lost time' – as if our time together had mysteriously disappeared, rather than been eaten up by the Terribly Important Job that she'd always loved more than me.

I stripped off Ella's dowdy black shirt and trousers, and climbed into the roll-top bath, which was filled almost to the brim with hot water. The bath essence I'd found was soapy and floral, with hints of honeysuckle and jasmine. Mummy always smelled like jasmine . . .

God, why was I thinking about her so much today?

Spending the day with Ella's mum had unsettled me more than I cared to admit.

*

'Wake up!'

I'd started my Sunday with a strange woman shaking me.

'I thought you were up already!'

I opened my eyes and immediately regretted it. Darryl's cocktail hadn't quite put me in a coma, but the sunlight filtering in through the thin curtains felt like daggers in my eyes.

'Jesus fucking Christ,' I said, shielding my eyes.

'Ella!' A shocked note caught in the woman's voice. 'Language . . .'

'Sorry,' I muttered.

Plum forgot where I was, who I was.

Only a mother could imbue the caution 'language!' with so much fervour. I sneaked a look at the woman: over-plucked eyebrows, low-maintenance bob in greying blonde; her features betraying a hint of my own mother.

'We'll be late for church,' she said. 'Be outside in five minutes.'

She scuttled out of the caravan, closing the door behind her with a prim little click. I sat up in bed – my stomach heaved, but I gulped down the vomit – and reached for Twinnie's phone to check the time.

8:30?

8:30! On a Sunday!

I'd only got home from Darryl's at three, accepting a ride from the backwoods barman on his moped along bumpy country lanes. He'd offered to let me spend the night at his, but the novelty had already worn off by then.

(For the record: Darryl's body = 7/10, Darryl's sexual prowess = 5/10, Darryl's apartment = 2/10.)

I yawned. Maybe I could tell Ella's mum I was sick and go back to sleep? Hmmm. Something about our short interaction suggested she wouldn't be sympathetic. I swept aside the bed-clothes and stood up. I'd already spent enough of this weekend sleeping. Time to grab life by the balls.

I rummaged around on the floor, looking for clothes, aware that time was ticking by. What was I going to wear? How was I going to make myself up in five minutes? Didn't this woman know that it took significantly more than five minutes to achieve the Jemima Cootes-Mitchell Look?

Except . . . oh wait. Today, I was Ella. I rocked back on my heels, considering my options.

I was out of the caravan with a minute to spare, wearing slouchy jeans and a blue hoodie. No makeup. Hair in a ponytail. It was weirdly freeing not to care about my appearance at all.

Of course, Ella's mum started tutting when she saw me.

'That's what you're wearing? Oh, well, I suppose there's no time for you to change now . . .' She opened the car door of an ancient-looking silver Volvo.

From across the caravan park, a weedy-looking guy with messy blond hair hailed us. Was that Twinnie's brother?

'You think about that coin toss, yet?' he yelled. Ella's mangy dog was nipping at his ankles.

Before I could think of a reply, my new mum nudged me toward the car.

'Come on, get a wiggle on,' she said.

*

The church looked like something out of a cosy TV drama I'd flick past at speed on a Sunday night. Ivy grew up its stone exterior and, inside, the wooden pews were polished to a high shine. Now that the shock of the hangover had worn off (I'd chugged the last few centimetres of a gin bottle back at Twinnie's caravan), I was starting to enjoy this adventure. As we entered the church, I nodded to the other parishioners and called out, 'Beautiful morning!'

I'd never been to a church service, not even as a child. Mummy worked on Sundays. Privately, I'd always suspected she thought my dodgy genes meant I might burst into flames on consecrated ground.

My parents met at a bar, in the pre-Internet dark ages, but Mother might as well have selected Dada from the profiles on BitOfRoughToPissOffYourParents.com. He was tall, dark, handsome; a charmer, a chancer. He had money – most of the time – but he never had the pedigree to make it in my mother's world.

I used to hate her; now I just pitied her. There was something inherently unlovable about my mother. No wonder Dada had tossed her aside before I'd turned five.

'All! Things! Bright! And! Beauuuuuuuutiful! The! Lord! God! Made! Them! Aaaaaaaall!'

I sang with gusto, sometimes slipping into *lah-lah-lah* to cover the fact that I didn't know the words. I was a great singer. Maybe not in tune 100% of the time, but real singers – Janis, Patti, Florence – had character to their voices.

I closed my eyes and imagined myself up on stage, accompanied by an audience's adoring screams. I'd been contemplating it for a while, but now I was certain: acting was a waste of time. So what if Savannah fired me? She could take her poxy plays and downmarket dog food ads and shove them. I wanted people to love me for me, and being a singer was a much better way to achieve that.

When was our next band practice? It wasn't today, was it? Whatever. We could reschedule. It wasn't like they could do anything without me. I was the star.

Beside me, Ella's mum kept shooting me glances. I gave her a big smile as we sat down to listen to the sermon. She smiled back at me uncertainly.

'Life. Is. Sacred.' The lady vicar had a silver helmet of hair and loose jowls that shook as she punched out her emphasis. 'But how much is a life really worth? We're a capitalist society. Everything's worth something!

'In Luke 12:6, we read, "Are not five sparrows sold for two pennies?" Yet not one of them is forgotten by God. Indeed, the very hairs of your head are all numbered. Don't be afraid; you are worth more than many sparrows.

'How can we do justice to God in our lives? Is simply existing enough?'

I stifled a yawn and pulled Ella's phone from my pocket. I dashed off a message to Twinnie and waited for the bloop-bloop-bloop bubbles of a new reply.

Nothing.

What was Lil Mouse up to right now? Would Carlo pay her a visit? He didn't know my current address, so probably not. It would be funny if he did, though. The look on her tremulous face would be priceless. *No, it's not me! I'm not her!*

I covered up a laugh with a cough.

'We must respect life,' the vicar was saying. 'We must do justice to God. We must do justice to ourselves. Sleepwalking through this life is not enough.'

I shoved the phone back in my pocket and glanced around

at the coffin-dodging congregation. Most of these people were sleepwalkers. Some were actually asleep right now. The vicar was right. Some people didn't use their lives. They barely deserved to live.

*

'You look peaky.'

Ella's mum killed the engine of the car and turned to face me. We were back at the caravan park and it was raining. I swear, all it did in Cumbria was rain.

'I'm fine,' I said, thinking, *Nothing a line of cocaine couldn't fix.*

'You're not fine.'

She reached over and felt my forehead. I gave the tiniest flinch and then relaxed against her touch. It was so intimate. My own mother and I didn't have that kind of relationship. When she hugged me, it was at arm's length. Ella's mum, with her extra layer of fat, was probably a good hugger.

'Come inside, have some tea and crumpets. Got some of your favourite jam from Bev down the road yesterday.'

I was about to refuse – this bizarro day of church at the end of the Earth was already weirding me out – but then I found myself nodding. I'd been famished the last few days, without the coke to suppress my appetite.

Twinnie's mum wasn't like my mother, the perpetual calorie-counter. She piled a plate high with crumpets dripping butter. I slathered on blackberry jam for good measure (well, it was Ella's favourite – got to stay in character!) and sank my teeth into the gooey sweetness.

'Feeling okay?'

'Feeling great!' I said with my mouth full.

'Mmm . . .' She toyed with the lid of the jam jar. 'Might be worth making an appointment all the same.'

What kind of appointment? I slowed the pace of my chewing.

'Remember, you don't have to do this all on your own, Ella . . .' She reached over and squeezed my arm. 'We're here for you. We're all here for you.' She shifted closer and pulled me into a hug.

Yes, I was right. She was a good hugger. Her white jumper was fuzzy and warm against my face. She squeezed me tight, turning me back into a little girl.

I couldn't help it, there were tears in my eyes.

Jesus.

What was wrong with me?

I pulled away, but couldn't cover up the tears quickly enough. A big fat blob landed in my jam.

'Oh, Ella . . .' She used the back of her hand to wipe at my wet face. 'You just worry me so much. Even today . . . was that alcohol I smelled on your breath?'

'Umm . . . had a couple of drinks last night with Bethany,' I said.

This stranger was still touching my face. She was too close and I could smell her sour breath. She caressed my cheek and, honestly, I wished she'd stop now. We'd gone beyond comforting and into smothering.

'Remember what David said about making good decisions? Was that a good decision?'

Was David someone from the bible?

'Uh, I guess not?' I shifted in my seat, angling for a way out. 'I should probably push on. You know, can't waste the day.'

She let out a long sighing breath and finally dropped her hand.

'How's your caravan? Heating okay?'

I shrugged, my eyes flicking to the door.

'You know you can always move back in here for a couple of months,' she said. 'Safer, less lonely.'

It was certainly warm in here, much warmer than Twinnie's caravan.

'You still look peaky. Do you want me to make up the bed

in your old room?'

'Maybe . . .' Something about her soporific voice and intense gaze made me feel woozy. Could I really be getting sick? 'Might go and have a nap now, actually.'

'Now?' Ella's mum frowned and checked her watch. 'Do you have time? You can't be late for work.'

*

At the hotel, I soaked in the bath for almost an hour, until my fingers grew prune-y and the water turned clear. It didn't have the rejuvenating effect I'd hoped for. The flu-y feeling I'd experienced in the caravan with Ella's mum was still dragging at my feet.

I slumped low in the water and sank into my worst memory. It felt morbidly good to poke at the wound, the way your tongue obsessively finds the bad tooth in your mouth.

'You stay here and have fun, Bug.'

I remembered the squeeze as she gripped my shoulder. Her kiss didn't quite make contact with my cheek. She gave me a final look that contained relief not sadness.

'Have fun while Mummy's away.' Her voice floated back to me, but she didn't make eye contact again.

She was gone for six months, but it felt like an eternity. I'd wake up every morning and run to the window, standing on tip toes to see over the sill. I knew if her wine-coloured Audi was parked outside, that meant she was back. The sight of the street, packed tight with grey and black and blue cars, stabbed at me, the pain deeper every morning.

'Where she go?' I asked over and over.

'You know, honey,' the woman told me, patience wearing thin. 'The clinic.'

Clinic. At the age of five, I could barely even say the word. Those clicking C's garbled inside my mouth.

'She's just getting some rest, honey.'

That polite euphemism was the reason that, over those six months, I imagined my mother as a Sleeping Beauty figure, submerged in an otherworldly sleep, waiting for True Love's Kiss to awaken her.

Now, of course, I knew that Prince Charming wasn't the cure for her problems, he was the cause of them. Mummy married a con man and ended up with a daughter she didn't like very much. So, following the divorce, she nope'd out of the whole situation for half a year. Nervous breakdown? I preferred to call it a bad case of selfish-bitch-itis.

While she was at a clinic in Switzerland, I was sent to live with a 'family friend', Diana, a woman with frizzy white hair and sagging eyes like a Doberman. I'd never met her before the day my mother dropped me off. Diana hated noise and barked at me if she heard even a floorboard creak. I got used to creeping through the dim, high-ceilinged rooms of her Primrose Hill villa on the balls of my feet. My strongest memory was the smell of incense, mingled with a burning stench of herbs, which Diana used to ward off evil spirits.

By the time the burgundy Audi did appear on the street outside Diana's house, I didn't care anymore. When Mummy squeezed me tight, showering me with kisses, my own lips barely brushed the skin of her cheek.

In the bath, I slid right down beneath the surface, so that the water erased the tears in my eyes.

Everything about today was pointless. This job was pointless. This whole place was pointless. What did it matter if I didn't clean the rest of the rooms on Ella's rota?

I heaved myself up and pulled the plug from the bath. I got dressed and stared at myself in the mirror. My mouth sagged into a straight line. I thought of dead puppies; roadkill. Sad, sad eyes reflected back at me. Damp hair curled across my forehead and I raked it into a ponytail. I looked like the spit of Ella in her driving licence photo.

With a sigh, I let go of my hair and it fell loose in rats' tails around my shoulders.

As I wheeled my trolley back to the storeroom, I wondered if this role was better or worse than jumping out of a box at the eleven-minute mark of a play about climate change and aliens. It was certainly more immersive. The play's audience wandered in amongst the action, mingling with the actors and even speaking to us. But no one believed I really was an alien invader.

Here, now, in this birdshit backwater, I was fooling everyone. I was the perfect Ella.

What a riot, what a rush, what a God-like feeling.

But what was the point of a play with no curtain call? My interest in being Ella was waning. I was bursting out of her skin. She had no deep dark secrets to ferret out; no life at all, in fact.

In the storeroom, I ran into Vika ('have nice evening, Yella!'). Maybe I could go to Bulgaristan, find out what made her want to leave. Maybe it wasn't just Ella's life I was tired of inhabiting.

I was bored of being Jem, too.

26

REHEARSAL

Ella

Katsu and I took the Underground to a different part of London (I wasn't sure where) and arrived at a higgledy-piggledy building with a sooty sandstone exterior.

'This is where you live?' I asked, as he unlocked the door.

'Yep, mind the chandelier as you walk in,' he said.

My gaze lifted to the ceiling. Low enough to brush the top of Katsu's head, something had been strung up by its neck using a length of Christmas lights. He flipped a switch, bathing the dark hallway in white light. It illuminated the fact that the thing being strangled by fairy lights was . . .

'Is that a Dalek?'

'Yeah, those things are dangerous.' Katsu shook his head, giving an exaggerated frown. 'We killed it and kept the body as a trophy.' His face broke into a grin. 'I quit drinking on weeknights and life got really boring. Anyway, it distracts from the wallpaper, doesn't it?'

Now that I took a second look, I saw the hallway was papered with hideous green roses.

'Yeah, I guess it does.' A memory surfaced in my mind and I smiled. 'When I was at uni, our landlord gave us permission to repaint. We decided to do a mural, my housemate Cait and I. Sea life. Turtles and octopuses and stuff.' I mimed painting, my fingers brushing the green roses. 'We'd just finished and the first person we showed was a bloke from the electricity company who came round to read the meter. He took a long look at it and asked how many children we had.'

Laughter pushed up out of my stomach. I hadn't meant to tell the story. What did Katsu care? For that matter, what did I care? It was years ago. A youthful misstep: a day wasted on the mural, then another when we painted over it with magnolia. Yet the memory – painted over in my mind – bloomed inside me now. I missed the absurdity of crap house shares; the silliness of living with friends. I missed something deeper, too: a part of myself that I struggled to find these days.

Katsu joined in with my laughter. 'Do you have a picture? I need to see those turtles.'

I shook my head, brushing past him into the flat's living-room-slash-kitchen. It was standard-issue post-student grot. There was a threadbare sofa (purple) and a drum kit (black). Plates and bowls (dirty) had been dumped on every available surface (also dirty). Yet my eyes superimposed memories of house shares where I'd lived. Origami rabbits greeted me from inside cereal boxes. Notes were fixed to the fridge. *Ants in the bathroom again. Thx for doing the bins. Movie night tonight?*

Perhaps Katsu mistook my faraway expression for judgement. He began tidying up dirty dishes and stray cutlery.

'Sorry, this place is a dump.'

'No, it's great,' I said with too much feeling. I looked down, avoiding his gaze, worried I might embarrass myself.

I was saved from making more conversation by the thud of footsteps on the stairs, accompanied by a heated discussion. The back-and-forth of the argument got louder until two figures pushed inside the living room. They didn't bother to say hello. They were too busy fighting.

About Aretha Franklin.

'For the last time, we're not putting an Aretha song on the set list! We're a rock band!'

'Good music is about mixing genres, pushing the boundaries. I can't believe you don't get that.'

'If you're so mad on pushing the boundaries, how come you

only ever want to play Aretha Fucking Franklin?'

'She's the Queen of Soul!'

'We're a rock band!'

'We're a hyphenate band! There's no such thing as rock music anymore!'

'You are so full of shit!'

'You are so closed-minded!'

'You're obsessed with Aretha!'

'Hey, guys,' Katsu said, raising his voice. 'What's going on?'

The two guys turned to look at us. The obsessed-with-Aretha guy was stringy and hyperactive-looking, with pale skin and an extravagant coif of brown hair. He wore eyeliner and there was a safety pin threaded through his ear. The we're-a-rock-band guy was tall and black, with tight, springy curls. Two full sleeves of colourful tattoos stood out against his muscular arms.

'Fuckin Aretha,' the we're-a-rock-band guy muttered in Katsu's direction, but he was smiling.

The obsessed-with-Aretha guy also seemed bizarrely relaxed for someone who'd just been shouting at the top of his lungs.

'One day, you lot will understand my vision,' he said, thumbing his safety-pin earring. 'What's up, Katz? Jem?'

Katsu stepped forward to greet them – hand slaps and one-armed man hugs – but I hung back, giving an awkward wave and trying to smile. *Ricky and Anthony*, I reminded myself. Katsu had told me their names. Ricky was the scrawny pale guy, inexplicably devoted to Aretha. Anthony was the muscular black guy. (They were very laid-back when it came to every topic except for Aretha Franklin, Katsu had assured me.)

The doorbell rang and Katsu went to get it. Moments later, a woman in her early twenties appeared. She had a round face and short bubblegum-pink hair. *MollyMollyMolly*, I chanted inside my head. I offered her a nervous smile until I remembered I was supposed to be Titanium Jem, who never showed the slightest uneasiness.

'No one in the band even knows Jem all that well,' Katsu had told me. 'Anthony's my housemate, the rest are just friends of friends and people who replied to our ad. You don't need to worry.' He'd grinned. 'You just need to pick a side on the Aretha debate.'

Now the cramped living-room-slash-kitchen took on another use: performance space. Anthony and Ricky hefted the purple sofa out of the way. Molly dragged her keyboard in from her car. Katsu went to fetch his guitar from his room. (His room! I wanted to see his room, in that stupid teenage way, where you think that seeing someone's things might let you x-ray into their heart.)

Finally, the four of them shuffled into place, squabbling some more as they finished their tuning, throwing glances in my direction. *Okay? Ready?* I felt a prickle of anxiety. I wasn't a singer.

Molly had brought along some song lyrics and Anthony had a couple of melodies he'd been working on. The aim was to collaborate on a couple of songs. But first we needed a warm-up. Despite a full-throated argument in favour of Aretha from Ricky, The Beatles had been deemed the least contentious band to cover. Molly chose 'Eleanor Rigby'.

I had a well-thumbed Beatles songbook at home. I knew 'Eleanor Rigby', but I'd only ever really sung along to the melody. I hadn't stood at a mic and tried to sing it as the lead singer in a rock band.

I stepped up to the mic stand and adjusted it for my height, trying to tame my shaking hands. Behind me, the band began to play; too loud, too heavy for such a delicate song. I wondered what their neighbours thought about the noise and got my answer when someone thumped on the other side of the wall. Anthony made his guitar squeal in response and then the band resumed the melody.

I sang the first line of 'Eleanor Rigby' tentatively.

My voice wavered and I stopped. The band continued to play. I gripped the mic and, sucking in a breath, picked up the lyric.

The sad song about a woman living in a dream flowed out of me.

I closed my eyes and tried to concentrate on the melody. I ignored the frequent bum notes, the way that Ricky's drumming was always either a fraction too fast or too slow. I tried to imagine that I was in my caravan at home. 'Eleanor Rigby' was one of the first songs I'd learned to play on guitar. I'd played it every day for months. For a time, it had been more than a song to me. It had been a space to crawl into; a refuge. For two minutes, I didn't have to be myself; I could lose myself in the music. The same was true now. All I needed to do was lose myself.

Taking a deep breath, I willed my voice to stay steady and strong as I reached the chorus. I sucked air from deep in my lungs and half-yelled about lonely people.

The band played the song several times through. Each time, it seemed to improve. Ricky finally found his rhythm. The guitars stopped grating against each other. And I managed to wrench from my voice a level of power that I hadn't thought possible. I no longer felt like I was battling the other members of the band, or chasing them through the song. I was leading them.

'That sounded amazing!' Katsu said breathlessly, when we stopped for a break.

'Jem, you killed it,' Anthony said. His eyes slid over to Ricky. 'I mean, you're no Aretha, but . . .'

Ricky rolled his eyes, but he and Molly joined in with the compliments, too.

I ducked my head, embarrassed, wanting to demur. Then I remembered that I was supposed to be Jem. So I said exactly what I was thinking – and it was, I felt sure, exactly what my double would have said in this situation:

'Yeah, I was pretty great, wasn't I?'

*

When band practice wound down, I let myself be swept along with the others, as they set out on the streets to scavenge for food. The mood was boisterous; our chatter was loud. We were only rock stars in our own minds, but what did it matter? We were still rock stars.

After a short walk, we descended some steps into what looked like a subterranean cell. It was a café. The lighting had a warm, yellow hue and the air was sweet with the smell of bread, fresh from the oven. I thought nothing of the gleaming white tile that adorned the walls or the strange, ceramic wall decorations. The five of us crowded into a booth, ordering more food than an army of roadies could eat.

As we ate, the chatter continued. The subject, almost without exception, was music. Here, at last, I could contribute to the conversation without checking myself. I stomped out my shyness and held court, arguing happily about the Beatles and the Stones, Pharrell and Frank Ocean, Adele and Amy.

At some point during dinner, Katsu put his arm around me. It was a casual gesture, perhaps an unthinking one. He wanted to make more room in the crowded booth. Or he was still pretending, for the sake of the band, that I was his girlfriend, that I was Jem. Perhaps . . .

I didn't want to think too hard about it. I tore apart a warm hunk of bread and took a bite. For today, I wanted to exist in the moment and not up in my own head. When the conversation hit a lull, I was the one to stoke it back to life.

'What are these?' I asked, gesturing to the smooth curve of the ceramic wall art beside me.

Anthony choked out a laugh. 'Urinals.'

'What?'

'It's a public toilet, yeah?' Molly said, raising her eyebrows.

I looked around me, my vision resetting itself, so that I saw for the first time the windowless space, the tile walls, the bulbous white urinals. How. . . disgusting! Ella-ish primness welled up in me for a second – why would anyone want to eat in a toilet? – before amusement overrode it. I snorted out a laugh and, around me, the conversation moved on.

'Welcome to London,' Katsu whispered in my ear, his arm tightening around me.

'London is weird,' I said, grinning.

'No doubt.' I felt the low rumble of Katsu's laughter vibrate through his chest. He kept his voice quiet, so that the others couldn't hear. 'Y'know . . . this is probably the most fun I've had with Jem in months and . . . you're not even her.' He shook his head. 'You know what I mean. Today's been great.'

I didn't reply, because I knew my voice would betray me. I leaned into his embrace and let my toes curl inside my shoes.

*

'I know it's just a dumb band,' Katsu said to me later, 'but it's also basically the coolest thing I've ever done.'

Since leaving the public-toilet-turned-café, Katsu had been irrepressible, talking almost non-stop. I couldn't help but smile. His enthusiasm was contagious. We were walking to the Tube station, just the two of us, and though the day's light was fading, I didn't even feel the cold. The rock star glow still clung to me.

'I'm so bored of doing the uni thing,' he said. 'This PhD is killing me, the dissertation I have to write . . . I'm actually losing sleep over it, how stupid is that? And even if I do manage to crank it out, then what? Even more time in the lab.' He stretched upward onto the balls of his feet. 'I kinda want to ditch it for a while. Spend a year playing shitty little venues, put out an EP. Jem's dad knows some record producers. He can hook us up. I mean, who knows, right? Way shittier bands than us have got record deals . . .'

'Definitely,' I said, when Katsu paused for breath. 'What's the band's name?'

'We still can't agree on one,' he said.

'Average of Beverages?'

'Ha! Maybe. Jem likes Lace Steak.'

I laughed. 'Lace Steak? What does that even mean?'

'Okay, so . . . tell me something you ate today,' he said.

'Um. Sushi. Or Yorkshire pudding. One or the other.'

'Tell me what kind of underwear you're wearing.'

'What?'

Katsu grinned, impish. 'Just tell me. There's a reason.'

I flushed. Self-consciously, my hand went to my waist, feeling the line of my underwear. It wasn't even *my* underwear that I wore. It was Jem's underwear – a fact that had felt vaguely grimy when I'd got dressed this morning. It felt even more grimy now, because Katsu's eyes were following my hand, his gaze glancing over my waist, my hip, my arse. He was –

There was no mistaking it. He was checking me out.

'They're . . . striped,' I said at last.

Katsu's eyes snapped back up to meet mine. He looked like the kid who'd got his hand caught in the cookie jar. He wore not his usual, easy-going smile, but a new one. A smile that held intent.

'Okay,' he said. 'Striped Sushi. That's your band name. Your underwear, plus something you ate today.'

'Not Striped Yorkshire Pudding?'

'Maybe, except that sounds insane. Striped Sushi actually sounds pretty cool.'

'Striped Sushi,' I said, smiling.

'There you go. When you start your own band, you already know what to call it.'

It took me a second to process what he was saying. I nodded distractedly, as he continued talking.

'Seriously,' he said, 'you should do it. Find a couple of musos up there in Cumbria, get something going. You sounded amazing back there. Any band would be lucky to have you as a singer.'

I nodded again, but my excitement was cooling. I pulled my fawn-coloured coat (Jem's) tight around me, feeling the chill of the November day. I'd forgotten, for a short while, that this was not my band. I would not be playing gigs or touring. I would only ever sing 'Eleanor Rigby' to myself. For me, it would only ever be an anthem of loneliness.

*

I was quiet for the rest of the journey back to Chelsea. Katsu asked me to come out with him and his friends to see a movie. ('There's an arty Spanish film playing. Jem would hate it – subtitles and subtext and stuff – but you're welcome to come.') He sounded enthusiastic about the idea, but, to me, the invite felt hollow.

I couldn't get a read on Katsu. Was he simply being friendly? Did he actually enjoy hanging out with me? Was I just a curiosity to him? I couldn't tell.

He walked me home, and I tried to ignore the ripple of tension when we stopped outside of my double's apartment block. It nagged at me, the thought that, if I were Jem, if Katsu were my boyfriend, he would kiss me goodnight now – just as he'd kissed me hello earlier. He'd probably come upstairs, too, undressing me the moment we got in the door.

But he was not my boyfriend. And I was not his Jem. I gave a mumbling goodbye and let myself inside, leaving the outside door to fall closed after me.

I felt exhausted – by the day; by the whole weekend. I wanted to scrub my face free of make-up, sink into the depths of a hot bath and emerge from it clean; emerge as Ella again. I took the lift to the second floor, walking on instinct, barely looking where I was going. I had my key ready to unlock Jem's front door when I saw a man crest the staircase.

At the sight of him (olive skin, sleepy eyes, mouth set in a straight line), the hairs on the back of my neck stood on end.

The big-fucking-problem guy. He was here.

For seconds too long, I did nothing but look at him as he crossed the corridor towards me. He was speaking, but my brain registered only a whine, painfully high-pitched.

I forced my body to move. I plunged the key into the door and yanked it open. Darting inside, the door fell shut behind me.

Almost shut.

A second before the door closed, the guy grabbed the handle and followed me.

Only then did the door slam shut.

I was inside the flat. And so was he.

27

BULLETPROOF

Jem

In a gloomy back office of the hotel, I was soliciting the help of an admin grunt named Sayid.

'You want to stick it where?' I asked, mock-aghast.

'In here.' Sayid laughed, gesturing to the clocking-out machine.

'Oh, you bad boy, you want to take the virtue of my time card.' I mimed clutching an invisible pearl necklace.

Sayid was floppy-haired and dark-skinned, with darting honey-brown eyes. He tugged the time card from my hands and slotted it into the machine. With a click, it stamped the time.

'Oooh . . .' I said in a throaty voice, raising an eyebrow.

He shook his head, grinning, and handed the time card back to me. Before I'd interrupted him, he'd been photocopying some sort of report ('Why Walney Island Is the Most Depressing Place In England: An Urgent Enquiry'). Now he crossed the room back to the hulking grey copier, and I followed him.

It was fun to distract him. I was tempted to invite him to Jackdaw's and take him for a spin, but he'd already mentioned that he didn't drink. Jesus. Imagine living in a place like this and *not* spending half your time blitzed.

'Ella?'

I barely registered the voice behind me. I leaned against the copier and used my foot to sock Sayid playfully on the leg. He laughed and mimed stamping on my foot.

'Ella?'

Someone tapped on my shoulder. A woman with ugly tortoiseshell glasses and an owlish look of reproach was standing behind me. Oh, shit. Ella. That was me.

'Done your rooms already?' the woman asked.

'Oh . . . yeah, yeah, of course, Mrs – ' I coughed to cover up the fact I had no idea of her name. Then I threw in a wink. 'Boss lady.'

She cleared her throat. 'Good, good . . . but as I'm sure you know, there's the small matter of' – she dropped her voice, angling away from Sayid – 'Friday to discuss.'

'Right,' I said, nodding sagely.

This Friday? Last Friday? Wait, what had Twinnie said happened? Something about a rich bitch and a torn robe?

'I'd like to do things properly, formally. So, if you're free now, we could have a little sit-down in my office. Is that okay?'

Her eyes bored into me. The woman's whole demeanour was so schoolteacher-ish that I took an instant dislike to her.

'Ummm . . .' I put on my best 'serious' Ella expression, with furrowed brow and bitten lip. 'Would you mind terribly if we did it another time?'

She placed a hand on my shoulder. 'I think now would be best.'

Oh. So this was like when my mother asked if I was free and actually meant 'this is happening right now whether you like it or not'.

The woman's hand remained on my shoulder and she used pinching fingers to turn me around. She gestured to a door with a tarnished plaque that read *Fiona Brannan*. I cast a glance at Sayid, but he was pretending not to know me, punching buttons on the photocopier.

In Brannan's office, I took a seat, slumping against the hard wooden back of the chair. I remembered Twinnie's briefing on what to do. *Just say sorry a lot.* Ugh. Grovelling wasn't my style.

'I'm really struggling with what happened. This is a very difficult situation.' Brannan shuffled some papers on her desk and then paused to look at me. 'What you did amounts to gross misconduct. Do you understand what that means?'

'Never good to be gross!' I roused a half smile.

Rather than smiling, her frown deepened. 'It's a sackable offense.'

'Oh, okay . . .'

I thought of roadkill, dead puppies, and endeavoured to look remorseful.

'Look.' Brannan let out a sigh. 'You're a sweet girl, Bethany raves about you. I want us to get all this straight and move on.'

'Okay . . .'

'Let's work out a solution together.' (I wondered what business book she'd stolen that one from.) 'First things first, I need an apology.'

'I'm sorry,' I said, struggling to keep the boredom out of my voice.

'I need an apology to the guest.' Brannan's teeth clicked together, over-emphasising the letter T. 'She has, and I don't blame her, checked out early, but I'd like you to write her a letter.'

'Okay . . .'

God, homework. What a drag.

'The garment you soiled cost' – Brannan did more paper-shuffling, her sweaty finger coming to rest at the bottom of a page of scrawled notes – 'five hundred pounds, so I'm afraid I'll need to dock your wages that amount.'

Christ, who cared? Didn't this rich bitch guest have other clothes? I thought of Twinnie scrubbing toilets to pay for it – how much did she even make? twenty pounds an hour? – and I almost felt bad.

My overriding feeling, though, was one of intense irritation. Brannan's voice was a drone that reminded me of sour schoolteachers, my prissy agent Savannah, Mummy Dearest.

'Sure, sure,' I said, biting my tongue to keep from saying anything else.

I shifted in my seat. The wood made it impossible to get comfortable. My earlier flu-y feeling was back, making me woozy and fevered. Brannan gave me a long hard look.

'I know you made a mistake, and I'm ready and eager to listen to your side of the story.' When I didn't say anything, she prompted. 'Ella?'

Fucking hell, this office was claustrophobic. I wanted to wrap up this pointless meeting and get out.

'Yeah, I mean, I'm really sorry,' I gabbled, hearing the way my real accent surfaced on the words *really sorry*.

'I want to give you another chance to prove yourself, but there will have to be an extra level of supervision for a while.'

Bitch Brannan pointed a finger at me to stress her point. That was when my wooziness gave way to anger. I sat up straight, my lips twisting into a sneer.

'For God's sake, I didn't take a shit in someone's suitcase,' I said. 'You think other maids don't get up to worse?'

'Excuse me?'

Her eyebrows shot up and I choked out a laugh.

'You heard me,' I said.

'All the staff in this hotel are duty bound to maintain our establishment's high level of standards. Nothing goes on that I don't know about. And if you're not willing to play by the rules – '

'No, I guess I'm not.'

I stood up and pushed back my chair so hard it clattered backwards onto the floor. I rumpled a hand through my hair and produced a smile that was closer to a snarl.

'Fuck you,' I said. 'Fuck this job. Fuck this whole town.'

*

At Jackdaw's, I bounced against the wooden bar stool like there was itching powder in my minge. It was an hour since I'd stormed out of the hotel, bombing along the country roads back to Walney in Twinnie's car. I was still steaming. Something about Bitch Brannan had really triggered me. I hated having to cower like that; I hated being talked down to. I couldn't shed my sweaty, fevered feeling.

'Another?' Darryl asked.

I gave a jerk of my head, nodding without bothering to look at him.

'Make this one stronger, would you? The last one was like cat piss.'

Darryl grabbed a couple of bottles from behind the bar and began mixing me a new drink. He made a fuss of adding a cherry and a pink umbrella, placing the concoction in front of me, like I was going to be so delighted I'd drop to my knees right there and then.

'Thanks,' I said with a glower.

Within seconds, I'd discarded the umbrella and gulped down half the drink. It tasted like kirsch and triple sec. Disgusting. I made a face, but kept drinking.

The trouble was, it wasn't alcohol I wanted. Anger always sparked my cravings. When I was happy, I was fine. As soon as I got pissed off, all I wanted was a line of coke.

'I get off early tonight,' Darryl was saying. 'Maybe I'll get you off, too . . .'

'Yeah?'

I was barely listening. My eyes weren't focused on his face, but on an infected mole on his neck: brown ringed with white, spreading out into a blush of swollen red. I wondered if he was dying. Cancer. Would it even be a loss to this sad little town?

Darryl wandered down the bar to take an order from a ruddy-faced older gent. He was the restaurant's only other customer. On Saturday night, Jackdaw's hadn't been hopping, but at least it had been busy. Sunday night, it was deserted. The absence of people only added to the gnawing emptiness in my stomach.

'Hey,' I said, when Darryl returned. 'What's a girl do around here when she's got a little craving . . .'

I had money burning a hole in my pocket. It wasn't Ella's money. A handful of change and a two-stamps-away-from-a-free-muffin card were all there was in Twinnie's purse. But, while Ella's mum had been in the bathroom earlier, it's done a quick recce of her caravan. I'd found £100 stashed behind a cereal box. Not a lot, but it would keep me going.

'Huh.' Pouring the old gent's drink, Darryl let a long, showy stream of whisky splash into the glass. 'I got a cure for your cravings.'

'Hmmm, tempting.' I forced a giggle. 'But seriously. Know anyone who deals?'

Darryl raised his eyebrows and made me wait till after he'd delivered the other customer's drink to receive a reply.

'Who, me?' he said at last. 'I'm a good boy, remember?'

Darryl's faux innocent act scratched at my raw nerves. Of course he knew where to get something. When I'd been at his flat the night before, I'd noticed electronics (TVs and games consoles, by the looks of it) stacked against the peeling wallpaper. He'd mentioned an upcoming court date, like I was supposed to be impressed by his petty criminality.

I didn't know if cocaine was his flavour of danger, but I knew there had to be a drugs underbelly to this soul-destroying town. What else was there to do, except get high or get out?

'Do you have a number or not?' I said.

A few minutes later, my head was bowed over the bar. I rested my forehead against my hand and listened to the endless drone of a ringing phone. I let it ring long after it became obvious no one was going to answer.

My patience snapped. 'Forfuck'ssake.' I sent Ella's shitty old phone skidding across the bar. Darryl observed me with wary eyes. He stooped to retrieve the phone and handed it back to me.

'If you wait till I'm done with work, I'll drive you over there. He's probably home, just turned off his phone or something.'

'Gimme the address,' I said. 'I'll go now.'

It was weird, the way cravings worked. The distractions of the past few days had submerged my need for coke. Now I'd started thinking about it, it had become an alarm in my brain. *Get it now, get it now, get it now*, the siren blared.

'He won't know who you are . . .' Darryl said.

'No one ever says no to me.' I grabbed a white paper napkin and flung at him. 'Write down the address.'

Darryl huffed out a long breath, visibly resisting. Finally, he pulled a biro from behind his ear and began to write in a laborious mix of small letters and capitals.

'Draw me a map, too,' I said.

His brow furrowed. 'He lives right in Vickerstown, by the chip shop,' he said, like I was supposed to know where that was.

Even though I was drunk and rattling, I could still read Darryl's expression. I wasn't cute and alluring to him anymore. I was just another bitch.

Damn straight. Dress me up like a country mouse and you still couldn't change me.

He pushed the napkin over to me and I crumpled it into my fist.

'Toodle-loo. See you.'

I stumbled off my barstool and flung the words over my shoulder as I tottered over to the door. Darryl might have muttered something like *fucking crazy cunt* at me, but I didn't care enough to listen.

The blast of cold air surprised me when I stepped outside. It sobered me up for a moment. Was this a stupid idea?

I'd expected to find a row of taxis idling on the street outside, but there were none. The wind whipped at my dress as I walked. It was a blue one of Ella's I'd changed into after my shift and it was all wrong for the time of year, even with Twinnie's parka bundled over the top. Lampposts, placed at uneven intervals, provided the odd pool of light, but it was a lot darker than light-polluted London. The deserted feel of Jackdaw's was echoed out here. The streets were empty of people. There weren't even any cars on the road.

The cold made my ribs ache, a phantom stab of pain piercing my drunken numbness. The memory of Carlo's first strike made my heartbeat skip into syncopation. A whisper of fear breathed down my neck. 'You put yourself in these situations, Jem,' he'd said. 'You do it to yourself.'

Carlo. Motherfucking Carlo. He'd been bugging me for too long.

After the run-in with him at the theatre, I was sorry I'd never got my hands on a gun. Country folk had guns, didn't they? Hunting rifles, that sort of thing. Maybe I'd make another sweep of Twinnie's parents' Chateau de Misery when I got home, see what I could find. First things first, though.

On a darkened street on Walney Island, I wavered on the spot, smoothing out the wadded-up napkin with its address and scrawled map. In the dark, the squiggly lines were hard to make out, but it looked like I needed to follow the road as it curved around to the right.

Ready and . . . go!

Ahead of me, the street was growing narrower. I meant to stride confidently, but as I walked, my unsteady feet sent me stumbling into the gutter. The pavement was too uneven. I veered into the road and followed the dotted white line that ran down its centre.

I'm bulletproof, I reminded myself.

28

CROSS MY HEART AND HOPE TO DIE

Ella

I was trapped inside Jem's flat. And the big-fucking-problem guy was bearing down on me. Scrabbling at the latch, I tried to swing the door open again.

Get out, get out, get out.

I had to escape.

The door opened an inch. Then the man was at my back, his weight smothering me. With one hand, he pushed the door closed again.

'Where are you going?' he asked. 'Just having a nice chat, aren't we?'

My fingers slackened, hands dropping to my sides. I turned to face him. He wasn't poorly dressed – in the half-light, I saw that his black suit was crumpled but not threadbare – yet a smell of homelessness clung to him.

My stomach turned. I felt an automatic desire to get away from him, even if it meant retreating from the only escape route. I skittered sideways, bird-like and shivering, my feet scuffing against the wood floor. The hallway was dark and I couldn't remember where the light switch was.

'Not much of a welcome, Jems,' he said. 'Don't wanna offer me a drink? Ask how I am?' He affected a high-pitched voice, his body flopping into a theatrical bow. 'How *are* you, Carlo? I'm tickety-boo, thanks for asking.'

Carlo. Now I remembered. That was what Katsu had called him the night of the party.

'Rude,' he said, wagging a finger at me. 'You're a rude girl.

Always have been. Rude, rude, rude.'

'Sorry,' I said. My default forever, my boilerplate response.

I was sliding along the wall now, edging around him, down the hallway and further into the apartment.

He let out a hyena laugh. 'We're about ten grand past sorry, sweetheart.'

I thought of the affectionate way Katsu's mum had called me sweetheart. Carlo spat the word like an insult. My back against the wall, I slid another step sideways. He still leaned against the door, his face lost in shadow.

I couldn't get out the front door, but there had to be something I could do.

Climb out a window? No. All that would get me was a seven-metre drop to the pavement below.

I slid my hand down over my hip, to where my phone lay in my coat pocket. It was too risky to pull it out and try to dial 999 in the dark. Carlo might snap and kill me. But maybe I could run to the bathroom, lock myself inside, and call the police from in there?

It wasn't a good plan – the bathroom was at the end of the long corridor and I couldn't remember if it was on the left or right – but it was all I had.

Too scared to turn my back on Carlo, I shuffled another metre sideways. He didn't move. I darted another few steps. My windpipe was squeezed by fear and I could only take quick, shallow breaths.

Now was the time to do it.

Run.

I could make it to the bathroom. I was sure I could.

The lights in the hallway flicked on. After the darkness, they were dazzling. Bright spots danced before my eyes. I turned to make my sprint to the bathroom, but Carlo was advancing on me.

He clapped a big meaty hand on my elbow, his grasp tight

enough to hurt.

'C'mon,' he said, frog-marching me through to the kitchen and away from the bathroom. 'Get me a brew, old chum.'

In the kitchen, Carlo again found the light switch. He let out a low whistle.

'This your pad? Niiice. How come you never invited me round for a housewarming?' He yanked open the huge American-style fridge and pulled out two bottles of beer. 'Honestly, it's rude to make me follow you home.' He shoved a beer into my hand. 'Hey, do that trick where you open it with your teeth!'

On automatic, I bared my teeth in a grimace, but Carlo was cackling. He cracked his own beer cap against the lip of the worktop and it popped off, rattling where it fell. Then he did the same for me.

'What's up with this craft beer crap? Gotta have what's hot, isn't that right?' He took a long pull from his beer and licked his lips. ''Member that Icelandic liquor we had once? Stuff was fucking deadly, but you finished the bottle.' His hand was still locked onto my arm and he jerked me like a rag doll. 'Re-mem-ber?'

'Yeah,' I gulped out. 'That was . . . crazy.'

Up close, the sticky sheen of sweat on his face caught the light. His gaze zipped back and forth, pinprick pupils making his eyes look alien. My experience of drugs began and ended at the prescription pad, but I knew what high looked like. Carlo was so high, he might as well have been balancing on top of the Shard. And he appeared ready to take a swan dive off the edge.

He dipped his head and put his face right next to mine, wafting rank breath against my cheek. 'Tell me about the money,' he said.

My brain stuttered, a charge of static making me dizzy. Things like this didn't happen to me. Never in her life would Ella be cornered by a deranged man demanding money. If I were myself, what would I say? Here, take my guitar! Take my ten-year-old TV with the dead pixels in the middle! Take my laptop that crashes every 30 minutes!

Add up my whole life and it wouldn't be worth ten grand.

'I . . . I don't know . . .' I said.

My voice came out meek, Cumbrian. Worse, it was the wrong thing to say.

Carlo's fingers dug into the flesh of my arm. I squirmed away from him, shoulders bending inward, making myself as small as possible. But he wouldn't let me go. One jolt and he could snap my bones in two.

'You can afford all this' – his eyes bugged out, sweeping across the expanse of high-end, open-plan living that surrounded us – 'but you can't pay me?'

'I . . . I'll get it for you . . .' I whispered.

'Heard it all before,' he said with a growl. 'Play me a new tune.'

I didn't say anything for a long moment. The silence was filled with a loud hum. I thought it might be inside my head until I realised the fridge door was still open, gusting cold air over my bare flesh. My hand was particularly cold. It was the beer. Icy glass numbed my palm. Feeling as if the hand were detached from me, I watched as it lifted the bottle of beer to my lips.

Gulp, gulp, gulp. One, two, three mouthfuls.

In the time it took to make the final swallow, I pushed Ella deep down inside me and pulled out a different person. I lowered the bottle and met Carlo's gaze dead-on.

'I mean it this time,' I said with an impish smile.

Instead of squirming against his grasp, I gave him a playful nudge.

'Come on, you know me.' My voice was stronger now; my enunciation precise. 'I'm good for it.'

He let out a low moan, but his grip on me was loosening.

His hard face was slackening, tiredness showing in the droop of his mouth.

'Jem, man . . .' he said. 'I really need that money.'

'And you'll get it. Promise. Swear on my life.' The laugh that came out of my mouth was brash and puckish. 'Cross my heart and hope to die.'

'You got any of it now?'

'Uh . . .' My smile froze. 'I just need to . . . make a couple of arrangements.' I groped for excuses, straining to keep my voice light. 'Wait for the banks to open . . .'

My phone – Jem's phone – vibrated in my pocket. It made Carlo startle, his head bouncing back and forth as he looked around.

'What was that?'

'Nothing . . . it was just . . .'

My voice faltered; my hands started shaking again as I pulled the phone from my pocket with my left hand. Carlo smacked it from my grasp. It clattered on to the tiled floor. He kicked it for good measure, sending it spinning away from my feet.

His anger was back; teeth gnashing, hair-pulling rage, intensified into lunacy by the drugs. He slammed a fist in my direction and it caught me in the jaw. Shock overrode pain. Ella would have cowered in fright, but Jem was stronger.

I watched my hand as it shot out. I was on the offensive now. I spun the bottle around so that the thick glass base faced out. Beer sloshed in an arc across the kitchen floor as I brought the bottle down on his head.

My hit wasn't hard enough.

The bottle only glanced off the side of his skull. He swatted it away and it exploded against the floor in a glitter of glass shards.

'You stupid bitch!'

He grabbed me by both arms and shook me hard.

'Please don't hurt me,' I whimpered.

'Hurt you? Nothing else gets through to you!'

Carlo gave me another shove and I crumpled against the open fridge door. I dislodged a jar of mustard and it fell with a smash.

'You do this to yourself,' he said.

I closed my eyes and the overhead lights of the kitchen burned red against my eyelids. My back was chilled by the air from the fridge. Its hum roared in my ears. I waited for the blow of his fist against my face.

It didn't come.

When I dared open my eyes to look at him, I saw he was doubled over, fists grinding against his eye sockets.

'You're Chernobyl,' he said, a howling desperation in his voice. 'And everything you touch is totally and completely fucked.'

I waited a moment longer, for him to kick me, punch me, put me out of my misery.

When he still didn't straighten up – he was rocking back and forth, muttering 'you're Chernobyl' over and over – I edged past him. Making my steps as soundless as possible, I crept into Jem's bedroom and flicked on the light. The kitchen smelled like spilled mustard, but here, the sweet orange-zest smell of Jem's perfume was strong.

The make-up I'd applied earlier was scattered across the dressing table. Beside those tubes and pots, a metal tree was draped with necklaces and bracelets. Rings sparkled in a white ceramic dish.

I grabbed a handful of jewellery and hastened out of the room, not bothering to stop and retrieve the rings and chains that slipped from my grasp as I walked. Back in the kitchen, Carlo was leaning against the counter with a glazed look on his face. He took a swallow of beer and looked at me like he didn't quite recognise me.

'Take these,' I said, thrusting the jewellery into his free hand. 'Sell them. There's at least a few thousand there.'

Carlo examined a ruby ring and then shoved it over the thick knuckle of his pinky finger. He set aside the beer bottle and stuffed the rest of the jewellery into his jacket pockets.

'What about the rest?' he asked hoarsely.

'Tomorrow,' I said, hoping only that my promise might make him leave. 'I swear.'

*

I stayed in the kitchen for a long time, staring at the spot where Carlo had stood, wondering if he'd come back.

A fine gold chain lay twisted on the floor. It glinted, catching on the edge of my peripheral vision. Before he'd left, Carlo had bent down to snag some of the jewellery I'd dropped, but he'd missed that one. How much was it worth? A hundred? More?

I felt like I should go and pick it up, but I couldn't move.

It was the sound of my phone – Jem's phone – vibrating against the kitchen floor that roused me. Taking small, tentative steps, I crossed the kitchen and stooped to retrieve it. With numb thumbs, I opened up the new messages. Both of them were from Katsu.

You're missing a treat with this film

There was a ten minute long sequence of a chicken crossing the road. Scored with classical music and shot with a moody purple filter. Batshit.

I should've gone to the cinema with Katsu. I should've eaten stale popcorn and leaned my head on his shoulder. I should've been there with him to make fun of the chicken crossing the road.

Frustration stirred in me, my chest growing tight. Maybe it was the aftershocks of the last half-hour, but my cheeks were flushed, my head pounding. I was mad.

When there were parts of Jem's life that were so filled with light, why was she so keen to scurry into the darkness? She had everything – beautiful flat, easy life, loving boyfriend – and she was throwing it all away on drugs and skirmishes with guys like Carlo. She had enough money, why hadn't she paid Carlo and drawn a line under it? Her addiction obviously went beyond drugs; she was hooked on danger.

I knew the correct response to this situation. I should run. Run from Carlo. Run from London. Run from Jem's life. In Cumbria, I'd wrestle my identity back from her, call the police if necessary. It would be just another nutty story about doubles behaving badly for the glossy mags.

The phone buzzed again in my hand.

Hey, you around tomorrow night? 2 4 1 burgers at a place near my house. Fancy it?

I felt a hand clench around my heart.

Yes, I fancy it.

A chilled-out Monday night with Katsu. He'd tell me more about the arthouse film and we'd laugh, our feet getting tangled up under the table. There'd be a smear of ketchup on his lip and I'd lean in to wipe it away. And maybe, just maybe, I'd get up the nerve to kiss him – not as Jem, but as me.

That was the trouble with running away from Jem's life. It meant running from Katsu; running from friends like April and Stee and Imogen; running from cute outfits and admiring glances. If you removed the encounter with Carlo, the last few days were the best I'd felt in years. The heavy feeling I usually lugged around with me only came back when I imagined returning to Walney Island.

My brain snagged on one thought in particular. *Cute outfits . . .*

Sounds good. Looking forward to it, I sent back to Katsu.

Slipping the phone into my pocket, I went back into Jem's bedroom. I had a strange sense that she might be hiding in here, ready to jump out from between a row of expensive coats. When I pushed my arms deep into a rack of clothes, I found nothing but fabric – smooth and rough; satin and wool. I pulled out garments out at random, checking the labels and then letting the clothes fall at my feet.

Chanel. Prada. Gucci.

I didn't know much about fashion, but I remembered the price tags on the second-hand clothes at the shop I'd visited yesterday. Four hundred pounds for a dress. Five hundred for a coat. Six hundred for a handbag. Jem's wardrobe might as well have been lined with fifty pound notes.

Footsteps sounded nearby.

My hand squeezed tight around a grey silk dress, my fingers crushing the fabric.

I wanted to believe I was imagining things. Maybe it was an echo from another apartment. But the footsteps were getting louder. It was the unmistakable sound of someone walking the wood floor of the hallway.

It was Carlo. He'd come back for me. With a gun, perhaps, or a gleaming knife. When I'd imagined dying, it had always been quiet. Pills, poison, water closing over my head; a final breath and then sleep. Carlo would kill me with a bang, with blood and screaming.

I leaned against a rack of clothes in the walk-in wardrobe. Should I try to hide – slip between the folds of fabric and hold my breath – or get it over with?

The bedroom door sighed as it was pushed open. Footsteps clicked closer. I felt like I was about to faint.

29

STRANGERS

Ella

'Why is your front door wide open?' a clipped female voice asked. 'Jemima, I'm assuming you're in here somewhere?'

A figure appeared in the doorway of the walk-in wardrobe.

'There you are,' Mum said. 'Your father has a lot to answer for. His whole strangers-are-just-friends-et-cetera thing.'

She shook a few tendrils of honey-blonde hair out of her eyes.

'Strangers are just friends who'll break into your house and rob you,' she said. 'For heaven's sake, lock your door – or at least close it. We are in London.' She waved her manicured nails in a dismissive gesture and glided over to me. 'All that money I spent on your schooling and you still don't have any common sense.'

I don't know whether she intended to hug me, but I collapsed against her, craving warmth like a puppy scrabbling for body contact. My jaw still throbbed from where Carlo had punched me. I closed my eyes and clung to her, breathing in her jasmine-scented perfume.

'Sorry,' I whispered.

'Not to worry.' Her tone was surprised; the words reflexive.

Not to worry, not to worry, not to worry, I chanted inside my head.

My heart was still beating too fast; a shadow of anticipated death lurked at the corner of my eye. The darkest whispers in my mind still wanted to beckon death closer, but the raw nerves of my body thrummed with relief. I was alive. On its most visceral level, all my body wanted to do was survive.

Leonora gave me one final squeeze and gently disentangled herself from my embrace.

'I was on my way home from the office,' she said, 'I know, I know, always working, tut tut, but I thought I'd pop in, wanted to talk to you about the car . . .'

'Oh . . . okay . . .'

I was barely able to stutter out the words. A tear escaped the corner of my eye. I turned away to hide it, but Leonora reached out to grab my chin with her thumb and first finger.

'What's wrong?'

Her eyes bored into mine and, this time, I felt a tremor that had nothing to do with Carlo. I stared into her grey eyes and waited for the façade to crumble.

Surely, this woman . . .

Surely, this woman who gave birth to Jem would be able to look into my eyes and see an imposter?

'Tell me what's wrong.' The chilly, longsuffering tone to her voice was gone; she sounded genuinely concerned. 'Bug, just tell me.'

Bug. A childish nickname. I imagined a five-year-old Jem careening around a big house in Chelsea, causing havoc and offering up an impish smile to say sorry. Bug. It suited her. My parents had never really gone in for terms of endearment. I was always just Ella.

'It's nothing, it's nothing . . .' I tried to paste a big fake Jem smile onto my face, but my lower lip wobbled and more tears leaked out of my eyes.

'It is something, I want you to tell me.'

Leonora's voice was forceful – she was obviously the type of woman who made demands and made sure they were met – and I felt a strong urge to tell her everything. Tell her about Carlo, about changing places with Jem, about who I really was.

But then what? She'd be repulsed, shove me away. *You're not my daughter!* I wasn't sure I could handle it. Not right now. All I wanted was to please her, to remain in her circle of jasmine-scented warmth.

'Had a fight with Katsu,' I mumbled, improvising.

'Ah, of course.' A grim smile broke across her concerned face. 'Smart women and all we do is spend our lives crying over men.'

She drew me into another hug and I let the tears fall freely. I didn't even know what I was crying about. Part of it was the stress of the past hour, but these tears came from somewhere deeper, too. Sadness followed me like a shadow, yet I hadn't cried – properly cried – in a long time. I spent my life sucking up my tears, burying my feelings deep inside. Now that I was crying, I couldn't seem to stop.

Leonora smoothed circles against my shoulder and murmured, 'I'm here, Bug, I'm here.'

*

We ended up in the kitchen. Leonora – high-powered career woman, take-no-prisoners bitch (Jem's description) – was making me cheese on toast.

I perched on one of the chrome breakfast bar stools. My feet hung several centimetres from the floor and I kicked them idly, feeling like a kid again. My face was probably blotchy from the tears, red from Carlo's fist, but I didn't care. Melting cheese under the grill made spitting noises; the smell of bread turning golden brown wafted through the kitchen.

I was starving.

'This used to be your favourite meal,' Leonora said, pulling the pan from under the grill in a flourish. 'Our cook would whip up the most beautiful dishes – salmon, lamb shanks, gorgeous fillets of veal. You'd wait for her to leave and then beg me to make you cheese on toast. My little philistine.' She smiled. Then a shadow passed across her face. 'You probably don't even remember that.'

'I remember,' I lied.

Just like that, I almost did. The memory filled itself in. I imagined sitting in a bright, modern kitchen like this one – one that wasn't a miniscule corner of a caravan; one where the heating worked all the time – and kicking my heels, small hands leaving sticky prints against the polished worktop. Begging, begging, begging for my favourite snack, until my mother laughed and said, *yes, yes, okay!*

Leonora served up the humble cheese on toast on a plate inlaid with tiny silver and blue flowers. She refused to eat any herself ('oh no, I mustn't'), but she watched me with an indulgent smile as I gobbled up the food. Eating should have aggravated the injury to my jaw, but I could barely feel it anymore. It was like it had happened to someone else.

The broken glass, the pool of beer, and the smear of mustard on the kitchen floor were the only reminders of the altercation with Carlo. Leonora stepped around them in high heels ('slovenly as ever, I see, mind you don't cut yourself before Gabriela comes'), but didn't move to sweep it up. Of course. Rich people didn't clean.

'I'm surprised you haven't badgered me about your car yet,' she said.

My mouth was full of cheese on toast, so I just raised my eyebrows in a questioning expression.

'Those voicemails you left for me were rather colourful.' She paused, as if anticipating a tirade. I kept eating, chewing more slowly as I reached my last crust. 'Don't worry,' she said. 'I called the company, paid off what was outstanding. They'll drop it off to you in a couple of days.'

Still I didn't say anything, but Leonora sighed as if I'd argued with her.

'I didn't react well,' she said. 'As my therapist says, I'm prone to overreaction.' She gave a frowning, ironical smile. 'I know, I know. Passed that one on to you. I only . . . want you to know the value of things, that's all.'

I nodded, still not feeling on firm footing. What had happened to Jem's car? What kind of lesson had her mum tried to teach her?

'I know you think I don't have time for you, but I went to see your play a couple of nights ago. Imagine my surprise to find some other girl jumping out of a box. I chatted to an odious young man afterwards who actually owned up to directing the thing. He told me you'd parted company with the show. Didn't use those words.'

'Yeah, um, I quit,' I said, brushing crumbs from my fingertips. Jem would've said the words proudly, but I looked down, evading Leonora's gaze.

'And what are you doing with yourself now?'

'I don't know . . .' Well, it was the truth.

Leonora took a deep breath, as if readying herself. 'I know what you'll say, but I have something that might interest you.'

Carefully nonchalant, she made a show of tidying up my plate (though she didn't wash it up, just placed it in the sink).

'It's a little arts venue, south of the river,' she said. 'There's a gallery, a theatre, all up and coming talent, that bleeding edge nonsense you love. A friend of mine – Tom; he's the primary investor – told me they need a creative assistant. It's a job, an actual job. Where you have to show up at the same time every day and wear tights that don't have holes in them.'

She put the bread and cheese back in the fridge, creating a gust of cold air. An echo of my earlier panic raised goose flesh on my arms. My body tensed. I only stirred back to life when Leonora reached over to touch my arm.

'Heaven forbid,' she said, 'I think you'd be good at it. I know academia never sat well with you. But it might be nice to put that brain of yours to use.'

'Sounds great,' I said blankly, still half-thinking about Carlo. Leonora raised her eyebrows. 'Sounds great, *but . . .*'

'No, I'd love to do it,' I said.

It really did sound amazing. In my final year of uni, I'd scoured online listings of similar jobs, but they all required internships and experience (none of which I had). To have a creative, interesting job fall into my lap made me feel dizzy.

Leonora's voice was so strong and confident. *I think you'd be good at it.* She sounded like she believed it. My mum never thought that much of me, and she was proved right when I dropped out of uni. Useless. I was a child to be protected, to be worried over, because she'd always known I couldn't make it on my own.

'Now, it doesn't pay much.' Leonora was struggling to conceal her delight, talking faster, her face more animated. 'But I'd be happy to top up your earnings. Get back to our old system.'

Jem's voice bubbled up in my throat. 'You're bribing me.'

'Not a bribe, Jemima.' A sharp note sliced through her voice. 'I just need a sense that you're on the right track.'

Her narrowed eyes met mine and I could see that she was expecting a fight. I knew what was supposed to happen. Jem would tell her to take her job and shove it. Take her money and shove it. Decades-old resentment would rise to the surface. Headstrong Jem would be wilfully blind to the fact that the money could be used to pay off Carlo; she'd ignore the reality that this job might actually be good for her.

'When would I start?' I asked, my voice even.

Leonora blinked. 'I'll need to firm everything up, so why don't we say a week tomorrow? I'll get Tom to email you the address.'

'Okay.'

'Well . . . wonders never cease,' she murmured, taking a step closer to where I sat on one of the breakfast stools. 'I know you're upset about that boyfriend of yours, but you're . . . more lucid today, more like yourself. Ever since you got back from the States, it's been hard to have a straight conversation with you.'

She reached over and stroked my cheek, before pulling me into a hug.

'I missed you very much when you were gone,' she said. 'Not sure I ever told you that.'

'I missed you, too,' I said, letting my shoulders relax as I returned her hug.

*

The next day, I heaved a bin bag filled with clothes over my shoulder and took the lift down to the lobby. It reminded me of leaving university, packing up my things like they were rubbish, leaving behind another life. The difference was that the woman I was today wore a bright smear of orangey-red lipstick and clomped along in a pair of heels that revealed grinning skulls on their soles.

At the trendy boutique in Soho, I dumped the black bag on to the counter and said, 'How much?'

The shop assistant wore the same red-glitter lipstick as she had on Saturday. She flicked her black flat-ironed hair out of her eyes and offered a tight smile. Just over her shoulder, an antler's head, draped with fairy lights, also gave me a snooty look.

'Uh, the Salvation Army is opposite McDonald's,' she said.

As Jem, it was easy for me to meet her gaze dead-on, unsmiling. I made sure my expression said, *Don't get uppity with me, bitch*. When I emptied out the bin bag, garments flopped all over the counter, some landing on the floor in a heap. Using two fingers, the shop assistant picked through them. Her darkly-outlined brows rose as she noted the designer labels.

'How much?' I said again.

She gave a little sniff. 'Let me see . . .'

Ten minutes later, I walked out of the shop with a wad of bank notes shoved inside my bra. Next stop was the pawn shop. With speckled floor tiles underfoot and garish fluorescent lighting overhead, it was much less glamorous than the whimsical vintage shop. This was the sort of place that I was familiar with from Barrow-in-Furness. Even the forced cheerfulness of the bleached-blonde sales girl reminded me of life at home, memories of long days of jolly drudgery settling in my belly like a stone.

I stood hunched over the glass counter, like a pickpocket revealing my wares to Fagin. I'd found more tangled necklaces and forgotten rings stuffed inside a jewellery box in my double's room. There were earrings and bracelets, gold and silver (or were they platinum?), studded with jewels or engraved with patterns.

Jem's collection of jewellery was so vast, I wondered if she'd miss half of this stuff. I let the treasure fall onto the glass counter with a clatter. At the sight of this hoard, the blonde morphed from ditzy sales girl to hawk-eyed appraiser.

'The offer is one hundred for the bracelet . . . we can offer two hundred for the diamond necklace . . .'

I didn't bother to haggle with her, as Jem might have done. I nodded and yes'ed her, until she'd counted out more than two thousand in fifty pound notes. It felt like robbery. Maybe it was robbery. I thought of Helm's wallet and glanced up at the sign that read 'CCTV in operation for your safety'. Yet, in that moment, the camera was simply recording Jemima Cootes-Mitchell pawning some of her jewellery for extra cash.

'Selling that one too?' the assessor said, pointing to the over-sized, tarnished-gold locket that hung heavy around my neck.

I clutched it instinctively. 'No . . .'

The idea of handing over a locket that contained a tiny, secret picture of mother and daughter repulsed me. Plus, this locket had become part of my Jem costume and to give it up was to melt back into myself.

I walked home with a slow, meandering gait. The money shoved in my bra chafed against my skin. It was enough cash to get on a plane and go somewhere, anywhere. I pulled at my lower lip distractedly, forgetting it would smear my lipstick. Where would I go? Who would I become?

I rounded the corner onto Jem's road and panic flashed in my brain.

Carlo stood outside the apartment block, leaning against the iron railings.

30

FANTASTIC, CATASTROPHIC

Ella

The sight of him – crumpled suit and fedora, sweat-sheened face – made me want to whimper and fall to my knees. I forced myself to keep walking, stomping the pavement with skull-soled shoes.

'Hello, hello, hello . . .' he said with a jovial leer.

A tremor prevented me from speaking, but I nodded a hello.

'Great to get your message.' He rubbed his hands together. 'Always happy to get up early for business.'

It wasn't very early – around eleven a.m. – and Carlo looked like he hadn't slept in days, but I nodded again. With shaking hands, I pulled the roll of bank notes from my bra and held it out to him. My skin crawled as his fingers brushed mine. I could see the dirt wedged deep under his fingernails as he began to count the money.

'That's only part of it, but . . . I'll figure out a way to get the rest.' I gulped down another surge of panic. 'Soon.'

His hand closed around the cash and he looked up, meeting my gaze.

'Jem, why d'you always make me hound you?' he said with a frown. 'We have a good thing going on and you fuck me around . . .'

There was a beat and then he broke into a jovial smile.

'But things always just work out for you, don't they? Un-fucking-believable.'

He mimed clocking me on the chin, his fist only brushing my skin, but I flinched as if he'd punched me. I'd put on three layers of concealer this morning to cover up the purple bruise on my jaw. He appeared not to notice my cringing reaction. His eyes were unfocused, body loose, feet bouncing against the pavement.

'Wanna get a drink?' he asked. 'Some food?'

Carlo taking a swing at me would be bad. Carlo taking me out to lunch sounded even worse.

He draped an arm over my shoulders. I tried to wriggle loose, making a show of adjusting my shoe, but he wasn't letting go of me. Oblivious to my blank expression, he chattered on about bars and restaurants we might visit.

Should I scream? Shove him and try to run? I wanted to do both, but Carlo was acting so buddy-buddy now. To do anything except play along was to risk bringing out his inner lunatic.

A gunmetal-grey sports car pulled up at the kerb. I barely glanced at it, until I heard the whirr of a car window and a greeting.

'Hello there . . .'

I didn't respond. Carlo's arm still lay heavy across my shoulders.

'What's going on?' the voice asked.

The car door opened and a man climbed out. He was older, dressed in a sleek black suit. Though silver streaked his dark hair, there was a boyish slouch to his posture. With his designer stubble and chiselled jaw, he looked like he'd stepped out of a perfume ad.

I couldn't have pictured a more perfect knight in shining armour.

'Jem?' he prompted.

My voice was still lodged in the back of my throat, but Carlo spoke up instead, spouting a ridiculous Cockney accent.

'Nuffin, guv'nor . . .'

The perfume-ad man clapped a hand on Carlo's arm.

'Well, jog on, then,' he said, with a hint of sarcasm. 'There's a lad.'

He was clearly a man used to getting rid of people, used to getting his own way.

I felt a prickle of unease. Who was this man who knew my name? Was he really my rescuer, or someone as bad as Carlo from my double's past?

Carlo and the perfume-ad guy stared each other down.

Then Carlo's eyes darted away. He dropped his arm from around me and took a step backward.

'Yeah . . .' he said, his expression cloudy. 'Gotta be going.' He took another step back. 'Catch ya later, Jems . . .'

'Catch you later,' I echoed, robotic.

I watched Carlo amble away down the road, until the handsome man nudged my arm, offering up an easy smile.

'How was your weekend?' he asked.

'. . . It was okay,' I said.

'Just okay? Darlin, every day should be fantastic or catastrophic. Anything in-between's just boring.'

He gave me another grin, showing straight white teeth. That smile. It made my stomach flop. Who *was* he?

'So,' he said, 'fantastic or catastrophic?'

'. . . Maybe a bit of both,' I said truthfully.

He laughed. 'Those are the best kind of weekends.' He put an arm around my waist. 'You can tell me all about it, princess.'

His sudden proximity, the weight of his body pressed up against me, reminded me too much of Carlo. The hairs on the back of my neck prickled.

Was he a friend of Jem's, an acquaintance – a hook-up?

A familiar sense of vertigo engulfed me. It was another one of those moments: looking down and realising you'd strayed into quicksand. Again, I felt the desire to turn and run. I forced myself to move slowly, disentangling from him and taking a step toward the apartment block.

'Not feeling too well,' I mumbled. 'I should go inside.'

'Princess . . .' he said, reaching out a hand.

Then it clicked.

Princess.

I'd seen the term of endearment among Jem's messages, but it wasn't from any of her admirers. It was from . . .

Her dad.

*

Max put the pint down in front of me and a dribble of beer spilled over the rim. On automatic, I reached forward and caught the spill with my finger, licking off the sour taste. Jem's dad leaned back in his chair and took a deep slug of his own pint, regarding me from across the scratched oak table. He was still all smiles. All white teeth and perfume-ad good looks. It made me feel lightheaded.

'You believe me, right, princess? About last month?' Max said. 'It was a massive deal. Deal of the century. I couldn't miss it.'

I nodded, mute. I didn't know what he was talking about.

The bar he'd taken me to was also a bistro and, around us, couples were cosied into booths, considering their menus. The space was dimly-lit and heated by an open fire, creating an evening atmosphere, in contrast to the bright day outside.

Eleven-thirty on a Monday morning seemed a strange time to be drinking, but I was desperate for something to occupy myself. The silence between us stretched.

'Don't freeze me out, darlin',' he said, his smile finally fading.

'I'm not.' I fidgeted with my sleeve.

Over the past few days, even through the skirmish with Carlo, I'd begun to feel almost comfortable in my double's skin. This morning, I'd spent an hour studying YouTube tutorials and perfecting my Jem make-up. As I'd worked, Katsu and I had flicked messages to each other, like kittens batting a ball of yarn back and forth. It was stupid stuff – How's your morning? How's your life? How are *you*? – but each ping of a notification made my cheeks glow. I'd even begun fantasising about the job as Creative Assistant that Leonora had promised me.

I was able to put on her clothes, put on her face, and pretend I was Jem. In the process, I'd half-forgotten that this whole situation was monumentally insane. I remained ignorant of great swathes of my double's life. Now, sitting across from Max and having no idea what to say, I wondered if lunch with strung-out psychopath Carlo would be preferable.

'Might be starting a new job soon,' I said, just to end the silence.

'A job?' Max's blue eyes bored into mine. 'Alright, hit me.'

I told him about the arts venue, the cutting-edge theatre programme, Leonora's link with its investor.

'Careful, love.' Max's expression turned hard. 'You always said you'd never work for your mum.'

'Oh, it's not working for her, it's her friend – Tom, I think.'

'Right. That's what she's telling you now. Soon enough, she'll start meddling. You mark my words.'

I chewed the inside of my cheek, not sure how to respond. Max was back in full flow, though. He leaned forward across the table, eyes sparkling with excitement.

'This deal I've been working on,' he said, 'it's gonna mean I'll be spending a lot of time in Paris. I may as well get an apartment out there. You can come and stay. Live there, even. Ditch the job and spend some time in gay Pah-ree. *Oui, oui, oui, j'suis baguette.*'

'Um . . .' I said, overwhelmed by such an extravagant offer.

Max sighed as if I'd contradicted him.

'Look, I know what you're thinking, but . . . I'm serious. You and me, princess. Taking on the world.'

I tried to imagine a scenario where my own father would casually suggest moving to Paris over drinks at 11.30 a.m. Maybe it would happen. Maybe if he began an all-out descent into madness.

'What would I do in Paris?' I asked cautiously, taking a sip of my pint.

'Anything you want!' Max said.

His smile was back and, when he smiled, he didn't look old enough to have a daughter in her twenties. By comparison, my own dad looked ancient; hang-dog and worn-out.

'I know some modelling scouts,' he said, picking up speed. 'Get your pics done. Sexy girl like you, they'd love you in Pahree. You could do some travelling, if you want. Do some damage across the continent. Much more fun than Hollywoodland. When I was your age, I found a lot of trouble to get up to in Monaco . . . but then, I shouldn't be telling you all that . . .'

Max gave a lazy wink. My stomach did another flop. The artsy job that Leonora promised was tempting – the sort of thing I'd dreamed of as a uni student – but Max's ideas represented a whole new life. The way he talked, it was like every possibility in the world could be yours. Snap your fingers, become a model. Snap your fingers, tour the world. Snap, snap, snap.

'What else have you been up to, princess?' he asked.

'Um,' I said. 'We had band practice yesterday . . .'

'Yeah? That still going on? You just say the word, we'll set you up with some studio time.'

I let out a breath. I realised I was smiling.

'Really?'

'Yeah, yeah, yeah . . .'

My mind was racing. Maybe we could go into the studio this week. Maybe this could work.

I hadn't written any songs in years – simply existing had sucked up all my energy – but since yesterday's band practice, that part of my brain had started lighting up again. When I'd woken up in that big bed this morning, creamy light filtering into the room, the first whisper of a new song had filled my head. Now it was growing stronger, more extravagant. My fingers itched to scratch out lyrics, about running so fast your heart ached, about a guy who kissed you like you were the centre of his universe.

'How soon could we do it?' I asked. 'Go into the studio?'

'Soon as you want, baby.'

With the help of the beer and Max's easy chatter, I was able to relax. Over the next hour, he regaled me with stories of being in the South of France as a young buck. He told me about the restaurants and nightclubs we could go to in Paris. He talked to me like a friend, not like a dad. He was . . . cool. So much cooler than my own dad. So much cooler than anyone I'd ever met in Cumbria.

Later, he drove me home in his grey sports car that looked like it cost more than the entire caravan park on Walney Island

'Do you want to come inside?' I asked eagerly, when we stopped outside Jem's apartment in Chelsea.

'Can't do it, got a business meeting across town,' Max said.

I nodded, swallowing down my disappointment.

'We'll see each other soon, princess.' He reached across me to open my car door. 'Promise.'

I climbed out of the car and waved as Max accelerated hard and drove away.

Inside the apartment block, I rode the lift upwards in a fog. My thoughts were full of Paris and studio sessions, intercut by the insistent melody of the half-formed song. I pushed open the door to my apartment –

All the lights were on.

Orange-scented perfume hung thick in the air.

I didn't so much walk the corridor as watched myself do it. It was someone else – not quite me – who crept over the threshold into the bedroom.

'Ugh,' Jem said, glancing in my direction only briefly.

The song that had been playing in my head all day, sweet and mellow, turned discordant. Resentment crashed through me.

It was over. It was all over.

Without any nod to modesty, my double stripped off a cornflower-blue dress and flung it on the floor. The dress was stained, its once-white pattern of tiny flowers turned brown. My stomach clenched. I recognised the dress from my own wardrobe.

'No offence,' Jem said, 'but your life is really boring.'

31

SOUR MILK

Ella

I woke up and didn't know where I was. The curtains had fallen open an inch and, outside, there was only the blue-white glow of the streetlamp. It was night time. Everything looked unfamiliar in the murky light, like a nightmare had slanted through into reality.

My heart thumped in my chest. I fumbled for my phone on the nightstand. It was dead. The black screen reflected a smeared face that didn't quite look like me.

I scrabbled at the cord of the bedside lamp until light filled the room. Familiar, after all. My room. My life. There were the grannyish brown swirls of wallpaper leftover from a previous tenant, the lopsided MDF furniture I'd got via Freecycle. My heartbeat slowed to its usual sluggish tempo. Fighting the bedclothes, I stumbled out of bed.

It was late enough that all my uni housemates were probably asleep, yet still I crept through the house. In the kitchen, I swiped a bowl from the cupboard. Last one. I used someone else's cereal and someone else's milk. I ate standing up, by the light of the fridge. I didn't close it until the cold draught turned my fingers numb.

There was a Post-It on the stove top. *Ella's turn to clean the kitchen!* I crumpled up the paper and it pulsed in my hand, hot and spiky.

As I shuffled through the house, up the stairs, I wondered if I'd find Post-Its on everything.

Ella's turn to clean the bathroom!

Ella's turn to hoover!
Ella's useless!
Ella's the worst housemate ever!
For fuck's sake, Ella, do something!

I reached the sanctuary of my bedroom, carrying the bowl containing dregs of brown milk in one hand. The other hand still formed a fist around the Post-It note. I unclenched my fingers and threw the balled-up recrimination into the bin. It bounced off the rim and fell onto the carpet. I couldn't find the energy to stoop down and pick it up.

I took a final slurp of cereal-milk and then stowed the bowl on the floor. I clambered into bed. A spider crawled across my arm, but when I went to swat it away, it had already disappeared down the crack between the bed and the wall. Bone-deep tiredness settled in my chest. I pulled sour-smelling sheets over my head and went back to sleep.

*

When I woke again, sunlight streamed through the gap in the curtains. There was a tap at my door. I ignored it, but it turned into a knock, a sigh, an 'Ella, open up'.

'Come in,' I said, levering myself up in bed.

The hinges whined as the door opened. My housemate, Cait, stood in the doorway wearing a dip-dyed green dress and a Buddha necklace.

'So, like, I thought you should know,' Cait said, 'Tom just tried to eat cereal off a dinner plate. Didn't work out so well.'

Cait's words were fuzzy. I rubbed my ears. She looked wrong, too. There was a halo of wispy-white around her mass of curly brown hair.

'Can you, like, bring your bowls downstairs?' Cait said. She crossed her arms.

'What?'

I couldn't concentrate on her words.

'They're everyone's bowls,' she said.

Cait pushed into the room. She made a show of picking up her feet as she toed through a battlefield of dirty clothes and rubbish that hadn't made it into the bin.

'I'll wash these up,' Cait said with a sigh. 'As a favour, yeah?'

Bending down, she loaded her arms full of containers encrusted with old food. I cringed. Some of them dated back a month or more. The whiff of rot was strong.

'Y'know, we might never notice if you died up here, locked away in your room.' Cait gave a smile that showed deep dimples. 'Don't work too hard. What's the point, anyway? You're a complete fucking waste of space, Ella.'

I sank down against the bed. My fingers were cold. My body was trembling. Another insect had crawled up from underneath my bed. I could feel it on my shoulder blade. I made a big gesture to try and swat it, heaving out a whisper-scream. Cait looked at me strangely.

'You're not sick, are you?'

I turned my face away, checking my shoulder blade. The spider was gone. 'No, I'm fine,' I muttered.

Cait paused at the door, still haloed in a weird light.

'Owen texted me earlier,' she said. 'He was really blowing up my phone, said he couldn't get through to you. Did you miss an exam or something?'

It took such a lot of effort to think, to form words. My voice came out as a croak.

'No, it's not till tomorrow . . .'

'Alright' – Cait shrugged – 'if you say so.'

She let my bedroom door fall closed again.

I dragged myself out of bed and flicked on the main light. I surveyed the mounds of rubbish and laundry with new eyes. When had it got this bad? I saw another ten containers, bowls and Tupperware and mugs, hiding under the bed. In the airless room, the smell of sour milk made a hit of vomit rise in my throat.

I choked back the revulsion. It was just regular student stuff.

It was normal to keep your curtains drawn all day and let dirty dishes pile up in your room. It was normal to sleep till noon. It was normal to skip a class or two. It was normal to be unprepared for your exams. People bragged about it. I'd heard them down the pub. *I haven't even started studying yet . . . I'll just pull a few all-nighters.*

All I had to do was pull a few all-nighters. I'd clean my room after final exams. I'd fix my sleep schedule, return messages and emails. Get back to who I was.

I ran a hand through my dirty hair. I just had to study. If I studied hard and passed my exams, everything would be fine.

Without bothering to change – I was still in yesterday's clothes; I'd forgotten to shower – I sat down at my desk. I opened up my textbooks, grabbed a pen and paper, and began to write. Revision notes. A solid day and night of study and I'd be able to fly through the exam.

My hand ached, but I kept on writing. I was so intent on my task that I didn't hear the knocking on my door. The hinges whined and I finally looked up.

Owen.

He was haloed in the doorway, an angel lit by a preternatural light. My heart squeezed in my chest. Full to burst. I couldn't have loved him more in that moment. Owen! My laughter, my relief, my light in the dark. My love, my love, my love.

His lip curled. His eyes grew wide.

My gaze flickered down to look the page of notes I'd written. Nonsense. Words and words and words and none of it made any sense. I flipped back a page. More and more nonsense.

Owen took a step into the room and, reflexively, I covered the pages with my arm, scared that he'd see. He wasn't looking at what I'd written, though. His eyes were scanning the dirty room. It was weeks since I'd invited him over. We always hung out at his place, since it was nicer, bigger, closer to uni.

'Ella . . .' he said. 'Why aren't you answering your phone?'

'Forgot to charge it,' I said. 'What an idiot, right? What an idiot . . .'

I summoned a laugh, hoping I would sound light-hearted. It came out more like a witch's cackle.

'Ella . . .'

He reached out a hand to me, perhaps planning to draw me into a hug. But I was too busy trying to conceal my reams of gobbledygook notes. His hand landed on my shoulder, lying there awkwardly, unmoving.

'Ella, I talked to one of your friends on the course,' he said quietly. 'She said you haven't been to class in weeks. You didn't take your final exam.'

'It's tomorrow,' I said. 'I have to study.'

I shrugged off his hand and turned back to my desk, shuffling the pages away under my textbook.

'You had an exam today. I spoke to your tutor.' Owen crouched down next to my desk chair. 'I've spent . . . I've spent the whole afternoon running around, trying to figure out what's going on.'

His eyes were boring into me.

'Look at me, Ella.'

I didn't want to. I was sure my eyes would betray me. He'd look at me and realise I wasn't the girl he'd fallen in love with. That girl had worn lipstick and smiled and danced and argued politics. The girl in front of him was someone else entirely.

Owen made a noise in the back of his throat. Hurt or frustration or anger?

'Why didn't you tell me what was going on?' he said. 'Ella, I don't get it, you could've told me there was a problem. We can fix this, but only if you talk to me. You stupid bitch, you useless waste of space, why have you been lying to me?'

(Did he say that last part or was it just in my head?)

I clapped my hands over my ears. The ocean roared inside my brain. My skin was crawling. There were dozens of spiders, all over me. Crawling into my bellybutton, down the backs of my legs, behind my ears and across my scalp.

'Leave me alone,' I moaned.

Some of the spiders crawled in through my nose and began eating my brain matter. That was what it felt like. Either way, my memory of what happened next gets fuzzy after that.

'Where's your phone?' Owen said at one point. 'Ella! Your phone!'

He was shouting at me the way my dad sometimes shouted at my nan, who'd had dementia for the last five years. Owen even mimed making a phone call with his hand. I moaned and pressed my hands over my ears.

Eventually, he found my dead phone and plugged the charger into the wall. He scrolled through the numbers at speed and then jabbed at the call button.

'Hello, Mrs Mosier? It's Owen.' (A pause.) 'Hi . . . yeah, not too bad . . . okay . . . it's just . . .' (His voice trailed off and then became resolute again.) 'There's something wrong with Ella.'

*

The process of packing up my life took less than an hour. I let them do it, Owen and my mum. They made for a weird tag team; overly polite, talking about the weather, while I sat huddled in the corner.

In the two-and-a-half years we'd been together, I'd never introduced Owen to my family. When he'd asked to visit my hometown, I'd brushed it off. 'Oh, Walney's boring, you'd hate it . . . My parents work all the time, they're busy . . . Another time, maybe, another time, definitely . . .'

Now I knew the real reason why. This was what I was afraid of. Owen's parents were well off; he'd grown up in Brighton and gone to private schools. I'd known Mum would find him posh, perhaps even strange. 'Not our kind.' My mum, in her churchy best, looked frumpy, a permanent frown on her face. Her old shoes and ill-fitting brown skirt held an echo of the sad little caravan park on Walney Island where I'd grown up. It was a place – a part of me – that I'd never wanted Owen to see.

'Will she be all right?' Owen asked.

His gaze skated over me and then returned to my mum.

'She'll be fine,' Mum said.

'I should give student welfare a call. Set up a meeting. Get some signposting.'

'That won't be necessary.'

'Don't you think she should go somewhere?' Owen chewed on his thumbnail. 'To see a doctor? Or a clinic or something?'

'She'll go home.' Mum's voice was placid, assured. 'We'll take care of her.'

'Maybe we should just give it a few more days?' Owen said. 'I mean, she has exams . . .'

'I spoke to the office at the university. She hasn't been entered for her final exams, hasn't been doing the work. She'd have to retake the whole year to graduate.'

'Shit,' Owen muttered.

He swore in front of his parents all the time. They were laid back. I'd even witnessed his thirteen-year-old sister exclaim 'Oh, for fuck's sake', to a gleeful reaction from her mum and dad. Yet my mum's face darkened. She took Owen's comment as her cue to leave.

'I think it was probably a step too far,' she said, as if speaking to herself. 'We shouldn't have let her go to a university so far away. Not with her history. She's . . . fragile. Doesn't know what's good for her.'

Owen didn't reply.

Later, Mum bundled me into the passenger seat of her battered silver Volvo. She packed the boxes and bin liners filled with my university self into the backseat. The heat of the day had baked the inside of the car into a kiln. Its windows were dingy with dust.

Cait and my other housemates were out – it was exam season: frantic hours in the exam hall, followed by heady celebrations in the pub – so at least I was spared the humiliation of them watching me go.

Owen held out a slip of paper to my mum. 'Here's my number, can you ring me when you get her home?'

She took it between thumb and forefinger, as if it were contaminated.

As we drove away, Owen stood on the pavement outside the house. He was there to wave us off, I suppose. He didn't wave, though. I craned my neck to get one last glimpse of him. His shoulders drooped, arms floppy at his sides. Through the grimy windows, it was hard to read his expression.

Maybe he looked sad, helpless, grief-stricken. Maybe he looked relieved.

32

HANDLE THIS

Ella

'You lost your job.'

David's office was dingy, like the lightbulbs needed changing. The only window showed a brick wall.

I looked down at my hands and didn't reply.

'Ella . . .'

I turned my hands over, palm side up. I looked at the lines of my knuckles, like staves on sheet music; pink, like tiny cuts opened in the skin. My hands. They looked weird. Were they my hands, or someone else's? Staves . . . music marked in lines by tiny cuts. I touched my fingers to my lips, to make sure I wasn't bleeding.

'*Ella* . . .' David said.

At last, I looked up.

'Sorry,' I said.

David, his bald head like an egg, nodded. The room smelled like floral disinfectant, as if he believed that neuroses could be eliminated from the air by one long blast of Febreze. A rotten smell lingered beneath the flowers. He made an *ahem* sound in the back of his throat, but Mum started speaking before he could.

'"Sorry" isn't a reason,' she said. 'You said you liked that job. Why would you throw it away?'

Just like that, I was five years old again: smashed bowl at my feet, unfocused anger surging in my veins; Mummy scolding me, asking me why I did it.

'I don't know,' I mumbled.

It was three days since I'd returned home from London to find my life on Walney shattered into a million pieces.

The moment I stepped off the train, dazed after the long journey, it had begun. A bearded guy I didn't know hailed me from across the street in Barrow, 'Oy oy oy!' I hastened away, hiding my face. Did he know me? Did he know my double?

Back at my green caravan, Jem's orange-scented perfume lingered in the air. Even after I changed the sheets and washed the clothes that lay crumpled on the floor, I could still smell the fruity rich scent. Each time I caught a whiff of it, nausea turned my stomach.

A letter from the hotel arrived, terminating my employment. I'd planned to conceal this from my parents for a while, but in a town where everyone knew everyone, of course they already knew. When my mum looked at me, her eyes had that dark, wary shade to them. Since my first bout of depression aged 13, Mum had looked at me like an interloper. I was the thing that had stolen away her sweet happy daughter.

'I'm just trying to understand what's going on in her head,' Mum said to David.

This was an emergency session; a council of war. The two of them were figuring out what to do about me. I shifted in my chair and it gave a squeak, but they didn't spare me a look. It was my mental health, but I was too unreliable to be involved in formulating my own recovery plan.

'It's not just the job.' Mum was wringing her hands. 'She stole money from us, she's been out drinking, she's been bragging about it . . . She didn't come home at all on Sunday night. I was driving around looking for her, I hardly slept . . .'

David was fidgeting with his notepad. His energy was always rubber-band taut. He nodded, like *yes, yes, how awful for you*. Of course the words themselves sounded deserving of sympathy. Yet, for someone paid to read between the lines, David was stunningly bad at it. Because, the truth was, when

my mum made statements like this, she didn't sound sad or upset. She sounded irritated.

'It's the . . .' Mum's voice dropped to an over-enunciated whisper, 'self-destructive behaviour that worries me.' She touched her own chin and I mirrored the gesture without meaning to.

The place on my jaw where Carlo's fist had caught me had turned a beautiful shade of greenish-purple. I'd made up an excuse – 'I fell over, hit my face on the edge of the counter' – but Mum was suspicious of anything that stank of self-harm. I actually found it offensive that her knowledge of me was so limited she thought I'd hurt myself so ostentatiously. The pricks and stabs I made at my body were always discreet.

That was what I'd learned this week:

She didn't know me at all. She hadn't noticed the fact that I'd been gone. She couldn't tell the difference between her own daughter and a terrible actress.

I looked down at my hands again. Had they always been like this? Blunt finger ends, ragged nails? A fairground fortune-teller had read my palm once. She'd said I had a strong, straight lifeline, but today it looked crooked and strange.

'Ella, what would you like to say to your mother?'

I glanced up. David's green eyes, over-large and unblinking, stared me down. I looked down again, making the tiniest of shrugs.

Mum cut in, 'She always does this, she shuts down – '

David held up his hands. 'Let's not get caught up on blame.'

I'd been to so many counsellors and therapists and doctors over the years. When I'd dropped out of uni three years ago, the psychiatrist had recommended in-patient treatment. She'd thought it might not just be depression but a personality dis- order as well – there were even some signs of psychosis. Mum hadn't liked that. If I went away to a clinic, everyone on the island would find out.

It was embarrassing enough that Smarty-Pants Ella, who

always thought she was better than the rest of us, back to Walney with nothing to show for her years of u It would be worse if everyone knew she was a basket c

There was a thud. Rubbery David had dropped his n on the floor. Now he was scrabbling around to retrieve wished it was just me and him. Sometimes I actually felt be after talking to David. He was intense and a little weird, b he listened to me.

It was my parents that paid the bill, though. I'd received a few months of counselling on the NHS and then been signed off. The woman I'd seen had apologised and told me you got six months and that was it. She'd referred me to David, who cost sixty pounds an hour. Since my parents paid, my mum wanted to make sure the sessions were useful. She bullied her way in under the guise of 'family therapy', but it was only ever me under the microscope.

What was the time? There was no clock in the room and my phone was in my bag. Was the session nearly over? My seat squeaked as I shifted in my chair again.

'Ella, I'd like to dig down into the feelings behind your actions,' David said.

Your actions.

As if I were the one who got drunk, got fired and stayed out all night. It was offensive that none of them could tell the difference between me and my double. A flush of anger swept through my body.

'It wasn't even me!'

'. . . Who was it?'

As David leaned forward, his eyes boring into me, I slumped back into my chair. My anger was short-lived; I didn't have the energy to sustain it. I remained silent.

Beside me, Mum began muttering, 'I just don't know what . . .' but David cut her off with a wave of his hand. He gave me a sympathetic smile.

'We've talked about this before,' he said. 'The black dog, the way that depression feels like a thing outside of yourself. What we need to start reconciling is how to come to terms with depression as part of yourself, but not the defining part.'

I looked at him blankly. In that moment, maybe I could have told the truth. Maybe everything would be better if I told the truth.

Listen, there's this person in London who looks just like me . . .

It sounded far-fetched. It sounded delusional.

I slipped down an inch in my chair.

The truth? I wasn't sure they'd believe me.

What was it I'd said to Katsu, days earlier? *No one is primed to say: hey, you're an imposter!* It was true for Jem, perhaps. I hadn't reckoned on the fact that everyone in my own life was primed to say: *hey, you're sick again!*

That was the thing about being wrong in the head. It ruined your credit forever.

On my best days, I felt that my mental (un)health was a tiny part of who I was. But, regardless of what David said, for everyone who knew me, it had become my defining feature. It cast a permanent shadow of suspicion across my behaviour.

Have a bad day? Depressed. Act weird at dinner? Depressed. Stay out late, get drunk, lose a job? Depressed, depressed, depressed.

'A big part of recovery is taking ownership of your actions, both good and bad,' David was saying. I wondered what textbook he was quoting. 'Let's find a positive way to move forward.' His thumb bounced against his notepad. 'You. Need. To take. Control.'

David continued his monologue, interrupted at regular intervals with unhelpful questions from my mum. I stared out the window. The view was of a brick wall, but, the way the light hit the pane, the scene inside David's office was reflected in the glass. I watched the three of us the way you'd watch a mediocre film; impassive, even bored.

Part of me was waiting to see if the character who looked like me might get up from her chair and flip over the desk.

I watched for a long time, but she never did.

*

I sat huddled on my bed, wrapped in two duvets. The orange scent of Jem's perfume was gone, but the cotton smelled faintly rotten, like everything that went through the caravan site's industrial-sized washers. Outside, the sun was setting, but I couldn't bring myself to break out of my cocoon and draw the curtains.

I'd won a victory today, but it didn't feel like it.

I hugged a makeshift hot water bottle – an old litre-bottle of Pepsi refilled with hot water and wrapped in a towel – but my fingers were still numb. Independence or warmth? I'd chosen independence.

My mum wanted me to move back into my parents' three-bedder, because I 'wasn't well' and I could 'stay safe' with her on the other side of a thin wall. The idea was excruciating: her eyes following me wherever I went; continual well-meaning questions about how I was feeling.

No. I wouldn't do it. For the rest of the off-season at least, my caravan was mine. I was staying here.

The broken heating was my punishment for refusing the offer. It was the end of November and autumn rain had given way to frozen ground and biting winds. Even Archie, my dog, had deserted me for the warmth of the family caravan.

I let my eyes drift closed and tried to ignore the cold cramping my legs. I was exhausted, but sleep had been elusive recently.

Beside me on the bed, my phone buzzed.

wyd?

I stared at the message. The name listed in my phone was Darryl. I didn't know anyone named Darryl.

Wait.

Darryl who used to burp the alphabet in history class?

A bitter laugh made its way out of my nose. Presumably I had Jem to thank for reuniting the two of us. Last I heard, Darryl worked at Jackdaw's, that crappy Italian restaurant that sold bowls of tinned spaghetti and cheap wine. Oh, God . . .

What was it that my brother had said to me the day before? Simon had thumped on my door, looking to borrow money. ('What part of "I just lost my job" don't you understand?') Traitorous Archie weaved between his legs, but neither he nor Simon reacted to my glare. I was closing the door in my brother's face when he said:

'Y'know, my mate Pete saw you at Jackdaw's. You were slobbering all over that tosser who works behind the bar. Then you and basic Beth started kicking off.' He made a yowling noise. 'Full on catfight.'

So that was why, when I'd retrieved my phone from my double, there were no new messages from Bethany. Not the usual whinging about work or play-by-plays of her thoughts on *Corrie*. Nothing. I read through Jem's exchange with Bethany, where they'd planned their night out, and it filled in some of the blanks. But what had Jem said to cause a 'catfight'?

My double hadn't bothered to tell me. As the two of us had faced each other down in her bedroom, it couldn't have been more obvious: my life had been diverting for a while, but now she was bored of me.

I should've asked Bethany what happened. I could've pleaded alcohol-induced insanity; grovelled at her feet . . .

I didn't want to.

Being around Jem's friends had reminded me what it was like to enjoy spending time with people. Seeing Bethany was a routine; a brick in the wall of the life I hated. What was the point?

I tossed my phone aside and tried to ignore the message from Darryl. 'Slobbering all over him'? That didn't mean Jem had . . .? Mortification burned up my face. It wasn't me who'd slutted it up with Darryl, but as far as everyone I knew was concerned, it was me. I could almost taste the sour tang of wine, feel a foreign tongue in my mouth.

It was fully dark now, night time erasing my view of the ruins of Piel Island. My eyes caught the clock on my phone. 16:57. There was so long till sun-up. So many hours of enduring my own thoughts. I knew what David's suggestions would be. Yoga. Meditation. Lose yourself in a favourite activity.

Nothing was appealing.

I struggled loose of my duvet cocoon and got my guitar from where it lay propped against the far wall. My fingers whispered against the strings, the music swallowed up by the cold. I wanted to write a song about running so hard my lungs burned and laughter bubbled in my veins. In London, the melodies in my head had felt loud and ecstatic. Now, played in my bedroom, they sounded meek. Just another anthem to loneliness. I set my guitar against the wall and sank back onto my bed.

My phone buzzed again.

Wanna come over you hot bitch

Revulsion crawled across my skin. Darryl had pornographic memories starring me. He'd probably told his friends we'd had sex. He'd told his co-workers, people at the gym, a stranger at the bus stop. They were all talking about it: what Ella was like in bed.

Think u can handel this?

This message came with a photo. His black pubic hair looked

like a nest of spiders. I couldn't even laugh at the misspelling, at the crude overconfidence of thinking a blurry dick pic would get me in the mood. I felt only cold and numb.

My thumb hit 'block', but I couldn't block out the sensation of disgust. I wanted to pull the covers over my head and wait for it all to go away. If I could sleep for three months, four months – if I could sleep at all – maybe that would be long enough for the whole island to stop talking about me, for my brother to stop smirking, for my mum to stop clucking and tutting.

If I'd been stronger, maybe I would've told Darryl to fuck off. I would've gone further in my argument with my mum and told her she couldn't sit in on my counselling sessions anymore. I would've apologised to Bethany and Mrs Brannan and everyone else. I would've found the words to make everything right.

But I wasn't strong.

I pulled my rotten-smelling duvets up to my chin and looked for a distraction. Habit guiding my hand, I pulled up Facebook on my phone. I'd avoided checking it since my return – opening up Facebook always felt like stepping into a room where everyone was shouting – but the lure of peering into my friends' (former friends') lives was as addictive as ever.

A red bubble indicated that I had dozens of new notifications. That was weird.

I hadn't posted anything recently. I kept it simple on Facebook. I'd post pictures of the dramatic Cumbrian landscape with captions like, *Lucky to call such a beautiful place home.* Last month, I'd added a pic of the underground swimming pool at the hotel, its mosaic tiles glittering in mood lighting. *Perks of working in the leisure industry.* That one got lots of likes. (Of course, I'd never swum in that pool. Housekeeping staff didn't get perks beyond 'do your job and you won't get fired'. I'd failed that low bar.) I thought of snapping a photo of my guitar and writing something like, *Songwriting keeps me centred*, but that seemed farcical, even by my standards.

My feed was carefully curated, but I liked the fantasy of it.

Now, as I scrolled through 'my' recent posts, a scratching sense of anxiety filled my throat. Jem had cracked the illusion wide open. Despite her promise not to, she'd filled up my wall with misspelled ramblings and crude come-ons to boys that I barely knew.

The most recent post just read, *Ella is not herself today.*

That one had attracted a stream of comments. Obviously it had. It made me sound like I was having a breakdown.

33

0

Ella

My breath was coming fast and shallow now, little bursts of white in the cold air of the caravan. At least the meeting with David had only included my mum. No matter what had happened between 'me' and Darryl, there was a possibility he would keep his mouth shut. Word might get around the island that I'd lost my job, but it wouldn't go any further. Walney Island was a bubble. My uni friends didn't need to know anything had happened.

Except now Jem had sounded a klaxon on Facebook, one that blared, *something's wrong with Ella*.

Even the concerned comments underneath the post didn't soothe me.

stay safe
hang in there
u ok?

Scrolling rapidly, I zeroed in on the comment from Cait. Bright, untroubled Cait, living it up in Beijing.

u ok?

It was an accusation. I heard her voice in my head.

You're useless. Why can't you keep it together? What's wrong now? Why are you so – ?

(Depressed, depressed, depressed.)

(Wrong, wrong, wrong.)

My heart dropped.

At the bottom of the list of comments, there was a familiar profile picture. The very last comment was from Owen.

if you ever want to talk just let me know

A big breath pushed itself out of my lungs like someone had wrapped their arms around me. The hot water bottle in my lap, which had been cooling before, was warm again.

Owen.

His face bloomed in my mind: unkempt blond hair, broad shoulders, wide mouth stretched into an irrepressible smile.

So much of everything was fake – the smiles I forced out, the version of myself I created online, the 'I'm fine's' that I served up for my parents – but my feelings for Owen were real. The realest thing I'd ever experienced.

'Owen, I need you,' I whispered aloud.

I was on a dinghy in the middle of the ocean and I'd spotted a rescue plane. Shaking, I pulled up my contacts list on my phone. I got to O and I pressed call.

*

Three years ago, I'd stood on the Barrow-in-Furness train station platform in a cornflower-blue dress, wearing red lipstick, waiting for Owen.

I bit my lip and then caught myself, relaxing my mouth into a smile. The train slowed to a stop, brakes squealing. Autumn sunlight glittered on the tracks. The doors swung open and passengers crowded onto the platform. I craned my neck to see past them, worried I'd miss him. He might not recognise me.

Then I caught sight of that familiar face, sunburned and grinning. He caught me around the waist and pulled me close. My body, numbed by months of loneliness, stirred to his touch.

I leaned up to kiss him, long and deep. My thoughts were scattered, thrumming too fast in my head. I'd moved back into my parents' three-bed static caravan after returning from uni. Were they home right now? Could we go there? Could we find a hotel room? Snatch a couple of hours for ourselves? I wanted to crawl on top of him, blot out the world with sex.

Everything could be as it was before.

'Hey, hey, hey . . .' Owen laughed, disentangling from my limpet embrace. 'Let me look at you a minute.'

He held my hands and pinned me with a searching look. I noticed the skin on his nose was peeling. The sun had bleached his hair lighter than usual. An unfamiliar tattoo peeked out from under the collar of his T-shirt.

It struck me like a physical blow. He was different.

'How are you?' he asked.

I tried to nod and smile, but it was too late. Despair rose in my throat, tears flooded my eyes. I pressed my face against his chest and began to weep.

For this much-anticipated, much-delayed visit from Owen, I'd planned a quintessential Lake District day. We'd drive to Coniston Water and then take a long hike through the fells that surrounded the lake.

It was late in the tourist season – almost November – but the weather was mild, sun banishing the grey for today at least. The grasses would be a lush green after so much rain; the lake shimmering blue as it reflected the clear skies overhead. We'd have the place to ourselves. Eden. Adam and Eve roaming paradise unfettered.

I'd even packed a picnic. Cheese and pickle sandwiches. Oranges. A couple of slices of cheesecake. It was shop-bought dessert, with a plastic-y sheen, but I'd hoped it would make him laugh.

We never made it to Coniston Water.

Instead, we sat on a wall in the train station car park. My lipstick rubbed itself off. My blue dress twisted at my waist, sitting wrong on my hips. I was too upset to think straight. When I spoke, the words tumbled out, accompanied by sobs that were growing dry and painful.

'I can't remember how to be happy,' I said, 'and I know my parents are trying to help, but everything's so much worse here.

I hate this town. I feel stuck here. And, when I'm at home, my mum just *watches* me, waiting for me to mess up . . .'

Owen wrapped an arm around me and squeezed.

'I didn't know things were so bad,' he said. 'I figured . . . you know, you're home . . . a few months and everything would be all right.'

'Being here, it's making me worse.' I shook my head, a shudder that travelled through my whole body. 'Being away from you. It's . . . it's just too hard.'

'Honey, honey.' He rubbed a hand across my back. 'You know that whatever happens, I'll always be here for you.'

I tried a smile, but my bottom lip quivered.

'I've been thinking about London,' I said. 'Our plans . . .'

'London? Shit, really? I figured you'd want to go back to Durham, finish up uni.'

'Yeah . . . I guess, yeah . . .' I said faintly.

'You should call them up, ask about resitting,' Owen said. 'There are probably special rules for people who . . . y'know . . . have mental health problems.'

My voice curled up into a ball and stuck to the back of my throat. *People who have mental health problems.* That was me.

I grunted a response.

'It'll all work out, I swear,' Owen said. His lips pinched into a smile.

He was a guy whose voice always had an easy, relaxed quality. A natural optimist. Stridently upbeat. Today I heard a false note. Lies, lies, lies, and a fake smile.

A heavy feeling of helplessness settled in the pit of my stomach. When I tried to imagine myself attending lectures, taking exams, the image sputtered into static.

'I just want to be with you.' I reached for his hand, clawing my fingers over his.

He was silent for a long moment, his hand motionless beneath mine. When he did speak, I heard the same note of false cheeriness.

'So, listen, I have some big news. While I was travelling, I got talking to some guys. They run this pretty cool charity that helps political prisoners. They think maybe they could find a job for me.'

Nervousness fluttered in my chest.

'Where?' I asked.

'Uh, Berlin.'

The thing that hurt the most was that we'd planned to go travelling together: zooming from city to city on the train; drinking cheap beer and eating mystery foods, curling up together in narrow hostel beds.

During his solo trip, he'd sent me pictures and mini-updates (guess who just ate fermented shark and is now regretting it? yep that's right this guy), but they didn't make me feel any better. While Owen's world was expanding, mine was shrinking.

'You're moving to Berlin?' I said.

'Yeah, well.' Owen shifted, angling his gaze at the horizon. 'It's a really good opportunity.'

If he was waiting for a response, I didn't have one to give. There was a slick, unpleasant taste on my tongue, like pennies.

'The other thing is . . .' He pulled his hand away from mine and used it to rub at his face. 'God, this is hard, you have to believe me, I didn't mean it to happen at all, but . . . while I was away, I met someone.'

When I still didn't reply, Owen couldn't seem to stop himself from rambling on. His leg jiggled as he filled the silence.

'You'd like her,' he said. 'Sophie. She reminds me of . . . Well, she's cool, anyway. Maybe we can all be friends someday. Sorry, is that a crazy thing to say?' His eyes flicked over my face. 'Sorry, Ella, I'm really sorry.'

I wished I had enough energy to rage at him, to take out the cheesecake and mash it in his face. But it was all I could do to stand up. Wooziness roiled through my stomach, but I forced myself to stay upright and begin the long walk home.

If only I'd gone with him to Europe, he'd never have made small talk with some guys in Berlin and found a job. He'd never have met Sophie.

I hoped, as I stumbled across the car park, that he might call after me.

He didn't.

It was my fault. For being broken and sad and fucked-up. If I were still the happy girl he'd fallen in love with, everything would be different.

*

'Hello!' Owen answered the phone.

In my caravan on Walney, I sat up straighter, as if he could see me.

'Hi,' I said in a tiny voice. 'I just wanted to talk.'

There was a long pause. I heard traffic on the other end of the call, the blast of a horn.

'Could you speak up?'

I pushed past the lump in my throat. 'Owen?'

'Yes, this is Owen. Who's that?'

'It's Ella.'

If he'd said *who?*, I think a sinkhole might have opened up beneath me.

'Oh my God, Ella!' he said instead.

To hear him say my name made me feel dizzy. How many times had I thought about calling him? Hundreds. Thousands. I half wondered if I was imagining this conversation now.

'Wow, it's been ages,' he said. 'So great to hear from you.'

'Where are you?' I asked, my voice still faint. 'Berlin?'

'Nah, not anymore,' he said.

I pulled my knees up to my chest, hugging my legs with one arm. The room had grown foggy, a pale gauze fluttering at the edge of the darkness. I couldn't seem to focus my eyes on anything. Lack of sleep was catching up to me.

'I'm in New York for a couple of months,' he was saying. 'What are you up to?'

'Oh, same,' I said.

'Same?'

'Yeah . . .' A high-pitched giggle escaped my lips. 'Fifth Avenue, Central Park, seeing all the sights. Archie and I went up the Empire State Building today.'

Owen was silent for a long moment – the sound of traffic crackled on the line – and blood rushed to my face. Idiot.

'Ella . . . I didn't catch all that,' he said. 'Who's Archie?'

'Just making a joke.' I forced another laugh. 'Archie's my dog.' I'd told him that. He should've known.

'You're still on Walney?' he asked.

I didn't want to hear the pity in his voice, but it was there, unmistakably.

'Yep, yep.'

'Ah . . . well, it's just for now, right? What are you doing for work? Making some cash so you can move on?'

Just for now . . . Owen and his kind only stayed in crappy places and worked crappy jobs as a stop gap. They spent a month waiting tables in Mexico and then wrote a blog post about it. They lived in a shack in Vietnam for the 'experience'. For them, the future was a shiny pearl and they were striving striving striving for it. How could I explain that, when I tried to imagine my own future, all I could see was static from an old TV?

'Still writing songs?' he asked. 'It's crazy that you'd call out of the blue like this. Y'know, I had that song you wrote stuck in my head last week.' He began a rendition, a theatrical warble to his voice.

My toes curled, warmth spreading to my extremities.

He remembered.

'Pretty catchy,' he said with a laugh. 'That's a great song.'

That was yours, I wanted to say. Your song. The one I wrote for you.

'. . . Thanks,' I managed breathlessly.

My burst of elation was chased by dejection. My songs might linger inside his head, but in body and soul, he wasn't mine anymore.

'How's Sophie?' I asked, gulping down a tremor.

'Sophie? She's . . . God, I don't even know. Great, probably. Sophie always lands on her feet. But we're not – together anymore.'

I couldn't stop my rapid exhalation. My mind was whirring – fast enough that I moved beyond dizziness and into giddiness; something akin to childish glee.

It was fate.

God moves in mysterious ways, my mum always said. Everything happens for a reason.

It was divine intervention.

I was *meant* to meet Jem.

Jem was meant to come to Walney Island. She was meant to impersonate me on Facebook. Because, otherwise, Owen might never have been worried enough to leave me a comment. I might never have called him. We might never have reconnected.

I sucked in a breath and a feeling of incredible lightness filled my lungs. Gauzy white still hovered at the edge of my vision, but I was floating now.

I loved him.

He loved me.

But, if it weren't for this phone call from the blue, we'd never have known that there was still a chance for us.

'Yeah . . .' Owen's voice clarified, as if he'd stepped out of the wind. 'I meant to send you an invite. Or one of those save-the-date dealios, anyway.'

'What?' I tried to say, but it came out as a whisper.

'It's next summer,' Owen said in a rush. 'Getting married.

Ol' ball and chain. Her name's Claudine. She's a lawyer.' (My mouth had dropped open, but he was still talking, with that familiar, cheerfully-ironical edge to his voice.) 'I know, I know. You'd hate her. But she keeps me sane.'

The ground rushed up to meet me.

God moves in mysterious ways . . .

Everything happens for a reason . . .

'That's why I'm in New York,' he was saying. 'I'm doing a bit of work for her company.' His voice was relaxed; I could hear his smile. 'I'd never marry someone like you, Ella, you worthless piece of shit. I'm marrying someone gorgeous and successful.'

'Congratulations,' I choked out.

'Thanks. It's pretty crazy, I have to admit. But things can change pretty quick, can't they?'

'Yeah.' My voice sounded far away. Standing outside of my body, I watched my mouth move. 'What's the work you're doing in New York?'

'Just business development stuff.'

'Oh . . . cool. What happened to the non-profit?'

The voice coming out of my mouth was flat, but Owen didn't seem to notice.

'No money in it,' he said. 'Ha ha, right? But it's true.'

He sounded different, I realised.

It was his accent, maybe, which had taken on an American edge. Or the tone, a little more harried than he used to sound when we were students. But there was something else, too. I couldn't picture him speaking. It was like there was someone else on the end of the line. A different Owen.

The traffic noise on the phone was back. I heard the whoosh of motion. He was walking again.

'Hey, I have to get going,' he said. 'Dinner plans.'

'Anywhere nice?'

The question came out automatically, my voice bland. I wondered if he'd respond by asking about the weather on Walney.

'Not sure yet.'

'Well, just stay away from the cheesecake . . .'

'Tell me about it.' He made a little *ugh* sound in the back of his throat. 'I'm sugar-free right now, training for an Iron Man.' His laugh was easy, unconcerned. 'Stupid idea.'

It was a strike to my stomach and I felt it as a physical blow. I wasn't far away anymore. I was right back in my body, in the prison of my mind.

Owen had no idea.

He didn't remember the anniversary cheesecake made with salt not sugar.

It was like the memory had wiped itself away. Part of me had gone, too. What did he conjure up when he remembered me now? I was just a few snatches of song lyrics, a girl in a cornflower-blue dress at the edge of his peripheral vision. Those memories would fade, too, once he was married to someone else, once New York turned his accent into something different.

I'd fade away to nothing.

'It was so great to hear from you,' he said. 'Keep in touch, yeah?'

'Yeah,' I said. 'Of course.'

We both knew it was the last time we'd ever speak.

34

THE MEANING OF LIFE

Jem

'Oh ho ho!' Elgin said. 'Good news!'

I looked up from my phone when he entered the back office, but didn't bother to hide the fact that I'd been slacking. 'Yeah?'

'Another three followers!'

'Cool.' My tone was bored. I ran my tongue over my teeth and returned my attention to my phone.

'That's four hundred and eighty-six now!' he said, clapping his hands together.

It was embarrassing how pleased he was, like I was his social media monkey and I'd learned to balance a ball on my nose.

'Awesome,' I said, again without enthusiasm.

Elgin was hovering by my desk now. I knew this because the grassy smell of patchouli was making my nose twitch. I dragged a thumb up my phone and said, 'Just putting together the guest list for the big opening.'

'Ahh! Wonderful!'

His voice made it sound like it was the best news he'd received all year, yet still he remained standing at my shoulder, his considerable girth casting a shadow over me.

Elgin (no last name, like Cher) was the creative director of ZANG, a brand-new contemporary arts centre, with a gallery, café and performance space. I was his underling, although he told me often that if I worked hard and 'learned to attract positive energy', I could be doing his job in ten years.

It sounded more like a threat than an incentive.

'Just a little dicky-bird, Lady J . . .' He lowered his head and nudged his big body into my personal space. 'I had a complaint from the artist about how you described Lambeth Lament Number Three.'

'What?'

Elgin pushed his granny glasses up his nose and ran a hand through his baby-chick-blond hair. I'd spent the first week of my job convinced it was a wig and even orchestrated a plan to 'accidentally' knock it off. Disappointingly, it had stayed put.

'You captioned it, "Come and see some rubble at ZANG",' Elgin said.

I let out a bark of laughter. Yeah, that was a good one. The artwork in question was a single brick spray-painted blue. I'd 'grammed it as part of a marketing push for the artist's collection of 'poignant reminiscences of growing up in the shadow of consumerism'.

Elgin's face, usually pasted with a smile, was uncharacteristically solemn.

'It's funny,' I said, my own smile fading. 'That's why it got so many likes.'

He made a harrumphing sound, his brow furrowed. I stared him down, my hand tightening into a fist around my phone. I was hoping he'd start screaming at me. At least that would break up the day's monotony.

I could even snap a pic for Instagram. Come and see the Incredible Passive-Aggressive Elgin at ZANG! Be wowed by his snooker-player waistcoats and stench of cologne!

Instead, Elgin turned the harrumph into a throaty fake laugh. The permasmile was back.

'Love the energy, Lady J,' he said, giving my shoulder a squeeze. 'Love the drive for social media engagement. The, ah, execution needs some finessing.'

What followed was a long boring lecture on branding and social media strategy. Honestly, what a waste to fill your head with stuff like that. I imagined Elgin on his deathbed, his shock of blond hair sticking upwards, murmuring, 'What's the follower count? How many is it now?'

I nodded and 'uh huh'ed until Elgin went away, bustling through to the ZANG café to examine the cakes for uniformity. In the empty office – Spartan and grey in comparison to the luxe interior design of the rest of the building – I spun around in my wheel-y desk chair until I felt sick. I was desperate to feel anything except bored.

I could quit this job. I could quit it today . . .

But then Mother would cut me off. I'd grown used to having money again. It still wasn't enough money, but at least I had my car back and my credit cards were working again.

For a while, I'd even enjoyed playing at the worker bee role. After I'd binned the play and my agent had binned me, it was a relief to have something to do each day. I wore tight little suit skirts and fitted blazers, clicking around the corridors of ZANG in stiletto heels. In response to all the selfies I'd posted of this Brand New Jem, Imogen was ecstatic (business was her god and she was evangelical about bringing people to His light). April was sceptical. She said it didn't seem like 'me', a comment which needled me more than I cared to admit.

To be honest, I hadn't felt right since I'd got back from Arse-End Island three weeks before.

I'd arrived home to find half my stuff gone. On her way out, Twinnie had burbled something about selling my clothes and jewellery to pay off Carlo. Crazy thundercunt. That wasn't how things worked with Carlo. He was still messaging me all the time, telling me I owed him. You could give Carlo a kidney and he'd show up a week later demanding the other one, too.

It wasn't just my missing stuff that was the problem. It was like the atoms of my life had been rearranged in my absence. Science wasn't my strong point, but . . . the air felt different. It did. Ella had created a new life for me in my absence – she'd got me a job, she'd patched things up with Mother – and it made me feel itchy in my own skin.

Why had everyone thought that little automaton was actually me? My friends, my family, hadn't even bloody noticed the difference. And then there was Katsu.

I grabbed my phone and fired off a message to him. U busy?

Staring at the screen, I waited for the bloop-bloop-bloop that indicated he was typing. There was nothing, just my own words staring back at me, the newest message stacked beneath ten others he hadn't replied to.

Was the bastard ghosting me? He wasn't allowed to ignore me! He was supposed to be there for me, in sickness and in health, through times of incredible boredom.

Ugh. I levered myself up out of the desk chair and wandered through ZANG in search of entertainment.

We might have 486 followers on Instagram, but we didn't actually have any visitors. The café, with its stark white walls professionally graffiti'ed with sayings like 'creativity takes courage' and 'the world is but a canvas', was empty. Even the solitary barista seemed to have gone on a smoke break.

I peered at the cakes under glass. Elgin had evidently done his quality assurance testing and gone back to his office. I slipped behind the counter. The barista had left the till logged in. I tapped a few numbers idly and it popped open.

A little purr of excitement quickened my heart. I glanced around the empty café.

I hesitated for a split second.

Then I grabbed a wad of twenties and shoved them in my bra.

I bumped the till with my hip and it dinged closed. I sang under my breath as I sauntered away. It was an Aretha Franklin song that Ricky had insisted we play at last weekend's band practice. Usually, having it stuck it my head would've annoyed me, but today it buoyed my mood.

The band! A couple more weeks of practice and we'd be ready for our big debut. My dear dad – who'd popped up after six months in Shenzhen on 'business' that was definitely crooked and possibly make-believe – had pulled some strings and got us a slot at a club in Shoreditch. This job would be irrelevant soon. Jemima Cootes-Mitchell was meant for more than social-media-wrangling. She was meant for stardom.

I readjusted my boobs inside my bra. All this cash to burn. Finally my life was looking up.

*

Stee had a dealer in Mile End and, ever since Carlo had gone cuckoo, I'd been buying through him. Mistake. I think Mile End's Premier Gangster took Stee for a total fucking idiot and offloaded on him anything that wasn't selling.

I wanted coke. Stee turned up at my apartment that evening with ketamine. Talk about a slap in the face. Too bad there wasn't a returns policy on drugs.

'It's cool,' Stee said, fingering the crumbly white powder through its plastic bag. 'Lets you have a near-death experience, see the meaning of life and stuff.'

I rolled my eyes. Life was about having a good time. I'd already got that one cracked.

We did the ketamine anyway – what the hell else was there to do? – and either it was a bad batch, or it was exactly the same as it always was, because we ended up starfished on my living room floor.

'Hey Stee, you'll never guess where I went last month . . .' I said, flopping over onto my stomach. As I did so, the floor gave way. I began sinking through the wood, which had turned to jelly.

'The belly of a whale!' he yelled out. His teeth were chattering, but he was sheened with sweat.

'No, Walney Island!'

'I went to the Island of Flobberyjobbit once, think I was stoned, though . . .'

'You don't get it . . .' I said.

I wanted to continue, but my face had come loose and was floating in front of me. I had to work hard to even swallow without choking on my tongue.

We lapsed into silence and I let my body sink while my face floated upwards. Soon I'd lost sight of Stee completely.

When I'd been on Walney Island, I'd imagined I'd get a lot of mileage out of my stories of pretending to be Twinnie. Since I'd got back, I hadn't shared them with anyone. At first I'd thought I was just waiting for the right moment. Then days had turned into weeks and still I hadn't told anyone about the switch.

I wasn't used to feeling embarrassed, but it was mortifying that Ella had been able to become me so perfectly. She'd slipped into her role and become a better version of me; one that my mother liked more. It was humiliating, too, to think of what had gone down on Walney.

I wanted to pretend none of it ever happened.

No matter how much I tried to forget it, though, I kept getting flashbacks to the worst moments. Even as the ket wrapped its tentacles around me, dragging my limbs in different directions, my thoughts lodged on Walney.

'I'm looking for Darryl,' I'd said, wavering on the spot.

After leaving the crappy Italian restaurant and the back-woods barman, it had taken me almost an hour to find this street. The world was dark, poorly-spaced streetlamps creating a muddy yellow glow that barely lit anything. I was finding it difficult to focus on the house number, but I thought this was the right place.

'No. Shit. Not Darryl,' I said. That was the barman. I unclenched my frozen fingers and squinted at the napkin in my hand. 'Dan.'

The Walney woman in the doorway gawped at me. The pink bobble holding back her scraggly blonde hair made me guess she was young – younger than me, perhaps – but her eyes had the sunken look of someone much older. She didn't reply.

The wind was making my teeth chatter. It hadn't occurred to me to put on a coat.

'He here?' I asked.

She toyed with her hair bobble, and then yelled over her shoulder.

'Danny! Dannyyy!'

There was the sound of footsteps from up above. Nodding, she turned and drifted back into the house, leaving the front door wide open.

An invitation?

Any trepidation I felt was outweighed by a desire to score. I strode inside, letting the door slam shut behind me. What was the worst that could happen? They'd chop me up and feed me to their –

A dirty-white boxer with a mashed-in face growled at me.

I bared my teeth and growled back at him. He whined and then slumped to the floor, taking the opportunity to lick his arsehole.

In the air, I caught notes of fried food and muddy carpets and a big dollop of shit. A kid in a sagging nappy toddled toward me. If it were possible for a child to glare, that one gave me the stink-eye.

The woman picked up the baby and, thumping it against her chest, she slumped onto the torn leather sofa. I didn't really want to sit down – and she didn't invite me to do so – but my legs were numb from the cold and weak from the booze, so I folded myself into the seat next to her. The house reverberated, as someone – Danny, I guessed – came galumphing down the stairs.

Danny entered the room and the boxer rushed to meet him, harmless as a puppy now. The man had the same smashed nose as his dog, matched by a furrowed brow and a buzz cut. I smoothed out the blue dress of Ella's that I wore and summoned a smile, feeling bizarrely like a door-to-door sales-woman. Hello, would you like to buy some pots and pans? Maybe a glittery pink dildo?

'Darryl gave me your name,' I said, and it came out as Poplar Park Debate Team Champion 2008. I tried to remember how to speak Cumbrian as I added, 'Said you could hook me up.'

'Right.' His voice was low, reminiscent of a whisper-shout, as if he were permanently poised for an altercation. 'What d'you want?'

Now it was him who was the door-to-door salesman, show-ing me his wares. Instead of a leather bag of quality goods, he had a Sports Direct carrier bag that smelled like feet and contained a range of pills. Lots of pills. No coke.

I wanted to scream, but there was no point, because the toddler was already bellowing at the top of its lungs. The boxer scrabbled at my feet, chasing its tail.

I pawed through the bag's contents, hoping to find something better concealed at the bottom. Then, giving up, I shook some OxyContin and Dexedrine into my palm, added some Codeine for luck, and dry-swallowed the pills. Danny stared at me, his frown deepening. I fumbled in my bra and withdrew a couple of twenty-pound notes.

'Here,' I said, waving them in his face.

He grunted what might have been thanks and stowed the money in his back pocket.

'You want a cup of tea?' the woman asked.

Now that she'd established I hadn't come to steal her boy-friend, the famous Cumbrian hospitality had kicked in.

I shrugged, sinking back into the sofa. I figured the pills would give me an amphetamine streak of wakefulness that might last long enough for me to get the hell out of this situation. All they did was make me wide-awake and too numb to move.

Danny and I ended up playing *Call of Duty* for hours. The

dog took a shine to me and passed the time trying to hump my leg. The woman made me tea and toast. The baby screamed. My neurons were firing at 7,000 miles an hour and I forgot how to form words.

I woke up on the sofa the next day with a scratchy blanket draped over me. *Call of Duty* was paused on the TV screen. It emitted a faint buzzing that sounded like my brain short-circuiting.

I swiped a cup from where it was balanced precariously on the arm of the sofa and swigged cold tea. I kicked out a leg and heard a whine. The boxer had curled up on top of me.

He'd also pissed all over my legs.

Or . . . wait, that might have been me. I remembered being desperate for the loo and then, later, feeling immense relief.

The piss was cold and pungent, soaking the bottom of Ella's blue dress a deep shade of yellow-brown. I tried to stand and my thighs slithered together.

My legs wouldn't hold me up and I crumpled to the floor.

'Y'alright?' a voice asked.

It was the scraggly-haired blonde woman. She was wearing a pink dressing gown.

You put yourself in these situations, Jem. Carlo's words rattled around in my head. *You do it to yourself.*

'I'm fine,' I muttered, despite evidence to the contrary.

I couldn't stand up, so I crawled across the carpet towards the door.

'You've had an accident, love,' the woman said.

'I haven't.' I clenched my teeth together. Even after the tea, my mouth was still dry. 'It was your dog.'

'Don't be embarrassed . . .'

Crawling required too much effort, so I sagged back on my haunches, exhausted. I squinted up at the woman. She didn't look pissed off. She looked . . .

'You can borrow a pair of joggers if you want,' she said.

The look in her shit-brown eyes . . .

She pitied me.

Humiliation started at my scalp and raged all the way down my body, burning up my face and making my fingers tingle.

This scum-of-the-earth girl, downtrodden wifey to a small-time drug dealer, and she pitied me.

I had no choice but to accept her help. I was so fucked-up on drugs, it took me an hour and three slices of toast before I could even stand unaided. The woman tended to me like I was her child, but she never quite lost that expression of pity.

She looked down on me. And she had every right to.

Stop.

I didn't want to think about it. I didn't want to remember.

The ketamine was wearing off and the floating feeling was almost gone. My body wasn't melting anymore. It felt heavy and weird, like it didn't quite belong to me.

'Let's do another hit,' Stee said. His eyes were shiny, silver and round. Maybe the ket hadn't worn off completely.

'Yeah . . .' I said, though I didn't really want to.

When had Jemima ever turned down a drug, turned down a date, turned down a new experience? She was a non-stop party. If she started saying no, she'd be nothing at all.

I snorted a lot of the white powder, just to prove I wasn't a pussy, just to stop my mind from dwelling on bad memories. My nostrils were burning and the chemical taste made me gag.

The walls of my apartment were gone. The floor was gone. It was just me and Stee, lying on a blanket of darkness. Then Stee was gone, too.

I was floating towards a bright white light. It was so warm, so welcoming.

The realisation came to me with a jolt of euphoria:

I was dead.

I saw my funeral, the casket being lowered into rain-slick mud. Mummy's mascara ran down her cheeks in black rivulets.

The scent of jasmine filled the air.

Dying felt so, so good.

It was the ultimate rush.

I could do anything. I could become anyone. I was God himself.

35

A WALL OF FACES

Ella

'Come on, I'll sign you up, it'll be fun,' Bethany said.

It was August and her pregnant belly was a small swell under her clingy white camisole. She kept patting it distractedly, the way you'd pet a dog.

'It seems kinda lame . . .' I said, but my tone was mild. Secretly, I was intrigued.

The two of us, plus child (hers) and dog (mine), were out on the sands, taking a ramble to the ruins of Piel Island. I squinted against the hot sun, which was baking the ground dry under my bare feet. The air smelled salty and clean. Oystercatchers filled the quiet with their *peep-peep PEEP-PEEP*s.

''Course it's not lame!' Bethany said. 'It's a phenomenon, they're obsessed with it in London.'

I shot her a fond smile. A sure-fire way to impress Bethany was for a fad to be big in London – or anywhere she deemed 'cosmopolitan'.

Before I could reply, Talia bounded up to us, pushing a lock of chestnut hair out of her sun-flushed face. 'Mummy, Mummy!'

She was supposed to be collecting shells for a necklace, but she carried in her hands a sea-battered bleach bottle. Bethany tutted and tossed it away, diverting her attention towards a fragment of green glass. Its edges had been softened by the tide. 'Look, an emerald!' Bethany said.

Talia toddled off to look for more gemstones and Archie ran behind her, yapping.

'Don't go too far!' Bethany called.

The day was idyllic, the expanse of golden-brown sands giving the illusion you could walk all the way to the mainland, but there were still patches of sinking sand that could trap you.

'It'll take five minutes to set you up with a profile.' Bethany was watching Talia, but talking to me.

I swung my arms and let my gait turn loose and meandering. It was such a nice day, I couldn't bring myself to be annoyed by her terrier-like insistence. Sometimes I needed my best friend to bring me out of myself, force me to do things I'd usually avoid.

'Sure, okay,' I said. 'What's it called again?'

'MeetYourDouble.'

*

Rain was drumming on the roof of my caravan. It had been raining nonstop for all fifteen days of December. Through the windows, I could see Bethany out there, without a hat or umbrella. She pounded on the door for a third time and then settled back on her heels. One hand went to her back to support the huge weight of her pregnant belly, the other wiped the rain from her eyes.

'I know you're in there, Ella!'

Her face appeared in the window, blurred by the rainslick glass, but I stepped to the side, concealed from sight by the sliding bathroom door. Inside the caravan, it was gloomy. I'd stopped turning my lights on and started locking the door. People thought I wasn't home, gave up and went away.

It was such an effective strategy that I was beginning to wonder if I really was fading away. One day I wouldn't need to hide. You'd be able to see right through me.

The ebb of relief at avoiding another visitor turned to self-loathing, slick and yellow in my stomach. It was three weeks since I'd spoken to Bethany. She must be ready to give birth any day now. She was probably in pain. She must be frantic and hopeful and bursting with things to tell me.

I made a pact with myself. If she knocked for a fourth time, I'd let her in.

The knock didn't come.

Instead, I heard the shuffle of gravel outside, followed by the roar of a car engine. She was gone.

I sagged against the bathroom doorframe. What kind of person was I? To pretend I wasn't home? To leave my pregnant friend standing outside in the rain?

Cowardly. Worthless.

I crept to the window to check she really had left. The gravel parking area was empty. In the distance, the crags of Piel Island castle looked murky in the rainy mist. The tide was coming in, creeping up the over the sands. Today could be the day it didn't stop, it kept coming, the sea rushing through my caravan, washing it all away.

On my bed, I returned to huddling beneath duvets that were scented like rotting fruit. When I swiped a thumb across my phone, waking it up, a wall of faces greeted me. I scrolled, scrutinising each one.

The nose on this one was wrong.

On that one, the lips were too full. The forehead was too high.

The faster I scrolled, the more the photos blended together. They were a blur of Ellas, none of them quite right.

MeetYourDouble invited me to vote on which image was the closest match. I tapped big red X's across a dozen near-misses and then, when I reached the final face, the Chelsea socialite with the mischievous grin, I stabbed a reluctant tick.

Why was Jem the perfect match? Why her? The app was mocking me.

I switched to Facebook with a sigh.

Christmas had crept up on me. Tinsel and twinkly lights festooned the photos on my feed. My Facebook friends had hung stockings on their mantels, tasteful red-and-white ones for their partners, fuzzy Disney-themed ones if they had kids.

Even if I had a mantelpiece, who would I hang a stocking for? Me, myself and I?

My thumbs hovered over the Status Update box, but I couldn't think what to type. The top post on my own profile was still the one that read, *Ella is not herself today.* I hadn't bothered to delete it. What was the point? People had stopped commenting on it. I'd received no more concerned messages.

It was also perhaps the truest thing posted on my Facebook in years.

I clicked away from the Status Update box and began my usual stalkerish rounds of other people's profiles, checking I hadn't missed an update. My heart ached to see that Owen had added a photo. He had his arm around a rosy-cheeked girl with auburn hair peeking out from under a green woollen hat. They appeared to be at an outdoor ice rink. *A bit bloody cold!!* was the caption, but they were both smiling.

There was nothing new on Jem's profile, although I still felt a prick of jealousy at the entry she'd added two weeks before, under Employer. *Creative Assistant – ZANG.* A quick Google search had confirmed it to be an arts venue. This was the job Leonora had offered and I'd agreed to. My job.

Katsu's page was mostly memes, lefty political stuff or incomprehensible Internet in-jokes. These were interspersed with the occasional blurred shot of waving arms at a gig or a sunrise over the Thames. I drank in these glimpses of his life.

Today, there was something different. I didn't spot it immediately, but hiding there, in the comments of a concert photo, was a bomb.

Andrew Miller: got my tix for isle of wight festival. you and jem up for it?

Katsu Quinlan: Lemme check how broke I am and get back to you. Me and Jem are doing different things now, tho.

Doing different things? What did that mean?

It was code for 'break-up'. It had to be.

My heart was beating faster. I felt almost warm, despite the cold caravan.

Was it possible that our weekend together had meant something to him, too? In the month that had passed, I'd almost convinced myself it was nothing. Our conversations had been friendly, not flirtatious. (He'd never like someone like you, Ella.) He'd been entertaining himself while Jem was away. (You'll never match up to her, Ella.)

Now I felt a flicker of something like hope.

Should I send him a message? Just something casual? I chewed on my bitten fingernails, drawing blood. No. That was too obvious.

He wouldn't want to hear from me . . . It was my double he'd really wanted . . .

The arrival of a new email snagged on my peripheral vision. Probably just a promotion for a Christmas sale. I pulled up my email screen anyway. The name of the sender leered at me. Jem.

I sat up straight. The subject line contained four exclamation marks. Not the standard one. Not an excitable two or three. Four.

Subject: *Come along to my band's first show!!!!*

In my mind, each of those exclamation marks came with a sound effect – *chk!* They kept sounding in my head, in quick succession: *chk, chk, chk, chk!*

Hours after I'd opened the email, I could still hear them. They taunted me, but they gave me energy, too. I had drive for the first time in a month. The exclamation-mark sound effects turned to a drum beat.

Lon. Don. Lon. Don. Lon. Don.

I wanted to go.

I needed to go.

Shoved under my bed, I found the silver dress and heels I'd worn to the Seven Deadly Sins party. There were splashes of blue liquor down the front. It was also dingy with dust and, like everything in this caravan, smelled of mould.

In my tiny kitchen sink, I dipped silver fabric into hot, soapy water. It took me an hour to scrub the dress clean. As I worked, I heard the drumbeat in my mind.

Lon. Don. Lon. Don. Lon. Don.

My hands were wrinkled and red by the time I finished. I didn't care.

I flung out the dress, water droplets exploding against the tight walls of the caravan. I held up the damp garment against my body and examined the effect in the mirror. It looked good as new. My eyes, reflected in the glass, were bright. My smile was different.

I looked good as new.

36

PAST TENSE

Jem

It was Imogen who alerted me to what Katsu had written on Facebook. I didn't obsess over Facebook the way pathetic people did, so I'd probably never have noticed it on my own.

'Doing different things'? What the fuck was that supposed to mean?

Katz didn't reply to any of my colourful messages requesting clarification. In fact, he'd hardly texted me at all in the last month. He and I weren't the clingy types, texting back and forth all the time, but after I got back from Cumbria, his replies had grown shorter, vaguer. The last thing I'd received from him was a mealy-mouthed excuse about being 'really really stupid busy' with his dissertation.

Catch up soon, he'd written. I knew what that meant.

'You're dumping me?'

I leaned in to his personal space and pinched the flesh at his inner elbow. He flinched.

'Can we talk about this later?' he said in a low voice.

'No, we can fucking well talk about it now!'

A few feet away, Anthony looked up from tuning his bass guitar. When he met my gaze, he looked away again quickly and cleared his throat. Molly, who'd appeared in the doorway, both arms full of bottles of beer from the fridge, turned around and left the room, mumbling, 'Forgot the bottle opener . . .'

Of everyone at today's band practice, only Ricky seemed morbidly interested in what was going on with me and Katsu. He raised his eyebrows and let one of his drumsticks spin on the palm of his hand.

I'd used up the last of my coke this morning and now, mid-afternoon, all I felt was tired and sweaty. I didn't like the way Ricky was looking at me. There was a lump in my throat. I tried to swallow it away, but my mouth was too dry.

'Can we talk about it later?' Katz said again, his lips barely moving.

'Fine, whatever,' I muttered.

This was more embarrassing for him than it was for me. I'd be a humanitarian and spare him the public humiliation.

It was the week before Christmas and Katsu's rundown house share looked like it had been decorated by asylum inmates. Flashing red and green lights in the shape of stars were draped over the curtain poles. A half-bald Christmas tree leaned theatrically to the left, while a huge Santa statue in the middle of the living room bent over, showing us his crack.

The band had agreed we needed to practise nonstop to be ready for our show just after New Year's. I'd even cancelled my usual Christmas skiing trip with Imogen. I was sacrificing for my craft.

This practice session was also the only time and place I knew for certain I could pin down Katz. In the last few weeks, he'd become a master at arriving late for practice and edging out the door early with an excuse (even though it was his bloody house that hosted the band!). He never met my gaze, always mumbled excuses about why he hadn't been in touch. Today I wasn't going to let him get away with any of that bullshit. I kept my eyes trained on him for the entire three hours.

As we practised our set – a mixture of covers and originals – I thought we sounded amazing. Anthony was getting huffy and perfectionistic, though, complaining that I wasn't hitting the high notes. 'How about I knee you in the balls and hear you hit the high notes?' I said. That shut him up.

We were also supposed to be writing new material. I'd

scrawled song lyrics on my arm in eyeliner. It was something I'd thought of in the car on the way over. *Go, go, go, fast as an engine, go, go, go*. That sounded like a banger, right?

The idea was to fit lyrics together with the melodies Anthony was working on. He was a total prima donna about it, never satisfied, always moving bits around, like he was creating art. Ugh, please.

By the end of practice, I'd developed a raging headache. No matter how much beer I chugged, I couldn't get rid of my dry mouth. I shot off a text to Stee's dealer in Mile End, but he couldn't meet me till eight. What a fucking day.

'Let's go to Marco's,' I said to Katz, as he unplugged his guitar.

He shook his head. 'I need to swing by the lab. The Wall and Grace is on the way, let's go there.'

Three months ago, he'd have rolled his eyes, but given me a lovely smile and let me drag him halfway across London to my favourite coffee house in Chelsea. Today his voice was flat. He wasn't smiling.

*

The Wall and Grace, an indie café two streets over from Katsu's house, was the scene of a hundred Sunday mornings: me, hiding behind sunglasses and sipping dark roast; Katsu, laughing as he taunted me with crispy bacon. Today, we sat at our usual table, with its blue-and-green mosaicked surface, a single white calla lily bloom wilting in a vase, but the mood was sober.

'So you're binning me,' I said, scraping my chair against the floor.

'It's not like that.' A crease appeared between his eyebrows. His long fingers wrapped around his coffee cup, but he only sloshed the liquid around, without drinking. 'I've just . . . been thinking.'

I glowered. 'Don't strain yourself.'

The coffee machine behind the counter whistled and billowed steam. At the table next to ours, a baby started screaming – cue: flashback to Walney – and, in the commotion, Katsu's mumbled response was lost.

'What?' I said.

'It's not working anymore,' Katsu said, louder this time. 'The two of us, we're like . . . I don't know . . . a train coming to the end of the tracks.'

'Very philosophical,' I said with a snort. 'What, have you joined a cult?'

I busied my hands, pouring three sachets of sugar into my coffee.

'No . . . I ran into a guy,' he said.

'Wait, you're gay now?'

'His name's Lukasz.' Katsu grimaced. 'Sound familiar? We got chatting at a party. When I mentioned you were my girlfriend, that's when shit got interesting.'

Lukasz. At that moment in time, I couldn't even remember what he looked like, only that he chain-smoked and had a sexy accent, Polish edging into Scottish. He was an actor. We'd met at an improv workshop. We'd only had sex a couple of times.

Now Katsu was looking at me with sad, hooded eyes.

Was I supposed to feel bad? Katz knew he was my man. There was never anyone like him. Those other guys, they were just . . . entertainment.

'Like you've never been tempted,' I said.

I gulped down half a mug of my too-hot coffee, ignoring the burn, ignoring the sense that I might feel guilty after all.

Something flickered in his eyes and he looked away.

'Tempted is different,' he said.

'So go fuck someone else!' I pushed my coffee cup away and spread my hands wide, my voice rising. 'You have my permission. We'll have a threesome, go to a goddamn orgy.'

Out of the corner of my eye, I caught a horrified look from the woman at the next table.

For the first time that afternoon, Katz smiled, an ironical twist to his mouth. 'Now that is tempting,' he said.

The woman beside us bundled her baby, who was still hiccoughing grisly cries, into his pram and began packing up her many bags. I watched her blankly.

'. . . I fucked up,' I said, my voice settling into a sigh. 'What do you want? Me to grovel?'

'. . . I just . . . don't think I can be with someone who never even thinks about me.'

'What does that mean?!'

Katsu flinched at the volume of my voice. Angry again, I was doing a good job of clearing the café. The woman and baby had gone. A pair of older gents were also hurrying out the door.

'Why didn't you tell me you were going to Cumbria?' he asked.

That one took me by surprise. I shrugged, my eyes bugging out.

'You went off on some crazy adventure to steal a poor girl's identity and you never even clued me in,' he said.

'It was a spur of the moment thing.' I shifted in my seat. 'Last-minute getaway.'

Katsu exhaled hard through his nose. 'Just like when you moved to LA and you waited till the week before to tell me. You'd booked your flights, arranged a going-away party, told all your friends, but I was the last to know.'

We were dredging up ancient history now?

'That was three years ago!' I said.

He moved his head in acknowledgement, a flush creeping up his face.

I hadn't known how to tell him. I hadn't wanted to hurt him. I'd aimed to avoid a situation like this one: me, guilty and lashing out; him, sad-eyed and disapproving. In truth, he was right: I just didn't think about him very much. He was part of the furniture. I could set him down for a while and pick him back up again when I liked. That was how it had always been with us.

'I'm sorry, okay?' I jutted out my lower lip. 'I'll try to be less of a colossal fuckup from now on. What else do you want from me?'

He was quiet for a long time. He took measured swallows of his coffee, drinking until it was done, and then wiped his mouth with the back of his hand.

'This isn't even really about you,' he said at last. 'I think I need to be by myself for a while.'

'Oh, okay, Greta Garbo. *I vaaaant to be alone.*'

That raised a faint smile from Katsu, but it didn't reach his eyes.

'We're not good for each other,' he said.

I released a puff of air from my cheeks. 'You'll never meet anyone like me,' I said.

I wanted him to laugh, but he just looked tired.

'True, very true,' he murmured.

He was quiet a moment longer, and then he asked:

'You remember our first date?'

'Broadstairs,' I said, without hesitation. Overcast skies. Fish-and-chips on the beach. Katsu's face all scrunched up with worry for me.

His eyebrows lifted. 'What? No, that party. We were seventeen. End of the summer, no parents.' He rubbed his chin. 'First time I ever took E. You said I'd get to be someone different.'

I tried to remember that night, but it was fuzzy. Where had the party been? Imogen's house? Her mum had gone through a gothic-glamour phase and fixed wrought iron lamp holders to every wall. Hideous. The memory flickered like firelight in my mind.

Katz had been so uptight in those days. He was in my year at school, but we ran in very different circles. He was the perfect little Asian kid getting straight A's. I knew he'd be cute if he loosened up. It was a lark. Wind him up and watch him go.

But . . . our first date? No. When my cool fingers pressed the little white pill into his sweaty palm, I probably couldn't have told you his name.

'Did you?' I asked. 'Get to be someone different?'

'I guess so . . . I was a terrified little kid and you showed me what it was like to be reckless, to be brave.'

The way he was talking in past tense made me ache.

'Oh, shut up,' I said.

Katsu leaned back in his chair, stretching out his legs. His ankle brushed mine, and if we were still us, I would've rubbed my leg against his like a kitten with a scratching post and fixed him with come-to-bed eyes. We weren't us anymore, though. We were something else.

'You'll be back.' I meant it to sound jovial, but my voice came out stern. 'Can't resist me.'

'Maybe.'

His half-smile was wistful. I caught in his expression an echo of that day in Broadstairs, when he travelled 80 miles just to sit on a beach with a miserable, fucked-up girl.

What else was there to talk about?

Nothing.

We sat in silence while I drank the last of my cooling coffee. There was no pleasant jolt that accompanied the caffeine, no frothy memories of Sunday mornings past.

'Gotta get to the lab,' he said at last. 'Wasn't lying about being busy. This dissertation is killing me.'

A thought occurred to me. 'You're not giving up the band, are you?'

He shook his head. 'Can't get rid of me that easily.'

When he pushed back his chair to stand, so did I. There

was an awkward pause. Then he reached out and clapped a hand on my shoulder, pulling me into a hug.

We'd never hugged goodbye in our lives. We kissed. We groped. We rubbed our bodies together in an echo of sex. We didn't hug.

Maybe that was why I melted into it. He was so warm, despite the cold leather of his jacket. He smelled like earth and salt, with a hint of honey-sweet that made me think of summer.

'Promise you're not quitting the band?' I mumbled against his chest.

'Never. First Shoreditch – next, the world.'

I didn't say: We were supposed to take on the world together.

I wasn't used to keeping my thoughts to myself, but Katsu's comments had shaken something in me.

I rubbed a hand down his back and his body stirred to my touch. In that moment, I knew I could've tilted my head back and found his face there, waiting for me to kiss him. He would've kissed me back. We could've scampered the short walk to his house and fallen into bed. It would've been easy. Despite his angst, his emo kid existentialism, I knew I could've squirmed my way back into his heart with sex.

I tapped my fingers against his back and his grip on me slackened.

It was time to let him go.

'Bye, Ripper,' he said.

I rolled my eyes and gave a dismissive wave. I didn't trust my voice to stay steady.

Was it true? That we weren't good for each other?

No. That wasn't it.

He was good for me. I just wasn't good for him.

37

NEW YEAR, NEW YOU

Ella

I spent Christmas Day blitzing a turkey dinner into soup for the care home residents who couldn't eat solids. Mum got me the job. She'd worked at Three Oaks care home on the north side of Walney Island for fifteen years, and even been promoted to supervisor at one stage, making a decent wage. Then the care home had been sold and her new corporate overlords had cut her salary and placed her on a zero hours contract.

Out of some misplaced sense of loyalty, Mum had stayed on. Others weren't so cheerful after their bosses spat in their faces. The rate of staff churn was high; there was always a job going at Three Oaks, especially over Christmas. It was probably the only gig I could get, considering I'd been fired from my last job.

'Nice for us to work together,' Mum said with a tight smile, as she sliced open a box filled with incontinence pads. 'Good to keep an eye on you . . .'

I managed a small nod. Think of the money, I reminded myself. You need the money for a train ticket.

(*Lon. Don. Lon. Don. Lon. Don.*)

The long shifts at Three Oaks at least meant I could avoid too much 'family time' over the festive period. For our Christmas dinner in my parents' caravan, we ate dry ham. I was supposed to be doing the timings, but I zoned out, thinking about toilet-cafés and Sunday roasts of beef-and-sushi. The meal passed in silence, soundtracked by the false cheer of carols on TV and the whine of Archie begging for scraps.

Using my first pay packet from the care home, I'd bought my mum some perfume that smelled like oranges, my dad an electric screwdriver, and my brother a Swiss Army knife.

My gift from Mum (and Dad, although he clearly had no idea what was inside the silvery package) was a thick self-help book with a glossy cover of blue-and-green swirls. It was called *Unleash Your True Potential!* I mumbled 'thanks', feeling its weight in the palm of my hand like an accusation.

Willpower. Stick-to-it-iveness. Backbone. These were the traits that my family felt would overcome my depression. Just try hard enough and everything will be better. The subtext of this viewpoint was:

Not getting better? It's your own fault.

Simon's present came in a white envelope. He smirked as he handed it over. Inside was a meal-for-two gift voucher for Jackdaw's.

'That'll be nice,' Dad said, peering at it, oblivious. 'They do a good carbonara, they do.'

My face burned, but I swallowed down my humiliation. The taste on my tongue was metallic. Later, I ripped the gift voucher up into tiny pieces and screamed into my pillow.

*

New Year, new you!

On Facebook, the tinsel came down. Instead of eating, now everyone was dieting. Instead of thanking God for their families, now they were working on themselves. They'd strayed to other gods, motivational speakers and get-rich-quick gurus. Post after post blared about starting afresh this year.

What's stopping you from taking the life you want?
The only thing getting in the way of you is . . . you.
Using my thumb, I scrolled and scrolled and scrolled.
New year, new me?

*

The first two times I skirted the house, I didn't stop, because I thought I was lost. All the houses on the street – sandstone exteriors stained black from smog – looked the same. Maybe my memory was tricking me. I took another loop around the block. The third time I passed the house, I realised it might be the right place after all.

I climbed the step and rang the doorbell, but as I waited for an answer, my stomach dropped. I was about to turn and scurry away again when the door opened. A guy in a Batman T-shirt with shaggy red hair peered at me.

'Sorry, wrong house,' I mumbled.

I took a pace back. Forgetting there was a step, I felt the world drop out from under me. I just barely caught myself, scraping a hand against the pavement to keep from falling on my behind.

'Whoa . . . you alright, Jem?' He reached out a hand to me.

'Yeah,' I gasped, as he pulled me up.

The guy turned and bellowed over his shoulder, 'Hey, K-hole! Door for you!'

Red-headed Batman beckoned me inside. I followed him into the hallway, past the 'chandelier' of a Dalek being strangled by Christmas lights. My grazed palm throbbed.

I'd been excited about coming to London for weeks, ever since Jem's mass-email invite. It was what had kept me going through the festive period. Now all I wanted was to run away. The truth hit me in the face like a punch:

In this city, I'd only ever be an imposter. It had been stupid to come. I was a fool.

I heard footsteps upstairs and my stomach gave another jolt. 'Um, sorry . . .' I said in an undertone, edging backwards in the direction of the door.

Batman appeared not to hear me. 'You want a drink?' he asked. 'We have plum wine.'

Plum wine? I was trying to form a response when Katsu

appeared at the top of the staircase. My heart squeezed in my ribcage at the sight of him and I forgot all about leaving.

'Have a drink.' Batman leaned toward me conspiratorially. 'We have so much plum wine, it was on special offer.'

It wasn't even dark yet. And I had no idea what plum wine was.

Katsu bounded down the stairs two at a time. 'Stop trying to get everyone to drink that stuff.' He elbowed past Batman. 'You're turning into a pusher.' To me, he said, 'Hey, Ripper, what's up?'

The question was friendly, but there was a tired expression in his eyes. He didn't reach out to touch me.

My gaze flicked from Katsu to Batman and then settled on the floor. They thought I was Jem. Of course they did.

'Hi,' I said in a small voice, my eyes still fixed on the grubby green carpet at my feet.

I'd put on red lipstick while I was on the train, my hand trembling with the vibrations. I was wearing my favourite jeans and a pretty white camisole, but the day was cold and I'd had to cover up with a heavy wax jacket. I looked frumpy. My lipstick was probably lopsided.

Whatever I'd imagined would happen when I saw Katsu again, it wasn't this. I was in the wrong place – I was in the wrong place by 300 miles. I tugged at the sleeves of the jacket and wished I could rewind this moment, do it over again.

Katsu's hand reached out to touch my elbow. When I sneaked a glance at him, I saw that his eyebrows were raised, his blank expression clearing into a half-smile.

'Hey, you,' he said softly.

I met his gaze full-on and his smile broadened. Maybe I was where I belonged after all. I couldn't help but smile back.

*

'Fuck it, let's have some plum wine,' Katsu said. 'It is Saturday.'

We were in his bedroom and he slugged purple liquid into two mugs and handed one to me. The two of us cheers'ed – the ceramic making more of *clank* than a *clink* – and we took swigs of our plum wine.

I almost choked. It was sour as unripe fruit, with a kick of a synthetic-sweet aftertaste that reminded me of cough medicine.

'Yeah, it's disgusting,' Katsu said, his own mouth puckering. 'And cheap. That's how Frank ended up with six cases of the stuff.'

I nodded, not knowing how else to respond. Frank? I guessed that was red-headed Batman, who'd disappeared up a second flight of stairs in a haze of weed smoke.

Katsu's room had speckled-white walls and it was barely big enough for the small amount of furniture it contained, let alone the guitar, keyboard, and mandolin that had been jammed in. The bed, in particular, swamped the space. I stood with both hands gripping my mug, looking resolutely at the city view out the small window. The rumpled duvet kept catching my eye, even as I tried not to look at it.

I couldn't avoid the mental image of a sleep-sated Katsu rolling over in bed to reveal the sleek muscles of his back. And it was easy, so easy, to imagine myself lying beside him, pushing my fingers into his hair and –

I took another swig of plum wine just to occupy my hands. David would lecture me that it wasn't good to drink while in recovery, but what did I care about any of that now?

'So what brings you to London?' Katsu asked.

'I'm here for the show. Jem sent me an email. I don't even know if she meant to send it to me. I think she sent it to everyone she knew . . .'

Four exclamation marks.

'Yeah, that sounds like Jem.'

Katsu puffed out a long breath, like he was about to say

more, but then didn't. There was a long moment of silence.

'Sorry, it's rude for me to just show up like this,' I said.

'Don't be stupid, I'm happy to see you.'

He flopped onto the unmade bed and took a long swallow from his mug. I felt conspicuous to still be standing. There was nowhere else to sit. With a flutter of hesitation, I took a seat next to him.

'I just' – his eyes scanned my face rapidly; his voice was hoarse – 'had a crazy moment where I didn't recognise you. My bad.'

My stomach squirmed. I wanted to ask: What if you'd met me first? What if I'd joined a band and you'd been the guitarist? What if I'd moved to London and our eyes had met across a crowded bar?

Would you have ever liked me for me?

I couldn't voice any of these thoughts. I took another sip of plum wine. A bitter taste like pennies had been lodged in my throat for days, made worse by the unripe fruit tang of the wine, but the alcohol was warming me up. 'Don't worry about it,' I said at last.

'Did you have a good New Year's?' Katsu's voice was smooth and amiable once more.

'Oh, sure.' I cleared my throat and tried to mimic his light-hearted tone. 'Mrs Kent tipped me twenty quid for an exceptional sponge bath.'

Katsu laughed. 'What?'

'It was time for a bit of a scrub-up and she told me it was the best sponge bath she'd ever had and her dad taught her you should always tip for a job well done. 'Course, what she thought was a twenty pound note was actually a bookmark.' I paused for effect, courting more of his laughter. 'But I guess it's the thought that counts?' I shrugged. 'I've been doing some casual shifts at a care home, helping out over Christmas.'

'Just making some extra cash?' Katsu said. 'Sounds good.'

It reminded me of what Owen had said to me – *just for now, just for now* – and I had to swallow past the lump in my throat. I'd practised the Mrs Kent story in my head during the train journey. It really had been funny. It had also come at the end of a brutal 10-hour shift, during which time another resident had run away from Three Oaks. The police had returned her. She was sobbing hysterically about needing to get to the bomb shelter.

'What did you do for New Year's?' I asked, trying to banish the memory.

'I have no idea.' He squinted, scratching his chin. 'I woke up in Croydon, but how I got there is fuzzy. My buddy Drew thought I needed to let loose. He was buying me tequila slammers and I was the idiot who didn't pace himself.'

Katsu shuffled into a more comfortable position on the bed. Beside him, I was still perched primly. I made an effort to shake my limbs loose. The drab wax jacket I wore felt too heavy.

'Why did you need to let loose?' I asked.

I had a pretty good idea why, but I kept my voice casual, pretending not to be too interested. I shrugged out of my jacket, revealing my white camisole. It was something I used to wear a lot when I was at university.

'Me and Jem broke up.' He wasn't looking at me as he spoke, his eyes instead tracking my movements as I tugged my arms free of the wax jacket. 'It was a long time coming, but it finally happened.'

'. . . Why did you break up?' The question came out a touch squeaky; I couldn't seem to catch my breath.

'It was just time. Being with Jem is a hell of a ride, but I'm not sure I want that anymore. Pretty soon I'll be done with my PhD and then what – ? Still getting wasted and rescuing Ripper when she decides to jump out of a third-floor window?'

'Sounds . . . eventful.'

He groaned and didn't reply.

'Things seemed to be going okay with her,' I said. 'You know . . . last time I was here.'

'Yeah, Jem's pretty good at making you forget all the bad things about her when she wants something.'

Despite his ironical tone, there was a note of wistfulness in his voice. Jealousy clawed at my insides. Jem had everything and more to spare. Even after he broke up with her, Katsu still existed in her orbit. Reading between the lines, I guessed she could persuade Katsu to take her back whenever she pleased.

We were both quiet. My mug of plum wine was still half full, but I didn't want it anymore. I placed it on the carpet at the foot of the bed. Katsu's mug (empty) rested on the duvet, his hand wrapped around it. I reached for it and our fingers brushed. I lingered a moment too long before taking the mug and placing it on the floor next to mine.

'You know what's fucked up?' Katsu said at last. 'The best day I spent with Jem in months . . . and it wasn't even her.'

A dizzy, sickly-sweet sensation gripped me. I looked up and found his eyes were on me. His gaze swept up my body and settled on my face.

I was used to people's eyes glancing over me, their attention diverting even as I was speaking to them. People looked past me, looked through me.

Katsu was looking at me like he could see inside me.

'I forgot what it was like to feel normal,' he said. 'Feel good around someone. Not be stuck inside Jem's drama every minute of the day.'

'I felt good, too,' I said, with difficulty. 'Being with you.'

Katsu gave me another searching look and then he leaned forward, closing the gap between us. When he'd kissed me the first time, at Jem's apartment, the moment had been brief, breathless, over before it began. This was slow – an exploration. My eyes fell shut. The kiss was hesitant at first. Then my lips relaxed against his and my hesitation fall away.

I thought fleetingly of my last kisses with Owen. They'd taken on an antique quality in my mind; sepia-toned, submerged by grief. By contrast, this moment felt sharp, alive. Everything was snapping into focus.

As we kissed, I reached for Katsu blindly, drawing him closer. We half-fell back on to the bed, the rumpled duvet soft at my back, his body solid and warm as he pressed himself against me. I could feel his erection through the layers of clothes and I wrapped my legs around him, anchoring him to me.

He wanted me. He really did. He wanted me for me.

Our kisses grew more haphazard, our bodies frantic for more sensation. I was pulling my camisole up, even as he was pushing it down. It wadded around my ribs and he was fingering my bra, trying to tease the hooks loose at my back.

I undid the clasp for him and my bra sprang off, my breasts loose, my nipples hard. He tugged off his own T-shirt by the scruff of his neck and then it was all skin-on-skin-on-skin. I rolled my hips against him.

There was a tapping sound and, to me, it seemed to come from far away.

'Gonna order a curry,' a voice called through the closed door.

Katsu froze, one hand on the waistband of my jeans.

'Either of you want in?' red-headed Batman asked. 'K-hole? Jem?'

The sound of Jem's name cut through me like a knife.

Katsu drew back. My body turned rag-doll-limp, my grip on him slackening. He was breathing heavily, cheeks flushed, hair mussed. The ghost of my lipstick was smeared across his cheek. His eyes scanned my face a final time and then –

'No, it's cool, she's not staying,' he called out.

We were both silent, listening as footsteps trailed away from the bedroom door. When Katsu spoke again, his voice was quiet:

'Sorry, I shouldn't have done that.'

I swallowed hard. My heart was still beating fast, my lips

336

were still tingling, but the sweet-seasickness feeling in my stomach had churned into nausea.

'Sorry,' I echoed, even though I wasn't, not at all.

I scooted across the bed, grabbing my bra. Only one of the hooks caught, but I didn't care. I pulled the straps of my camisole back up over my shoulders and re-buttoned my jeans where Katsu had tugged them open. I hoped he might stop me, but the spell was broken. He struggled back into his T-shirt like he couldn't remember how clothes worked.

'I'm sorry,' he said again. 'This is all . . . too much. It's fucking with my head.'

He reached out to me – perhaps for a hug or some other conciliatory gesture – but then he seemed to think better of it. His fingers only brushed uselessly against my elbow.

Heat was building behind my eyes. It was becoming hard to see clearly.

'You get that, right?' he said. 'What this all does to me?'

'I get it,' I said, using every ounce of strength not to let the tears out.

'I know you're not her. But. It fucks me up how much you look like her.'

The final truth of it was laid bare and I couldn't keep from crying any longer. I would always be tied to Jem in Katsu's mind. He would never look at me and see just me.

'You're gonna find someone so great,' he said, his voice straining with false cheer. 'Someone right for you.'

'I don't want to find someone else,' I whispered.

I turned and stumbled out of the room, tears blinding me. I passed Frank on my way out of the house and the hearty way he said 'Want some more plum wine, Jem?' only made me cry harder.

38

THE SHOW

Ella

I stood at a sink in a McDonald's bathroom and splashed water on to my face. I blinked through tears and tap water, looking at my reflection. I watched as the woman in the mirror grabbed a paper towel from the dispenser and mopped up her face. The woman in the mirror took out a bag of make-up and began to paint over the blotchy surface of her skin. The woman in the mirror remade herself.

It was dark outside. After the over-lit restaurant, the rest of the world felt shadowy and unreal. I'd spent three hours at McDonald's, nursing a black coffee and picking at an apple pie that tasted burnt and metallic. The sugar and caffeine left me unsteady on my feet, clumsy in strappy heels, as I pushed out the door into the night.

'Alright, darling . . .'

'Got a smile for us, sweetheart . . .'

'Oi, I'm talking to you . . .'

A group of men stood on the pavement, smoking. When I'd entered the restaurant, in loose jeans and a heavy wax jacket, I'd been invisible to them. Those clothes, along with the pretty camisole that a different Ella had once loved, were shoved inside my backpack. Now I stood in the dipped-and-scrubbed silver dress. As the fabric caught the reflection of the brightly-lit window, it drenched me in my own spotlight.

After Katsu's rejection, all I wanted was to get away from myself for a while; crack my neck and climb out of my own self-loathing. Despite the wintry night, I didn't feel the cold. I brushed past the men and the spotlight followed me.

The club in Shoreditch where the band was playing was on the next street over, nestled within a stretch of bars and restaurants. Inebriated hipsters filled the streets, as Saturday night fired up. Yet my spotlight carried me through the crowds. Nothing could touch me.

On my way into the club, I caught sight of a handwritten bill, listing the names of the bands that were playing tonight and what time they'd be onstage. Third on the list was Lace Steak, 10:00.

Inside the club, the air was humid, sour with sweat. The black floor was sticky, pulling at the soles of my shoes. The band onstage pounded out bluesy rock music and their energy was contagious. It was still early – not yet nine – but there were at least 100 people dancing, clapping, stamping their feet to the music.

A bar ran along the back wall of the club and, tucked away in the corner, there was a coat check room. It was staffed by a bored guy with hound-dog eyes and a thick beard. I handed him my shabby backpack – the final trace of that other girl – and received a ticket in exchange.

'Hey, Jemster!'

As I returned to the dancefloor, someone slammed into me, a purple-haired girl who was gone a moment later.

'Good luck tonight!'

Someone else thumped me on the shoulder. Onstage, the band was finishing its last song and the crowd clamoured for an encore. My well-wishers were swept away in the tide of people.

In morbid moments, I'd often wondered how many people would show up to my funeral if I died. Family members, out of obligation; a few ex-friends, crying crocodile tears. It would be a quiet affair. By contrast, if this show was anything to go by, Jem's death would be a party. As I'd suspected, my double seemed to have invited everyone she'd ever met to the gig. And, apparently, most of them had shown up.

As I pushed through the crowd, more people smiled at me, patting me on the back or yelling. 'Hey Jem, you're gonna kill it tonight!'

I smiled back, buoyed by the attention. My spotlight was bright, so bright. They thought I was Jem. Who else would I be?

'*AIIIYEEEEEE!*'

Someone tried to jump on my back, piggy-back style. A voice screamed a war cry right in my ear. I staggered forwards, deafened and unbalanced.

'*Tonight's the niiiiiiiiiiight!*' the voice screamed, only fractionally quieter.

I turned to look at the banshee and realised that I did, in fact, know this face. It was Stee, the not-a-girl, with his pixie-ish silver-blonde hair. He was flanked by April and Imogen.

'You excited?' Imogen asked. She towered in stiletto heels, dressed in black sequins more suitable for a cocktail party than a gig.

'. . . Yeah!' I said.

'You don't sound excited!' Stee said, frowning. 'You should have a drink. Have mine!'

Stee thrust a glass of something dark and fizzy into my hand. I took a swig. It tasted like ginger, but with a bitter aftertaste. I handed the drink back to Stee with a slight grimace.

April leaned close to me, her mermaid blue-and-green hair tickling my face.

'Are you nervous?' she whisper-shouted, and I could hear the kindness in her voice.

I jerked my head. A sort-of nod. Of course I was nervous. I was always nervous.

My eyes scanned the crowd, which had swelled to perhaps 150 now. Where was the real Jem? The second band on the bill was onstage, setting up their equipment. That meant there was less than an hour until Lace Steak went on.

Beside the stage, half-obscured by the mixing console, there was a roped-off area, where five or six people were milling around. I guessed that was what passed for 'backstage', but I couldn't see my double there, either.

I was banking on the fact that Jem would be fashionably late. I wouldn't stay long enough to see her. I just couldn't resist taking a peek at this life I could only dream of. But, now I was here, to think of leaving made my chest ache.

'Remember when you lifted that old git's wallet?' April said.

The reference caught me off guard. I stopped looking at the crowd and returned my attention to her.

April laughed and the sound merged with the first rumble of the band onstage starting their set. 'You just need to channel that kind of crazy fearlessness,' she shouted over the applause.

She pulled me into a side-hug, crushing her body against mine. 'You'll be amazing,' she said in my ear.

The certainty in her voice made me glow. I couldn't speak. I just nodded. Pretending to watch the band, I let her drift back into conversation with the other two.

Crazy fearlessness? Was that what it was when I stole Helm's wallet that night in November? It hadn't been a mistake. It hadn't been a lapse into freakishness. I'd been fearless.

My spotlight flared and I had to blink against the burst of light.

'. . . But who wears sunglasses indoors at night?'

'Um, hello! Bulletproof wankers. Music industry wankers.'

'You're so full of shit.'

The conversation around me had sped onward. Imogen and April were talking about a man at the bar. A man wearing sunglasses. Indoors. At night.

'Maybe he's blind!' Stee cut in.

'He's not blind. He's an A&R guy. I'm telling you,' April said. 'Look, he's talking to Max.'

My head whipped around. Jem's dad. Sure enough, he was

leaning against the bar, talking to the man in the sunglasses.

Max's eyes lit on me. He slapped the mystery man's hand and left the bar, jostling through the crowd toward me. I felt a prickle of panic, the old urge to run away. Then Max assailed me with a glorious perfume-ad smile.

I summoned a smile in return. It was my new smile. The smile that didn't belong to me. 'Dad!'

He wrapped me in his arms. 'Princess, all these people here to see you . . . God, I love you so much,' he said, with the intensity of someone in a movie.

Close by, I was glad to see that Imogen looked dazzled, too. Yes, my dad was dazzling.

'Why aren't you drinking?' Max asked, releasing me from the hug. 'Let me get you a drink!'

He ambled back to the bar, without asking what I wanted.

'Bet that guy's here to sign your band,' Stee said to me, watching Max re-join the man at the bar.

'First show and you get a record deal?' Imogen said, her lips twitching into a smile.

'It could happen!' Stee said.

Neither of them sounded jealous or resentful, merely impressed. That was how things worked for Jem. She was someone who got the guy and the band and the packed-out show at the shit-hot club. Obviously she'd get a recording contract, too. Life was easy for her. She'd never known an emptiness so deep that even breathing felt like hard work.

I tried to maintain my smile, the glow of my spotlight, but it was flickering.

Jem would be here any minute. The jig would be up. And I'd go back to being Ella.

My triumph at proving I could impersonate her was gone. The old darkness tugged at the hem of my skirt. *You don't belong up there on stage*, it said. *You belong down here in the gutter.*

It was hard to breathe. The air was thick with heat. The band on stage was thrashing through a rock song, heavy with bass. People were still pouring into the club, packing us in tighter and tighter.

'I have to go!' I said, shouting to be heard above the noise of the band.

I didn't wait for a response from April, Imogen or Stee. I squeezed through the crowd, ignoring the stray greetings – 'Hey, Jem!' 'Break a leg!' – and trying to stay steady on my feet. Looking for some respite from the noise, I ended up in the corner of the room, near the toilets and the coat check.

It was quieter here and a little cooler. I sagged against a wall papered with posters for other shows. My eyes screwed shut as I tried to catch my breath.

In, out, in, out –

'Been looking for you,' a voice said, 'you're late.'

When I turned to face him, my voice lodged in my throat. There was a metallic taste in my mouth, the same one that had lingered all day. Pennies on my tongue.

'I texted you three times,' Katsu said. 'You were supposed to meet us at the back door at nine, help unload the equipment.'

I sucked in a deep breath.

'Time is just a concept,' I said, in Jem's voice.

I tried to smile, but my lips felt sticky.

Katsu didn't respond. He was checking his phone, making harsh swipes up the screen. Since I'd seen him last, he'd changed into a tight-fitting white T-shirt, which he wore with black jeans. His hair hung in his face, still downturned. I focused on his fingers, gripping his phone. Long fingers. Musician's hands. With a shiver, I remembered the feel of those fingers at my jaw, drawing me in for another kiss.

'Hey,' I said, reaching out to lay a hand on his arm.

He didn't react; he kept on swiping. Part of me wanted to come clean, to lean in and whisper, *Hey, it's Ella.*

Yet I remembered the frustration in his voice from earlier in the day. I could still hear it, his voice when he'd said to me, *It fucks me up how much you look like her.*

The words circled in my head. *It fucks me up. It fucks me up.* Each time they circled, I heard it differently. *It fucks me up how much I like her. It fucks me up how much you're not like her. It fucks me up.*

My nerve endings fritzed. There was lightning in my brain.

'Hey,' I said again.

This time, I moved closer to Katsu. I ran my hand up his arm, feeling the corded muscles beneath his t-shirt. I pressed closer still, into his personal space. As I moulded myself against him, I felt the way his breathing changed, the way his muscles tightened. I felt the way he reacted – to Jem.

I pressed my body against his side, hooking my chin on to his shoulder. My arms reached around his waist, tightening into an embrace. I exhaled slowly, warm breath against the side of his neck.

He still held his phone, but he'd given up the pretence of looking at it. His face, in profile, was blank; eyes hooded, lips unsmiling. Yet there was a sense of wavering; my power overcoming his. Katsu was not giving in yet, but he was teetering on the edge.

Jem took what she wanted.

And Katsu was there for the taking.

I remembered the silly guessing game we'd played in Jem's bedroom, all those months ago; how easy it had been for Katsu to tell me and my double apart. It was not so easy anymore. I'd fooled him. I'd fooled them all.

Time for a final test.

Katsu turned his head, looking me dead in the eyes.

'Jem . . .' he said, his voice low and throaty with longing.

'Yes,' I said.

I leaned up and kissed him hard on the lips. It was a fleeting kiss, but it was hot. An exclamation mark. A kiss that sounded in my head like *chk!*

I knew the truth of it now: Katsu didn't want me; he wanted Jem. The kiss proved it.

'Yo, ten minutes!'

The air beside me was disturbed by a clicking of fingers. I thought perhaps it was inside my head, until Katsu reacted, too. My eyes darted left and I saw Anthony, already turning to walk away again.

'Shit . . . showtime,' Katsu murmured.

There was a crackle in my brain. The flash of a spotlight.

My double might be late for the show, but she wouldn't miss it altogether. She craved the attention too much. My gaze cut across the dancefloor to the club's entrance. What would happen when she strode in the door? What if there were two Jems here instead of one? Would reality short out and one of us end up vaporised on the spot?

Katsu's arms were still around me. I leaned my body against his. He was strong, warm, decisively real. And, in his arms, I was Jem. I was a Somebody. The lead singer of a band playing at a London club. I was loved, desired.

I mattered. I existed.

But as soon as Jem showed up, I'd cease to exist.

'Come on, we've got to do our set-up,' Katsu said, reaching for my hand, guiding me toward the roped-off area by the stage. I allowed him to do it, unwilling to let him go.

Yet something was dragging at me in the opposite direction, an invisible force. My hand dropped from his.

'I have to go,' I said in an undertone, turning away from him.

'Wait . . .' Katsu's voice drifted after me.

I walked away, trying to stride purposefully but failing. My legs rebelled against me as I walked; the energy was being sucked from me.

My spotlight had flickered out.

39

SHARDS

Ella

Slipping back into the club's crowd, I became one among many; anonymous, invisible. I was almost at the exit when a commotion erupted at the corner of my eye.

The noise of the club meant it was too loud for me to hear Jem's laughter, but when I caught sight of her, I heard it in my head. Machine gun fire. She stood in the thick of things, holding court like a queen. Her face was ecstatic, as she bathed in the glow of attention.

By contrast, I was fading. The two of us – Jem in the middle of the crowd; me at the edge – were separated by a few metres, but the distance between us felt like a chasm. I ducked my head and turned away. My foot went sideways in my strappy silver shoe as I stumbled onward.

I remembered that my tatty backpack was at the coat check. I needed to get it back, retrieve the version of myself that was shoved down deep inside.

'Ticket?'

There was a blonde girl behind the desk of the cloakroom now, tattooed rose stems curling over her wrists. She gave me a bored look and prompted again:

'Ticket?'

The slip of paper – where was it? On automatic, I patted down my dress, even though it didn't have pockets. I'd held the ticket in my hand. I remembered that much. And after that – ? I had no idea. I imagined it fluttering from my grasp, before being stamped underfoot.

'I don't . . . I mean . . . I must've . . .' My voice came out in a whisper, panicked, distinctly Cumbrian.

The girl's bored expression softened.

'Don't worry,' she said, 'I remember you.'

She turned and rummaged through a rack of coats, extracting one and handing it to me. Fawn-coloured and expensively-cut, the coat was heavy in my arms, the rich wool soft against my bare skin.

It was my coat.

Of course it was.

A man elbowed past me, shoving his ticket at the coat check girl. I took a step away, and then another. Three more steps and I'd pulled my arms through the sleeves of the fawn coat, plunging my hands into its pockets. My fingertips brushed against something cold and jagged.

I kept my head down, fighting against the crowd, as I made my way to the exit, but a voice punctured my numbness.

'Heyyy! Jem!'

Someone slapped me on the back. A grinning face loomed in front of mine. It was just another stranger who thought he knew me. He voice slurred out a question:

'Where are you going?'

My fist tightened around the keys in my coat pocket.

'Home,' I said.

*

On the street outside the club, I breathed in smoke. It smelled sweet, like oranges. I brushed past the woman who was vaping by the door and stumbled onward. My eyes felt too big for my head, my brain pounding inside my skull. I scanned the traffic, looking for an opening in order to cross the road.

'Jem!'

I took one step out into the road before a black cab screeched toward me, chasing me back onto the pavement. The driver sounded his horn.

'Hey, Jem!'

I half-ran, half-hobbled another twenty metres, thirty metres, away from the voice that was calling my name. I took a turn onto a side street. There were fewer people here, less traffic. It was the wrong way, but I wanted an escape. I didn't want to talk to another of Jem's admirers. I needed quiet. Calm. The sanctuary of home.

'Hey, Miss Marilyn Monroe . . . slow the fuck down.'

A hand grabbed my shoulder. I recognised his voice now. I recognised his smell. It was an unwashed, almost-spicy-al-most-sweet stench that slammed me back against the memory of a brick wall.

His big meaty hand spun me around to face him.

Carlo.

'Congrats on the big gig. Gonna get that big fat record label money, right?'

He was grinning, but his eyes were unfocused and his hand wasn't letting me go. I tried to shrug him off, but he used his other hand to clamp down on the back of my neck. Next to my ear, a car roared past. In too-high heels, I was teetering at the edge of the pavement.

'Go away,' I whispered, but he didn't seem to hear.

'Remember that song we used to sing back in the day? Drove everyone on set crazy. When I grow up, I wanna be – I wanna be – ' He bellowed the final word at the sky. 'Famous!'

Carlo's fingers dug into the base of my skull.

'You owe me,' he said, 'a drink.'

You owe me. His words exploded in my head, memories jarring with the present. *You stupid bitch, you owe me. I have to hurt you. Nothing else gets through to you!*

The echo of a punch made my teeth chatter. Carlo was still singing, but I could feel his hands beating me down. I sucked in a breath, scanning the street for someone who could help me. Now that we were off the main drag, the crowds were gone. The only people visible were far away, oblivious to what was going on. Another car rumbled past. I stuck out a hand, a vague attempt to wave it down, but it just kept going.

'Come on, then,' Carlo said and, though he was smiling, it looked more like a dog baring its fangs.

Ella would have cowered before him. She would have stuttered and pleaded, her body crumpling inward. But Jem? What would Jem do?

Jem squared her shoulders and shook him loose.

'I don't owe anyone' – I delivered the words through clenched teeth – 'anything.'

He raised his eyebrows, mouth slack. He was swaying on his feet now that he didn't have me to lean on.

'Fuck you.' I spat the words at him and my spittle flecked against his cheek.

'Don't talk to me like that, you little bitch . . .'

His anger was back and he grabbed for me again. I pressed my hands against his chest and pushed him away.

There was no reasoning with this guy. He was a junkie, a waste of space. He was nothing.

I pushed him again. Harder this time, so he took a stumble-step off the pavement. My blood churned with a strength I hadn't known I possessed. He was no match for me.

Another car passed us, a white sports car, but I didn't try to flag this one down. I didn't need a knight on a white charger to save me. I could save myself.

I squared my shoulder and shoved against Carlo sideways, my elbow hitting his kidney. Grunting, he stumbled again, doubled over in pain. One final push and he was out in the road, down in the gutter like the trash he was.

He fixed me with a glassy look of confusion and surprise.

That was when the taxi hit him.

Forty miles an hour. Direct impact.

His body flopped against the car bonnet like a rag doll. There was a squeal of brakes, but it was too late. The damage was done. A smell of blood bloomed in the air. I realised now what the persistent taste in my mouth was. Not metal, not pennies. It was the taste of blood.

I heard a scream.

It might have been me. I don't know.

My hands were shaking, so I thrust them deep into the pockets of my coat. My fingers rubbed the set of keys like a magic charm. I hastened away from Carlo's body, retracing my steps back onto the main thoroughfare with its throngs of people. It was easy to slip back into the flow of foot traffic, become invisible again.

I heard commotion building at my back – 'Oh my God!' 'Shit, what happened?' 'Is someone calling the police? Someone should call the police!' – but my legs held firm as I strode away.

Home.

Time to go home.

*

'Evening,' a silver-haired gentleman greeted me.

'Good evening,' I said.

'Beautiful night, isn't it?' When he smiled, his twirled moustache tickled the corners of his mouth.

I nodded and he held open for me the heavy door to the Chelsea apartment block.

'You stay safe now, Jemima.'

'Oh, I will,' I said.

The old man saw a woman wearing Jem's exquisitely-tailored fawn coat. She held Jem's keys in her hand. She lifted her chin and gave a Jem smile.

Maybe what the old man saw was true.

In that moment, I was almost sure I really was Jem.

I glided across the marbled entrance hall and ascended the

staircase like a movie heroine.

The keys turned in the lock of Jem's front door like magic, like Abracadabra, open sesame.

Inside, it was dark, but I felt no trepidation. The long shadow that fell down the centre of the hallway belonged to me. And the darkness had a cool, satin quality, like expensive material draped across my skin.

I didn't bother to turn on the lights. I could see through the darkness; I was a part of it. As I roamed the empty apartment, my tread was soundless against the wood floors. My feet didn't touch the ground. I was floating.

I passed the arty pictures on the walls, the carelessly extravagant furniture. On the table in the living room, there lay a roll of cash, tossed aside like Monopoly money. I thumbed through the wad of notes: twenty . . . forty . . . sixty . . . eighty . . . a hundred . . . more. I shoved the notes into my bra.

In Jem's bedroom, my gaze was drawn to the fuck-you green wall, dyed grey by the darkness. A stray beam from the streetlamp outside glinted against the metal of the ceremonial swords and daggers mounted on the wall. The inscriptions on them were foreign, maybe Japanese; unreadable to Jem.

I felt a wave of contempt. What relationship to her did they have? They were another quirky affectation. Everything here was fake. Pretentious. Every part of Jem's life was designed for maximum shock value. She had everything and she valued none of it.

I reached up and unhooked from the wall a small, dainty dagger with a sharp point. I pressed its edge to my fingertip. A line of blood appeared, black and slick in the darkness. I still wore the fawn coat and I wiped my finger across its lapel, leaving a smear of blood. I slipped the dagger into my pocket for safekeeping.

My eyes raked over the contents of the room again. Her bed was unmade, white sheets tangled into ropes.

351

Memories that weren't mine slanted through my mind. Jem's laugh, machine gun fire, filled the room.

'That little mouse, little twinnie . . .

'Did you see the look on her face?' Jem flopped on to her belly on the bed, waving her bare feet in the air. 'What a riot.'

Katsu, naked, stretched across the bed and pulled her on top of him. 'Jem . . . Jem, I love you,' he murmured, his lips brushing over hers. 'I could never love anyone like her.'

I watched them kiss. They paused only to laugh at me, at the fool I'd been, what a fool. My face burned and tears blurred my vision.

I turned away, but couldn't escape her. She was everywhere, her laughter hanging in the air. I couldn't stop her memories from flooding my head. I saw her onstage at the Shoreditch club, the rapturous crowds, the performance of a lifetime.

In that darkened bedroom, I saw the future, too: arena shows, fans in their thousands chanting her name. The noise filled my ears, deafening me.

I wavered on my feet, reaching out to steady myself. My fingers grasped the edge of Jem's dressing table. Its surface was cluttered with make-up. When I overturned it, the crash was almighty, almost enough to drown out the chanting fans.

A pot of blusher hit the floor in a puff of pink powder. Bronzing beads went rolling. Make-up brushes fell like pick-up sticks.

I stooped to grab a bottle of perfume that had survived the crash. Without hesitation, I threw it.

It exploded against the wall in a glitter of glass shards. One of the shards bounced back against my leg, slicing into my skin, but I barely felt it. The room was drenched in orange scent. The smell was so strong that I could see it, turning white and gauzy in the air. The initial fragrance was sweet, but the smell that lingered was one of rotting, like orange peel left in the bin for days too long.

The rotten stench followed me as I stalked out of the room. I flung my arms wide and watched ornaments tumble to the floor. Pictures lurched off the walls. Glass shattered. Each crash was satisfying.

I swept into the hallway like a movie heroine in a film where the world was ending. Everything was rewinding. Erasing.

A snatch of light illuminated someone caught in my peripheral vision. I whirled around.

I wasn't alone.

I glimpsed another face in the hallway.

Carlo. It had to be Carlo. My stomach lurched.

I hadn't killed him, after all. He was back. And he wanted to kill me.

'Please . . .' I whispered, screwing my eyes shut. 'Just do it.'

I waited for the deadly blow to come. But there were only spiders, crawling over my skin, pulling at my scalp with their pincers.

When I opened my eyes, the intruder had drawn closer. It was a woman, pale-faced, with shoulders hunched. She glared at me.

I was looking in the huge gilt mirror. The other woman was my reflection. I hadn't even recognised myself.

The woman in the mirror looked feral.

I let out a scream and lunged at her. My fists pummelled her face, shattering her nose, her mouth, her eyes. My knuckles bled as, shard by shard, she fell to the floor.

Afterwards, I stood motionless. I stared down at my broken reflection, the life draining out of me.

How long passed?

I don't know.

Minutes. Hours. Years. A whole lifetime played out and then rewound itself.

*

'Bollocks.'

The sound pierced my consciousness.

'*Bollocksss.*'

The familiar voice roused something in me. Limbs creaking, I crept backwards. My elbow hit a door handle, but the pain was remote. It belonged to someone else.

'Shitting fucking bollocks *suh-suh-*smothered in cum sauce . . .'

Her silhouette appeared in the doorway.

I yanked at the door handle blindly and slipped into a room off the hallway. The door eased shut behind me.

It was the laundry room. The trapped air inside was warm and stale. It smelled like fresh sheets, fabric softener. I crouched down next to the washing machine, making myself small.

Footsteps trampled along the hallway. My double's monologue continued:

'That crazy bitch, stole my coat, stole my keysss . . .'

I could hear the slurring in her voice. I could imagine her weaving through the apartment, taking in the devastation.

The footsteps faded and then grew louder again. She was circling back around to the hallway and, off it, the laundry room.

What would I do if she found me?

My whole body trembled. I sucked my knuckles like a child. They were bruised and bloody from where I'd punched the mirror.

'Fucking lunatic!' Jem said.

It sounded like she was on the other side of the laundry room door. In the darkness, huddled down low, I willed myself to disappear.

Fumbling in my pocket, I found the dagger I'd taken from Jem's wall. The skin of my thumb and forefinger burst open as I pinched its tip. Blood made my hands slippery.

I'd already killed Carlo tonight.

Did I have the courage to lunge at Jem, as I'd lunged at the woman in the mirror?

When I'd fantasised about killing myself, it was always pills. Line them up, drink them down, and the result was like going to sleep. That was the theory. Except, you were more likely to wake up in a hospital bed with a tube down your throat.

It would be cleaner, perhaps, to use a dagger. Stick a blade in your throat and it was all over in seconds. My own blood churned with bad feeling. Jem's would probably flow out of her like champagne.

I gripped the hilt of the dagger with both hands and waited for the laundry room door to open.

'What a fucking mess,' Jem said outside the door.

What a fucking mess, I mouthed in the dark.

I waited for her to come, but a moment later, I heard footsteps trailing away.

My whole body sagged – with relief, but also with disgust. Disgust at myself. This was who I was now. A murderer.

*

Silence settled over the apartment.

Minutes passed, perhaps an hour. In time, the satiny quality returned to the darkness. It wrapped itself around me, making me into a wraith.

Hands pushed at the laundry room door. They had blunt finger ends, ragged nails. They didn't look like my hands, but I watched them twist at the door handle, I watched them grip the dagger in a fist.

In the hallway, shards from the mirror glittered on the floor. I caught a glimpse of my face, mixed up like a Picasso.

I stole through the apartment and my feet didn't touch the floor. There was no sound at all in my double's bedroom.

Jem slept like the dead.

Her posture, spread-eagled on top of the bed covers, reminded me of a crime scene outline. Her slack face was serene, hair fanned out across the pillow. I stood over her, listening. The room was so quiet. I strained to hear her breathing.

Maybe she really was dead.

She let out a snort, sucking in a laboured breath. The image reset itself. Not dead, after all.

My double's body gave a fit, an electric spasm, and she flung out an arm, as if reaching for me. I wondered again what I'd do if she woke up and found me here, in her bedroom.

Scream?

No . . .

She wouldn't scream. She'd laugh.

My scalp prickled with humiliation. She'd laugh, machine-gun-fire spraying itself around the room.

Twinnie, what the fuck are you doing here?

Even as she slept, I saw her rise up on her elbows and tip back her head, laughing.

You think it's clever, playing dress up with my life? Well, here's the bottom line, Twinnie. You're not me. You'll never be me.

You're a pathetic little mouse.

Scurry off home, little mouse.

A sob rose in my throat.

You're right, Jem. I'll never be you.

I'll never be anything at all.

40

DARK SPOTS

Jem

That crazy bitch.

I woke up with the hangover from hell, but it wasn't hard to figure out what had happened.

Every table, shelf and surface in my apartment had been swept clean. The walls were bare, picture frames languishing broken on the wood floor. I stepped out into the living room and surveyed the damage.

Who else could have picked up my coat at the club?

Only the girl who shared my face.

Twinnie apparently harboured a secret penchant for home invasion.

'Ow!' As I stomped across the floor to the kitchen, I crunched against a sliver of glass. 'Motherfuckingshittinghell.' I hopped on one leg like a deranged flamingo and examined the bottom of my foot.

The sunlight slanting in through the sash windows made the smashed glass on the floor flash and shimmer. It also revealed an inch-long cut on my foot that oozed bright-red blood.

When I lowered my leg, pain pulsed up through my body. My head was pounding, too. My mouth was dry. If the alcohol hadn't squeezed out every drop of water from my body, I might've cried.

The real Jemima Cootes-Mitchell didn't cry, though.

I gritted my teeth and continued across the floor to the kitchen, ignoring the pain in my foot. Flipping open the fridge, I grabbed a glass bottle of icy water. Glug, glug, glug. For good measure, I grabbed the vodka from the fridge, too.

My body was craving something harder, but short of some ketamine Stee had stashed in my laundry room, I didn't have anything. It was such a drag that Carlo hadn't shown up to last night's gig. I'd made nice with him, paid him the last of his money, invited him to the show, but he'd skipped it, the arsehole.

I swiped my phone from the kitchen counter. I didn't remember putting it there. But then, much of my memory of last night consisted of bright flashes and dark spots of nothing. After the show, I'd got absolutely ruined.

I rocked back on my heels, the vodka bottle swinging from my fingertips. God, this place was a fucking mess. What did I ever do to Twinnie to make her play interior decorator like this?

In the silence of the apartment, there was a *crack*.

The hairs on the back of my neck stood on end.

What was that? A footfall? A dropped weapon?

She wasn't still here, was she? Little Mouse, hiding in the shadows, waiting to come out and nibble some cheese.

There was another *crack*.

I twisted to look behind me, half-expecting to see a figure lunging towards me.

Then I realised.

It was just the vodka bottle. I bumped its base against the kitchen cabinets again. *Crack*.

I laughed, the sound over-loud in the empty room.

Let her come. If Twinnie lunged at me, I'd hit her round the head with this bottle. That would serve her right.

I spent the next five minutes searching the rest of the apartment to be sure she wasn't still there. The gash on my foot left a bloody trail of footprints behind me. When I'd finished searching and found no one, I was almost disappointed. My muscles were tensed and ready. Anger was making my blood pump hot in my veins, loud in my ears.

Fuck you, Twinnie. You don't know who you're dealing with.

I took a swig of vodka and scrolled through my phone. I stabbed at the little phone icon next to her name and listened to it ring.

'Hello, this is Ella Mosier. Please leave me a message.'

'Oh, hello, Ella Mosier, otherwise known as the craziest cunt from Birdshit Island. This is your absolute best friend, Jemima. Do give me a call back when it's fucking convenient to you. In the meantime, I'll be thinking of ways to pay you back for your top-notch design efforts.'

I almost hurled my phone across the room, but I didn't need another broken thing to add to my collection.

Picking my way through the shattered glass, I slumped onto the sofa. I swung my legs up so that I was half-sitting, half-lying. A thick, hot trickle of blood ran over the arch of my heel and soaked into the caramel-coloured fabric. For a moment, I watched the blood turn brown and spread. Then I hit call on my most-dialled number.

I took a long pull of vodka and counted the rings.

One. Two. Three. Four. Five.

'Fucking answer,' I muttered, my lips already beginning to go numb.

Six. Seven. Eight –

'Hey.'

'Ella was here,' I said, not bothering with a greeting. 'You saw her?'

On the other end, Katsu let out a long breath. The whoosh of a passing car drowned out the beginning of his sentence.

'. . . way to the lab, can't really talk.'

What time was it? Midday? Later? I craned my neck to look at the gaudy red 60s-style clock on the wall, but Twinnie had smashed that, too.

I pulled the phone away from my ear and held it in front of me, like it was Katz himself and I could reach out and shake him. 'She trashed my apartment!' I shouted.

'Are you sure?' Katsu's voice came back muffled.

'She stole my coat, my keys, went on a fucking rampage!'

Another gulp of vodka calmed me enough to put the phone back to my ear and listen for Katz's reply.

'Listen, I don't know what went on,' he said, 'but that doesn't sound like her.'

'So she *was* here last night.' I waved the bottle of vodka for emphasis, building my case for an invisible jury.

'Yeah, she was . . . upset.'

On Katsu's end of the call, a siren throbbed out a single shriek.

It occurred to me that maybe I should call the police. That was what a normal person would do. But it wasn't like there was a mystery that needed solving. The embarrassing fact was, the culprit was a pathetic slip of a girl who'd probably had her first sexual experience with a sheep.

There was also the minor issue of the ketamine in my laundry room, the weed in my underwear drawer, and the fact that I hated pigs. No, I wasn't going to call the police.

'You saw her last night and you didn't tell me,' I said to Katz.

'It was . . . confusing. I didn't know what was going on.'

I thought back to when I'd arrived at the club the night before. I'd been stone-cold sober at the beginning of the night, so I actually remembered what had happened. Behind the rope, at the steps to the stage, Katz was jangling with nerves, tuning and retuning his guitar. When he said hello to me, he had a weird look on his face.

'Why are you wearing that?' he asked. 'When did you get changed?'

I was wearing skin-tight leather trousers and a Vivienne Westwood corset that made it look like the bones were on the outside of my body.

'What?' I said.

'That silver dress . . .' he said.

A dress? Who the hell wore a dress to a rock show? I was Joan Jett; I wasn't Katy Perry.

'What silver dress?'

He met my eyes for a long moment. A staring-into-your-soul look. It was the type of look he used to unleash when we were in bed: searching, insistent; like he wanted more from me than just an orgasm.

'Nothingdoesn'tmatter,' he muttered, turning away.

I felt the loss of his gaze; a twang in my stomach. Whatever he wanted, I couldn't give it to him. Never had been able to.

'Stay off the crack pipe.' I forced out a laugh. 'And get your shit together before we go onstage.'

Now, hungover in my post-apocalyptic apartment, it all clicked into place.

Silver dress. Hadn't I loaned Twinnie a silver dress for the party a few months ago?

It explained, too, the disjointed conversations with Imogen and the rest; the feeling I'd had all night that I was missing something. Without realising it, I'd been half a person, cleaved in two by Ella, who was creeping around town impersonating me.

'That stupid fucking bitch,' I growled down the phone. 'She smashed up my flat. Who does that?'

Katz was silent for a long moment. Then he said:

'Sure you didn't do it yourself? Remember what happened a few years ago? You broke every plate you owned.'

'Only 'cause I was high!'

I hated that Katsu had catalogued all my mistakes. He used to laugh with me about that night, the first time I tried LSD. Now I could imagine his solemn, frowny face. Mr Grown-Up, tutting his disapproval.

'If you really think it was Ella, you should let her give her side of the story,' Katsu said with a sigh. 'It's probably not what you think.'

I flexed my toes and a fresh blob of blood leached out of the gash in my foot. 'Why are you taking her side?'

You're my boyfriend, I wanted to shout. *Ex-boyfriend. Whatever. You belong to me.*

'Did something happen between you two?' I said.

I remembered that very first day Twinnie and I had met. I'd found her shy-girl act funny, as she'd sneaked glances at Katsu. He'd been all over her at the Seven Deadly Sins party, too, playing the gallant protector to her instead of me.

For that matter, what had happened while I'd been on Birdshit Island? She'd probably seduced him, the little slut. After all, Katsu had only ghosted me after Ella's jaunt through my life.

'Nothing happened.' Katsu's tone was long-suffering, edging into irritation.

'Liar.' I knew him well enough to recognise that huffy tone. 'Pretty pathetic of you to hook up with her. Pretty creepy.'

I was tired of being grown-up about how things had ended with Katsu. I didn't want to be civil. I wanted to hate him. Maybe we weren't right for each other, but he wasn't allowed to take up with my shadow.

'You were the one who cheated on me, remember?' Katz said.

'This again? It was one time, maybe twice, I don't even – '

'Great talking to you, Jem.' There was a sneer in his voice. 'Great knowing you.'

The bastard hung up on me.

This time, I actually did fling my phone across the room – another addition to the wreckage – and it bounced against the floor, landing with a sullen thump.

I felt the urge to cry again, but I screamed instead. My horror-movie howl echoed around the bare walls.

*

This time last year, on a rooftop in Los Angeles, someone had the idea to howl at the moon.

It was yet another party, one held on top of a six-storey building downtown. I'd thought it would be like something out of a movie – twinkling lights as far as the eye could see – but it was smoggy and I could barely see as far as the strip club's illuminated red sign down the block.

There was no moon to be seen. I ended up wailing at nothing at all.

When my voice grew hoarse, I leaned over the flimsy railing at the building's edge and craned my neck to see the ground below. Maybe I'd fall and fall and keep falling, right through into another dimension.

'Babe . . . baby,' a voice said, hot breath close to my ear.

I righted myself, tottering in high heels, struggling to remember how to stand. The guy who was talking . . . I couldn't seem to make his face stay still. It kept moving, eyes reshuffling beneath his nose, lips dancing on his forehead.

What had we taken? Coke, definitely, but something else, too. I didn't remember. I'd stopped caring of late.

'Katz . . .' My voice came out as half a murmur, half a moan. 'Katz, let's go home . . .'

'Who the fuck is Katz?'

I laughed as he flounced away, the guy whose face wouldn't stay still and whose name I couldn't remember. But there was an ache inside. I wanted Katsu. And, more than that, I wanted to be the girl Katsu had always seen when he looked at me.

LA was supposed to be my place. In the movie biz, I was sure I could out-smile, out-charm, out-sass everyone. It was cutthroat, but so was I. Toss me a grenade and I'd eat the explosion, swallow fire and come out smiling. As I packed up my life in London and headed for the sun, I felt sure it was only a matter of time before I made it.

The reality was smog and parties and powder I couldn't name.

LA made me realise I wasn't special. For every movie, every

TV show, every dog food commercial, there were a hundred other Jems lined up ready to audition. Each one of my clones was ready to launch themselves into the movie meat grinder and get spat out by the Hollywood machine.

Toss me a grenade and watch the fire eat up my insides.

'Jemma? . . . Jemma, can you hear me?'

Dawn was breaking as I weaved along the pavement barefoot, shoes hooked over the fingers of one hand, phone clutched in the other hand. I peered at passing cars, trying to figure out which one might be my Uber driver.

'Jemma, are you there?' the voice on the phone said.

'Yeah, I'm here.'

No matter how many times I reminded my agent my name was Jemima, she still always called me Jemma.

'Did I wake you up? You sound sleepy.'

My agent, Savannah, was a dark-haired beauty who looked like a Bollywood starlet. She was bi-continental (which I'd always thought made it sound like she was hot for land masses) and flitted between London and Los Angeles. I had no idea which city she was in today, but regardless of where she was in the world, she'd probably risen at 5 a.m., chugged a kale smoothie, and done her sun salutations. Pretentious cow.

'I'm fine,' I muttered.

'Last minute,' she said brightly, 'but I squeezed you in for an audition in the new Tarantino film. Can you make it to Burbank for eight?'

I blinked, my bad mood clearing.

'Yeah! Shit . . . yeah, I can make it.'

My stomach roiled with unexpected happiness. One audition was all I needed to make it. One good audition . . .

At that moment, a black sedan slowed to a stop at the curb. The smoked-glass window lowered an inch, revealing a slice of a tanned male face. 'Uber? You call an Uber?'

I said goodbye to Savannah and hastened over to the car.

'Hold on,' I said to the driver, 'I just need to throw up. Gimme two seconds.'

*

Savannah emailed me the sides for the part and I read them on my phone in the car. I was auditioning for the role of a wayward girl who partied a little too hard and ended up dead in a dumpster. Combing my fingers through my tangled hair, I grinned. I could sell my dishevelled appearance as method acting. I reapplied my orangey-red lipstick with a jerky hand and recited my lines under my breath.

Dammit, Mack, maybe all there is to life is staring into the abyss and picking out a maggot or two to eat from the darkness.

Traffic was bad, but I only arrived 20 minutes late to the cool, grey halls of the studio. Still, the blonde handling the sign-in sheet sucked her teeth and said she'd let me in only as a favour to Savannah, who'd been 'kind of a mentor' to her. (A mentor in pretension and bitchery?)

'Dammit, Mack . . .' I whispered under my breath, as I took a seat next to the other would-be partygirls who'd probably never swallowed more than an aspirin in their beige little lives.

I was going to kill this audition.

I was going to be famous.

I was going to breathe fire.

*

The lights on stage burned yellow and then, when I shut my eyes, red against my eyelids.

I blinked my eyes open again. I didn't expect it to be so bright. I didn't expect to be able to see the faces of the crowd, packed in close and each one visibly waiting.

Waiting for me to fail.

I stood at the microphone, but I didn't say anything.

Finally, it was Katsu who leaned over and pulled the mic stand toward him. 'What's up, London, we're Lace Steak.'

He let the mic stand ricochet back toward me and arced his hand down to play a squealing electric note on his guitar. The rest of the band started up, noise reverberating underfoot. I heard my cue a second too late. My fingers wrapped around the mic, but I couldn't find my voice.

A few feet away, Katsu continued strumming, his rhythm a shade too fast – I could feel his waves of irritation – as the band played the song's opening through once more. Nerves stuck in my throat like a fist, but I gasped out the first line.

I thought it might get better, once we got into it. It was a bad idea to open with an original song – the *fast as an engine, go, go, go* one, which sounded tinny and tentative in the room – but once we started hammering out our cover of Celebrity Skin, the energy would pick up.

It got worse.

The sound mix sucked. Ricky couldn't find the beat on the drums. No one could stay in time with each other. And I . . . I couldn't breathe. The crowd was yelling, but it didn't sound like support, it sounded like fury.

They were all looking at me. It was Los Angeles all over again. A piece of meat in the audition room. They were judging me. Not thin enough. Not pretty enough. Need bigger boobs, whiter teeth, glossier hair. They demanded perfection and nothing less.

'Hey there, Jemma, how are you today? . . . Great, great . . . So good to have you here . . . Now just stand on your mark and give the camera your best . . .

'We're ready when you are . . . Hey, Jemma, you okay? . . . Stand on the mark, sweetie . . .

'You're gonna have to speak up . . . Okay, try again . . . The camera's not catching it, hon . . .

'I think it may be time to move on, honey . . .'

It wasn't my last audition in LA. It wasn't even my worst. But it was the one that came screaming back to me when I was onstage at the show last night.

The guy running the audition was named Garrett and he wore a baby-blue sweater-vest, despite the fact that it was over 90° F in Burbank that day. He spared me a look of pity when I stumbled out of the audition room after stuttering and whispering through my lines.

Dammit, Mack . . .

*

It was a bad idea to be sober.

I had a stupid notion that I should try to enjoy the band's first show with a clear head, not submerged in smog. Me, up on stage, performing. Just me, no chemical modification. Me, doing what I was built for.

We bombed. Our first show and it was a fucking disaster.

Afterwards, I stumbled off stage, shell-shocked, listening to everyone lie and tell me how great it was.

The rehearsals had been bad. I wasn't oblivious. I'd noticed. But so what if I didn't always hit the notes? I was a rock star, it was cool to be raspy and off-key. Teething problems were temporary; I'd thought it would all come together in the end.

Sober, with the bravado stripped away, I couldn't lie to myself anymore.

I was a shitty singer, just as I'd been a shitty actress.

Katsu didn't join in with the platitudes. He was stony silent. I hadn't just ruined this for myself, I'd ruined it for him, too.

When he caught my eye, he gave me that weird look again. It was far from the worshipful look he'd given me during the first few years of our relationship, as if he couldn't believe he'd won a girl like me. Nor was it the stare-into-your-soul look that characterised the last few on/off months, like he was hoping to x-ray through layers I wasn't sure I had.

This was a new look.

In my ruined apartment, with blood drying on the sole of my foot, I realised what that look meant.

I wish you were different.

I wish you were . . . more like Ella?

41

PRESAGE

Ella

At the base of ruined Piel Castle, I huddled into a nook shaped by tumbled stones. Even in this hollow, the wind was fierce, pulling at my shabby wax jacket. The day's cold crept down the back of my neck, chilling my bones.

In the summer, locals might spend an afternoon on Piel Island. Tourists might make a day trip here, nosing around the castle where pretender to the throne Lambert Simnel had once hidden out. On this January day, there was no one. Even Ol' Roy, the pub landlord, tended to vacate the island in the depths of winter.

The wit-wit-wit of a bird call was the only sign of life.

I drew a notepad from my pocket and spread it open at a clean page. My fingers, gripping the blue biro, were numb. When I started to write, the result was a wonky row of childish cursive that didn't resemble my own neat handwriting.

I'm sorry, I wrote. *I can't do this anymore.*

I'd written letters like this before. The first time, I was sixteen. I wrote a note, tucked it beneath my pillow. It was past midnight and my parents' caravan was dark and cool and quiet. The tearing of blister packs of pills sounded deafening to my ears, but no one stirred.

I emptied out all my antidepressants and, when that didn't look like enough, I popped out twenty or thirty ibuprofen onto my pale pink duvet as well. I drank them down with half a bottle of my dad's whisky.

I was ready to die. I'd made the decision.

I'm sorry, the note read. *I'm so, so, so sorry.*

I woke up the next day, a Saturday, to Mum pounding on my door. My whole body was heavy. I couldn't get my breath. I doubled over, wheezing, and the vomit washed out of my throat, splattering whisky-brown across my duvet. The smell of it was sour, disgustingly human.

Later that day, I tore up the note and buried the pieces underneath the orange peel in the bin. Fear shivered through my body, stronger than my self-loathing, stronger than my desire to die. I was a coward. I couldn't even kill myself right. I was too weak.

Here, now, on Piel Island, I wasn't scared anymore.

How had April termed it? Crazy fearlessness. I was crazy fearless.

I finished writing and ripped the page from my notebook, shoving it in my pocket. My limbs cracked as I stood up. When I was a teenager, climbing the castle walls was a popular dare on sun-baked, skunk-scented summer evenings. Today, it was impossible to remember how it was to feel warm, to feel drowsy or contented, but I wanted to stand at the highest point and . . .

And what?

I climbed.

In the mist, the grey stones were slippery against my palms. Tufts of green grew out of the castle walls and I buried my fingers in these crevices, climbing, climbing, climbing.

The castle resembled a stone box with no roof. Parts of its walls had collapsed onto the beach, as if the pressure of standing up straight for so many hundreds of years was simply too much. This created a rough-hewn ladder of sorts that you could use to reach the apex of the walls, some three storeys above ground level.

At the top, I drifted along the walls, looking out to the murky grey horizon and thinking of the imposter boy king Lambert Simnel, the men ready to die for him. My foot lodged in a crevice and I wavered.

If I fell from this height, I could crack my skull open. It would be quick. Quick, like being struck by a taxi, head smashed against the tarmac.

I'm so, so, so sorry . . .

My arms shot out, helping me to regain my balance. It was an instinct to save myself, rather than a concerted effort.

The note in my pocket had a heartbeat all its own. I could feel it thudding against my thigh, the vibrations travelling all the way to the tips of my toes and beyond. The whole of Piel Castle ruins were shaking.

I'm sorry. I can't do this anymore.

I'm trapped and there's no way out. I've felt like this for so long and I can't take it anymore.

I don't think anyone ever really saw me, ever really knew me, ever really loved me.

The world will be a better place without me in it.

Since my return from London, I'd been busy. No more long hours of lethargy; no more days that disappeared like smoke. I'd been filled with a clear, pure, merciless energy like nothing I'd experienced before. There was so much to do before I died.

In my caravan, my ragged fingernails had caught the edge of the faded floral wallpaper. I'd dug in and tugged. Hard. The wallpaper came off in jagged strips. I tore at the poster, too. The Paris skyline split in two as I ripped it apart.

I cleared the walls of the person I'd once been and repainted in magnolia. My mum was complimentary when she found me dragging half-empty paint tins from the shed.

'Good to see you with a sense of purpose,' she said.

I gifted her a clear, pure, merciless smile. She smiled back and pulled me into a hug. I felt nothing. What a relief, to be empty of everything; to be skin hanging on a skeleton.

Time for a spring clean. I wanted everything to be clean and painted fresh. No sense in leaving the caravan to moulder without me.

Everything sentimental – a silver necklace with a tiny cross that had belonged to Mum, notebooks full of scribbled song lyrics, a faded-blue origami rabbit made by Owen – went in the bin. I couldn't quite bring myself to smash the guitar to pieces, rock star-style, but I also didn't want to look at it anymore.

'Hey, Simon,' I said to my brother. 'You want my guitar?'

'What's the catch?' he asked.

He was stretched out on his bed in my parents' caravan, playing a game on his phone. He didn't look up at me, he didn't invite me inside the room. Archie was curled up asleep at the end of the bed. In months past, I would've tried to entice him back to my side, but now I let him sleep. He wasn't mine anymore. Nothing was mine anymore.

'No catch,' I said.

I propped my guitar against the doorjamb and waited for a response.

'Alright, I'll take it,' Simon said. His thumbs stopped skimming his phone, but he still didn't look at me. 'But if you go crying to Mum, saying I stole it from you – '

'I won't,' I said. 'You want to do that coin toss thing?'

That got his attention. 'Serious?' He tossed his phone aside and scrambled off the bed.

'Yeah,' I said. 'The caravan. We'll flip for it.'

'Fuck yeah!'

Simon jangled with loose change as he thrust his hands into his pockets and pulled out a grimy two pence piece. He gave me an eager nod and I returned a beatific smile.

The coin arced high in the air before I could say anything more. As soon as it landed on the carpet, Simon was whooping.

'Heads! Heads it is!'

He pulled his jumper up over his head like a footballer

celebrating a goal and charged around the small room, blind.

I didn't bother to point out that we'd never called heads or tails. Let him have the caravan, magnolia and smelling of paint. I didn't need it anymore.

*

I'm sorry . . .

I made it down off the trembling ruins of Piel Castle as the sun was setting. Mist and drizzle combined to create a smothering wet-weather-grey that erased Walney Island ahead of me. Now the greyness was tinged with rust-orange as the light faded.

I can't do this anymore . . .

I hastened across the sands and my wellies sank with each step. When I glanced over my shoulder, I saw the footprints behind me had disappeared, swallowed up by the soft sands.

I'm trapped and there's no way out . . .

The wind whipped my hair around my face. My nostrils filled with the scent of salt and earth and, beneath it, a sweetness of rotting fruit. I swallowed, and all I tasted was blood.

I don't think anyone ever really loved me . . .

When the edges of the tide pools frothed with tiny white bubbles, you knew it was time. Presage, they called it. Hurry, hurry, keep going, get home safe now. When the brown puddles turned white at the edges, that meant the tide was coming in.

Death was coming.

First it would arrive in a trickle and then in a torrent.

One rush of seawater and her legs would buckle.

Ella would die gasping, the cold taking her voice away, the water filling up her lungs, the sands sucking her under.

In the shadow of the island of an imposter king, another imposter would die.

For her parents, it would be a relief. They'd finally be free of the shackles of a depressed daughter who couldn't seem to feel better. As for Bethany, Simon, the rest of the people in her life? It was hard to imagine they'd care at all that she was gone. They'd cry a few crocodile tears at the funeral and then they'd move on.

The world will be a better place without me in it.

42

EVERYONE GETS A TURN

Jem

There was a crack down the centre of my phone screen, like a lightning strike. I pressed the phone to my ear and listened to it ring. Lounging on my stomach in bed, I kicked my clumsily-bandaged foot in the air. On the eighth ring, there was a click and then, *Suuuuuuuuuup. Carlo.*

He sounded embarrassingly stoned in his voicemail message. It made me imagine him raking a hand through dirty hair and blinking at me from beneath heavy eyelids.

'Hey, fucker, where are you?' I said into the phone.

It was either the fifth or sixth message I'd left for Carlo today. Mummy Dearest had come through and deposited my monthly allowance in my bank account, following the goodie-goodie work I'd been doing at the gallery in my Big Girl Job. Now that I was flush with cash, I had coke on my mind.

Papa had given me some pocket money on Saturday night, as well, right before he'd disappeared off the face of the Earth. **Business in Dubai – back in a couple of months. Stay sexy, princess,** he'd texted me. Wasn't Paris where he was supposed to be going on business? Big surprise. Dada was marvellous at making plans and even better at breaking them.

I called Carlo once more, on the off chance that he might still be sleeping at – I glanced at the time – eleven on a Monday morning.

'Charlie, Charlie, Charlie,' I sang into my phone, 'I need some jelly beans. Call me back.'

I was still wary of Carlo, but at least he'd never tried to sell me ketamine and called it coke.

The time caught my eye again. 11:04 a.m. Bleurgh. I wanted to go back to sleep, but I'd already slept for 18 hours and now it felt like my bones were ready to jump out of my skin. I was still hungover – maybe even a little drunk still – and the drone of hoovering from the living room was reverberating around my skull cavity.

'Too loud!' I yelled, and then regretted it. A slime of pre-vomit coated the back of my throat.

A second later, the bedroom door cracked open and Gabriela's head appeared, brown curls falling out of a top knot. The vacuum continued to whine at her feet, louder now that it was closer.

'Sorry? What was that?' she said.

'It's too loud,' I mumbled, cradling my head in my hands. 'Can't you use a broom or something?'

Gabriela nodded sagely. 'Broom,' she repeated.

'Uh . . . now?' My eyes bored into her, until finally, she cut the power to the vacuum.

Blessed, blessed silence.

Gabriela bumbled away, letting the door fall closed. She'd arrived an hour ago, surveyed the broken glass and bloody footprints and, without raising an eyebrow, gone to work. In fairness, she'd seen worse.

Once, I'd got so fucked up, I wrote the lyrics to Head Like a Hole across the living room walls in red lipstick. When I finished, it looked like blood. A scene from the Manson murders. The sight made me laugh so hard I threw up.

Gabriela cleaned it all – the lipstick, the vomit – and never even clucked her disapproval. Good old Gabriela. She was like the mother I never had.

Actually, Gabriela's primary drawback was that she was paid by the mother I did have. She spent most of her time removing non-existent dirt from the soulless Kensington townhouse that my mother checked into every night like it was a hotel. Mother never had any friends round, because she didn't have friends. She never entertained any boyfriends, because she was a dried up old prune. Yet Gabriela cleaned it top to bottom twice a week like it was a public toilet.

I half-suspected Gabriela reported on my behaviour to Mother, as well. Maybe my hangover was making me paranoid, but I thought I'd heard her whispering to someone on the phone.

My own lightning-strike phone vibrated on the bedspread. I flipped it over, hoping to see Carlo's name. Instead it flashed up 'Elgin', a new message.

What's going on Lady J? Where are you?

Bollocks.

I'd thought maybe my boss at the gallery wouldn't notice one day's absence. That relied on him having other things going on in his sad little life, which, naturally, he didn't.

I could phone him, lay my illness on thick, and claim a sick day. My hand hovered over the call icon, but I couldn't bring myself to do it. Sluggishness crawled across my skin. I flopped over onto my back and stared vacantly at the messy green wall of my bedroom.

What was the point?

I'd failed as an actress, failed as a singer. I might as well fail as a worker bee, too.

It was only a matter of time before I fucked it all up anyway.

Mother was surely expecting it. I'd always been Daddy's Little Girl in that sense. Big plans; no results.

I stared at my phone, waiting for a new message to come through. I almost wanted Elgin to send me another text, berating me. A call from Carlo in the throes of psychosis would at least break up the monotony. I wanted a message from Stee or April or any of my friends. I was so fabulous, why weren't they texting me?

It was Katsu's voice I heard in my head: *Because it's Monday morning, and they have jobs, they have stuff going on. It's not all about you, Ripper.*

I wrapped myself in the duvet and burrowed down into bed. I imagined him saying it in his new disapproving tone. Serious, grown-up Katsu, who didn't have time for me. The image gnawed at me.

What I wanted most of all was to see Katz's name flash up on my phone. I wanted him to apologise for yesterday. I wanted him to tell me he loved me.

I wanted to know that someone, somewhere, loved me. Because I wasn't sure anyone ever had.

'All done.'

Gabriela's voice broke through my thoughts. Leaning against the door jamb, she gave me a big smile.

'Good as new,' she said. 'I'll be off now.'

A lump rose in my throat. *No, stay,* I wanted to say. *Don't leave me here alone.*

'You didn't bring any cake, did you?' I asked.

'No, no, no, Albert's on a diet,' she said, making a clicking sound with her tongue. Was Albert her husband? Her cat?

'I could order something.' I fidgeted with my phone. 'Cheesecake or macarons . . . or . . . or cookie shots. We don't have to tell . . . Albert.'

I fixed her with a megawatt smile, but my mouth drooped at one corner. It didn't matter. She wasn't looking at me. She was coiling the power cable around the vacuum.

'So much work to do, but you enjoy your cake,' she said distractedly, backing out of the room.

There was a muffled clatter as she collected up the rest of her cleaning supplies. Then she was gone, the front door bumping shut behind her.

I jammed my fists into my eyes to stop the tears before

they fell.

God. Just grow up. The woman is a bloody cleaner. She's not your mummy, she's not your buddy; she's the help.

I broke out into a laugh.

Pull yourself together. All you need is a cocktail and a snort of something.

I reached for my phone again, ignoring the pang as I realised I'd still received no new messages.

I'd throw a party. A Stuff-Your-Stupid-Job party. What did it matter that it was a Monday? I could put the notice up on Facebook right now.

It was the first time in a while that I'd logged in. Facebook was for people like Elgin who didn't have lives of their own, so they were constantly sticking their beaks into other people's.

'Bitch,' I said idly, swiping past a grinning redhead.

My head still rested against my pillow, while my thumb twitched against the screen. I scrolled through a feed populated with sort-of-friends and people-I'd-once-fucked.

'Tosser . . .'

Fake smiles. Posed pictures. Everyone desperately glossing over their fucked-up emptiness.

'Bitch . . . tosser . . .'

My thumb stopped when I spotted Carlo's face. He looked handsome instead of hollow-cheeked. His mouth was open mid-laugh and amusement lit up his whole face. It wasn't a photo, after all. It was a clip from the indie movie we were in together. When I hovered over the still, Carlo came to life, shuddering into a genuine, full-body laugh.

Underneath the clip, there was a notice:

Charlie Bove – In Memoriam.

Oh, my God.

In memoriam? Fucking hysterical. Carlo was pulling a prank or something. I bit out a laugh and, in the clip that looped over and over, Carlo laughed with me.

Come to think of it, a fake funeral would make for a great party. Everyone would dress up in their best goth-chic, complete with black veils and eyeliner tears. We'd drink bright-red Bloody Marys and tar-black liquorice-stick cocktails. Surely I could find a funeral home that would lend me a coffin for the evening. Come on, guys! Climb inside and pretend you're dead! Everyone gets a turn!

Grinning, I tapped my phone to expand the post. I expected the comments to be cry-laughing emojis and *hahahaha good one*. But no one seemed to be getting the joke.

Gone too soon rest in peace brother

Cant believe ill never see him again

Soooo tragic omg

I kept scrolling, waiting for the penny to drop among these wailing simpletons. None of them were getting the joke. Some were even discussing sharing rides to the funeral.

I read the post again.

. . . fatal collision on Saturday night . . . rushed to the hospital . . . heroic efforts . . . but tragically died a few hours later . . . donations requested instead of flowers . . . raising money for Battersea Dogs Home . . . Charlie loved dogs so much . . .

Jesus.

My phone trembled in my hand.

He was actually dead.

43

BAD BLOOD

Ella

What would Jem do?

The old me was dying. I'd left her out on the sinking sands that day.

I hadn't completely got rid of her, though. I was still stuck inside this body, with its churning bad blood. But soon, my blood would flow rich like wine, fizzing like champagne. Life would be so good.

What would Jem do?

I was starting to know, instinctively. I was ready to be reborn.

I could access her thoughts and feelings now. There was a door in my mind that led to Jem's.

The night I'd gone to her apartment after the show, I'd been terrified. Jem's taunts had driven me out of the apartment. But I wasn't scared anymore. A new strength was boiling inside me. It had allowed me to kill Carlo. It had opened up a new world to me.

When the mirror in my double's apartment had smashed, the door had sprung free. Since then, during the intervening week, I'd found I could open it anytime and step through.

Sometimes it was only for seconds at a time. Three days ago, at a family dinner, I'd looked down at the iceberg lettuce and cucumber on my plate and said, in a sharp, haughty voice, 'This salad is ghastly.'

'Well, next time, you go to Tesco and see what you can find, young lady,' Mum said.

I wilted back into Ella, my shoulders slumping, my mumbled

381

apology soft with Cumbrian vowels.

Sometimes, though, I could be Jem for hours at a time.

Yesterday, I'd run into Bethany near the park. Her squalling new-born was in the pram and Talia was attempting to climb her leg like a monkey. Bethany gave me a tremulous smile, her mouth opening as if she were about to say, *hi y'alright?*

I brushed past her, sweeping my hair over my shoulder and stalking onward down the street like I was on a catwalk.

It was so easy being Jem.

Jem didn't give a fuck. She didn't make nice. She didn't concern herself with the opinions of sheep.

I turned my face up to the sky for a moment and let the sun warm the length of my neck. On this January day, it was still cold – I walked with my hands thrust into the pockets of my fawn-coloured wool coat – but at least it wasn't raining.

Sunshine had brought the people from the homes and the streets were busy. A group of lads showed off their muscles in T-shirts even as their fingers turned blue with cold. I smiled brazenly at them, coquettish in orangey-red lipstick.

One of the guys crossed the road, falling into step next to me. 'Alright, beautiful? Get your number?'

I laughed him off, toying with the tarnished-gold locket that hung between my breasts.

'I'm not from around here,' I said, and kept on walking as his pace slowed.

I don't fuck losers, I thought.

Maybe I should've said that out loud?

The question stuttered in my mind. Maybe Jem would've taken his number? Maybe she would've considered it a laugh?

Maybe . . . Maybe . . .

Despite the cold, I felt too hot in my coat. Blood boiled in my veins.

I scurried over to a nearby bus shelter. It was a relief to sit down. I clutched the sides of the red plastic seat and willed myself to remember who I was.

'Where's a pretty girl like you off to today?' the woman seated beside me asked.

'Oh . . .' I murmured. 'Nowhere special . . .'

'Really? Can't believe that's true.'

The woman's white hair was styled in tight curls and her pink lipstick was smeared. With her quavery voice and rheumy eyes, she was old enough that the aura of nosiness that radiated from her was supposed to be endearing and not rude.

I took a deep breath. 'Just going to meet my dad.'

'Lovely, lovely! Bit of a daddy's girl, are you?'

'Yeah . . . yeah . . .'

I scanned the street, almost expecting to see his gunmetal-grey sports car come racing over the bridge.

'He'll be picking me up,' I said vaguely.

'Good dad, is he?'

'The best,' I said, turning to meet the woman's moist blue gaze. 'He's really cool, y'know? Not like other dads.' My voice was growing stronger now. 'He's great at business, very successful. Moving to Paris soon – I'm probably going with him.'

'Paris? Well, ooh la la! You lucky duck.'

'Yeah, I'm lucky.' I broke into a smile. A Jem smile.

'I went to France on my honeymoon.' The woman matched my smile with a gappy one of her own. 'Few years ago, mind. You been before?'

'Oh yeah, lots of times. My dad is very well travelled.'

I tossed my hair over my shoulder and pulled a compact from my bag to check my make-up. In the process, I noticed the man sitting next to me. He was a geography teacher type, balding and dressed in an ugly patterned jumper. He was also listening to every word I was saying.

I knew him.

No. Ella knew him.

My face flushed, sweat prickling up my neck.

It was Tim Something. He always sat on the front pew at church. He'd offered me his handkerchief once when I had a cold and couldn't stop sneezing.

I knew him. He knew me.

In this town, I'd always be Ella.

Beside me, the white-haired woman was burbling on about her honeymoon, but Tim Something was still looking at me. I waited for him to interrupt, to say, *What you talking about, Ella? Your Rory's a brickie, what's he want to go to Paris for?*

Noise roared in my ears like the ground beneath me was opening up. No. It was the bus pulling in, its engine rumbling. My head drooped and I cradled my skull in my hands. I remembered the feel of Carlo's meaty chest as I'd pushed him. His expression of shock seared against the back of my eyelids.

'Y'alright, dear?' the woman asked.

'Fine, fine,' I muttered. It took a lot of effort to lift my head and look at her.

A spider was crawling across my hand, but when I swatted at it, it was gone.

The woman tottered to her feet and, with slow, slow steps, climbed aboard the bus. Tim Something followed her. He had his phone pressed to his ear. Was he calling my parents? The police?

Even though I felt sick, the thought propelled me to my feet. I scurried away from the bus stop, keeping my head down. I passed the group of lads in their too-tight T-shirts. They didn't seem to notice me.

Maybe they couldn't even see me.

Ella was dying, dying, dead. I had to get out of this body and find a new one. Yet her hands still clamped around my throat, threatening to pull me back into this old life.

I couldn't let her.

I had to become Jem once and for all. And the only way to do that was to kill the imposter.

44

RUMOURS

Jem

On the day of Carlo's funeral, I wore a black satin-and-lace dress that looked like vintage lingerie (but came with a designer price tag). My left foot was still bandaged, but I wore heels anyway. I decided against drawing eyeliner tears beneath my eyes (too tacky), but I did find a black veil in my wardrobe that I'd once worn for Halloween. Carlo would have appreciated the drama of it.

That became the mantra of the day.

It's what he would have wanted.

Carlo would have liked my tits in the dress. He would have laughed at the veil.

It's what he would have wanted.

Behind a locked door, the guy raised his eyebrows at me and held up the bag of coke. Was his name Jake? Jace? I'd met him a few times before, but I couldn't remember.

He was tall, with a buzz cut, and muscles bulged beneath his black T-shirt. Though he was even whiter than I was, there was a studied 'street' vibe to him, set off by a whispery moustache and soul patch.

I swiped the bag from him and shook out a crumbly mass of cocaine onto the porcelain. We were shut inside a small communal bathroom in the basement of the church. The stink of the enclosed space had layers to it: bleach, covering up piss, covering up something else – the smell of death?

The weather was bitterly cold, but I hadn't been able to find my favourite coat this morning so I'd shoved a fake-fur stole over my shoulders. Even indoors, I was shivering. I knew the cocaine could fix that. It could fix everything.

I used a credit card to cut up the powder into lines.

It's what he would have wanted.

'Here's to the big man,' I said.

When I surfaced after snorting my line, my veil was twisted around the back of my head, like a frizz of black hair.

'Here's to him!' Jake-Jace bent his head to get his own commemorative snort.

I leaned against the basin, closing my eyes and rolling my neck as I waited for the drugs to hit my bloodstream. Through the ceiling, there came the shudder of distant organ music. The service was starting. Even clad in coke's bulletproof armour, I didn't want to go back out there.

Carlo was dead. He was really dead.

People our age weren't supposed to die. We were supposed to live forever. Worst case scenario, our bodies would die and we'd upload our thoughts and memories to the cloud for future resurrection.

Charlie wasn't going to be resurrected. He was gonzo.

I was thinking of him as Charlie more and more now. Carlo was his would-be gangster persona; a lunatic who took his addiction too far. Charlie was my friend. For two years, we had a standing Saturday breakfast date at a hole-in-the-wall in Clapham. I always hated the way he poured ketchup over his eggs, creating a disgusting wound of red sauce.

I heaved out a sob.

I missed him.

'Shit, you okay?' Jake-Jace asked.

He had long arms and a tendency towards king-of-the-swingers arm movements. Now he tried to hook me close in an embrace, but I shrugged him off.

'Yeah.' I blinked rapidly. I wasn't going to let a stupid memory ruin my make-up. 'You wanna do another line?'

'It's what he would have wanted,' Ja-Ja said solemnly, shaking out more cocaine.

Afterwards, we were jangling. Blood thrummed in my ears. Ja-Ja's foot was tapping a too-fast rhythm on the tile floor and it felt like my heart had synced to match it. Without preamble, Ja-Ja began telling me about the old-timey car he was rebuilding from scratch. His voice came out rapid-fire. He gave no signal that he was changing topics, but suddenly he was telling me about the three months he'd spent in Thailand.

'Ever been to Thailand?'

'No,' I said, rolling the hem of my dress between my thumb and forefinger in quick, obsessive flicks.

'So you heard the rumours?' he asked, without pause.

'About Thailand? That it's a hippy shithole? Yeah, I've heard.'

'Rumours about Charlie.'

I squinted. 'What rumours?'

'Said it was an accident.' He leaned in close. His eyes, pupils dilated, looked almost completely black. 'Not an accident. No way.'

Ja-Ja tapped two fingers against my temple. His breath, moist against my face, smelled like Doritos. When I swallowed, all I could taste was the harsh chemical taint of the cocaine.

'Police don't have anyone for it,' he continued. 'But that's what I heard.'

I sucked in my cheeks and swept my tongue over numb teeth. The cocaine was churning heat through my bloodstream, but somewhere in my core, I felt a shiver.

There was one person who I knew for certain had gone on a rampage last weekend. I'd left Twinnie a bunch more voicemails over the last few days, but I'd still received nothing in return.

Could Ella have been involved in Carlo's death?

No. It was too ridiculous to believe.

'Shoreditch is full of crazies on a Saturday night,' I said, lifting my chin.

Ja-Ja shrugged. He had apparently grown tired of the conversation. He was looking at me intently, his hand coming to rest oh-so-casually on my hip. I ignored his gaze, my fingers toying instead with the still-half-full bag of coke.

'How much do you want for this?' I asked.

'Oh, we can work something out . . .'

Ja-Ja affected a husky tone that was neither convincing nor sexy. He rubbed a hand over my satin-encased thigh. Then, in a swift movement, he tugged at the lace hem, sliding his hand up my bare leg.

I let out a snort of derision and wriggled away from him.

'A hundred will cover it, I'm sure,' I said.

I snapped open my teeny-tiny black satin handbag and withdrew a couple of notes. I dropped them in the basin and grabbed the bag of coke. Ja-Ja's expression was already twisting from surprised to nasty, nose lifting into a sneer.

It was Carlo all over again and I wasn't going to take the chance that he had Carlo's violent streak.

'Nice meeting you!' I said sarcastically.

I scraped the door lock across and burst free of the bathroom, not waiting to hear Ja-Ja's inevitable *hey bitch* reaction.

*

Upstairs, in the church, the atmosphere was hushed. I still walked with a slight limp, thanks to the cut on my foot, and my clattering footsteps down the centre aisle drew glances. I tossed my hair and revelled in the attention. A couple of people waved or shot me covert smiles.

We were all supposed to be looking at a wispy, grey-haired woman who was reading a long poem celebrating Charlie's life, but her eyes remained downcast and she spoke at a barely audible volume.

God, why did funerals have to be so depressing?

Mine would be a party; a three-day bacchanal, with wine

and sex and a good dollop of insanity.

I dropped into a seat next to Stee, who gave me a small smile. With a jolt, I realised that Katsu was sitting next to him. He'd known Charlie through me – back in the day, the three of us used to hang out occasionally – but it hadn't occurred to me that he'd come to the funeral.

He looked good, too. He was one of the only guys our age who was dressed in a suit. Black jacket, white shirt, skinny bootlace tie. His hair, which fluctuated between chin-length and shoulder-length, was long enough to be knotted at the back of his head. The resulting look was austere – and surprisingly sexy.

I reached across Stee and nudged Katz's elbow with my hand. He didn't react. My eyes bored into him, but he wouldn't meet my gaze. I pinched his arm through his suit jacket, but still nothing.

'Leave it,' Stee muttered.

That made me flush, the realisation that maybe they'd been talking about me. Katz had been complaining to Stee before I'd arrived.

I retracted my hand and sat up straight, staring dead ahead. The wisp of a woman at the front had stopped reading now, tears dripping down her face in big fat blobs. She wavered on her feet, like she might collapse.

I sniffed loudly, though not from crying. My eyes felt dry and itchy, incapable of tears. My right foot bounced rhythmically against the stone floor.

Inside the handbag in my lap, my phone whistled.

I had a wild thought that it was Katsu messaging me. We used to do that – sit next to each other and send x or hi or ♥. So cheesy. I'd slap him and mime vomiting. Now all I wanted to do was look down and see an x from him on my phone screen.

The name that came up wasn't Katsu.

It was Twinnie.

I read the message and the flush that lingered on my cheeks

turned to fire.

Got your coat.

My Burberry sable coat, monogrammed on the breast pocket with JCM; wool that melted between your fingers like the fur of a teddy bear. My dad gave me that coat.

Someone else was standing at the lectern at the front of the church now. It was a balding man, his paunch thrust forward. His voice boomed through the high-ceilinged space, reciting the words to Do Not Stand at my Grave and Weep.

My thumbs flicked across the screen of my phone.

Thief, I typed, give it back

The reply from Ella came back seconds later. My phone's accompanying whistle, loud in the silent church, made the balding man falter, but I didn't care. Twinnie's response read:

Come and get it

I had to bite my tongue to stop from screaming.

That bitch.

That crazy bitch.

Surreptitiously, I licked my finger and dipped it into the bag of coke hidden in my handbag. I feigned a cough, covering my mouth with one hand and using the other to rub the white dust into my gums.

So Twinnie thought she could ransack my flat. She thought she could come into my life and steal my coat. My eyes slid sideways. She thought she thought she could steal Katz.

I wanted to show her how wrong she was. That coat was mine. Katsu was mine.

Despite the heat that chased the cocaine, the cold of the frigid day crept through me. I rubbed my bare arms hard, till they flared pink. Then I circled the thumb and finger of my right hand around the wrist of my left and squeezed.

Would she fight if I grabbed her?

How hard would I have to hit her before she screamed?

I thought of Carlo and his bicycle pump and almost laughed.

Could it really have been Twinnie who killed him? If so, she deserved everything that was coming to her.

I'd found her online. I'd invited her into my life. Now I was ready to put Twinnie back in her place.

45

THIEF

Ella

Got your coat

Phone clenched in my hands, I sat cross-legged on the bed in the airless caravan. I'd finished painting it this morning, but when I breathed in deep, all I could smell was oranges, undercut by vanilla and ginger.

For a second, I was sure my double must be right behind me. I even felt her arm slip through mine. My head whipped around.

There was no one there.

'Just me,' I whispered. 'Just me . . .'

I returned my gaze to my phone. I stared at the message for a long moment and then pressed send.

Got your coat

The reply came back immediately:

Thief give it back

My fingers glided over the phone's keyboard.

Come and get it

It was easy to lure her here; easy to know what to say to make her come.

What did Jem care about? Stuff. Useless stuff.

I knew the thought of the fawn-coloured coat in my possession would rile her. Her tarnished-gold locket hung heavy around my neck, too. I wound its chain around my wrist, twisting tighter and tighter.

Bitch im coming

The message appeared on my phone just as I'd known it would. Four hours by train from London to Barrow-in-Furness. Five hours if she was driving. The clock was ticking.

What would Jem do when she arrived?

She'd scream and shout and stamp her feet like a brat. Jem defaulted to aggression and degradation whenever someone crossed her. I imagined her storming over to the caravan park, hammering on my door, on my parents' door.

She'd relish the opportunity to shake her finger in Mum's face. *Do you know what your daughter's been up to? Do you know how pathetic she is?*

Of course they knew. They knew Ella was worthless. Mum would agree with every vile word that spilled from Jem's lips. *She's pitiable*, Mum would say. *We can't stand her.*

Tears sprang to my eyes. Using my sleeve, I wiped them away roughly.

It didn't matter. Ella was dead.

The phone vibrated in my hand. Another message from the imposter.

Better watch out bitch

I checked the time. It was just past noon. Four, five hours till she arrived.

I wasn't going to let her run amok. I wasn't going to let her ruin my plans. Jem was in my power now. I could read her

393

thoughts and pre-empt her every action. It was easy to know what to say to control Jem.

After all, I was her.

*

Dad went down to the pub to watch the footie on Saturday afternoons. Mum attended her church group. I could be almost sure that neither of them would be at the caravan park when Jem arrived. Simon was the wild card.

He showed up at my door at two o'clock, crowing about 'his' caravan, demanding to move his stuff in. As he talked, I found I could look right through him. I could see the strange shape of his skull, the holes in his cheeks above his smile, the hollows cradling his eyeballs.

'When are you gonna be out of here?' he asked.

I stared at his fleshless face a moment longer and then pulled a twenty pound note from inside my bra.

Money. Money could solve all problems.

Simon grimaced, but he took the twenty anyway. It was some of the cash I'd grabbed from the London apartment. Plenty more where that came from.

'Get out of here' – my voice came out haughty – 'go to Barrow and get some burgers or something.' I gave a dismissive flick of my hand. 'Don't come back for a while.'

'Moving tomorrow, yeah?' Simon bounced on the balls of his feet. 'After church, you'll get your stuff out?'

'Tomorrow,' I echoed, and my brother gave a self-satisfied grin.

Today, no one would notice I was gone, but tomorrow –

Tomorrow, Mum would barge into the green caravan, demanding to know why I wasn't ready for church. The bed would be empty. Her irritation would tick over into panic. She'd call for Dad.

My mind was wide open. I could see everything. I could

see the future. It hadn't happened yet, but I could watch them ransacking Ella's caravan, pawing through the sad remains of her life.

Clothes all there? Then she's not run away . . . She's just having a funny five minutes . . . She'll be back soon . . . What's that? A note –

I'd placed the suicide note placed beneath my pillow like a letter to the tooth fairy. By the time they found it, their daughter would be dead, once and for all.

*

Four o'clock arrived and my body was rebelling against me. Inside the caravan, I peered out the window for the hundredth time, scanning the gravel drive for signs of a car. My fingers drummed against the window pane. I couldn't stay still.

Was this how Jem felt when she snorted whatever it was she snorted? Like she could crawl out of her own skin?

The spiders were all over my body now. Tiny fangs nagged at my earlobes. They were biting at the flap of skin between my thumb and forefinger. Their hairy bodies burrowed into the hollows behind my knees.

I scratched at my legs and glanced down at my phone to see if there were any new messages. Nothing. I re-read our last exchange. Goading Jem had provoked her into action, but I knew that grovelling would work best now.

Im sorry, I'd typed. im so sorry let me apologise in person

I imagined her scowling as she'd shot off her reply to me:

Leaving the motorway now. Not an apogee I want from you ill be there in an hour

So she was driving, not on the train. The timestamp was 3:22 p.m. Right now, it was 4:07 p.m. My mind opened up and I saw her, bombing along the country roads of Cumbria at 80mph, eyes on her phone not on the road, courting her own death with every casual swerve of the steering wheel.

I let the phone screen darken. I wasn't sure I could wait much longer. My whole body craved it: a renewal, a rebirth.

I lifted the fawn-coloured coat from the peg by the door and slid my arms into its smooth lining. Glancing in the mirror, I tousled a hand through my hair and smacked my orangey-red lips. The gold locket, hiding its photo of a mother and daughter, glinted in the light. I made a final sweep of the caravan – misery painted up magnolia – and then I was gone, door slamming shut behind me.

The gravel cracked beneath my soles as I strode across to the caravan park's entrance. Beside the faded Paradise Point sign, Simon's one-armed doll was still nailed to a post. Her greenish skin had turned grey over the last couple of months; her painted eyes were peeling.

The sight of her suddenly bothered me more than I could stand. I grabbed her by the neck and pulled. With a pop, she came loose from the post. There were gaping holes in her neck and arm from the nails. I was contemplating what to do with this grey creature when there came the rumble of a car.

I jumped, startled enough that the doll leaped out of my hands. It landed in a puddle at my feet. A red car tore along the road. Its windows were tinted. I waited, fingers bouncing, skin seething, for the car to turn into the caravan park.

It didn't slow down. It didn't stop.

It wasn't her.

I hugged my expensive wool coat tighter around myself, balling my hands into fists to stop them from shaking. Where was she? I felt so lightheaded I might float away. I didn't exist anymore, I was sure of this fact. I needed to slip into her body or I would die.

I checked the time on my phone (no new messages). It was almost half past four and the day had turned colourless, the sky blanketed in cloud, the light fading. Now the first few drops of rain slicked against my face.

Snab Point, where the rocky edge of the island turned into the sands of Walney Channel, was a short walk along the road that hugged the shore. There were no more cars, but I kept close to the verge, my ears straining for the sound of an engine.

A quarter of a mile later, the grass-tangled dunes fell away. An expanse of sands opened out before me. The low-tide path to Piel Island uncoiled like a snake. This well-trampled track cut through the spiky green salt marsh, leading away into the mist.

On a fine day, cars would be packed into the makeshift parking spot by Snab Point. Today, it was deserted.

An oystercatcher cried *peep-peep-PEEP-PEEP* and, as if in answer, my phone vibrated in my pocket.

On the bridge

The sun was setting, the sky clinging on to the last of the day's light. My eyes flicked to the left. A mile away, the road bridge from Barrow to Walney was dotted with lights that glimmered in the late-afternoon gloom. I still felt dizzy, my heart beating too fast and too loud in my chest, but the future was so clear to me now. I saw myself in London, I saw myself on stage, I saw myself falling into Katsu's arms, falling into a different life.

I waited at the side of the road. There were puddles at my feet and, at the edges, they frothed with tiny white bubbles. Presage. It would be foolhardy to go out on to the sands now – a death sentence. The drizzle in the air turned to real rain and the minutes drained away.

There came the roar of an engine. A pair of headlights blinded me. The car was cutesy-yellow and travelling much too fast for such a narrow lane.

I took a step forward into the road and waved my arms

over my head.

'Stop . . .' I said, but my voice was whipped away by the wind.

The car made a swerve and came careening towards me. I glimpsed a face –

Her face –

My face –

And then I saw only Carlo's face. There was a smell of blood in the air. My tongue turned bitter with the taste of metal. This time, when I tried to speak, the word exploded out of my mouth.

'Stop!'

Maybe she still didn't hear me. Maybe she was too high to control the car.

There was a squeal of brakes. The car made another swerve.

I closed my eyes, waiting for the impact, wondering if it would be better this way after all.

The car screeched to a halt. The engine vroomed one final time and then cut out, the silence of Walney deafening in its wake. I sucked in a breath and opened my eyes. The front wheels were ten centimetres from the tips of my boots.

A car door opened and then slammed shut.

'Hello, Twinnie.'

Jem, dressed in a ridiculous black satin nightie, a fur stole and heels, leaned against the yellow exterior of her car. She ran a hand through her bird's nest hair and rolled the balls of her shoulders in her sockets.

'Got a death wish, have you?' she said and barked out a nasty laugh.

'I've . . . I . . .' My voice trembled and then gave out.

Rain dribbled down my cheeks, down my neck, past the collar of my coat. In front of me, Jem's eyes were zeroing in on what I was wearing. Her fleeting look of amusement was gone. Those orangey-red lips twisted, her face darkening into a scowl.

'My father gave me that coat,' she said.

'I know,' I whispered.

The memory filled itself in: my handsome father tucking the soft wool coat over me as I slumbered in the passenger seat of his sports car on long drives through the mountains of northern Italy, across the desert of southern Spain. I murmured the words under my breath. 'My father gave me that coat . . .'

My double stared at me, her eyebrows raised. Then she reached out to grab my arm.

'Give it back!'

When she touched me, I felt an electric shock. I jolted backwards. Jem raked her gaze over me once more.

'That necklace!' she said. 'That's mine, too. What else did you steal, you crazy cunt?'

I clutched the locket into my fist, like it was a talisman, and took another few steps backward. My feet stumbled against the rocks that led down the winding path toward Piel. Jem followed me, tottering in heels. There was a bandage on one of her feet.

'Katz.' She let out his name in a howl. 'You stole him, didn't you? You fucked him, you little slut.'

My double, waving her arms like a madwoman, reached out to try and grab me again. Another electric shock.

'You turned him against me!' she yelled.

She lunged forward and got a grip on my forearm. Her fingers clawed at the sleeve of my coat, pulling hard enough that the seams ripped. I struggled against her, gasping out 'please' and 'don't'. I felt her touch like the whip of electric wires.

Jem snarled in my face: 'Give. It. Back.'

Her accompanying slap was hard enough that it sent me reeling. My whole cheek stung. All the blood rushed to my face, the sound of it roaring in my ears.

My double looked like she'd surprised even herself with the force of the slap. One of her arms dropped limp to her side;

the other rested on my forearm in a loose grasp.

Her eyeballs bugged out, huge in their sockets. Up close, I noticed it for the first time: Jem's irises were black. None of their usual blue-green-grey colour was visible. Only black. They were demon eyes.

Terror shot up my spine. I wanted to cower and hide, but I had to stay strong. It was do or die.

And, in that moment, I knew exactly what to say. I knew what would make her rage boil over.

'Take it.' I contorted my shoulder so that my left arm popped out of the sleeve. Then I spun free of the coat entirely, leaving it bunched in Jem's fist. 'But Katsu told me the truth. He never loved you.' My voice wavered, but I forced out my next words. 'No one has ever loved you.'

My double was silent. Her black eyes stared back at me.

I took a step backward. Still she said nothing.

When she finally spoke, it was in a low voice, the words delivered between gritted teeth.

'You'd better run, bitch.'

I ran.

46

LIVE OR DIE

Ella

Soft sand squelched beneath my boots as I ran. The mix of gravel and rock turned to wet silt. I hit a slippery patch, slid, and almost fell. My arms windmilled and I kept going, along the winding path out onto the channel's sands.

Behind me, I didn't see Jem take off her shoes, but, in a snatched glance over my shoulder, I glimpsed her throw them at me.

'You smash – up – my – place!' One of the shoes whipped me around the thigh. 'You take – my – man!' The other shoe missed my arm by a few centimetres, landing with a thud in the sand. 'You stupid – stupid – bitch!'

Barefoot and fuelled by drugs and anger, she was faster than I'd expected. I stole another glance over my shoulder – I had to blink through the rain, which slashed against my face – and sucked in a gasp. She was only a few metres behind me.

I sped up, running so hard my lungs burned. I was past the knotty green grasses of the shoreline now, past the churned-up track. Around me there was only the wide open expanse of the sands. The ground was firmer beneath my feet now, part of the illusion that it was harmless out here, that maybe you could run all the way to the lights of the mainland a mile and a half away.

It was just that: an illusion.

But I knew the safest route. Even now, with the light leaking out of the sky, the sun reduced to a smudge of orange at the horizon, I could intuit the subtle differences in the sands.

There were the firm parts you could walk on, and the patches of cow belly softness that could suck you in.

I slowed down fractionally, my eyes darting left to right, just to make sure I was on safe ground. Half a mile ahead loomed the craggy, unloved ruins of Piel Island, but around me there was nothing. The wind howled in my ears. Rain matted the hair to my scalp. Without my coat, the cold was intense, making my teeth chatter.

My legs were rubbery. I wasn't sure I could run much further. I sneaked a look behind me and that was when—

'Stupid! Bitch!'

She grabbed a fistful of my wet hair and yanked. My head jerked to the side. My legs were slow to receive the message to stop running and I toppled backwards, slamming against her.

Jem just barely stayed upright. Letting out a splutter of frustration, she twisted her wrist, pulling my hair, digging her nails into my scalp.

'You don't just take' – she was breathing heavily, but she spat the words into my ear with venom – 'from other people. That's not how – the world – works.'

I yelped in pain and this seemed to anger her more.

With one hand still tangled in my hair, she used the other to form a fist. It connected with my cheekbone. Pain exploded across the side of my face.

'I was only ever nice to you,' she said, 'but you're all wrong.'

She released her grip on my hair. Without her to hold me up, I flopped onto my knees, the sand cold and hard beneath me. She bent down, towering over me, hands on my shoulders, and put her face close to mine.

'You're. All. Wrong.'

A few flecks of spittle hit me in the face when she spoke, but that wasn't what made me recoil.

Her eyes weren't black anymore. They had turned to mirrors. They showed a perfect reflection of me.

Her voice was mine. She was me.

And she was telling the truth.

Ella was wrong. She had always been wrong.

I ducked my head, not wanting to look into those mirrored eyes. My hand crept up to cradle my throbbing cheekbone. There was blood in my mouth, a tooth dislodged.

Since the moment of her birth, Ella had been a drain on the world. A loser. A worthless little crab living in the grit and shit of Walney Island. All these years, she'd been waiting for death and now it was time to give it to her.

'You pathetic little mouse,' Ella said, spitting out the words.

My head snapped up.

All my life, Ella had been taunting me. I was sick of it.

'Shut up, bitch,' I said.

I didn't whisper it. I didn't tack a note of uncertainty on the end. I spoke it loudly and clearly.

'Shut up!' I said again.

Ella actually laughed. It was the same taunting laughter that had always accompanied my worst moments.

'Don't try and grow a spine, Twinnie, it doesn't suit you,' she said.

Without thinking, I reared up and grabbed her around the neck. My thumbs dug into the hollow of her throat. It was gratifying, to hear the *gurgle*, to feel the way she shuddered like a wounded animal.

I was strong. I was powerful. As Ella, I'd only ever been weak.

The other girl, the other Ella, she was clawing at my hands. Her legs kicked out wildly. She caught me in the ankle and the shot of pain made me let go.

I collapsed on the ground, my hands scratching at the rough compacted sand. Sucking in air, I inhaled the smell of rain and sand. There was something else, too. A rotting, foul stench. Death was coming for one of us.

When I turned my face up to the sky, Ella was gone.

From ten metres away, I heard her voice rise to a yell.

'Where the everloving fuck are we?'

Darkness was descending. The sun was completely gone now, leaving only twilight and driving rain.

Ella set off at a run – another twenty metres from me – and then slowed. She veered left, then right. Even from this distance, I could see the sand was pulling at her heels. It was the wrong kind of sand.

I sat back on my haunches, watching her. The sand beneath me was wet, cold – and hard.

By contrast, Ella was floundering in cow belly.

'Fucking, fucking, fucking mud,' she shouted.

Her black dress transformed her into a shadow. Soon enough, she'd be nothing at all.

I could just wait . . .

The quicksand was dragging at her ankles, each step an effort. The road – where we'd come from – didn't look far off. That's where the yellow car was parked. The imposter thought she could run, reach safety in a matter of minutes, but she didn't know she was taking the wrong route.

She was straying into sands that would trap you there until the tide came in.

Nearby, the tide pools were frothing with white foam.

Not long now.

I blinked. There was a light in the darkness.

It seemed to be shooting out of the palm of her hand. Mystical.

Then I realised what it was: her phone.

The light juddered upward as she held the phone to her ear.

She was calling for help.

I scrambled to my feet and set off at a run. Just like my double, the sands pulled at my every step. The heavy tread of my boots helped, but I still had to wrench myself forward.

She was talking into the phone.

It could only be 999. Who else would she call?

Oh, God.

All she needed to say was 'Help, I'm stuck in the sands by Walney Island' and everything would be ruined.

I reached her, gasping. Icy rain whipped across my face. My boots were smeared with grit right up to where the rubber met my calves.

'Hello?' she shouted into the phone. 'Hello, can you hear me?'

She pulled the phone from her ear and let out a howl. 'Motherfuckingshittinghell.'

No signal.

Relief ebbed through me.

Of course there was no signal, not out here at the edge of the Earth.

She turned to look at me with mirrored eyes.

'You killed him, didn't you?' There was a whimper in her voice. 'You killed Carlo . . .'

'No,' I said honestly. 'You killed him, Ella. Now it's your turn to die.'

I reached for her, grabbing a fistful of her hair as she'd grabbed mine. I intended to push her to the ground.

She was too quick for me. Her palm connected with my bruised jaw and I recoiled, releasing my grip on her automatically. When she pushed me, the force of it knocked me off my feet.

This time, when I fell to my knees, the soft sand sank beneath my weight. Cow belly.

'No!' I gasped out.

Scrabbling to get purchase, my knees churned uselessly. My hands grabbed at Ella like a beggar. My fingers closed around the satin hem of her dress. When I yanked, she fell to her knees, too.

The phone, slippery from the rain, slid from her hand. With a sound like an inhalation of breath, it was sucked beneath the surface of the sand.

Ella screamed. Her hands dug for it, but it was no use. The

phone was gone.

She turned on me, mirrored eyes glinting in the half-light. Dusk was almost dead, the sky growing blacker every minute.

'What do you want?' She clawed at me, her fingers tangling in the locket chain around my neck. 'My stuff? You want my stuff? You want money?'

'My name is Jemima,' I said in silky newsreader English. 'I don't want for anything.' Despite the desperate situation, my lips stretched into an impish smile. 'Born with a silver spoon in my mouth.'

'You are actually insane.' Her grip on my locket tightened. 'You fucking lunatic.' Sand coated her forearms, rain running in rivulets past her elbows. 'Stop talking like that. Stop talking like me!'

By pulling on my locket, she was choking me. My fingers scratched at her knuckles, trying to pry myself free of her grasp, while my knees slid against the sand.

If I could just get back on my feet, if I could just find the path again, I'd be safe. The imposter would be swept away by the tide, and I could start my new life.

But Ella was bearing down on me. In a renewed effort, her hands were pushing at my shoulders, her feet scrabbling against my stomach.

'You think just 'cause you look like me' – she clawed at my face – 'you *are* me? You're nothing. No one.'

Ella's fingernails bit into the skin of my face, drawing blood, but I barely felt it. Nor did I react when her knee hit my ribs. My body remained limp as her bare foot pushed against my thigh.

For a moment, she was actually standing on me, using my body as leverage to get to her feet.

Then she was gone.

Rain lashed at my face, droplets rolling into my eyes like tears, spilling over my lips like blood.

I struggled into a half-sitting position, propping myself up on elbows.

I thought I saw her, a shadow in a black dress, but maybe it was my imagination.

Maybe . . .

Maybe she'd stumbled to safety, intuiting the right way back to Walney. Maybe she was lost in the darkness, the quicksand dragging at her heels, trapping her there for when the tide came in. It was impossible to know.

My elbows slipped against the soft wet sand. Water was trickling around me. Too much water for it to just be the rain. This was saltwater. First it would come in a trickle and then in a torrent.

If I did nothing, I'd die.

The story would tell itself: the suicide note, the possessions given away, a woman slipping beneath the surface of her own sadness.

If I tried to get up, I still might die. The tide still might claim me. But perhaps I'd live, slip into a new skin and begin my life again.

It was time to decide once and for all.

Did I want to live or die?

CUMBRIA NEWS NOW

Death on Walney sands ruled a suicide

Stephanie Lease

Police have ruled a woman's death on the sands off the coast of Barrow-in-Furness a suicide.

The body of Ella Mosier, 24, was recovered on Wednesday 17 January, five days after the local woman was reported missing. The apparent cause of death was drowning after being immobilised by the sinking sands.

Following interviews with friends and family of the deceased, investigators with the Barrow-in-Furness police department have concluded that she walked onto the sands intending to end her own life.

Mosier's brother, Simon Mosier, said his sister had been struggling with depression for more than ten years. "Ella received lots of help, lots of support, from the people in her life. It's tragic that she felt she had nowhere else to turn. We're all in mourning."

A candlelight vigil is planned for Mosier tonight, at Paradise Point, the family's caravan park, near where the young woman's life came to an end.

To reach a suicide prevention team in your area, visit
www.samaritans.org

MoneyMagnt

MeetYourDouble raises £72.5m to take its platform global

Adam Wagner

Social media start-up MeetYourDouble has already made a splash in the UK market, scoring high download figures in the key demographic of adults aged 18–34, but a new round of venture capital investment will see it expanding its global reach.

The app, which utilises facial recognition software and user votes to connect people who look alike, raised £72.5 million this week in a Series B round led by GBX.

The cash injection will allow MeetYourDouble to improve customer experience, sharpen its patented facial recognition software, and aggressively target a new base of users.

This drive for additional users includes a widespread advertising campaign, to be rolled out across Europe and the USA, starting next month.

Late last year, the success of MeetYourDouble looked set to be derailed by stories of financial fraud, romantic turmoil, and even physical harm. The so-called Brawling Doubles video became a media sensation.

However, the app has reported healthy month-on-month growth rates since. An unnamed source at the start-up confided in MoneyMagnt, "All publicity is good publicity. Obviously we don't condone violence, but our download rates went through the roof following the Brawling Doubles."

Executives at MeetYourDouble are also rumoured to be shopping a reality show concept to several interested TV production companies, with so-called doubles invited to live together in a

Big-Brother-style house.

"The future looks bright for MeetYourDouble," comments Jack Orozco, co-founder of the app. "The idea of meeting another version of you is something that has captured the public's imagination in the UK, and I can't wait for folks oversees to have the same positive experience."

47

EVERYTHING CHANGES

Jem

'Big day,' Katsu said.

On the pavement outside my Chelsea apartment, he stamped his feet. The ground was still icy, clumps of dirty snow piled up against the railings, but the sun was bright.

'Every day's a big day,' I said, flicking open a pair of over-size sunglasses.

Katsu raised his eyebrows. 'Even you cannot be blasé about this.'

I gave him a haughty look through dark lenses. Then I let out a bark of laughter and grabbed him by the elbows. I spun him around, once, twice – until my heels hit a patch of ice and I skidded. 'Shiiiiit,' I yelled, my grip on him tightening.

We kept spinning, him holding me up. Our shared laughter was brash in the quiet of the morning.

'We're meeting a record company!' I shouted for all the world to hear. 'We're meeting a record company!'

I collapsed against him, my face coming to rest in the hollow of his neck. His arms wrapped around my back, pulling me into a hug. The leather of his jacket was smooth and cool against my skin, but his heartbeat was strong, his breath warm.

'We're meeting a record company . . .' I whispered the words this time, closing my eyes.

He raked a hand through my hair. I thought for a second he was going to slide his fingers over my jaw, tilt my face upwards for a kiss.

But no. We were friends. We were trying to be friends.

For now, anyway.

I pulled away and rearranged my hair. I'd spent an hour that morning blow-drying and curling it, so it gave the effect of sexy-messy effortlessness. Katsu put his hands in his jeans pockets, fixing his eyes on the horizon, and we set off.

The offices of the record company were in Kensington, close enough to walk. Anthony, Ricky and Molly were meeting us there. We swung by Marco's for a dark roast and I chugged mine rather than sipped it, the caffeine zipping through my veins.

'So ZANG was in the *Sunday Times*,' I said. 'Our Instagram followers jumped by, like, two thousand. Elgin is over the moon, past Jupiter, orbiting Uranus . . .'

During the walk, I jabbered on about ZANG, about what I'd done at the weekend, about what I was doing next weekend, about my shopping trip to Paris with Mummy, about flying to Dubai to see Dada, about all the songs I was writing, about the great bar I'd just found, about –

Katsu slung an arm across my shoulders. He nosed into my personal space.

'It's okay to be nervous,' he said in a low voice.

I shrugged off his arm. 'I'm not nervous.'

As well as the meeting, we'd also been invited to play at a showcase event this evening. There would be lots of industry people there. The record label liked our demo – the three songs we'd recorded last month at a studio in Camden – but the unspoken caveat was that they wanted to see how we performed.

It would be my first real performance since that night in Shoreditch. Huge crowd, judging eyes, nowhere to hide.

Big day. Big day. Big day. The words circled in my head.

I kicked back my coffee cup for a final slurp, but it was empty. Should've got the bigger size.

I took a deep breath. Sure, it was a big day, but every day was a big day in my life.

Katsu was looking at me like he could tell what I was thinking. They unnerved me, those looks, like he could x-ray inside of me.

'I'm fine,' I muttered. After a pause – an *uh-huh* nod of the head from Katz – I said, 'What's going on with you, how's the PhD?'

He snorted. 'Like you care.'

'Tell me' – I rolled my shoulders, swinging my arms to get rid of my excess energy – 'it'll put me in a stupor. Like meditation through extreme boredom.'

When he laughed, something warm squirmed in my belly. I'd always loved being able to make him laugh.

With another sighing chuckle, he said, 'I just got the results of' – my brain hummed and all I heard was *science science science* – 'need another six months to write up my findings.'

'Six months? We'll be touring Japan in six months,' I said.

I gave him a sidelong look. He'd shaved the sides of his head a couple of weeks ago, so his remaining hair fell down in a floppy approximation of a Mohawk. God, he was sexy. He didn't look like a chemist. He looked like a rock star.

'Is that right?' he said.

'Yeah . . .' I said dreamily. 'It's going to happen for us, I know it.'

I looked away, but I could feel his gaze lingering on me. I thought I felt him caress the back of my hand, too, but maybe it was just a stray hair.

*

Backstage at the venue that evening, it was packed. The basement room was windowless and lit with strip lighting, giving off a prison vibe. The other inmates were talking, laughing, drumming out rhythms on the wobbly Formica tables. On one wall, a flatscreen blared adverts broken up by reality TV bollocks.

Tonight's bill featured six different bands, all of whom were preparing to play a breathless twenty-minute slot that could make or break their career. Everyone was clustered in groups. No one was here to make friends.

The rest of Lace Steak were hanging out at the dilapidated pool table, but I'd staked out a spot in front of a grimy mirror. I was touching up my make-up. Someone jostled past me. The eyeliner in my hand nudged past the corner of my eye. The effect was less 'winged eyeliner' and more 'kid with crayon'.

'Fuck's sake!' I swivelled around, planning to stab my eyeliner pen through the jostler's jugular.

'Who are you wanting to murder this time, Jems?' Stee asked me with a laconic grin.

It emerged that he and Imogen had sneaked backstage to wish me luck. I laughed, feeling my irritation recede. I'd been on edge all day. The fact that the meeting had gone well hadn't calmed my nerves, only shredded them further. This was happening. It was actually happening – provided I didn't screw it all up this evening.

Imogen took over make-up duties ('your contouring is all over the place today,' she said, clucking), while Stee kept up a biting commentary of all the people around us. 'Well those definitely aren't her real lips . . . I saw him last week, passed out in the pisser at Ubiquity . . .'

I let his voice tune in and out. Sometimes I listened to him, sometimes I focused on the TV, partially visible over Imogen's shoulder. My stomach was all knotted up, and I didn't need Imogen to tell me that I was in danger of sweating off my make-up.

On the flatscreen, my eye caught a familiar logo. A woman with a Roman nose and an extravagance of curly hair stepped into the frame. 'Seven billion people in the world,' her voice filtered out through the speakers, half-obscured by the noise of the room.

A second woman, with the same nose, the same curly hair, joined her.

'Find out how many look just like you!' she said with a grin. 'Download the MeetYourDouble app today. See your life from a different perspective. Just think who could be waiting for you out there!'

Those adverts were everywhere now. I couldn't fucking avoid them. I swung my body around, away from the TV screen. Imogen let out a loud tutting sound. I had lip liner on my jaw. I scrubbed it off with my fist. Waving away her protests, I stood up. 'I think I'm done.'

'So Jem's in a snit,' Stee said to Imogen, arching an eyebrow. When I made a face, he leaned in close to me. 'Want something to put you in a better mood?'

I noticed for the first time that there was a gaunt look to Stee tonight. Once so dapper, with his bright bow ties and pocket squares, he now looked almost dowdy in dirty jeans and a black hoodie. He kept running his tongue over his front teeth, a lizard-like obsessive motion.

Going a bit Carlo.

'No, I'm just fine,' I said, affecting a little shrug. 'I'll grab a beer to see me through.'

Stee returned my tight smile with a blank stare. He mumbled something about going to the bathroom and left.

Maybe it was time to drop him. I had plenty of other friends, anyway. If I was going to make it in the music biz, I needed a clear head and loyal foot soldiers.

Imogen and I pushed across the crowded room to unite with Katsu and the rest. Just as we reached them, a man clambered up on a chair and cupped his hands to make a megaphone. He had bottle-red hair and wore a mauve velvet jacket, a clipboard clenched under his arm.

'First band's up in ten minutes,' he yelled over the noise of the room. 'First band, head to the stage to do your set up.'

He checked his clipboard. 'Lace Steak? Everyone here from Lace Steak?'

*

As we trooped through the rabbit warren of corridors, I almost regretted rebuffing Stee. I'd slept like shit last night and my nerves were jangling, despite the lie I'd told Katz. Cocaine would give me courage and energy; it would make everything sparkle. Yet I realised the truth now. When I snorted cocaine, it made me into someone else – someone I didn't like.

In February, I'd spent two weeks at a clinic on the Pembrokeshire coast, courtesy of my mother's credit card. The place was a glass-and-steel monstrosity perched on a cliff, miles from civilisation (miles from a dealer). Inside, it was done out like a spa, with skin treatments and daily massages, but the staff wore white coats like doctors. I was there to get some rest.

In my daily 'one-to-ones' (never called counselling or therapy) with a thin-lipped lady named Julia, I recounted my nightmares. With my knees pulled up to my chest, I rocked against the chair back and told her about sinking in wet sand, the wind ripping my screams from my throat. In my dreams, a woman with my face tried to pull me down, time and time again. Each night, I woke up gasping.

'Completely normal,' Julia said in a clipped voice. 'The woman represents your past, the quicksand is your addiction.'

I gave her a sceptical smile. I wanted to ask about her qualifications. She probably had a PhD in seaweed wraps and had been shunted over from the beauty therapy wing.

It was a nice fiction, though. Ella was a metaphor. She existed only in my mind.

A few days after my return from Walney Island, I'd run a Google search that had kicked up a news story: 'Death on Walney sands ruled a suicide'. I pictured her body out there on the sands, bloated by the tide, tinged blue with cold. My stomach rebelled against me and I barely made it to the kitchen sink before I threw up.

I could've gone to the police, I suppose, and told them that Twinnie was psycho as well as suicidal. What good would that have done, though? It would only have incriminated me. My phone had been swallowed up by the mud, but our text-exchange still existed on a server somewhere. The police would see my messages and think I'd threatened the little mouse.

No, I didn't want to get dragged into all that.

'Are you ready to change?' Julia asked on my last day at the clinic.

I gave a noncommittal grunt. All this 'embrace the change' mumbo-jumbo, all the healing mud baths and transformative vibration massages – I couldn't stand it. Yet, when I slid into the black Mercedes hired to take me back to London, I found that Julia's question followed me home.

*

As I stepped on stage, I could feel the hum, reverberating up through my legs. It started at my feet and became a quake when it reached my stomach.

I was going to throw up. What an entrance.

No, fuck that.

I'm Jemima Cootes-Mitchell and I am invincible.

I lifted my chin and walked out into the glare. I couldn't see anything, but the tremble of the bass line carried me along.

When I reached the mic, my voice lodged in my throat. A metallic taste coated my tongue. My teeth ground together, like I was chewing on pennies.

Help me, help. There was a whimper in the back of my mind. I hiccupped, sure I was going to freeze.

But what came out of my mouth was a battle cry.

'Whaaat's up, London? Are you ready to get loud?'

The screams from the crowd were rapturous. Blinded by

the lights on stage, I couldn't see them, but I knew they were there. Friends had come out in droves. They stamped their feet and yelled my name.

The whole stage was vibrating now, like a natural disaster, but I was ready to ride the tsunami.

Watch out. Here I come.

To my left, Katsu played the opening riff of our first song. I cast a mischievous smile in his direction – you love me, you know you do – and he returned an exasperated one of his own. I was about to miss my cue.

I didn't care. They'd wait for me.

When I did open my mouth to sing, my voice was velvet, melting over the jagged guitar. The applause grew so loud I could barely hear myself, but I knew I sounded divine.

It was a new song, one about coming back from the dead and embracing life.

The audience didn't know how literal it was, but they sang along with the catchy chorus about facing down your fears. The execs at the record company thought this could be our first single. A summer smash.

I'm ready. Ready to change. Ready to become the person I was always meant to be.

Nicola Martin studied at the University of East Anglia and the University of California, Berkeley. She lives and works in Bristol. *Dead Ringer* is her first novel.

ACKNOWLEDGEMENTS

The publisher would like to thank Tom Ashton, Paula Beaton and Rosie Hilton for their editorial work during the preparation of this book, as well as Andrew Forteath for the cover design.